Praise for *A Lot Like Adiós*

"Alexis Daria's *A Lot Like Adiós* i[...] novel! Between Mich and Gabe's crackling dialogue and their palpable yearning, I fell hard and fast for this book, racing through its pages until I finally closed it with an overflowing heart and a deep, happy sigh. Romance readers, this is your new favorite book!"

—Emily Henry, #1 *New York Times* bestselling author of *People We Meet on Vacation*

"A sexy and sweet tale that tells us home is more than a place—it's where our heart lives."

—Bolu Babalola, *Sunday Times* (London) bestselling author

"Second-chance romance perfection! I was under this book's spell from start to finish, fanned myself several times (in the first hundred pages, no less), and fell completely in love with Mich and Gabe. A TBR must-have."

—Tessa Bailey, *New York Times* bestselling author

"*A Lot Like Adiós* is the quintessential read-in-one-sitting book. You will not want to put down this fresh, sexy take on the childhood-friends-to-lovers trope. I adored every page!"

—Farrah Rochon, *USA Today* bestselling author of *The Boyfriend Project*

"*A Lot Like Adiós* is a thoroughly satisfying second-chance romance with the heat turned all the way up to MUY caliente. Gabe and Michelle's journey back to one another is brimming with moments of scorching passion and deep yearning. A love letter to fanfiction, the old neighborhood, and that one person from your past you could never forget."

—Adriana Herrera, *USA Today* bestselling author

"Scorchingly hot and irresistibly sweet, Alexis Daria's friends-to-lovers tale is a sexy masterpiece that'll make you wonder what your childhood best friend is up to these days. Michelle and Gabe's chemistry sizzles right off the page."

—Hannah Orenstein, author of
Head Over Heels

"*A Lot Like Adiós* is a shining example of what a contemporary romance in the hands of a talented author can be: funny, sexy, inclusive, and real. I absolutely adored it!"

—Mia Sosa, *USA Today* bestselling author of
The Worst Best Man

"Gabe and Michelle are my favorite hot nerds in the galaxy. This wildly sexy, emotional trip through their lives will tug at heartstrings—and elicit pants feelings—across the cosmos."

—Andie J. Christopher, *USA Today* bestselling author

"With *A Lot Like Adiós*, Alexis Daria has crafted an on-brand romance filled with friendship, heart, and sexy situations that will singe your eyebrows. Her lovely Latinx story explores the pressures of family expectations on relationships before expertly delivering a satisfying and heady HEA. Michelle and Gabe are the two out-of-the-box romance characters readers want. A delight. A breath of fresh air. An absolute joy."

—Diana Muñoz Stewart,
award-winning and bestselling author of *I Am Justice*

A LOT LIKE ADIÓS

Also by Alexis Daria

You Had Me at Hola

What the Hex (novella)

Take the Lead
Dance with Me
Dance All Night (novella)

A LOT LIKE ADIÓS

A NOVEL

ALEXIS DARIA

AVON

An Imprint of HarperCollins*Publishers*

Excerpt from *Take the Lead* by Alexis Daria. Copyright © 2017 by Alexis Daria. Reprinted by permission of St. Martin's Press. All Rights Reserved.

This is a work of fiction. Names, characters, places, and incidents are products of the author's imagination or are used fictitiously and are not to be construed as real. Any resemblance to actual events, locales, organizations, or persons, living or dead, is entirely coincidental.

A LOT LIKE ADIÓS. Copyright © 2021 by Alexis Daria. All rights reserved. Printed in the United States of America. No part of this book may be used or reproduced in any manner whatsoever without written permission except in the case of brief quotations embodied in critical articles and reviews. For information, address HarperCollins Publishers, 195 Broadway, New York, NY 10007.

HarperCollins books may be purchased for educational, business, or sales promotional use. For information, please email the Special Markets Department at SPsales@harpercollins.com.

FIRST EDITION

Designed by Diahann Sturge

Title page illustration © adisetia/Shutterstock Inc.

Calendar illustration on page 1 © MCruzUA/Shutterstock, Inc.

Chat head icons © popicon; notkoo; Kuttly; oculo/Shutterstock, Inc.

Library of Congress Cataloging-in-Publication Data has been applied for.

ISBN 978-0-06-295996-6

21 22 23 24 25 CPI 10 9 8 7 6 5 4 3 2

For my grandmothers

A LOT LIKE ADIÓS

Chapter 1

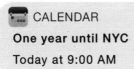

📅 CALENDAR
One year until NYC
Today at 9:00 AM

"Fuck." Gabriel Aguilar scowled at the reminder on his phone screen before swiping it off with this thumb. He hated calendar alerts—the damned things ruled his life these days—but he especially despised this one. New York was the last thing he wanted to think about, today or ever.

Shoving the phone into his sweatpants pocket, Gabe pulled open the glass double doors leading into Agility Gym and strode inside like he owned the place.

Which, technically, he did.

Cool air and the faint scent of lavender greeted him, a welcome change from the blistering Los Angeles heat. The gym felt like home, more so than Gabe's minimalist apartment in Venice did. Located near Bergamot Station in Santa Monica, Agility Gym was well ventilated and spacious, with clean lines, high ceilings, and large front windows that let in lots of sunlight. All around, trainers and physical therapists worked one-on-one with clients on everything from stunt work to knee rehab.

There were ups and downs to being a business owner, but Gabe wouldn't trade it for anything. He'd built this. It was *his*.

The lavender scent grew stronger as Gabe neared the front desk where Trung, a former acrobat of Vietnamese descent who managed client scheduling, chatted with Charisse, one of Agility's best PTs. Trung swore by the soothing effects of the essential oil diffuser, and while Gabe didn't have strong opinions about aromatherapy, he could appreciate that lavender was an improvement over typical gym smells.

Despite the calendar alert urging him on, Gabe went over to greet them.

Charisse, a tall woman with a small 'fro and dark umber skin, returned Gabe's fist bump with a wide smile. She and Gabe were gearing up to co-teach a class on hand therapy for the many clients who complained of repetitive strain injury from overusing their phones and computers.

"Lots of new sign-ups," Charisse said, before turning to Trung. "Can you pull up the list?"

"Sure thing." Trung's purple-tipped nails clattered on the keyboard before they spun the screen around, revealing a color-coded spreadsheet. "Here you go."

"Almost at the stretch goal," Gabe said with a grin. "We might have to open more spots."

Scanning the long list of names gave Gabe a rush. It was the kind of thing he missed doing, since most of his time now went toward the administrative and managerial tasks of running the gym. Speaking of, he had a shit-ton of such tasks waiting for him.

"I'll see you two later," he said, and headed for his office in the back of the building.

As Gabe approached, his business partner, Fabian, Charles stuck his head out of his own office.

"That you, Gabe?"

Gabe started most of his mornings at a gym closer to his apartment, where he could be just another person sweating it out with the weights, and not the face of the business. They'd worked out a schedule where Fabian came in earlier, but Gabe stayed later.

"Yeah, it's me." Gabe had met Fabian while playing baseball for UCLA, and all these years later, the guy was still his best friend. Fabian was Haitian by way of Boston, with coppery skin and dark locs pulled back with a rubber band. He was first-generation like Gabe, whose parents had been born in Mexico and Puerto Rico.

Fabian waved him into the office. "Did you see the calendar alert?"

Gabe bit back a frustrated growl. Thinking about New York made him think about his family, a topic that always tanked his mood. "How could I miss it?"

"I figured you'd say that. Come on, I've got some updates."

Gabe followed Fabian into the office, trying to ignore the piles of paper on Fabian's desk. And floor. And chair.

Fabian claimed having everything out where he could see it

counted as an organizational system, and while it made Gabe twitchy, he couldn't deny that the guy was a genius at what he did.

They'd started Agility together when they were twenty-six and filled with the fire to build something of their own, a gym focused on physical therapy and rehab. Gabe had gotten interested in sports medicine after blowing out his knee and working on his recovery with the UCLA team doctor. After graduation, Gabe worked as a personal trainer and went back to school for physical therapy. Fabian had followed up undergrad with an MBA. The gym itself was Gabe's vision, but Fabian had the skills to make it happen. And so, Agility Gym had been born. Five years later, it was now a hot spot for Hollywood stars.

And at thirty-one years old, Gabe was tired as fuck.

But there was no rest for the wicked, and there was still work to be done. He waited for Fabian to move a pile of papers from the guest chair before he sat down. Fabian took his place behind his desk and pulled a few brightly colored sticky notes off his computer monitor. Gabe, who'd gone paperless three years ago, withheld a comment.

"Ah, here we go." Fabian held up a blue sticky note. "Today marks one year until we have to open an Agility Gym branch in New York City, as per the terms of our investment agreement with Powell."

Gabe crossed his arms and waited for Fabian to get to the point. Richard Powell, their first investor, had insisted they open a location in New York City within six years, mainly so Powell could use it while he was on the East Coast for work. They'd met Powell through an investment competition for recent grads, and he'd been the first one to give them a chance. At the time, they'd been thrilled that Powell had taken such an interest in the gym. But lately, his involvement left Gabe wondering who was actually in charge here.

"I know you don't want to, but you've gotta get started on this, dude," Fabian said, a note of apology in his voice. "I can hold down the fort here, but I can't travel back and forth like we'd planned."

Resentment simmered in Gabe's gut. When they'd made the agreement, Fabian had assured Gabe he'd handle it when the time came. He was the one with the vision for the New York location, and the drive to get it done. But Fabian's life had expanded in ways they never could have foreseen. Since then, Fabian had gotten married and bought a house. His wife, Iris, an entertainment lawyer, was pregnant with twins, and their home renovation project had turned into a beast. On top of all that, Fabian's parents had moved in with him in advance of his father's open-heart surgery, which was scheduled to take place in a few weeks.

Gabe was happy for him. He really was. Fabian had always wanted to be a dad, and even though Gabe didn't feel the same impulse, he could still be happy for his friend.

But Gabe *wasn't* happy about what it meant for him.

For all his messiness, Fabian was a great business partner, and an even better friend. He knew about Gabe's issues with his family, and he'd never have stuck Gabe with this task if there'd been another choice. Gabe hadn't been back to New York since his sister's wedding nine years ago, where he and his parents had made a scene and his father had yelled "Don't come back!" at his retreating form.

"I know I have to do it," Gabe said, shaking off the memory. Managing the New York launch was something he'd resigned himself to once he'd realized the one-year mark was coming up and Fabian was in no position to go anywhere.

"I'll help how I can from afar," Fabian offered. He held up his other hand, which had three pink sticky notes stuck to his fingers. "That's what I wanted to update you on. I've made some inquiries."

Gabe shifted in the chair, getting comfortable. "Let's hear it."

Fabian peeled a note off his finger and squinted at whatever he'd written there. His notes looked like they were written by a two-year-old who'd decided to try writing upside down.

"I've reached out to a real estate agent to help us find a space, a contractor to give us a renovation quote, and . . ." Fabian wiggled his middle finger, which held the final pink sticky note. "I found the mastermind behind the Victory Fitness rebrand."

At that last bit, Gabe leaned forward. "Really? You found them?"

Victory Fitness was a bicoastal gym chain whose clout had skyrocketed three years earlier thanks to an ad campaign that went viral. At the time, Fabian had tacked up the magazine ads on his office corkboard, and they'd kicked around the idea of hiring whoever had come up with the concept. There were already a lot of gyms in New York, but if they could bring that person on board, it could be exactly what they needed to make the expansion a success.

As much as Gabe didn't want to return to New York, if he had to do it, he wanted to blow it out of the water, to have the name of his gym—a take on his own last name, Aguilar—splashed everywhere.

Especially where his father could see it.

"It took a little work to track her down, because she's freelance now. But I got someone at her old firm to give me her contact info. Her name's . . ." Fabian peered at the sticky note. "Michelle . . . Amato."

Gabe's heart leaped into his throat and his skin prickled like someone had dumped a bucket of ice water over his head. "What did you say?"

"Michelle Amato. She used to work for a marketing and advertising firm—"

"Oh shit." Gabe put a hand on his forehead and fell back into the chair, the strength draining out of him. Even though they'd been out of touch all these years, the last thing Gabe had heard about Michelle was that she'd gotten a job in marketing. "It's Michelle. It has to be. Goddamn."

It was a small fucking world after all.

"What is it, dude?" Fabian tossed the sticky notes onto the desk and got up. "You look pale."

"Michelle's my . . ." What were they? "We used to be friends. Best friends. She—"

"Wait, this is *that* girl? *The* girl? The one who you—oh damn." Fabian pulled out his phone while Gabe stared into space, swamped by memories.

Of playing in their adjoining backyards. Of dinner with her family. Of her keeping him company during his shifts at his father's stationery store.

Of her taste on his lips the last time he'd seen her.

"This is the one you wrote that sci-fi fanfiction for?"

Gabe narrowed his eyes at Fabian's question. "I wrote it *with* her, not *for* her. We were fifteen. And I told you never to bring that up again, pendejo."

"Not my fault you spill your deepest, darkest secrets when you're drunk." Fabian's eyebrows rose. "Daaaamn. She's smoking hot, dude."

"What?" That snapped Gabe out of his reverie. "How do you know?"

Fabian turned the phone to face him. "Her Instagram."

Gabe grabbed the phone, suddenly ravenous for a glimpse of Michelle after all these years.

Fabian stuck his hands on his hips, mouth agape. "You mean you haven't Internet-stalked her?"

"Not . . . not in a long time." He had in the past. But it had been too painful, and scrolling through her photos without commenting made Gabe feel like a creep. It had been more than five years since he'd last looked her up. And shit, Fabian was right. Mich was gorgeous.

She was pale, but there was a warmth to her skin, offset by her long dark hair. Her light brown eyes held that glint he remembered, like she knew a secret and didn't you wish she'd tell you.

The photos in her feed were a collection of selfies, family pictures, a black cat, and Manhattan street photography. Gabe zeroed in on the selfies, which showed her giving the camera a range of looks that went from sultry to silly.

It was, in essence, Michelle. Just as he remembered her.

He'd always thought she was the most beautiful girl in the world, and age had only made her hotter.

"Stop it." Fabian snatched the phone back. "You're torturing yourself."

"No, wait—" Gabe reached for the phone, but Fabian held it over his head.

"I'll email her to apologize and say we found someone else," Fabian went on. "No harm, no foul."

Gabe was already pulling out his own phone to look her up through the gym's Instagram account, taking care not to accidentally like one of her photos with an errant thumb tap. "Did you mention my name in the email?"

Fabian hesitated before answering. "I might have."

Gabe sent him an exasperated look. "Is that yes or no?"

Fabian sighed. "It's a yes, but let me handle this. For your own good."

Gabe shook his head, suddenly filled with certainty, and . . . some light feeling he couldn't name. "Nah, I gotta email her."

"Son, listen to me. This is the one who got away. You're not thinking clearly."

Fabian was right, but it didn't matter. "I have to," Gabe said, getting to his feet. "The way I left things, and now this . . . I'll be a total dick if I don't even email her to explain."

He'd already ghosted her as a friend. He wouldn't add professional ghosting to the list of his sins where Michelle was concerned.

Had he really thought he could keep his old life separate

from this expansion? He should have known better. It was only day one and a gigantic piece of his old baggage had already been dredged up. Now he had to address it.

Gabe grabbed the duffel bag he'd set beside the chair. "I'm gonna email her."

"Let the record state that I think this is a terrible idea," Fabian told him. "This is my fault. You should let me fix it."

"You have enough work to do trying to manage everything from here so I spend as little time in New York as possible." Gabe's phone dinged with another fucking calendar alert.

"Conference call with the managers in ten minutes," Fabian said, glancing at his computer screen.

"Yeah, yeah." That meant Gabe had ten minutes to reply to Michelle. "Forward me the email you sent her."

Fabian let out a soul-weary sigh and dropped into his desk chair. "Fine."

Gabe left his partner's office and headed to his own.

He dreaded returning to New York, dreaded facing Michelle. But somewhere deep inside, he also felt . . . glad. All the times she'd reached out to him over the years, he hadn't known what to say . . . so he hadn't said anything. Now he had a real reason to reply.

He was nervous as all hell, but also . . . he still missed her. After all this time, an ache still formed in his chest at the thought of her.

Mouth set in a grim line, Gabe sat at his own desk, which contained not a single piece of paper or sticky note, and pulled the ergonomic keyboard closer. Then he began to type.

Chapter 2

To: Michelle Amato
From: Fabian Charles
Subject: Marketing campaign inquiry

Ms. Amato,

I'm contacting you in regard to the Victory Fitness campaign you spearheaded with Rosen and Anders a few years ago. My name is Fabian Charles, and I am writing on behalf of myself and Gabriel Aguilar in our capacity as co-owners of Agility Gym in Los Angeles to see if you are available to consult on the campaign for our upcoming expansion to New York City. I'm attaching a document with further information. Please contact me at your earliest convenience.

Fabian Charles
Co-owner of Agility Gym, Los Angeles
he/him/his

To: Michelle Amato
From: Gabriel Aguilar
Subject: Fwd: Marketing campaign inquiry

Hi Mich. It's Gabe.

It's been a long time.

I didn't know Fabian had reached out to you, and we'll understand if you pass on this.

I've missed you.

—G
Gabriel Aguilar
Co-owner of Agility Gym, Los Angeles
Pronouns: he/him

Michelle Amato struggled for breath as she reread the emails that had landed in her inbox only moments before.

No. No no no no. How could he do this? Crash into her life again like the goddamn Kool-Aid Man, like he hadn't completely wrecked her when he'd left? Fuck him.

And with this? With a *job offer*? The motherfucker wanted to *hire her*?

"Everything okay?" Ava asked from over by the stove.

Michelle glanced up from the phone and tried to control her facial expression. She was babysitting her sister Monica's three children for the day, and her cousin Ava Rodriguez had come over to help. It was summer break, so Ava, a middle school teacher, was off, and Michelle, as a freelancer, made her own schedule. Ava was cooking a big pot of arroz con gandules for lunch, and Michelle was supposed to be slicing plantains to be made into tostones.

Thank god Ava was there, because after these emails, Michelle needed a minute alone. The kids—eleven-year-old Phoebe, nine-year-old Danica, and six-year-old Henry—were busy in the living room with screens of various sizes, but they'd each been in and out of the kitchen three times in the last hour.

"Work email," Michelle said, holding up the phone. Technically, that wasn't a lie. "I'll be right back."

Michelle opened the basement door and jogged down the steps, intending to sit at the desk her father had put down there. They were in her parents' house in the Bronx, the house Michelle had grown up in. Mom and Dad were currently in Florida at their beach house, and Michelle was staying here while her one-bedroom apartment in Manhattan underwent a bathroom renovation.

If she'd been thinking clearly, the basement was the last place she would have gone to process an email from *Gabe*, of all people. She stopped short halfway to the desk, glancing down at the carpet under her chancletas.

Back to the scene of the crime, she thought. Or at least, the moment when everything had changed between them.

It had been a hot summer day, barely a week after high school graduation, and this basement had been Michelle's bedroom then. Gabe had come over to smoke up while her parents were at work. They'd huddled together in the backyard, just on the other side of the sliding glass doors, and gotten super fucking high. Afterward, they'd retreated inside to watch some nineties action movie on TV, giggling and making the kind of commentary only very high teenagers do. Michelle had been sprawled out on the floor right here, propped up by colorful throw pillows, and Gabe had been sitting on the edge of her bed.

She still didn't know what had possessed her to ask the question. Maybe something on the TV had sparked the memory. Or maybe it had been on her mind ever since Lizzie DeStefano, Ava's school friend, had put it there a few days earlier. Either way, Michelle had been feeling giddy, from marijuana and the prospect of the whole summer stretched out before them, when she'd turned to Gabe . . .

And asked if he had a big dick.

It made her cringe with embarrassment to think about it now. What a totally inappropriate thing to ask one's best friend! But at the time, she'd felt like a little flirting between friends was okay, especially friends whose eyes sometimes lingered on each other's body longer than they should. It didn't have to mean anything, right?

Hey Gabe, I got a question for ya.

Yeah?

You got a big dick?

Do I—what?

Lizzie DeStefano, Ava's friend from St. Catherine's, said she thinks you've got a big dick.

I barely know Lizzie!

Well, do you?

. . . Do I what?

Do you have a big dick?

Gabe had evaded the question, but Michelle hadn't missed the way his gaze had been glued to her boobs. He'd been so adorable, and playful banter was part of their dynamic, so she—and this was totally on her—had gone and sat next to him on the bed . . .

And asked if he was *hard.*

You do, don't you? Oh my god. Are you hard right now?

Looking back, Michelle wanted to shake herself. At the time, she'd thought she was being so edgy and cool. Talking about penises, without a care in the world! Like a real grown-up! But before she could laugh it off or apologize, Gabe had answered her in a voice gone low and deep.

Yeah.

Yeah, he was hard. For her? The thought had given her a thrill.

Michelle could never remember who moved first, but in the next second, they were kissing, and it was the most amazing and stunning thing she'd ever experienced. She'd kissed a couple of other boys before, but this was *Gabe*—*her* Gabe—and his mouth was like heaven. Soft lips and frantic kisses that tasted like the wintermint gum they always chewed post-joint.

As Gabe's hands roamed her body, Michelle had straddled his lap and reached into his sweatpants to find out firsthand just how hard he was.

And it turned out Lizzie DeStefano was right. He *was* big.

From there they'd been caught in a cyclone of teenage lust. Michelle's shirt and bra were lost to the whirlwind, and then

Gabe's mouth was on her, driving her wild with need. And just as she'd started to rearrange everything in her mind—like moving Gabe from the category of *best friend* to *potential first lover*—she'd spotted the piece of paper sticking out of his sweatpants pocket.

Michelle often wondered what would've happened if she hadn't seen the paper at that exact moment. If she'd been too far gone to be curious, or if she just hadn't noticed it. Would they have had sex?

Would he have stayed?

She'd never know. Because she *had* found the paper then, and it had been a one-way plane ticket to Los Angeles for the following week.

All the excitement at discovering this new aspect to their relationship had drained away as the truth he'd come over to tell her spilled out. Gabe wasn't staying in New York for college, as she'd thought. Instead, he'd gotten a scholarship to UCLA, and he was leaving *soon*.

To make matters worse, he'd *lied* to her about it. For *months*. He'd told her he was going to Hunter College in Manhattan. That he would be here, right next door, when she drove down from SUNY Binghamton on holidays and the occasional weekend.

They were supposed to spend the whole summer together. They'd had *plans*, damn it.

Anger had won out over tears. Michelle said some things she wasn't proud of.

You said college wasn't going to be goodbye, Gabe. Well, this sure feels a hell of a lot like goodbye.

Heart breaking, she'd ripped up the ticket—just a printout, but it gave her some small satisfaction—and told him to leave and never come back.

And he had.

Until now.

Michelle sat right there on the floor and pulled up the email again, staring at the words.

Hi Mich.

The greeting pinged the memory of her name on his lips, with a soft *ch*, like *Mish*. She kept reading.

It's Gabe.

Her Gabe. Her best friend. Once.

It's been a long time.

No shit, Sherlock.

I didn't know Fabian had reached out to you, and we'll understand if you pass on this.

The Victory campaign had been Michelle's greatest professional achievement, and also the beginning of the end of her time in corporate America. Somehow, Gabe's business partner had found out Michelle had worked on it, and Gabe was giving her an out. He didn't think she'd take the job because of him.

But then there were those final words.

I've missed you.

"Fuck you, Gabriel Aguilar," she whispered at the phone as tears welled in her eyes.

How dare he miss her? *He* was the one who'd left, the one who'd ignored every single email or text she'd sent him.

Sure, she'd accept some of the blame, but after the initial anger faded, she'd tried to reach out. To bridge the distance. And he'd never replied. And now, thirteen years later, he showed up in her work email out of the blue wanting to *hire her*?

Michelle had imagined this moment so many times over the years, often while lying awake at night, consumed by anxiety over things she couldn't control, reliving the final moments of their friendship.

In some of her fantasies, she bumped into him by chance on the street, like she still randomly ran into former classmates all over New York City. Sometimes she saw him first, and she'd stop, turn, and say, "Gabe?" with a mix of wonder and surprise. A light laugh and an "Oh my god, how are you?" And then a hug, both of them shaking their heads, a sort of *Wow, what a small world* moment. Other times, she imagined him spotting her first, her name on his lips. In her dreams it was always her full name, Michelle, which didn't make any sense, because once they'd gotten to middle school, he'd started calling her Mich most of the time.

When she was really in a mood, she imagined running into

him somewhere like a bar, and stalking up to him with an indignant "You bastard!"

Never had she guessed he would reappear like this.

Michelle blinked hard and stared up at the ceiling. She hardly ever cried, and she certainly wasn't going to shed any more tears over *him*. Taking deep breaths until the pressure behind her eyes abated, she dabbed at the corners with the tips of her fingers to wipe away the moisture.

She should say no. She was a freelance graphic designer now, and she didn't even take marketing jobs anymore, no matter how much some of her current clients hinted that they'd be happy to pay for those services.

She should ignore him. After all, that's what he'd done to her, wasn't it? She'd been fine all this time without him. What could he possibly add to her life now?

Then a more disturbing thought occurred to her. If she turned him down, what was to stop him from hiring the rest of the team who'd worked on Victory? Clearly Gabe and his partner knew about her old firm, Rosen and Anders, which meant they could easily reach . . .

Nathaniel.

"Fuck," she hissed between her teeth.

Not Nathaniel. Anyone but that backstabbing asshole.

Getting up, Michelle went to her dad's desk and grabbed a yellow legal pad and a pen. She took them to the sofa and plopped down on the worn leather cushions. It was time to make a Pros and Cons list. Normally she'd involve Ava in this, but she didn't want to tell her cousin about Gabe's email just yet.

After writing headings on the page and drawing a line down

the middle, Michelle wrote "Marketing burnout" in the Cons column. She'd quit for a reason, after all.

Below that, she added "Working for Gabe." They'd collaborated well on school assignments, and on the long-running fanfic they'd never finished, but they were older now. Plus, she'd be working *for* him, and she didn't know how she felt about that.

Pressing down hard with the pen, she scrawled "Screw over Nathaniel" in the Pros column. She'd be damned if he got a job that should've been hers.

Again.

The pen tip hovered over the page, and before she could overthink it, she wrote "Closure with Gabe" underneath.

Because even after all this time . . . yeah, she missed him too. And more than that, she wanted—no, *needed*—to know why. Why everything had gone so wrong between them. Why he'd left and never come back.

This might be her only chance to get it.

And then, in a fit of vindictive pique, she wrote, "Ruin his life."

Okay no, that was too much. She crossed it out.

What did she *really* want?

She wanted to see him. To spend time with him. To find out if there was anything left to salvage . . .

With a lump in her throat, she wrote in tiny, reluctant letters, "Friendship 2.0."

Their relationship was complicated, mixed with love and affection, anger and hurt, and unfulfilled desire. But when she thought about Gabe, it was like a cavern opened up in her chest, a gaping emptiness where her heart and vital organs should be. If she had the chance to replace even a bit of what she'd lost, she had to take it. Maybe if he could just be in her life again, somehow, she wouldn't feel the ache of loneliness as acutely as she had since he left.

Sure, she had other friends. She had her cousins. But she didn't have anything like the friendship she'd had with Gabe. Someone she could be silly around, and say all the weird ideas that popped into her head. Where she knew he'd never . . .

Well, she *thought* he'd never leave her. That they'd always be friends, *best* friends, forever.

She'd been wrong.

Michelle blinked hard at the list. How about that? The Pros column outweighed the Cons.

In the back of her mind, a plan began to form.

The new gym location would be in New York City, and Gabe would have to come back at some point. She could arrange to see him in person, but where? He wouldn't have an office here. Would they meet at a gym? A café, where so many freelancer meetings took place? A hotel lobby?

Michelle couldn't envision herself getting the answers she wanted in a public place. Gabe was squirrely when it came to talking about his feelings, and she wouldn't put it past him to act like his silence over the last thirteen years had never happened. She needed to catch him off guard, to keep him in close proximity for longer than a consultation meeting. In the past, she'd let other friends crash on her sofa during their visits to New York, so it would be perfectly normal to offer the same for Gabe.

The plan solidified in her mind. This was it—she'd insist he stay with her, mostly to work on the project, but also to wear him down until he told her why he'd completely abandoned her.

The renovation on her bathroom was due to finish soon. Her tiny one-bedroom apartment was the perfect place to achieve the closure she so desperately needed.

Michelle turned on her phone but instead of replying to the email, she grabbed Gabe's cell phone number from the signature and sent him a text.

Michelle: I'll do it.

Chapter 3

Michelle: I'll do it.

Gabe: Mich?

Michelle: Who else?

Gabe: Right.

Gabe: Um, hi.

Michelle: Don't "hi" me. If I help you with this, you have to meet my demands.

Gabe: Okay. Hit me with them.

Michelle: 1) I want a lifetime membership.

Gabe: To the gym?

Michelle: Yeah, to the gym. You know what gym memberships cost these days?

Gabe: . . . yeah. I do. I own a gym.

Michelle: 2) You pay my full rate. No friend discounts.

Gabe: You got it.

Michelle: 3) You stay with me while you're in New York.

Gabe: What? Why?

Michelle: It's one of my conditions. If you want my help, you have to agree to it.

Gabe: I have to come out there soon to look at locations. But I'm staying at a hotel.

Michelle: No. You have to stay with me.

Gabe: Why can't we just meet up somewhere?

Michelle: Gabe. I haven't seen you in 13 years. You were my best friend, and you disappeared on me. You want my help? This is the least you can do while I work on your campaign.

Gabe: Where do you live?

Michelle: Hell's Kitchen.

Michelle: That's on the west side, in case you forgot.

Gabe: I know where it is.

Gabe: Fine. I'll stay with you.

Sixteen years ago

Celestial Destiny: Initial Planning Session

Michelle:

OMG

Gabe:

WTF

Michelle:

Pure basura. We finally get Latinos in space . . .

Gabe:

And they canceled it! On a cliffhanger!

Michelle:

I can't accept this. We have to know what happened to Zack and Riva in season 2.

Gabe:

What can we do? Beyond the Stars has been canceled already. This one season is all we get.

Michelle:

Wait a second.

Gabe:

What?

Michelle:

I'm a genius.

Gabe:

What??

Michelle:

WHAT IF WE WRITE IT???

Gabe:

. . . I don't understand. You mean write for the show?

Michelle:

Fanfiction, Gabe! We'll write our own Beyond the Stars fanfic!

Gabe:

Right. With all the free time we have.

Michelle:

It won't take that long. We'll work on it together!

Gabe:

Between baseball and working at my dad's store, I'm already drowning in homework.

Michelle:

Come on, Gabe, it'll be fun! Like when we used to pretend we were Luke and Leia fighting Stormtroopers on the swing set.

Gabe:

I miss that swing set.

Michelle:

Me too. This can be our new swing set.

Gabe:

Okay. ☺

Chapter 4

Picking someone up at the airport in New York City was the biggest of favors, and Michelle hoped the big jerk appreciated it. But not even the nighttime traffic leading into LaGuardia Airport or BTS blasting positive-energy K-pop from her car's speakers could distract from her jitters about seeing Gabe again.

What would he be like? Would it be weird to be around him again, or just like old times? She wasn't sure which she preferred. It might hurt more if they slipped right back into their old dynamic, but she also harbored the hope that they could pick up where they'd left off. Although, the last time she'd seen him, they'd had their tongues in each other's mouth. Were they going to pretend that hadn't happened? What was the etiquette for reuniting with a former best friend you'd almost banged?

The music was interrupted as her Fiat's Bluetooth called out, "Call from Ava."

Gripping the wheel tight, Michelle debated whether or not to answer. Her stomach was a bundle of twisted-up knots, her teeth clenched tight. Ava would know something was going on, and Michelle didn't want to explain what she was doing, especially since she wasn't totally sure herself.

She declined the call and BTS resumed.

"Get your shit together," Michelle told herself. "We're thirty-one, not eighteen. We can be adults about this."

Right. They were adults now, which meant Gabe was absolutely not going to freak out when he found out the plan had changed, and that instead of staying in Michelle's apartment in Hell's Kitchen, they'd be staying at her parents' house in the Bronx.

Damn, who was she kidding? He was *totally* going to freak out.

If she told him, he'd refuse to get in her car. He might even turn right around and hop on a plane back to Los Angeles. Her whole plan hinged on keeping him close, so that's what she'd do.

And hope he didn't notice where she was driving.

It was wrong to trick him, but what else could she do? Despite repeated claims that her bathroom renovation would definitely be completed by now, her apartment still had no toilet.

As the line of cars and taxis pulled to a standstill, Michelle flipped her mirror down and looked herself right in the eye. "Do not let him see you sweat. He doesn't deserve it."

Better to make *him* sweat. Michelle unclipped her hair from its messy bun and let it tumble down over her shoulders and back. Then she grabbed a tube of lipstick out of her purse and freshened up her lips. The deep red was striking against her summer tan, and with her signature dramatic eye makeup, it created what Ava called her "witch look."

By the time Michelle had finger-combed her dark locks and pouted at her reflection a few times, traffic had started moving again and she was feeling a little more confident.

Sure, she was an emotional mess inside, but at least she felt pretty.

The music stopped again.

"Text from Gabe," her car said, and Michelle tensed as his words were repeated in a robotic voice. "Almost there."

"This doesn't have to be a big deal," she told herself, speaking out loud as she navigated her way around a stopped rideshare SUV. "He's here to work. It doesn't have to be weird."

She tapped on the wheel along with the music, trying to ignore the sick feeling in her gut.

If only she could talk to Ava and Jasmine about it instead of giving herself a pep talk alone in her car. Her best cousins, her Primas of Power, were her biggest support system. But for some reason, when it came to sex and relationships, Michelle just couldn't open up to them.

It wasn't fair. She gave them shit about not telling her when they were having romantic troubles. Yet, when it came to herself, she clammed up.

She could guess how they'd react, though. They'd tell her to stay away from him. She'd been a fucking wreck after he'd left for California. Her primas had stuck to her side the whole summer before college—the summer she'd planned to spend with Gabe.

The summer that might have gone differently after they'd kissed.

Not this time. She wouldn't let him affect her like he had. This was for closure, and to assuage her curiosity. That was it. She'd pick him up, drive them home, and tomorrow they'd work on his project. She'd stay cool and she'd get the answers she deserved.

And maybe an apology too. It was the least the pendejo could do.

Even with her plan in mind, Michelle's nerves sizzled as she approached the pickup area. A car in front of her pulled away from the curb and then . . . there he was.

Her heart thumped like it had taken a hit. He was . . . gorgeous. And *here*. Gabe was here!

Six feet of hard-muscled Latino Superman, with the deepest dimples you ever saw and the softest lips she'd ever kissed.

Michelle's mouth literally watered at the sight of him. It was stupid. She'd looked up his gym's Instagram account to get a sense of the brand, and it of course featured photos of Gabe, along with his business partner, Fabian. Gazing at Gabe's sweet smile had broken her heart all over again, but she'd told herself it was better to be prepared. He'd been a hottie at eighteen, but back then, he was still just the boy next door, her best guy friend who'd somehow grown up to be cute.

But seeing him in person again, after all this time . . .

Yowza.

In black track pants and a white T-shirt that was unaccountably stylish on him, and the backward baseball cap that had always been his staple, Gabe was really, really ridiculously good-looking.

And he was searching for her, his dark eyes scanning the line of cars.

What would happen if she didn't stop? If she just drove past him and went back home? It wasn't too late. Gabe could hail a taxi, find a hotel, hire somebody else—maybe even Nathaniel— and Michelle could go back to her life as it was before she'd received his email.

And wonder "what if" for the rest of her days? No gracias.

Michelle tapped the horn to get his attention, then gave a little wave when he turned his head. She pulled the Fiat up to the curb and popped the trunk with shaking fingers.

Gabe moved around to the back of the car, rolling his gray hard-shell suitcase behind him.

Inside, Michelle turned down the music. Then she turned up the AC. And then, because she couldn't stand it a second longer, she got out.

She hadn't planned to. The LaGuardia curbside pickup was a logjam of cars and people and luggage, and it was best to get in and out as soon as possible. But she couldn't take the thought of sitting next to him in the car without . . . something.

Gabe hefted the suitcase into the trunk with ease, then shut the hood. He turned as she came up beside him and without a word, Michelle reached up and threw her arms around his neck in a tight hug.

She hadn't planned to do this either, but she couldn't stop herself. She *needed* it.

His arms came around her, enveloping her in his embrace. It felt good, so freaking good.

Gabe still gave the best hugs.

He smelled good, too—clean and fresh, like soap. And his hug felt strong, warm, and safe.

But he wasn't safe. She had to remember that.

From the feel of his body pressed to hers, Michelle noted the ways he'd changed. He'd grown a few inches taller than the last time she'd seen him, and put on . . . a lot of pounds of muscle. Holy hell. It was like being hugged by a living, breathing, flesh-and-blood wall. Or a marble statue, one of those sexy ones with defined muscles, an air of self-important boredom, and an accommodating fig leaf. Something without an ounce of softness, but you still wanted to cuddle up against it because the beauty was so staggering and alluring.

But it hurt too. Oh god, did it hurt. Heartbreak and longing and arousal and love and anger and sadness whirled around inside her like a tornado of conflicted feeling, fascinating and destructive.

He'd been her best friend. And he'd *left* her.

But it was hard to stay angry when he held her like this.

Just as Michelle became too aware of her breasts pressed to his hard chest, of her face nestled into his shoulder, and his breath on her neck, a car horn blasted behind her, making her jolt. She pulled away, dropping back down on her heels. And got her first good look at that handsome face.

Gabe had a jaw square and sharp enough to cut, with killer cheekbones leading down to dimples that could ruin your life. Dark eyes narrowed with a hint of wariness, and his thick, straight brows gave nothing away.

"Hi," she said, trying not to sound as breathless as she felt.

"Hi." His voice was deeper than it had been, and something about that made her want to cry. "Thanks for picking me up."

"You're welcome. Let's go before somebody yells at us for being parked too long."

She berated herself as she got back behind the wheel. *That was real fucking stupid, Michelle.* He hadn't deserved that hug.

But she had. After all this time, it was the least of what she deserved.

GABE TRIED NOT to stare, but he was pretty sure he was doing a terrible job of it.

Part of him was positive this was all a huge mistake—coming back to New York, staying in Michelle's apartment, hell, even opening a new gym. The other part just wanted Michelle in his arms again.

On the flight over, he'd tried to brace himself for how things might be different between them, preparing himself for an extremely awkward car ride to her place. But then she'd surprised him with a hug. He hadn't expected it, but once his arms were around her, it had felt as natural as breathing.

He knew what it felt like to hold her. Michelle was affectionate, and they'd hugged often when they were younger. And then, of course, there'd been that one time, the last time, when—

Gabe pinched his thigh to interrupt the memory. These pants wouldn't hide a hard-on, and that's what had gotten them into trouble in the first place.

He should've worn jeans. Or a cup. But he preferred comfortable clothes for travel, and he hadn't expected to get turned on by Michelle immediately.

She was stunning, though. There was no denying that. Some things he remembered—the spill of long, dark hair. Honey-colored eyes. The smattering of light freckles across her nose and cheekbones. He tried not to think about the enticing swell of cleavage revealed by her tank top, or the way her faded blue jeans hugged her lush, round ass. Michelle had been sexy before— and his dirty teenage-boy mind had noted the changes as they'd grown up together—but now, he just wanted to take a bite out of her.

He'd always thought the phrase *a body that wouldn't quit* sounded stupid. Looking at Michelle . . . he got it.

They were quiet as she navigated the traffic leaving the arrivals terminal at LaGuardia, but when they hit the highway, Gabe finally said what was on his mind.

"You look good, Mich."

Her eyes cut away from the road for a second, giving him a quick, sweeping, up-and-down glance. Just as he thought she was going to say "You too," her gaze returned to the road and she said, "I know."

Gabe let out a low chuckle. It was such a Michelle thing to say. She'd always had an abundance of confidence. It was one of the things he used to adore—and even envy—about her.

"How was your flight?" she asked, keeping her eyes trained on the road.

"Not bad. I had the row to myself."

She nodded. "Cool. Did you sleep?"

He shook his head. "Nah. Wasn't tired."

He'd also been too wired to relax enough to sleep. Instead, he'd caught up on emails and indulged in a few episodes of *Spaced Out*, the latest original sci-fi series on ScreenFlix.

If he could avoid seeing his family on this trip, he'd call it a success, but at least . . . at least things seemed to be going okay with Michelle.

She turned to peer out the back windows and Gabe finally got a good look at her shirt. It showed Queen Seravida, one of the lead characters from *Beyond the Stars*, a sci-fi TV series from the mid-aughts. It had been canceled after one season but had since attained a cult following.

Had Michelle worn that shirt on purpose? As a reminder of their shared history and the fanfic that had consumed their teenage years?

"I thought of you when she died," he said.

Michelle frowned. "When who—oh." She glanced down at her shirt. "Tamara Romero. Yeah, I was devastated."

Me too, he thought. When he'd heard the news of the actress's death, he'd thought of reaching out to Michelle. But he hadn't done it.

"Are you still in contact with any of the others?" he asked, referring to their *Beyond the Stars* online fandom group from back in the day.

Michelle shook her head. "I'm Facebook friends with a few of them, but we don't interact much. I don't know what happened to the others—I never knew their real names."

Gabe was quiet for a moment, remembering all the hours he and Michelle had devoted to their favorite fandom. "We never finished our story."

"No, *you* didn't." She gave him a little smirk.

By the end, Gabe had basically been writing all the chapters of their fanfic with Michelle leaning over his shoulder, making comments and suggestions. Those had been some of the happiest moments of his teenage years, which was pretty fucking nerdy to admit, but it was true. Just the two of them, with all their inside jokes, making up a world of their own.

They'd been close to the end when he left. The plan had been to continue writing the story together while they were in college, but things hadn't worked out that way. Just one more thing Gabe had abandoned when he'd left New York.

He peered out the window, idly scanning the signs along the side of the highway. And frowned. It had been a long time since he'd been here, but he was sure he remembered this route.

"This is the Whitestone Bridge."

Michelle didn't even blink. "Excellent deduction."

"But you live in Manhattan."

"Yup."

"Shouldn't we be taking a tunnel or something?"

"We would be . . . *if* we were going to Manhattan."

Gabe stared at her impassive expression. "Michelle. Why aren't we going to Manhattan if that's where you live?"

She sighed. "Because I'm not staying there right now."

His gut plummeted like he was on an out-of-control roller coaster. "Why not?"

"There's no toilet," she replied bluntly. "My bathroom renovation is taking twice as long as expected. They were supposed to be finished already, but you know how it goes."

Gabe sucked in a breath as panic set in. No, they couldn't be going where he thought they were going. "I'll pay for a hotel. A suite. For both of us. You'll have your own room. Room service. Open bar. Whatever you want."

She snorted. "Don't be ridiculous. Why would we stay in a hotel when I have a perfectly good house for us to use?"

House. *Shit.* That confirmed his suspicions.

Michelle was taking them to her parents' house in the Bronx.

Suddenly the car felt even smaller as desperation kicked up his pulse. "Fine, then *I'll* stay in a hotel. Drop me off somewhere. Anywhere. Side of the highway is fine. I'll hitchhike."

She shot him a dark glare, her mouth tightening into a hard line. "You agreed to stay with me. Since I'm staying at my parents' house, that's where you're staying too."

He narrowed his eyes back at her. "You did this on purpose."

She let out an exasperated sigh. "Yeah, Gabe. I demanded that my contractors take extra time to renovate my bathroom just so I could trick you into staying at my parents' house. I *love* not having a working toilet in my apartment. It's the *best*."

Sweat prickled Gabe's forehead under the band of his cap. He adjusted it, trying to wipe it away, but more sprang up. "My parents live *right next door* to yours."

She kept her eyes on the road. "So what?"

Gabe slumped as much as the seat belt and mediocre leg room would allow, as if someone else driving on the highway might recognize him and rat him out. "They can't know I'm here."

"Then don't tell them."

Trust Michelle to oversimplify the problem.

"I mean, I don't want them to see *me*."

"I hardly ever see them. It'll be fine. We'll keep you out of sight. Stop worrying so much."

"What about your family? They'll tell my parents the second they lay eyes on me."

"My parents are in Florida at the beach house. No one else knows you're here. Don't murder me, 'kay?"

"You haven't told anyone?" That surprised him. He was sure she would have at least told her cousins.

"No way." She gave a mock shudder. "The last thing I need is all of them breathing down our necks. They'll read too much into it and the next thing you know, my mother will be planning our wedding."

She made it sound like a fate worse than death. But she was right. They'd already dodged enough invasive questions when they were younger. People assumed they would eventually get together, and while Gabe had dreamed about it often, it would never have worked. Michelle was firmly based in New York City, and Gabe couldn't live here. Not even for her.

"You know I wouldn't have agreed to stay with you if you'd told me we were going to the Bronx," he said.

"Oh, I had a feeling," she replied. "That's why I didn't tell you."

Gabe threw up his hands. "This was a trap!"

"Okay, Admiral Ackbar, calm down."

"Still with the *Star Wars* jokes, huh?"

She smirked. "You know it."

"Well, it's nice to see some things don't change."

Michelle was quiet for a long moment. "I'm not the one who changed."

Direct hit. He was the one who'd lied, and then left. And she wasn't going to let him forget it.

But he'd left for a reason. He'd stayed gone for a reason. And that reason was living in the house right next to the one she expected him to stay in for four days.

Fuck their agreement. He couldn't do it. This was beyond what he could tolerate. He'd sleep there tonight, but in the morning? He was leaving to find a hotel.

No matter what Michelle said about it.

Sixteen years ago

Windows Messenger Chat Transcript

Celestial Destiny: Episode 1 Planning Session

Celestial Destiny: A Beyond the Stars Season 2 Fanfic
Episode 1
By BxGamer15 and ChelleBlockTango

Disclaimer: We don't own the rights to Beyond the Stars, we're just two fans who are mad that we finally got Latinos in spaaaaace but they were canceled after one season.

Gabe:

What the heck is up with your username?

Michelle:

It's "Chelle" for my name plus the song "Cell Block Tango" from the musical Chicago. Have you seen it?

Gabe:

You know I haven't.

Michelle:

Cool. We can watch it this weekend.

Gabe:

Can't wait . . .

Michelle:

Is that sarcasm? From someone with the username Bronx Gamer 15 years old? Why don't you add your social security number while you're at it?

Gabe:

I take it back. Your username is awesome. Let's move on.

Michelle:

Where should we start?

Gabe:

Zack escaped when he was young, so we should pick up where he is now, since we saw that glimpse of him right before the cliffhanger ending.

Michelle:

Did they ever say where he'd been hiding?

Gabe:

No. I guess they were going to show it as flashbacks in season 2?

Michelle:

Okay, well, if YOU were a prince with a murderous dad whose mom had just faked her own death, where would you go?

Gabe:

Hmm . . . The Mos Eisley Cantina.

Michelle:

LOL this isn't Star Wars! They're not in a galaxy far, far away!

Gabe:

Yeah, but somewhere like Tatooine seems like a good place to disappear. Worked for Obi-Wan, right? Everyone has secrets and no one's gonna ask too many questions. Maybe Zack became a bartender. He hears all the gossip but he's basically invisible to everyone around him.

Michelle:

Can Riva be a bounty hunter now? And Queen Seravida, who is also in hiding, hires her to find Zack.

Gabe:

Does Zack recognize Riva?

Michelle:

Maybe not immediately, but they were best friends, even though she was a commoner. Part of him would recognize her, right? I mean, I'd recognize you, even if years had passed.

Gabe:

Same. Riva finds him, but he doesn't go quietly. He thinks his father is the one who hired her.

Michelle:

Then Riva tackles him, stuns him, and drags him to her ship.

Gabe:

Um, Zack is a trained fighter. And the actor is like half a foot taller. How is Riva doing all that?

Michelle:

Hello, she's a badass bounty hunter who never loses a target. Besides, she's his BFF, so his guards are down.

Gabe:

Fine. So he's like, "Tell my father I'm never going back." And she's like, "I would, but it was your mother who hired me."

Michelle:

And then he's like, "AY DIOS MÍO, my mami is alive?!"

Gabe:

Uh, maybe not exactly like that.

Michelle:

And Riva stuns him anyway!

Gabe:

Of course she does . . .

Chapter 5

Gabe kept his gaze glued to the windows as they exited the highway at Pelham Parkway and drove down the tree-lined avenue through the streets of the Bronx to their old neighborhood. Faded memories clashed with the reality lit by yellow streetlights. There was something disconcerting about being back—an underlying sense of comfort, but also of *wrongness*. He didn't belong here.

As they turned off Eastchester Road onto Morris Park, he twisted in his seat to look out the window at a familiar green-and-white logo.

"Was that a Starbucks?"

Michelle let out a muffled snicker. "Yes, Gabe. Even the Bronx has Starbucks now."

As they crossed Williamsbridge Road, Gabe was hit with a pang of grief. That was where his father's stationery store had been before it'd closed, shortly after Gabe left for college in California.

That move—along with the way he'd dropped the news— had been the beginning of the end of his relationship with his parents.

It had been right after Michelle ripped up his flight printout and kicked him out of her room. He'd gone home to pack and make dinner, and he'd blurted it out the second his dad was done eating.

I'm going to California.

His parents hadn't been happy, to say the least. The shouting match that followed had spanned two languages and countless old arguments about school, Gabe's choices, and family obligations. His father had dismissed Gabe's accomplishments—like graduating with honors and getting a scholarship to UCLA were nothing—and his mother had called Gabe ungrateful.

And then he and his father had their last big fight about the stationery shop.

You are part of a family, Gabriel. Families make decisions together. You need to stay here and help with the store.

Pop, the store is going under. It's only a matter of time.

The store will be fine if you help—

Nothing I do is going to help the store!

It would if you tried!

The store is your dream, Pop. I'm going after mine.

To do what? Play baseball? What are you going to do, join the Yankees?

I don't know. But it's not working at a card shop in the Bronx. I'm leaving. And there's nothing you can do to stop me.

Gabe had seen them a few more times after that, but it had only gotten worse. After the incident at his sister's wedding, he'd been done with his parents for good.

Michelle turned on their street, and Gabe's pulse spiked. Familiar houses, barely changed in the last decade, pinged his memory one after the other, each a little pinprick of grief.

No. There was no way he could spend four days here. It would kill him.

Who was it who'd said "You can never go home again"? Whoever it was, they were right. This wasn't his home anymore. And he couldn't—wouldn't—go back.

The Amato and Aguilar families lived on a block with a few small stand-alone houses—a combo of red brick and aluminum siding—that had driveways, but no garages. Predominantly an Italian neighborhood, the demographic had shifted a bit over the years Gabe had lived there. He had no idea what it was like now, except that his Puerto Rican and Mexican parents and Michelle's Puerto Rican and Italian parents still lived there. Michelle's mother was one of the reasons his own mom felt comfortable moving next door.

After Gabe left for the last time, the only person he'd stayed in touch with was his older sister, Nicole.

Nikki was a mom now, with two children—Oliver, who was seven, and Lucy, who was nine and had transitioned two years earlier. Gabe had met his niece and nephew for the first time when Nikki had taken the kids to Disneyland. Gabe bought their tickets, since they'd made the longer flight to Disneyland in California, as opposed to Walt Disney World in Florida, just to see him. It was the first time he'd seen Nikki in person since her wedding, and he'd had fun with her and the kids. And when Nikki and her husband, Patrick, took a family trip to Colorado, Gabe had flown out to join them.

He FaceTimed with Lucy and Oliver regularly, but when he thought about his own uncles, he couldn't help but feel like he was remiss in his Tío Duties. Tío Marco, Gabe's godfather, had always been around when he was a kid. His father's younger brother, Marco, had helped Gabe's parents when they'd moved to this neighborhood, had picked Gabe up from baseball practice and gone to his games, and intervened when Gabe's dad got on his case about working more hours in the stationery store.

Stop thinking about the store, Gabe told himself. It would only make this worse.

As Michelle pulled into the driveway of her family's house, Gabe scrunched down as much as he was able to. He peeked out the car window at his parents' house, to the right of Michelle's. It was too close, the car and steps too visible from the front windows.

"I can't do this," he muttered in a strangled voice.

Michelle shut the car off. "Don't worry, your parents go to bed early."

"Their bedroom light is still on."

"Why on earth would they be looking out the window to check when I get home?"

"You don't know my mother."

"I'm sure it's fine," she replied breezily, and got out of the car.

"Wait." He reached across and grabbed her wrist before she could close the door. Her skin was cool against his. He was burning up with anxiety. "I'll go in through the back."

"Suit yourself." Taking her keys out of her purse, Michelle rounded the car and climbed the steps to the front door. After a deep breath, Gabe opened the car door as quietly as he could and slunk out. Shutting it gently, he crept along the side to the trunk. This would be easier if he weren't wearing a white T-shirt, but he hadn't expected to sneak inside under cover of darkness, now had he? He slipped his suitcase out but when he closed the trunk, it made a loud *thunk*, and he winced. He didn't dare drag his luggage, so he cradled it against his chest, trying not to think about airport germs as he crouch-ran toward the gate on the left side of the house.

By now Michelle was unlocking the front door. When Gabe opened the gate, the hinge creaked loudly, and she shot him an amused look. He ducked through and finally, with an entire house separating him from view of his parents, he straightened to his full height.

Pausing to take a breath, he looked around, unable to believe where he was. For the first time in nine years, he was in the same space as his parents. They were home, and so damn close. He'd seen an SUV in the driveway, and his mom's car—the one she'd bought right before he graduated college—was parked at the curb.

Bitterness blossomed in his chest, and a strange tension took hold of him. For all these years, he'd tried not to think of them. It had been too painful. And it was painful now, but also . . . some small part of him really wanted to see them. Wanted them to see *him*.

It wouldn't go well. He knew that. His interactions with them hadn't gone well since he was fourteen years old, marked by yelling and criticism. There was no reason for that to have changed.

Adjusting his grip on the suitcase, Gabe made his way to the back of the house. Here, he had to be careful. Michelle's back-yard was separated from his by only a low chain-link fence, and the sliding glass doors leading into Michelle's basement would be easily visible by—

He stopped. The fence he'd climbed over countless times as a child was gone, replaced by a stylish wooden lattice covered by climbing plants.

This, more than anything else, triggered a fresh wave of grief. What else had changed in his absence?

He heard a door open and nearly leaped out of his skin, but it was just Michelle opening the kitchen door, up a short flight of steps from the mostly concrete backyard.

"Come on," she hissed.

He'd expected her to open the sliding doors to the basement, but of course she had to make this even more difficult for him. With a muttered curse, Gabe hefted the suitcase and tiptoed across the yard to the steps.

A bright light flashed on and he froze. On the tiny deck outside the kitchen, Michelle gestured frantically for him to get a move on. Realizing it was just a motion sensor light, Gabe tucked the suitcase under one arm and jogged up the steps as quickly and quietly as he could. He slipped past Michelle into the dark kitchen and finally, with great relief, put the suitcase down.

"You could've warned me about the light," he said with a growl.

"I forgot. It's been a long time since I had to sneak someone into this house." She pointed at the mat just inside the door. "Shoes off. You know the rules."

In the dim light permeating the windows, Gabe toed off his sneakers while Michelle slipped out of her sandals and slid on indoor chanclas. Something brushed Gabe's ankle and he jumped as a dark shape appeared and began to sniff his shoes with gusto.

"That's Jezebel," Michelle said. "She's hard to see in the dark."

She moved to the light switch and turned it on, flooding the room with light. Gabe dropped to the floor like he was doing a push-up, and a sleek black cat he recognized from Michelle's Instagram feed poked her nose—which had just been in his sneaker—into his face.

Michelle stared at him. "What are you doing?"

"Close the curtains," he hissed, annoyed at her surprised look. The cat—Jezebel—bumped her head against his temple, so he shifted to scratch her ears.

"Gabe, your mom isn't going to look into the kitchen—"

"Yes, she is. She used to do it all the time. Close the fucking curtains!"

Michelle sighed but did as he asked. "Better?"

"No." Gabe got up from the floor, breathing like he'd just run a five-minute mile. He couldn't go through this every time he had to enter and leave the house. And he couldn't stay locked inside either. He had meetings to attend and locations to look at—in Manhattan.

Michelle stood at the kitchen counter, watching him with a pensive expression. It was the first time he'd gotten a good look at her, head to toe. A familiar sense of desire rose up. He still wanted her, but mixed up in it was longing and anguish, anger and heartache. The strength of his feelings threatened to choke him.

He'd always thought she was pretty. When they were little,

they'd had fun together, and that was enough. Her prettiness didn't mean anything except that he'd adored the sight of her smile.

As they'd gotten older, they'd both changed, and his gaze started to linger on her in different ways. Their bodies had matured, and he no longer thought nothing of her easy touches, the way she leaned against him when they watched movies or sat on his lap when the bus was crowded. Back then, he thought *a lot* about those touches. And he'd eventually admitted to himself that he was in love with her, beyond friendship. He loved listening to her talk and watching her dance around her room when her favorite songs came on the radio. He loved arguing with her about movies and sharing food from the same plate.

He loved to see her smile.

She wasn't smiling now, though.

"What are you thinking?" he asked, the words tumbling out before he could question whether or not they were wise.

Her gaze dropped to the counter. "It's weird having you back here."

Gabe looked around the kitchen he'd once known as well as his own. "It's weird being back here."

"I wondered if it would be like it used to be."

"I don't think we can go back to how it used to be." He said the words gently, knowing they had the potential to hurt her. She was more emotionally fragile than she pretended to be. But to honor their friendship, he had to give her honesty. He wasn't the same person he'd been then, and neither was she. They'd grown up. They couldn't slip back into the easy camaraderie that came from seeing each other daily.

"I guess we can't," she murmured. Then she opened the fridge and waved him over. "Anyway, I made these for you."

He stood next to her, trying to ignore the enticing woodsy fragrance that clung to her, and peered into the refrigerator.

On the main shelf, uniform stacks of Tupperware containers were piled four high. Michelle selected one and removed the lid. Scents of lemon and pepper wafted up to him. Inside the container, which was separated into two compartments, sat a baked chicken breast and a side medley of sauteed vegetables—zucchini, mushroom, and green pepper.

Gabe stilled. "What's this?"

"Meal prep." Michelle replaced the lid and put the container back in the fridge. "I figured you're probably on some kind of bodybuilder diet, so I looked up food recommendations and portion sizes. Some blogs suggested a lot of lean proteins and veggies throughout the day, so I did some cooking in advance."

A warm feeling spread through Gabe's chest. "How did you know?"

She gave his torso and arms a pointed look. "Instagram."

Of course.

"Anyway," she continued, "we obviously don't have a full gym, but there's a weight bench and a couple machines downstairs."

"Thanks." Gabe didn't have the heart to tell her he wouldn't be staying here more than one night. It would lead to an argument, and Michelle had clearly gone to a lot of trouble to prepare for his stay. The premade meals were more than he ever would have asked for.

Michelle gestured at the containers. "Do you need dinner?"

"Nah, I had a sandwich on the plane. I'm just tired."

It wasn't a lie. And the sooner he went to bed, the sooner he could sneak out in the morning.

"All right," she said, shutting the fridge. "You're going to stay in my brother's old room."

He nodded. Junior's room was upstairs, so Gabe would at least be far away from Michelle's room in the base—

"Next to me," she added.

Gabe frowned. "¿Qué?"

"I'm staying in Monica's old room."

"What happened to the basement?" The words were out before Gabe could stop himself. The basement was where their friendship had both leveled up and shattered, all in one fell swoop.

Michelle busied herself at the sink. "It was my dad's dream to convert it into an entertainment room. Big TV, a bar, plus a desk and the exercise equipment. Once I moved out, he got his wish."

"Oh."

Shit. How was he supposed to function knowing she was sleeping in the room next to his? For some reason this was worse than the idea of sleeping on the sofa in her apartment. Maybe the memories of her family occupying this house, of *his* family right next door, would be enough to quell whatever thoughts his libido tried to conjure. Gabe could only hope.

But when Michelle took him upstairs, he saw something he'd forgotten. The bedrooms shared a bathroom.

Gabe stood inside it, the peach walls and tiles reflecting off his skin and making his image in the mirror look yellow and sallow, but all he could focus on was the explosion of bottles and jars on the bathroom counter. Michelle's makeup, her lotion, her face stuff. All the things she used on her body, on her skin and hair, when she stood in this room *naked*.

He shut his eyes. Being here was reverting him back to his teenage self, and he didn't want that. That Gabe had been unsure of himself, worried about what other people thought of him and his choices, too afraid to act. When he'd moved to Los Angeles, that had been one of the biggest changes he'd made. Alone, away from his family and everyone who knew him, he'd finally had the space to take decisive action, to not give a fuck what anyone thought. It had worked for him.

That was why he was here. Taking decisive action to open the New York location of the gym. Yes, it was part of his investment agreement, but he'd made a deal and he was confident Agility Gym could make the jump to a new market.

So why was he hung up on the simple task of brushing his teeth in the room where Michelle showered?

He sent his reflection a resigned glare. He knew why. Because he wanted her. Still or again, it didn't matter. It had been a long time since he'd felt this level of wanting for someone. He didn't know how much of it was old, leftover desire or some fucked-up part of him that wanted what he couldn't have. But he wanted her, *now*. And there was no getting around that fact.

As Gabe got ready for bed that night, exhausted from a day of travel and riding the emotional roller coaster that had become his life, he reminded himself that this was why he'd left. Being here, around the people he'd left behind, pulled him into a hurricane of drama and doubt. Yeah, there were times he felt alone, but he was strong in his convictions, and that mattered more. Better to be alone and focused than surrounded by people who didn't believe in him.

With that in mind, Gabe picked out his clothes for the next day, zipped his suitcase, and set an alarm for early the next morning.

He didn't need these reminders of who he'd been. As much as he still wanted her, he couldn't let Michelle trap him here, in such close proximity to painful memories.

Tomorrow, he was leaving.

Chapter 6

Michelle woke early the next morning. Too early, but she couldn't get back to sleep, her mind full of thoughts of Gabe. Beside her, Jezebel was curled into a warm ball.

The summer morning light seeped past the bedroom curtains, which at one time had been pink, like the bedding, walls, and carpet. She'd shared this room with her sister before Monica had gone off to college and Michelle eventually moved down to the basement. Since then, it had been repurposed as her mother's craft room and painted a soft yellow with white furniture and plastic drawers full of jewelry-making supplies and washi tape.

To an extent, Michelle understood how Gabe felt. It was weird to be sleeping in her parents' house in her now-unfamiliar childhood bedroom. It had to be even stranger for Gabe, who hadn't been back for many years.

When Michelle had conceived of this plan, some part of her hoped that having him here would make her feel . . . happy. She remembered being happy when they were young, whereas these days the best she could hope for was mild contentment. Plus, she'd missed Gabe more than she cared to admit. She'd expected some nostalgia, some reminiscing about the good old days. Excitement about the Agility project and catching up on what they'd been up to since they'd last seen each other. After all, they had college and all of their twenties to rehash.

What she hadn't expected was the simmering arousal. Like all of her cells prickled with awareness of him. Like he was a giant magnet pulling her inexorably toward him, and she was power-less to stop the attraction. It was a force of nature, undeniable in its strength, laughing at her to *just give in.* To stop fighting it. *You want him, dummy.*

Michelle shoved the blankets aside and slid from the bed. This line of thinking was doing nothing but making it impos-sible for her to get back to sleep, and now she had to pee. Jez-ebel immediately burrowed into the warmth Michelle's body left behind, making herself at home in the center of the bed.

Michelle stepped into her chancletas and left the room si-lently, making sure to avoid the creaking floorboards under the hall rug and on the stairs. She used the downstairs half bathroom so as not to wake Gabe by flushing the toilet on the other side of the wall from his bed, then went to the kitchen to make a cup of tea. If she was going to be up and about, she might as well caffeinate.

She was taking her first glorious sip when she heard the toi-let flush upstairs. Odd, it was the hall bathroom closer to her parents' room. The pipes made a different sound in that one. Maybe Gabe didn't want to wake her up?

It was barely 6 A.M., and for Gabe, it would be three hours behind. She stayed quiet, sipping her tea slowly. He would probably go back to bed. But then the ceiling creaked overhead, followed by the sound of footsteps moving toward the stairs.

Setting the mug on the counter, Michelle left the kitchen to greet him, intending to ask if he wanted tea or coffee. She hadn't thought he'd be up yet, so she'd made only the one cup for herself.

"Morni—" she started, then stopped short when she saw Gabe, frozen mid-step, right on the middle stair that always creaked.

He was already fully dressed . . . and carrying his suitcase.

Surprise and a rising wave of anger made her heart pound.

Eyes narrowed, Michelle propped a hand on her hip. "And just where do you think *you're* going?"

Oh god, she sounded just like her mother.

And like a teenager caught sneaking out—because really, *what else* could he be doing?—Gabe cringed. His shoulders hunched up near his ears and his lips parted in a grimace.

"Um . . ."

He seemed to be at a loss for words, but despite the early hour and minimal caffeine, Michelle was not. Besides, she didn't need an explanation. His intention was clear.

This motherfucker was leaving her *again*.

Michelle stomped to the bottom of the stairs and glared up at him. "You're sneaking out. Don't even try to make up some bullshit excuse."

Gabe's eyes flashed, anger rising in their dark depths, and he straightened, setting the suitcase down on the step beside him. "I'm leaving."

Michelle scoffed and crossed her arms under her breasts. "Yeah, I can see that. You're really fucking good at it."

His gaze flickered to her breasts. She hadn't put on a bra yet, and her pose had pushed up her ample tits.

Her nipples tightened as she thought of how, the last time she'd seen him, he'd had his hands and mouth on her breasts. She adjusted her stance slightly to make sure he could see the points of her nips poking through the thin fabric of her sleep tank. Why should she be the only one plagued by sexually frustrating memories? Besides, she was *pissed*.

"Get your ass back upstairs," she said, in a tone that brooked no argument.

Gabe's lips tightened, and he gave her an exasperated look, one she remembered well. It was the look that said he thought she was being a bitch but wouldn't dare tell her so.

And fine. Maybe she was. She hadn't told him they'd be staying here, suspecting that he never would have agreed to it if he'd known about the change in plans. But she'd also hoped that the familiar surroundings, the nostalgia, would bring them closer together than staying in a bland hotel room would.

Well, so much for that.

Gabe picked up the suitcase but instead of going back up, he started down the rest of the stairs. "Michelle, you know I can't stay here."

She held her ground and used the only leverage she had. "What I *know* is that you agreed to stay with me in exchange for me taking on this project."

He came to a stop where she blocked the bottom of the stairs like Gandalf on the bridge declaring, *You shall not pass.* They faced each other, him towering over her from his greater height and the added boost from the last step, her gazing up at him with nothing but cleavage and chutzpah as her weapons of choice.

Michelle fought a shiver of awareness. He was so close, the sleepy annoyance in his eyes too fucking endearing. And she was wearing practically nothing, just a thin tank top and little shorts. Her pulse fluttered, and she saw he was breathing hard too. She didn't think it was from exertion, since he was still holding the suitcase like it weighed less than Jezebel had when she was a kitten.

"I agreed to stay with you in Manhattan," he said, breaking into her thoughts before she could undress him with her eyes. "I did not agree to stay with you here."

"So you're leaving again." Michelle couldn't help the emotion in her voice, although she would have banished it if she could. "Just like that. Without a word."

"Michelle. You lied to me about where we'd be staying."

Ah, so they were on *Michelle* now instead of *Mich*. He must really be mad. She supposed she couldn't blame him. Maybe she hadn't set out to deceive him, but in the end, that's what she'd done. Still, she wasn't letting him go without a fight.

"What were you going to do? Sneak out while I was asleep, call for a car, and have them drop you off at a hotel?"

"What else am I supposed to do?" From his defensive tone and the look on his face, she could tell she'd hit the nail on the head.

"You're supposed to stay and deal with your problems instead of running away again," she shot back. "You and I have a lot of unfinished business, Gabe."

He stepped down to the floor and set his suitcase beside him.

Michelle didn't back up, though, and the move left them toe to toe, both breathing hard.

Her heart thumped at his nearness, at the spark of anger in his dark eyes. Maybe it was perverse, but she liked him like this, pissed off and prickly. The Gabe she'd known had shied away from conflict, never raised his voice, and let her take the upper hand in all their arguments. This Gabe wasn't backing down, and it was as sexy as it was infuriating.

He leaned down to look her right in the eye. In a deceptively soft voice, he asked, "Do you know why I left?"

"No, I don't know why!" The memories flooded back—the betrayal, the hurt. How much she'd missed him. The missing had been like a sickness, taking up permanent residence in the pit of her stomach. "You didn't even talk to me about it."

"I did, actually." His jaw was like granite. "I tried to talk to you about my parents. But every time I brought it up, you defended them. You didn't see that I was drowning here. If you had, it wouldn't have surprised you that I wanted to leave."

"Fuck your parents!" She pressed her hands to her face, embarrassed by the outburst. "Sorry, I don't mean that. But this isn't about them. You also abandoned *me*."

In a nervous move she remembered, he took off his Yankees cap and smoothed a hand over his hair. "I had to get away from here, get out of this life."

"That doesn't explain why you ghosted me." Her voice hitched, and she hated it. "It doesn't explain why you didn't reply when I reached out, why you—"

"Michelle." Gabe interrupted her tirade and wrapped his fingers gently around her wrists. She hadn't even noticed she'd been waving her hands around. His thumbs stroked her skin, right over her pulse, and she calmed slightly.

"I needed a clean break, and you . . ." He let out a sigh that seemed to come from the depths of his soul. "You were the only person with the power to drag me back here."

The silence that followed his words settled onto her skin, making her feel tight and tense.

"Why?" she whispered.

He released her wrists. "What do you want from me, Mich?" He sounded tired. Defeated.

But he'd called her *Mich*.

She stepped closer, if such a thing were possible. Their bodies brushed, the points of her breasts nudging his torso.

"Why was I the only person?" she pressed, her tone insistent. "*Why*, Gabe?"

The spark in his eyes was her only warning.

"Because of this!" The words burst out of him like a storm. He curled his big hands around the thin straps of her tank top, clinging like they were a lifeline, and lowered his forehead to hers. His voice was harsh with longing. "God, Michelle, I want you so fucking bad I can't think straight."

Desire coursed through her, hot and dizzying. Was it the answer she'd expected? No. Would she take it?

Hell yes.

She leaned in further, pushing her body into his. Her hands came up to grip his thick forearms. "This is why you ignored me?" she demanded, her voice breathy. "Because I'm too sexy and amazing?"

He groaned, his fingers tightening on the delicate straps of cotton. She imagined him ripping them, her shirt falling off her body.

Yes. Take it off. Touch me.

It was what she'd said back then, the memory burned into her brain. She was very close to saying it again now.

"It's because I can never say no to you," he ground out. "Seemed smarter to keep my distance, in case . . ."

"In case of what?"

His voice was low, the backs of his fingers hot against her skin. "In case you asked me to stay."

"And what if I had?"

"I . . . I don't know."

"Why didn't you ever do anything about it before that day?" This was another thing she'd wondered about. She'd known him too well to think he was just an opportunist taking advantage of her teasing.

"We were friends."

"Well, we're not anymore," she murmured, searching his expression as if it held more answers.

"You're right. We're not." He sighed and some of the tension left his body. In a move that surprised her, he pressed his lips to her forehead in a soft kiss. "I never wanted to hurt you, Mich. I'm sorry that I did."

Her pulse beat heavy and thick in her throat. The moment held a note of unreality. Gabe was here, his hard, hot body pressed to hers, his hands wrapped in her clothing, his cheek resting against the top of her head. The scent of his cologne was faint, the world around them quiet, save for the light chirping of birds outside.

I want you so fucking bad.

The words she'd pulled from him mingled with her own feelings, her own memories, her own needs.

"Gabe?" She waited for him to meet her gaze again. When he did, she licked her lips and said, "I think it's time we finished what we started."

He blinked, eyes going wide. "You mean . . ."

"We're never going to move on until we get this out of the way." And then she went up on tiptoe, leaning her body flush against his. Lowering her voice, she whispered in his ear, "*Let's fuck.*"

Chapter 7

At some point during the argument, angry tension had turned to sexual tension. Gabe's jet-lagged brain couldn't pinpoint when it had happened, but it was impossible to mistake where they were now.

Let's fuck.

Michelle's words rang in his ears, heating his blood. His need for her overwhelmed his senses, and even though some part of him knew it was a bad idea, he preferred to see the logic in her suggestion.

He'd held back in the past, but once he'd known the taste of her, he couldn't stay in touch, because he'd always be drawn back to her.

Like now, a voice whispered in the back of his mind, but he slammed a mental door on it.

They wanted each other. They were alone together. And right now, she was pressing those stunning tits right into his body.

Let's fuck.

Well, okay then.

Curling his hand around the back of her head, he slid his fingers into the warm mass of hair clipped up in a messy bun.

She leaned into his touch and he moved closer, backing her against the wall, where a framed photo showed seven-year-old Michelle dressed in white, holding a tiny children's bible and a pink rosary. She looked angelic, with her head bowed and her eyes downcast—except for the slight smirk twisting her mouth.

Gabe grimaced. "I'm going to hell. Why is this picture still here?"

"My mother believes it's my greatest achievement. And no, you probably shouldn't sex me against the wall under my First Communion glamour shot."

Gabe looked into her eyes while his hands roamed down her curves to cup her sweet ass. "Is that what I'm doing, Mich? Sexing you?"

She sucked in a breath and he was gratified by the way her lashes fluttered when he squeezed. "I will be severely disappointed if you don't."

He glanced over his shoulder at the living room. "Sofa?"

Michelle gave a firm shake of her head. "My mother will kill us if we have sex on her new couch."

"Upstairs, then."

He grabbed her hand to pull her up the stairs, but she tugged him back and sent him a withering glare.

"Bring the fucking suitcase," she hissed. "You're not going anywhere."

He gave her a long look, then grabbed the suitcase and stepped back, extending a hand toward the staircase. "Lead the way."

That sexy glare shouldn't have turned him on as much as it did. He was still angry with her, still didn't want to stay here, but he'd never stopped wanting her. The thought of getting her naked and finally learning his way around that hot little body of hers was convincing him that maybe he could stay here for just a little longer.

The one who got away, Fabian had called her. And even though they'd never technically dated or had sex, Gabe couldn't deny that it felt that way with Michelle. She was the one person who'd haunted his thoughts all these years, who made him wish things had been different so they could be together.

Michelle ascended the stairs like a queen. Gabe followed with his eyes glued to her shapely butt—barely covered by her pajama shorts—as it swayed side to side, entrancing him. He gripped the wooden bannister so tight, he wouldn't have been surprised if it splintered under his hand. His heart felt like it was going to burst from needing her, and his cock was rock hard, tenting the front of his sweats.

Holy shit.

They were really doing this.

Really about to have sex.

He was *really* about to have *sex* with *Michelle.*

At the top of the stairs, she grabbed his hand and they moved down the hallway, but when he would have turned to her old bedroom, she pulled him toward the room he'd slept in the night before. Gabe balked, rearing back like a horse spotting a snake.

"I can't have sex with you in your brother's bed," he whispered.

"We're definitely not doing it in my mom's craft room," Michelle shot back. "She'll know. And why are you whispering?"

He didn't know why he was whispering. Something about

being in this house full of old memories made him feel like a kid again.

"Come on." She pulled on his hand. "It's not my brother's room anymore and besides, the bed in there is bigger, and you, my friend, are a very big boy."

And then she shot a look at his crotch and smirked.

For years, Gabe had imagined this moment. Never in his wildest dreams would he have guessed it would go quite like this. Shit, it wasn't even seven in the morning.

Gabe took a deep breath and let Michelle draw him into the room, which thankfully no longer looked like it had when her brother, Junior, lived here. The posters of cars and Janet Jackson had been replaced by watercolor paintings of Old San Juan and Rome. And the window overlooked the backyard, which meant he didn't have to worry about his parents being able to see inside.

He couldn't remember the last time he'd had to consider something like that.

Michelle ducked into the adjoining bathroom while Gabe stored his suitcase in the corner by the closet. When she came back, she carried an unopened box of condoms. Moving to the nightstand, she ripped the box open and set it down.

Gabe raised an eyebrow, but she stood with her back to him. He waited near the end of the bed, unsure how to proceed. Should he go up behind her? Wait for her to come to him? Fuck, this was awkward.

Before he could decide, Michelle stripped her tank top over her head. Gabe's breath backed up in his throat at the sight of her bare back, and he almost choked when she shoved her shorts and panties down, giving him a full view of that gorgeous ass of hers. She reached up to pull the clip from her hair. Raven waves cascaded down her back, obscuring the bird tattoo below her neck. He'd have to examine that more thoroughly later. And then she turned to face him.

Chest tight, he didn't move. Her body was a revelation— narrow shoulders, full breasts that had always held a siren song over him, dusky pink nipples that he knew were as soft as rose petals, round hips that flared out from a trim waist, and strong dancer's legs. She was thicker than she'd been in high school, but she looked strong, confident, and sexy as hell.

Staring at her breasts, all he could think about was the last time he'd touched them. Tasted them. And how it had all gone so wrong.

This was probably a mistake, but he didn't fucking care. Years of pent-up desire screamed at him to close the distance between them.

Instead, he growled, "Get over here."

A mischievous light sparked in her eye, and she pounced on him. He caught her in his arms and their mouths crashed together.

Unlike their friendship, the kiss picked up right where they'd left off all those years ago.

Back then, their kiss had been breathless and exploratory, fueled by surprise and marijuana. This kiss was rough and angry, and unbelievably hot, inflamed by years of unresolved sexual tension and emotions Gabe didn't want to name. He ate at her mouth with his lips and tongue, unable to get enough. Michelle knocked his hat off, skimming her fingers through his short hair. Her arms wrapped around his neck as she arched her body against his. Gabe held her close, fusing them together, reveling in the feel of her tight little body pressed to his. Her curves fit perfectly against the planes and angles of his frame, and his cock hardened further, nudging at her belly. She was like living fire in his embrace, and he didn't care if he got burned.

"I'm still mad at you for trying to leave," she mumbled between kisses.

He nipped her lower lip with his teeth. "And I'm still pissed at you for trapping me in the Bronx."

She had the nerve to laugh, a deep throaty sound that shot heat straight through him. Then she grabbed the waistband of his pants and yanked them down. "Let's go."

This was what happened when you worked in a gym. You started to view gym clothes as real clothes, which made it way too easy for a naked woman to pull your pants down.

It made quite the case for sweatpants as day wear.

Clad in a T-shirt and boxer briefs, Gabe glanced down at his pants around his ankles. "¿Así?"

"Don't be sentimental," she said with a teasing grin.

"All right, it's like that." He grabbed the hem of his shirt and pulled it over his head, taking care to flex as much as humanly possible while he did it. Once the shirt was off, he grinned at the stunned look on Michelle's face.

"Holy fucking shit, Gabe. Do you even lift, bro?"

That startled a deep laugh out of him, but it turned into a

strangled gasp when she pressed her palms to his pecs and ran them down his muscles—straight toward his cock.

"Mich—" he gasped, and she shook her head.

"We've wasted enough goddamn time, Gabe. Don't mess around."

God, she was amazing. As direct and irreverent as she'd always been, but somehow even sexier. "Whatever you say, babe."

Her hair was loose, so he sank his hands into the long mass of it, holding on for dear life as she gripped the waistband of his underwear and carefully peeled them off him.

He was already rock hard. He'd been fighting off an erection since the moment she'd confronted him at the bottom of the stairs in a skimpy little pajama set. From his higher vantage point, he'd gotten a good look at the valley between her breasts. Then she'd had to go and cross her arms, and the sight had nearly brought him to his knees.

If she wanted him on his knees, all she had to do was ask. He'd never been able to deny her anything.

"Fuck, you're big," she said, her eyes glued to his cock.

He suppressed a groan. "That's what got us into trouble in the first place."

She met his eyes, hers holding a glint of humor. "Goddamn Lizzie DeStefano."

"Did she really ask you if I had a big dick?"

"No, she said she *thought* you had a big dick, and then I . . ." She glanced at his cock again, her cheeks turning pink. "I was curious."

Michelle circled his length with strong, capable fingers, her expression pensive. "It turns out she was right."

"She didn't know from experience," Gabe ground out, because this part had seemed important all those years ago. "She and I never—"

"Shh. I know."

And then Michelle gripped his cock tighter and gave it a lazy stroke. Gabe's muscles tightened and he bit back a curse.

God bless Lizzie DeStefano.

Michelle's gaze snapped back to his, as if she were waking from a spell. "Come on," she said, letting go of him and moving to the bedside table. She took a condom out of the box and passed it to him. "Put that on."

He ripped it open and rolled the latex on while she flipped the comforter back.

"What are you doing?" He'd made the bed before trying to sneak out, figuring it was the least he could do.

Michelle sent him a bland look as she climbed onto the middle of the bed. "I'd rather not have to explain weird stains to my mother."

He blanched at the reminder of where they were. "Oh. Right."

She patted the sheets. "Now lie down."

He raised an eyebrow at her command but complied, stretching out on his back next to her. He reached for her, but she threw her leg over his hips, straddling him. When she rose up, positioning herself over his cock, he gripped her waist to hold her in place.

"Espera," he said.

She shot him an incredulous look. "Wait for what?"

This was going way faster than Gabe had expected. Yeah, he was ready for her, but was *she* ready? They'd barely touched each other, and unless you counted angry banter, there'd been little in the way of foreplay.

Gabe *loved* foreplay. Learning every inch of someone's body, losing himself in their kisses, hearing the sounds they made as they came. He desperately wanted to do those things with Michelle.

Not only that, he *was* big. He wanted to make sure she was ready to take him.

When she rubbed her pussy along his cock, he groaned, fighting for control. "I don't want to hurt you, Mich."

She leaned down, her breasts a warm, heavy weight on his chest. "You won't."

Just to be sure, Gabe reached between them to check for himself, finding her hot and slick with desire.

Before he could explore further, she sank onto him, her core enveloping his cock inch by inch. They worked together—Michelle angling her pelvis, Gabe holding her hips to keep her steady—until he was fully sheathed inside her. Michelle let out a long sigh, like she'd been holding her breath, and Gabe flexed his fingers on her round ass, trying not to move.

"*Fuck*," they said in unison, then laughed. Something between them lightened in that moment, despite the vibrating tension in his body and hers. They'd always laughed easily together.

Michelle pressed her face into his neck, but his mouth found hers and he kissed her long and slow, one hand skimming lazily up and down her back, the other sliding into her hair, massaging gently.

"Don't worry," he whispered against her lips, holding her close. "I've got you."

She propped herself up with her hands on his shoulders, leaning away from him. He couldn't read her expression, but then the corner of her mouth curved in a smirk he'd seen a million times before.

"You ready?" she murmured with a devilish lilt.

"Fuck yeah." The words rasped like sandpaper, pulled from the deepest part of him, where he'd locked away all his feelings for this woman. He'd dreamed about this moment, and his imagination had nothing on the reality. The feel of her clenched around him, her thighs clamped tight on his hips, her hand exploring the contours of his muscles—he couldn't hold back another second.

He slammed his hips up into her and she gasped, her head falling back, fingernails digging into his biceps. When he paused, thinking he'd hurt her, she smiled dreamily.

"I'm okay. You just surprised me."

He slid his hands up to cup her breasts, letting her control the rhythm. "Move on me, mami."

She rolled her eyes. "Dude, you did *not* just call me *mami*."

He let out a chuckle that turned into a moan when she rocked on him. "You can take the boy outta the Bronx . . ."

She pursed her lips, as if holding back a smile. "Shut up. *Papi chulo.*"

And then she started to move, setting the pace, taking him slow but deep. Her breasts swayed in front of his face, and he raised his head to capture one nipple in his mouth, dragging his tongue over it. He ran his thumb over her other nipple, relishing the feel of her softness filling his hand, her warm skin against his lips and tongue.

She dug her nails into his arms again, the tiny pinpricks anchoring his body as waves of pleasure threatened to carry him away.

"*Fuck.*" Gabe slammed his head back against the pillow. His hands fisted in the bedding. This was nothing like how he'd imagined this morning going and, right now, he didn't fucking care. He didn't care about anything except the feel of her body moving over his.

"Michelle." His voice was hoarse with need. He wrapped his arm around her, drawing her down to kiss her deeply. With his other hand, he worked his thumb between them, groaning when he found her clitoris. She moaned against his mouth, her movements becoming less fluid, more erratic.

She buried her face in his neck but he gently cupped the back of her head. "Look at me, baby," he murmured. Whether it was instinct or memory, something told him she was trying to hide. "Let me see you."

Her eyes opened, heavy-lidded, almost reluctant. He sped up his ministrations, rubbing circles over her clit. Her lashes lowered again and he kissed her face, whispering, "Open your eyes."

He wanted to make her come, wanted to see her as she shattered. But when she opened her eyes, he saw a flash of something that might have been fear in their honey-colored depths. Then she bit her lip as her body twitched on top of him. She was close to climax.

Gabe closed his own eyes and kissed her. As much as he wanted to watch her reaction, there was something too intimate about it. Yeah, his cock was currently buried inside her, shuttling back and forth in the wet heat of her pussy, but being eye to eye while she came? It was more vulnerability than either of them was ready for.

He kissed her through it instead, swallowing her soft cries. He held her tight as her core spasmed and her body shook with tremors of release on top of him.

And when she was done, her body draped limply across his, he gripped her hips. "Baby, I gotta—"

"Do it," she murmured.

He flipped her over and fucked her.

It didn't take long, just a few more strokes. He'd barely held it together while she'd come apart on his cock. With his face pressed into the curve of her neck, with her limbs wrapped around him like vines, he gave one last thrust. And came with a low groan.

Breathing harshly, he felt his pulse thundering in his ears like an oncoming 2 train rattling along the elevated track. All the strength drained from him, and with it, the impulse to run.

As his scattered thoughts returned, he was aware of every inch of his skin against hers. Her soft breasts pillowing his chest, her strong thighs hugging his waist, her hands resting on his lower back, her breath tickling his ear.

And in the back of his mind, all he could think was that they'd finally done it. *They'd had sex.*

As much as Gabe loved the feeling of being inside her, he was softening. He had to get rid of the condom, and Michelle probably didn't enjoy being crushed by him.

With great effort, he rolled off her, flopping onto his back.

I just had sex with Michelle, he thought, staring at the ceiling. *I just. Had sex. With Michelle.*

Fuck. Now what did they do?

Michelle cleared her throat. "Did we just have angry sex?" she asked softly.

"Not angry," he replied. "Just . . . mildly disgruntled."

She huffed out a laugh. "Well, this is awkward."

Gabe swallowed hard. His heart still pounded his rib cage like fists against a punching bag. "You're right," he rasped.

"I know."

He shook his head. "No, I mean . . . we do have unresolved . . ."

"Issues?" she suggested. "Baggage? Tension?"

"All of that." He turned to look into her eyes, and his heart flip-flopped in his chest. How was it possible to feel utterly satisfied but also terrified about what was to come? "I owe it to you to stay here and work this out."

Her expression softened and she looked away to gaze up at the ceiling. "For how long?"

"Until I leave on Friday." He didn't know if she meant staying or screwing, but either way, Friday was the end.

She nodded, still not looking at him. After a moment, she asked, "What are we doing here, Gabe?"

"I don't know. But I don't regret it." Sex had unlocked something between them. Or maybe that kiss all those years ago had turned the key, and now they were finally opening the door to see what was inside.

Michelle let out a soft sigh. "Neither do I."

"I did miss you," he admitted.

"You said that in your email."

Gabe slid his hand over sheets warmed by their bodies until he found hers on the bed between them, then he laced their fingers together. "And I'm sorry."

Her lips curved, but she still didn't look at him. "You already said that too."

"I needed to say it again." He waited until she turned her face to him before he went on. "Mich, I'm sorry I lied about leaving. I didn't know how to tell you, and it took so much finagling—a private scholarship, scraping together loans—I didn't know it was happening for sure until late in the process."

Her mouth tightened. "You still could have told me what you were planning."

"I could have. But I also had this feeling, like if I said it out loud to anyone, it would fall apart. Or my parents would find out and somehow put a stop to it."

"You were already eighteen."

"You know that didn't matter in my house. My father was in total control, and if he knew . . . You remember how he was."

She squeezed his hand. "I guess he was pretty hard on you."

I'm eighteen now.

What, you think that's some magic number?

You can't control me anymore!

Gabe shut his eyes against the memories. "He'd have worn me down, day after day, with lectures about family and responsibility, about being realistic and not making stupid choices."

"But *I* wouldn't have done that. And I wouldn't have told your parents."

He opened his eyes again. "What if you'd tried to stop me?"

"I didn't, though. When you finally told me—or, rather, when I found out—I didn't tell you to stay."

"Because you were angry. If I'd told you earlier, you might have persuaded me not to leave." He'd hated the thought of leaving her, but he'd also been terrified that he would throw away all his carefully laid plans if she asked.

Michelle arched a brow. "Well, I guess we'll never know, will we? You didn't tell me until the last fucking minute, and then you cut me out of your life."

Gabe's throat tightened as he remembered the way they'd argued that last time, remembered how much it had hurt. "Because I would've come back for you."

She shook her head slowly. "I don't know if I believe you."

He gave a little shrug. "I'm here now, aren't I?"

"Only because you need me to work on your gym launch."

He sighed. "I wish that were the only reason. It would make all of this easier if it were."

"You said downstairs you never made a move because we were friends."

"That's right."

"You mean because you didn't want to ruin the friendship?"

"That, and I didn't want to make you uncomfortable. And what if you . . ." He trailed off, unable to voice his old fears, even now.

What if she didn't love him back?

"What if I wasn't attracted to you?" she asked.

Sure, that was good enough. "Yeah."

"Don't be silly, Gabe. You were, and are, *very* attractive."

"Then why didn't *you* make a move?"

"I was about as obvious as someone could be. How many times did I sit on your lap or ask for a back massage?"

"I thought you acted that way because we were best friends."

"It *was* because we were best friends. I trusted you. I was closer to you than anyone else outside of my family. And I thought the attraction was just . . . a natural offshoot of my affection for you, as my friend. I didn't really think about it more than that."

"Oh, I sure the hell thought about it. A lot."

"It did cross my mind, but as a . . . future thing. Like maybe someday we'd take that step, but I didn't need to force it. You were a constant. My hot best friend. It didn't bother me that we dated other people. You were still mine, and I was yours. That was all I needed. And then . . ."

"And then." He knew exactly what she meant.

"I didn't know it would be like that. Like *this*. And once I knew . . ."

"It changed things," he agreed.

"It didn't have to change as much as it did." Her eyes shone with emotion. "You really hurt me, Gabe. By lying, by leaving, and then by completely ignoring me. I know I didn't respond well to your decision, but do you know how hard it was to reach out to you after that? Every single time, only to receive nothing. But I kept trying. That's how much you meant to me."

Meant. Past tense.

He lifted their joined hands to his lips and kissed her knuckles. "I'm sorry. I needed . . ." Space. To escape. To forget. "I needed to start over."

"I get it. And I want to be angry at you. I *am* angry at you. But . . ."

"But?"

"I'm just so damn happy to have you back." Her tone was raw and wistful. "And it feels better to forgive you than stay mad."

A slight pressure eased in his chest. "I'm not sure I deserve it."

"I'm not sure you do either. But here we are."

Michelle slipped her hand out of his and got off the bed. "I'm going to shower," she said in a quiet voice. "I'll leave towels out for you."

It was on the tip of his tongue to suggest they shower together, but if she'd wanted that, she would have said so. So Gabe just nodded and watched her leave.

Sixteen years ago

Celestial Destiny: Episode 2 Planning Session

Gabe:

Holy shit. I can't believe so many people read the first chapter.

Michelle:

Fucking amazing. We need to get started on chapter 2!

Gabe:

I have science homework to do.

Michelle:

You can copy mine.

Gabe:

You don't even take notes in science class.

Michelle:

Fine, you can check mine and let me know what I got wrong. 😊

Gabe:

How is that saving me time to write chapter 2?

Michelle:

Let's just plan it out now and we can write it later.

Gabe:

Okay. We left off with Zack unconscious on Riva's ship. Where are they going?

Michelle:

His mom hired her to find him, so Riva will be taking him to Queen Seravida. And I think there should be a tía.

Gabe:

Like the Queen's sister?

Michelle:

Sure. They're Latinos in Space TM. You know they'd have lots of tíos y tías. I think you should put one in this scene.

Gabe:

I should? What about you?

Michelle:

You're better at world building.

Gabe:

Sounds like somebody's gotten a lot of "include setting details" notes in their Creative Writing class.

Michelle:

I see the details in my head, I just don't write them down. Is that so wrong?

Gabe:

Since Ms. Shapiro isn't telepathic—yeah, that's wrong.

Michelle:

Whatever. You're still writing this part. And I think it should also be from Zack's POV, like chapter 1.

Gabe:

So Zack and Riva arrive on this planet, and there's a random auntie waiting for them there. It's a big moment. The first time Zack's seeing his mother again, after thinking she was dead all these years.

Michelle:

Zack's Latino. He should call her Mami.

Gabe:

   She's a queen!

Michelle:

   Doesn't matter. She's his mami.

Gabe:

   I guess.

Michelle:

   While they're there, the queen gives Zack a mission.

Gabe:

   To go after a MacGuffin.

Michelle:

   A what?

Gabe:

   It's the thing people in movies are always after.

Michelle:

   What kind of thing?

Gabe:

   Anything. The Holy Grail. R2-D2. The One Ring. Doesn't matter.

Michelle:

   So Queen Seravida tasks Zack with finding the MacGuffin that's
   making his father a total monster.

Gabe:

   If only it were that easy.

Michelle:

   Everything okay over there?

Gabe:

   Yeah, it's fine. Zack's powers are uniquely suited for this quest. But he
   hasn't used them in years, and he's not convinced he even wants to
   get sucked back into his family's drama.

Michelle:

Luckily he has Riva to be his guiding star.

Gabe:

Yeah. Lucky guy.

Chapter 8

What.

The hell.

Were you thinking?

Michelle stood with her hands braced on the kitchen counter and stared at the bubbling water in the glass electric kettle, as if it were a crystal ball that would turn up a snarky answer like *I predict you were thinking with your hormones.*

Sex was *not* the kind of closure she'd intended when she insisted Gabe stay with her. And she couldn't even blame it on being high this time.

Making bad romantic choices wasn't new for Michelle. It was why she'd given up on dating, opting instead for flings, affairs, or fuck buddies. Whatever you wanted to call them, her sexual entanglements never lasted long and barely touched her heart.

In her more self-reflective moments, Michelle could admit she tended to have sex with guys who were kind of boring because it allowed her to maintain emotional distance even while letting them into her body. And while she'd gone out a few times with women, she hadn't gotten to the bedroom with any of them. Even at thirty-one, her bisexuality was still something she was figuring out on a practical level, beyond a lifetime of easily dismissed crushes on female celebrities.

But this was *Gabe*, not some rando from college, or work, or from an app. And she'd fallen into bed with him less than twelve hours after reuniting.

This didn't have to be a big deal. After all, she was queen of keeping her emotions separate from sex. Why should this time be any different? Sex was just sharing your body with someone. It was as natural as breathing. They'd scratched the itch, gotten it out of their systems, and never had to mention it again.

Oh fuck. Who was she kidding? Sex with Gabe was *totally* a big deal. Her inner teenager was freaking the hell out, bouncing off the walls and cheering, "He likes me! He really likes me!"

But there was danger here too. Gabe had fucked her how she liked to be fucked, hot and fast and a little rough. This kind of sex was impossible to ignore. It was too good, too intimate. It grounded her in the moment and forced her to be present, forced her to confront how she felt.

She didn't want to think about how Gabe made her feel. Despite forgiving him, she couldn't let him mess with her head, or her heart. Like he said, this was only until Friday. She had to remember that.

And while part of her wanted whatever she could get of him, it was better all around if she maintained emotional boundaries.

The kettle turned off with a soft *click*. Michelle went through the familiar motions of making a cup of tea and tried not to focus on how much had changed since the last time she'd done this very thing earlier that morning. She scooped loose leaves into the strainer, soothed by the familiar scent of vanilla Earl

Grey and the scratch of the dried tea leaves rustling in the tin. She set the strainer in the mug—one of her dad's, with the FDNY logo—and poured water over it, leaning away from the steam that rose into the air. Then she opened an orange prescription bottle and set her daily low-dose anti-anxiety pill on the counter next to the mug.

Michelle occasionally drank coffee, but she didn't love it like she loved tea. She wouldn't go so far as saying a hot cup of tea cured all ills, but it came close. The meds helped too.

The sound of water running through the pipes upstairs shut off. Gabe was done with his shower. Damn, he was fast.

Michelle set a timer for three minutes to let the tea steep and imagined Gabe coming downstairs when the timer went off. How was she supposed to harden her heart to him in such a short time?

Jezebel butted her head against Michelle's ankle, and Michelle crouched down to pet her. Things were much better when it was just her and Jez. She needed to remember that.

The timer beeped. Michelle shut it off, then heard footsteps overhead. She removed the strainer, squirted honey into the mug, gave it a stir, and added oat milk. By the time she washed down her pill with the first decadent sip, Gabe entered the kitchen.

Michelle stayed at the counter, scared to look at him. Maybe if she didn't, she could pretend he was less attractive. Or that he hadn't just fucked his way past her emotional walls.

Or that his apology hadn't settled something inside her that had been off-kilter for far too long.

He came up behind her, his big hands landing on her hips,

warm through the denim of her shorts. She sucked in a breath, which trembled out as a sigh when his lips touched the sensitive place at the top of her spine, right over her tattoo.

"What's this?" he asked, tracing his fingers over the image she could see in her mind's eye—a stylized barn owl, with wings outstretched, and a tiny crescent moon over its head.

"It's a symbol of Athena," she murmured, and hurried to take a steadying sip of tea. "Greek goddess of wisdom, among other things."

Not that any of Michelle's choices that morning could be considered *wise*.

"I like it." Gabe stroked the little owl again and Michelle tried—and failed—to fight off a shiver.

"It's still early for you," she said, cupping the mug with both hands so she didn't give in to the urge to touch him. "If you want to go back upstairs and sleep some more, that's okay with me."

"I'd be happy to sleep with you more." His deep voice—and that Bronx accent that had apparently never gone away—was a seductive rumble in her ear. She shivered again, but stepped away, giving him a stern look.

"That's not what I meant," she said primly. "Here I am trying to be a good friend and look out for your beauty sleep—not that you need any help in that department—and you try to get more sex out of it."

He grinned, flashing those dangerous dimples at her, and Michelle could have kicked herself. *So much for never mentioning it again.*

The teasing light in his eyes softened. His tongue darted out and he licked his bottom lip like he always did when he was nervous. She filed that away in the "same" category. Also in the "cute" category.

"Did it feel good?" he asked, voice quiet.

On the floor, Jezebel reached up to paw at his knees. Michelle's heart thumped when he leaned down to pick up the cat, but she just shrugged and turned back to the sink. "Yeah. Fine."

"Fine?"

She bit back a laugh at his aggrieved response. "Maybe more than fine," she amended.

He stared at her for a second longer, then his eyes narrowed, and he said, "Michelle."

Just that. Just her name, in a low growl with a tinge of exasperation and humor, like he was trying not to laugh. He'd said her name like this before, but the growl . . . that was new.

She filed it under "different" and "sexy."

"You hear that, Jezebel?" he muttered behind her. "She says it was *just fine*. Next time I need to show her what I can *really* do when it's not three-thirty A.M. my time and she's not rushing me."

He put the cat down and opened the fridge, taking out the containers of cottage cheese and blueberries Michelle had bought for him.

Next time? Hell, she'd barely survived the first time with her self-control intact. How would she handle a second time?

Michelle really hadn't planned to let him make her come. Her intention had been to get in and out—so to speak. Wham, bam, thank you, man. She'd thought rushing him into the penetration part and being on top would have helped her stay in control, but then Gabe had to go and call her "mami"—

which should *not* have been so adorable—and whisper sweet nothings in her ear.

Don't worry. I've got you.

Damn it, how was she supposed to keep her head when the man said things like that while holding her in those massively big, strong arms? It just wasn't fair. Even a hard-ass like her couldn't keep her cool under that kind of seduction.

The easiness of their banter should have made her happy—this was the closest to "old times" she'd felt since picking him up last night. Sex should have complicated their interactions, made things *more* awkward. Instead, it had torn down a wall between them—a wall Michelle desperately wished would stay up. She felt closer to him now, like she could say or do anything around him. And that was dangerous.

Maybe Gabe wasn't leaving today, but he was still going back to Los Angeles on Friday. She couldn't let herself get used to this.

No matter how good it felt.

Chapter 9

Gabe ate his breakfast and tried to keep his hands to himself. Michelle clearly didn't want to get all snuggly, and her "fine" comment bothered him.

She was holding back. He could tell from the way she'd rushed him and used humor as a defensive tactic, even when he was inside her. She'd held back during sex, and she was trying to put distance between them now. It was smart. Whatever they were doing here was only temporary. He had every intention of returning to his life in Los Angeles at the end of the week, and handing the New York reins over to Fabian whenever the guy was ready. Gabe wasn't back for good.

All the same, he just wanted to be close to Michelle again.

It was stupid to want her like this. There was still too much baggage between them, too much distance, and she was too tied to his old life. For twelve years' worth of memories, she was a constant fixture. In college, he'd struggled not to start sentences with "my friend Michelle" whenever he talked about something from his childhood. Each time had been a reminder that they weren't friends anymore. Eventually he just stopped talking about his life in New York altogether. It was one of the things he loved about Agility Gym—it was entirely rooted in his life in California. There was no overlap. No reminders of who he'd been, or of the people who hadn't believed in him.

Until now, when his worlds were colliding.

Gabe put his bowl and spoon in the sink and gave them a quick wash with the sponge before setting them in the drying rack. Then he turned to bring up something that had occurred to him in the shower.

"I probably should've asked earlier, but I'm assuming you don't have a boyfriend who's going to show up at any minute, right?"

"No boyfriend. Or any other kind of friend, for that matter." Michelle raised an eyebrow. "And you? No secret wife back in LA?"

Gabe held up his bare left hand. "No wife, no husband, no spouse. I don't want to get married, and even if I did, I don't have time to date anyone."

Michelle propped a hand on her hip, her jaw dropping open in surprise. "Gabriel Aguilar, do you mean to tell me we're both bi?"

He grinned. "Looks that way."

"Huh. Wish we'd figured that out in high school. We could've had some *amazing* conversations."

"I kinda knew," he said with a shrug. "But it wasn't like we had too many people around us to provide an example, you know? And I never would've told my parents."

"True. My tío Luisito didn't come out to the family until a

few years ago, after his divorce. Everyone was more chill about it than I expected them to be. He's married to Tío Archer now, and he's never looked happier. Plus, Abuela adores Archer."

"I came out to my sister," Gabe said. "My niece Lucy is transgender, so I wanted to make sure she knows someone else in the family is queer."

Michelle's smile softened. "I'm sure that made a huge difference to her."

"I hope so."

"Ava and Jasmine kind of know about me, but I don't talk about dating at all, so who knows what the rest of my family thinks."

His brows creased. "Why don't you talk about dating?"

"Because I don't date." Her tone was matter-of-fact.

"Why not?"

"Why don't you?"

"Like I said, I don't have time."

"Maybe I don't have time either."

Gabe raised an eyebrow, and she expelled a sigh. "Look, love and romance just aren't for me."

"But you deserve those things." And more. Michelle deserved to be worshipped and adored.

"If that were true, my romantic life wouldn't have gone the way it has." She shrugged again. "It's fine. I don't plan to ever get married or have kids. I love my nieces and nephews, but I don't feel any urge to have kids of my own."

"Same. I'm content to be an uncle." Gabe pulled up a photo on his phone and turned it to show her. "Lucy and Oliver. My niece and nephew."

Michelle smiled at the picture of the children, but her eyes were a little sad. "I know," she said. "I've met them."

"Oh. Right." Of course she had. She'd been here all the years he hadn't.

"How come I never saw you?" she asked quietly. "On holidays or summer break?"

"I didn't come back often. When I did, I usually stayed with my uncle or my sister."

Michelle turned away to fuss with the stuff around the sink. "Was it me?"

"What?"

She shot him a direct look, but her voice was tight. "Were you hiding from me?"

He sighed. "Maybe a little. But things with my parents got worse after I left for school. It was hard to stay with them."

"So you're saying it wasn't because I'm so sexy and amazing?"

He laughed at the repetition of her words from their earlier argument, grateful that she'd lightened the mood. "You *are* sexy and amazing."

"Thanks. Too bad no one else knows that."

"I have a hard time believing other people don't see it. At least two-thirds of our high school baseball team was in love with you." *Including me.*

"Then why didn't I date anyone on the baseball team?"

"Because I said I'd go after them with a bat if they messed with you."

"Ah. You always were an excellent hitter. But what about you? With that face and body, you must be kicking people out of bed left and right."

He snorted and shook his head. "A few, here and there. I actually broke up with someone about a year ago. Well, I guess she broke up with me."

"Was it serious?"

This was something he almost never talked about, but it was easy to open up to Michelle. "I think she wanted to get married eventually. And I don't."

"What happened?"

"The gym was more important." Gabe knew how it sounded, saying that right after sex. It was laying down a boundary, but it was what he did now, what the people he had sex with needed to know about him. The business was his number-one priority.

Liv, his ex, had never understood that. She'd come from money, and work had been a lark to her, something to pass the time between vacations. She'd hated that Gabe couldn't take off on "weekend getaways" with her whenever she felt like going to Napa or Vegas or Sedona.

Michelle didn't ask him to elaborate. She just unplugged her laptop from where it was charging on the kitchen counter. "Then we'd better get started."

"I've gotta get my stuff," Gabe said, glad for the chance to get out of the kitchen. He needed to shake the feeling that he'd revealed more of himself than he'd intended. Sharing with Michelle felt too easy, too right.

He ran upstairs to the bedroom that once again held his suitcase. He should've known his attempt to leave would be met with failure. With a sigh, Gabe pulled out his laptop and ergonomic Bluetooth mouse and mouse pad. He knew way too much about hand and finger-joint injuries to use the touch pad, and even the laptop keyboard, despite being a larger one, was pushing it. It was why he was going to teach the hand therapy class with Charisse when he got back to LA.

Downstairs, he sat across from Michelle at the old wooden dining table where they used to sit side by side doing homework. It wasn't ideal positioning, since they'd have to spin their laptops around to show each other something on the screen, but having the table between them was symbolic of the distance they were trying to maintain.

Michelle had her laptop, a mouse, a fancy notebook, and at least half a dozen pens in different colors spread out next to her.

Once Gabe finished setting up, Michelle spun her laptop to face him.

"There's a bit of a disconnect with your branding," she said, getting right to business. The screen showed a website he was very familiar with—the Agility Gym home page.

"The design is . . . fine," she went on. "But it's very cold."

There was that word again. *Fine*. And the website had cost over two thousand dollars.

"What's wrong with it?"

"It's . . . okay. I would have done better, but not everyone is me."

Gabe frowned at the website, which showed an artsy photograph of a fitness model lifting weights. "What do you mean?"

She gave him a look like she couldn't believe how dense he was being. "It's light blue, slate blue, and navy blue."

"That last one is Yankees blue," he pointed out. He'd been proud of that choice.

"Gabe. This branding was clearly designed by two dudebros. It's boring."

Before he could dispute being called a dudebro, she moved the cursor and opened the "About Us" page on the website.

"Look here," she said, pointing at the photo of Gabriel and Fabian. "This looks like it's out of some beefcake calendar, like 'Real Househusbands of the Los Angeles Gym Scene.'"

Gabe groaned and covered his face. "It was our investor's idea and that's exactly what he was going for."

"Really?" Michelle gave the picture a skeptical glance. "You look like two guys from the high school wrestling team about to win the dance battle that will save the rec center."

A teen movie reference was absolutely not what Gabe was going for. "It's not great."

"The first thing we have to do is reconcile what your brand is saying about you and what you *want* it to say about you."

"Me?"

"The gym, Gabe. Keep up. You're the face of the gym. It's named after you, right? Aguilar. Agility."

He nodded, pleased that she got it.

But then she shrugged and added, "It's a little heavy-handed but I guess your clientele doesn't care, or doesn't notice."

Before he could comment, she shoved a sheet of paper at him.

"Fill this out and let me know when you're done." She took her laptop back and popped on a pair of noise-canceling headphones.

Gabe stared at her for a moment, then shook his head and looked at the paper. Michelle had always been this way. Her brain moved a mile a minute, especially when she was working out a problem.

When he reached for one of her pens, she swatted his hand away. After digging in a black zippered pouch that literally said *Don't Touch My Pens* on it, she passed him a regular ballpoint pen with a bank logo on it.

He accepted it with a sigh and got to work. But after skimming the questions on the paper, he scowled. Shit like "What are your brand's core values?" and "How would you identify your ideal customer avatar?" made him sweat. How did you even put such abstract concepts into words? He flipped the paper over to make some notes and saw—god help him—that there were questions on both sides.

He was almost at the end—having skipped at least half of the questions—when Michelle shifted the headphones down to rest around her neck.

"Here's a question for you," she said. "Fabian is Haitian, right?"

"Yeah."

"And you're Mexi-Rican. Except none of that Latinx flavor is present in your brand. Why is your website full of photos of white people?" It was clearly a rhetorical question, because she kept going. "Have you done any TV commercials?"

Gabe shook his head. "Not yet."

Michelle tapped a pen against her lower lip as she skewered her laptop screen with a look of fierce concentration. "Maybe we could do something fun with music . . ."

Gabe tried to imagine playing merengue music in the gym. It was nearly impossible to picture. "I don't think that fits the brand," he said.

"Don't you get it? *You* are the brand. You and Fabian. And there's nothing of you guys in the messaging aside from this eighties porno picture."

"It's not—" He bit back his retort. She was trying to get under his skin. And of course, now that she'd said it, he couldn't see the photo any other way. Fuck. "The brand reflects the clientele."

She just raised her eyebrows in a way that said *Whatever you say, asshole* and went back to clicking with her mouse.

A few minutes later, Michelle's phone chirped with an incoming call. When she glanced at the screen, her lips compressed into a thin line. She pressed the side button and it stopped ringing. Then she turned the volume off and placed the phone back on the table screen-down.

"Telemarketer?" Gabe asked.

"Ah, no." Michelle made a show of looking at her laptop. "It was Ava."

Gabe narrowed his eyes. "Since when do you ignore Ava?"

When they'd been kids, he'd been Michelle's best school and neighborhood friend, but Ava and Jasmine had been her best cousins. He couldn't imagine that had changed.

Michelle's shoulders hunched. "Um . . . she still doesn't know you're here."

"Really?" That surprised him. "Did you ever tell your cousins about . . ."

"About the day we got high and ripped each other's clothes

off?" Michelle capped her pen with a sharp snap. "Oh yeah. They know about that."

Gabe shut his eyes. And prayed he didn't run into Jasmine or Ava while he was here.

Next to him, his own phone buzzed with a text.

Fabian: How's it going over there?

Fabian added an emoji of peeking eyeballs that managed to be nosy as hell for just a few pixels.

Michelle had popped her headphones back on and wasn't paying attention to him, so Gabe lifted the phone and snapped a photo of her and her laptop, to prove they were working. But when he looked at the picture, all he could see was how beautifully Michelle's cleavage was framed by the low V-neck of her *Not Today, Satan* tank top. If he sent that, Fabian would immediately suspect the truth. Instead, Gabe sent a photo of the half-filled branding worksheet Michelle had given him, and a short reply.

Gabe: We're working.

Fabian: Have fun! But not too much fun.

And then he followed it with an animated GIF of Robert De Niro pointing at his eyes and then the camera with the caption *I'm watching you.*

With a weary sigh, Gabe turned back to his laptop. Fabian was right. He had to stay focused on the project. In this place full of memories, it was easy to forget the rest of the world still existed, and he needed to remember that he was here to do a job, not have a sex vacation with his childhood best friend. But despite his determination to keep his eyes on his own screen, Gabe's gaze kept wandering across the table to Michelle. After a while, he leveled a glare her way. "This isn't working."

She blinked up at him. "What's wrong?"

"You *know* what."

Michelle glanced down at her cleavage, impressively displayed by the skimpy top. Her lips curved in a sly grin. "Oh. Am I distracting you?"

"*Yes.*" He ground out the word through clenched teeth and she laughed.

"Don't you work in a gym? I'm sure you see sexy people in spandex all the time."

They're not you, he thought, but didn't say it.

Actually, fuck it. What did he have to lose?

"They're not you." His voice was gravelly with desire. Shit, she turned him on so quickly.

Michelle gazed at him from under her lashes. "You can't keep your eyes off me."

He shot her a look full of exasperation. "Michelle, I've been attracted to you since we were fourteen. I've *never* been able to keep my eyes off you."

Her lips pressed together and she looked down at the laptop. "Maybe you were better at hiding it."

"Maybe you were better at ignoring it," he retorted.

She shrugged. "Maybe both. Get back to work."

Gabe tried. He really did. But the questions were frustrating him, and he had approximately eleven million emails coming through. He didn't know how much time had passed before Michelle spoke again.

"How do you feel about some rebranding?"

Gabe looked up just as Michelle spun the laptop. Now the screen showed the Agility logo in red instead of blue, with a white star worked into the design. And while the website still retained some of its original blue tones, there were some bright pops of red balanced by green, white, and gold.

"How did you do that?" he asked, surprised by how much better it looked.

"A quick mock-up in Photoshop," she replied. She tapped the touch pad and the flags of Puerto Rico, Mexico, and Haiti appeared on the screen. "Incorporating the color scheme and design elements of the flags is a subtle way to get the background of the owners into the branding."

Gabe nodded. "Makes sense."

She tapped the touch pad again and the picture from the "About" page appeared in a collage with some screenshots from Agility's Instagram account.

"You two are also trainers, right?" she asked.

"I'm a physical therapist and Fabian studied sports medicine and business. But yeah, we're also trainers."

"Let's show you both in action. Working with clients. Helping them achieve their best bodies and selves. Not posed and looking at the camera, but in the moment, doing what you do best. Which is not, I'm sad to say, modeling."

"Hey, I did a little fitness modeling back in the day."

"I believe it. You have a fantastic body. But this, Gabe, is your moneymaker." She reached across the table with the pen and dug it gently into his cheek, where his dimple would be. "You're not even smiling in this picture."

He glanced at the photo of him and Fabian on Michelle's screen. He'd felt so uncomfortable during that photo shoot, from the way they'd styled his hair to the tight outfits to the awkward poses.

And she was right. Gabe had been working his dimples since he was a teenager. Senior year, he'd taken a second job as a valet for an Italian restaurant. Most of the other guys had adopted a bored, lazy air, but Gabe had smiled at every single person who pulled into the lot. He asked about their day when they arrived, and when they left, he asked if they'd enjoyed the meal. Those tips had contributed to his "Get Out of the Bronx" savings fund.

The annoying thing was, it was something he'd learned from his dad. "A smile is your best customer service skill," Esteban Aguilar used to say, and Gabe had spent years watching his father charm customers into buying more than they'd planned on when they walked in.

Too bad Esteban used up all that good humor at work. By the time he'd gotten home every night, he'd been tired and unapproachable.

"They told us not to smile," Gabe said, gesturing at the picture.

Michelle shook her head. "They were wrong."

If Gabe had previously harbored any doubt that Michelle was the right person for this job, it vanished in that moment. Hiding a grin, he went back to clearing out his inbox.

ANOTHER FIFTEEN EMAILS appeared and Gabe closed the browser tab. He couldn't concentrate like this—sitting in the Amato house across from Michelle and her low-cut shirt, inundated by admin work. He usually got in a workout first thing in the morning, and while sex counted, he still had too much pent-up energy to sit here answering branding questions and vendor emails.

Besides, there were still things left unsaid between them, and the words were piling up in his throat. Things like *I used to love you and maybe I still do.*

He shot to his feet. "You said there's a weight bench downstairs?"

Michelle glanced up from her screen. "Yeah. Plus an elliptical and a rowing machine."

They would have to do. "Thanks. I'm going to take a break."

She shrugged, so he went upstairs to change. When he came back down in basketball shorts and a loose tank top, Michelle slapped her pen down on the table and glared at him.

"Okay, now you're just showing off."

Gabe froze. "Excuse me?"

"You heard me." She picked up the pen and used it like a pointer, indicating his attire. "Who's being distracting now, huh?"

His lips twitched as he glanced down at his outfit. "Oh, this old thing?"

She shook her head and returned her attention to the laptop, but as he headed down the stairs, Gabe heard her mutter, "Two can play at that game."

Downstairs, he paused for a second to take in the changes. The last time he'd been here, it had been Michelle's bedroom, with her bed against one wall and posters of the Gorillaz and *Star Wars* tacked up above it. She'd had a desk with an oval mirror over it. Photos of the two of them at various ages had been tucked into the frame of the mirror, along with pictures of Michelle's older siblings, her cousins, and both sets of her Italian and Puerto Rican grandparents. Gabe wondered where those photos were now, and if she kept them on display in her apartment.

Even when everyone started using digital cameras, Michelle had still made an effort to get pictures printed, sometimes dragging Gabe along with her to the one-hour photo booth at the local pharmacy.

She'd made a framed collage of the two of them, for him to remember her by while she was away at school. At the time, she'd thought he was staying at home in the Bronx, but it turned out he was the first to leave.

He still had that collage, in a drawer in his apartment in LA. As much as it hurt to look at it, and despite his commitment to minimalism, it had never occurred to him to throw it away.

Now, the basement was a man cave. A leather sofa sat where Michelle's bed once had, and a huge flat-screen TV hung on the wall over the place where Michelle's boxy little screen had been. She'd had a cable box and a DVD player, and they'd watched the one and only season of *Beyond the Stars* countless times on that TV, putting it on in the background while doing homework, along with hours of music videos and raunchy cartoons. As they'd gotten older, they'd smoked weed in her backyard while all of their parents were at work, huddling against the sliding doors, hidden from view by the deck stairs.

Teenage Gabe had needed to be diligent about his smoking schedule because of his baseball plans, but he'd gotten a kick out of watching Michelle roll a blunt. Even the way she'd licked the paper to seal it was sexy. They'd pass a joint back and forth, giggling, the distance between them narrowing the higher they got.

On the far end of the basement, a home gym had been created in one corner. Interlocking foam mats made the floor, and as Michelle had advertised, there were a couple machines and a weight bench, along with some adjustable weights that might get heavy enough for his purposes. A narrow mirror, probably the one Michelle had used in high school, was fixed to the wall behind the bench.

Starting on the elliptical to get his heart rate up, Gabe then moved to the rowing machine. He was on the weight bench doing curls when the basement door opened.

Gabe glanced up and almost dropped the weight on his foot as Michelle jogged down the steps in an outfit that had him instantly going hard.

He'd seen a lot of sports bras in his day. Most were functional, but not fashionable. Some were cheap spandex that didn't do the job. And some were designed to support while still looking fantastic. Michelle's was the latter. Her sports bra gave her an impressive amount of uplift and cleavage, and her yoga pants clung to her curves, emphasizing her hips and butt.

She crossed the room and began to unfurl a yoga mat on the floor right in front of him.

Setting the weights down, Gabe dropped his head into his hands and groaned out her name.

"Micheeeeeeeelle."

"What?" she asked, all innocence. He heard rustling, and

when he finally looked up, she was on her hands and knees on the yoga mat, her beautiful butt in the air, with a resistance band tight around her thighs.

He sent her an exasperated look. "What are you doing?"

"You're the personal trainer. I should think you'd know." And then she had the nerve to smack her ass and give him a saucy wink. "Gotta keep this baby in prime condition."

As if all that wasn't enough, she started doing fire hydrant leg lifts.

Gabe watched her for a few moments, mesmerized. His trainer brain noted her perfect form, the way she kept her core engaged and taut while rotating her leg and hip out. And her body was . . . everything he'd ever wanted. Not even because of what she looked like, but because of Michelle herself. She'd always moved with easy confidence and total trust in her own body. It was rare, and it was sexy as hell. Something he tried to help others learn.

Gabe rubbed his hands over his face to snap out of his trance. "Are you trying to provoke me on purpose?"

Michelle shot him a sassy grin. "Maybe."

That was a yes. She *was* trying to drive him wild. Wild with need, with wanting her. How had he ever spent so much time around this gorgeous, maddening woman without losing his mind?

Because he'd thought she wasn't into him. He hadn't wanted to push her, hadn't wanted to ruin the friendship, hadn't wanted confirmation of what he'd feared—that they really were *just friends*—followed by rejection.

But she hadn't rejected him. Then or now.

"Actually, I just remembered I have to do push-ups." Dropping down to the mat, Gabe caught Michelle around the waist and flipped her onto her back. She let out a peal of laughter, but made no move to push him away. Gabe braced himself above her, doing push-ups that brought his mouth an inch away from hers. On the third one, Michelle lifted her chin and kissed him.

Fire spiraled through him. He loved her playful side, the way she enticed him to take things less seriously. Lowering himself to his elbows, their bodies touching, he murmured, "Time for planks."

She raised her eyebrows as his pelvis pressed into hers. "Someone's already got a plank, I see."

His cock surged against her, inexplicably turned on by her bad jokes. "And someone didn't warm up first," he said, then closed his mouth over hers.

She kissed him back fully, her hands coming up to cup his face. Shifting his weight onto one elbow, Gabe slid his other hand down her body, molding over her breasts and belly before delving his fingers into the tight space between her thighs. They were pressed together by the resistance band and his own legs. The spandex pulled taut over her pussy, making it easy for his fingers to find her crease. He stroked her through the fabric, loving her heat, swallowing her gasps as he continued to kiss her.

Her hips bucked against his hand. Little moans issued from her throat as her kisses became more intense. The fabric against his fingers grew damp. And then she bit his lower lip, letting out a high-pitched cry as her body shuddered beneath him.

When she stilled, her head falling back to the yoga mat, Gabe drew his hand away.

"I'm warmed up," she said weakly, and he managed to laugh, despite his raging hard-on.

"Never let it be said that I don't look out for my clients."

She reached down and brushed a hand over his dick through the thin fabric of his sweatpants. "Are you looking for round two?"

He bit back a groan. "No condoms down here." And he was a little worried about her earlier "it was fine" comment. It had always been impossible to know what she was really thinking.

"Ah. Right. Well, I guess we should go to the zoo."

His eyes widened. "The *zoo*?"

She sent him an impish grin. "This is your first time back in how many years? You didn't think I was going to let you get away with working the whole time, did you?"

He had thought that, but in hindsight, it was pretty naive of him. Of course Michelle was going to cart him around to do some sightseeing.

Sitting back on his heels, Gabe tugged the resistance band down her legs and set it on the weight bench. Clearly his work-out was over. Then he got to his feet and gave her a hand to help her stand. She wobbled a little.

"You okay there?"

"Just a little weak in the knees." She sent him an enigmatic smile and headed for the stairs.

He was sweating, and since he'd forgotten to grab a towel, he pulled off his shirt and wiped his face with it. Then he followed Michelle up the stairs a few paces behind.

When she reached the top, she let out a bloodcurdling scream.

Gabe's heart leaped into his throat. He bolted up the rest of the way and into the kitchen where he saw—

Fuuuck.

Michelle's cousin Ava stared at him in horror. Before Gabe could say anything, Ava's brows drew together, and she shrieked in an accusatory tone, "Michelle! Is that *Gabriel Aguilar*? And, Gabriel, *where is your shirt?*"

Chapter 10

Despite the riot of sensations in her body caused by Gabe's rather efficient orgasm delivery, Michelle tried for a nonchalant tone. "Oh, hi, Ava. What are you doing here?"

Ava's brows creased in annoyance. "You didn't answer my calls last night or this morning. I was worried you were dead."

Michelle pressed her fingers to her forehead. She was really in for it now. "Gabe, why don't you go upstairs?"

He moved toward the doorway while Ava gave him that menacing Latina Mom stare that asked "¿Tú quieres la chancleta?" It was the look you got when you'd been bad and you knew it, right before Mami took off her slipper and hurled it at you like a missile. Then Ava turned the look on Michelle, who hunched her shoulders and made a beeline for the electric kettle.

"I'll make you some tea," Michelle said, retrieving a mug from the cabinet.

"Why is it so dark in here?" Ava moved to open the shades, but Gabe leaped toward her.

"No, don't!" He slapped a hand over the shade to keep it down while Ava stared at him like he'd lost his mind.

"He's worried his mom will see him in here," Michelle explained.

"Oh, she absolutely will," Ava affirmed, letting go of the cord that controlled the shade. "I've seen her peeking in while I was watching Monica's kids."

"See?" Gabe hissed, giving Michelle an *I told you so* look.

"Okay, okay." Michelle waved him off. "Ve y ponte tu ropa."

He raised an eyebrow at her command that he go put some clothes on. And then he was gone and Michelle was alone with her cousin.

The second they heard his bounding footstep on the stair that creaked, Ava whirled on Michelle, eyes wide and mouth agape.

"What is he doing here?" she whispered. "Ay dios mío, is this some kind of sex pact?"

"Sex pact? What are you talking about?" Michelle busied herself making tea the way Ava liked it—strong, milky, no sweetener.

"Like if you're not married by thirty, you'll marry each other. Or you meet every few years to get it on. Come on, I know you've seen those movies."

In hindsight, Michelle *wished* she and Gabe had made such a pact. At least then there'd be clear parameters for whatever was happening between them. "I'm helping him with a project for his business."

"Oh really? You're 'helping' him with a 'project'?" Ava's voice dripped with skepticism, and she made air quotes around the words.

Michelle cut her a glare. "It amazes me that everyone thinks *you're* the nice one."

"Compared to you, I am." Ava shot her a wink and leaned her elbows on the kitchen counter. She was the tallest of the Rodriguez girl cousins, towering over Michelle's five-three by a good six inches. "But come on. You came upstairs wearing *that* and he's got no shirt on."

"We were exercising," Michelle said defensively, glancing down at the sports bra she'd bought on their cousin Jasmine's recommendation.

Ava snorted. "Yeah. Okay."

"And . . . other stuff." Michelle sent Ava a severe look. "Don't tell Jasmine."

Ava accepted the mug Michelle handed her. "Fine. I won't. But you're not going to be able to keep this quiet. And even if you are, at what cost? Remember last time?"

"Of course I do."

"I just want you to be happy," Ava said softly.

"Don't worry," Michelle said, not sounding anywhere near as confident as she wanted to.

"Ha. Like I could ever stop worrying about you."

"I know. That's why you're mi prima favorita."

"Don't let Jasmine hear you playing favorites."

"She's my prima favorita too. But for real, do *not* tell her about Gabe."

"You know I can keep a secret." A shadow passed over her expression, and Michelle guessed Ava was thinking about the years she'd suffered in silence in her marriage. Michelle still felt guilty that she hadn't noticed Ava's unhappiness sooner. "Is Gabe moving back?"

"No. He's only here until Friday."

"Right before your parents get back. That's cutting it close. And what about his family?"

Michelle shook her head. "They don't know he's here."

"Whatever happened between them, it must have been really bad."

"Yeah, it sounds like it." Michelle stirred her own fresh cup of tea as Ava's words sank in. No wonder he'd been pissed at her for bringing him here.

"But for real." Ava lowered her voice. "Did you and he . . . ?"

Michelle's heart pounded, but before she could try to play it off, Ava's jaw dropped.

"You *did*," she said with a gasp. "You're blushing."

Michelle slapped her hands over her hot cheeks. Damn her pale complexion. "It doesn't mean anything," she hissed. "Don't get excited."

Except . . . maybe that wasn't entirely true.

Don't worry, I've got you.

I never wanted to hurt you.

Maybe it meant . . . something. What, she didn't know.

She'd gone down to the basement to tease him. It hadn't been smart, but on some level she wanted clear evidence of how much he wanted her. To know if what they'd done had been a onetime thing or not. If he'd ignored her and continued working out, she would have handled it like a grown-up and locked her feelings away.

But he hadn't. He'd climbed on her and brought her pleasure right there on the yoga mat, without pressuring her to do anything for him in return. It was stupid to pretend their emotions weren't involved, but she was going to try anyway.

"What are you two doing next?" Ava asked innocently, raising her eyebrows as she sipped from her mug. "Since you're done *exercising*?"

"More work." It wasn't entirely false. Michelle did have a good reason for taking Gabe to the zoo, and it wasn't just for nostalgic shits and giggles.

Although she hoped there'd be some of those too.

"ALL RIGHT, ALL right, I get it. The Bronx Zoo has much better branding than my gym does."

Gabe had been walking around the zoo with Michelle for two hours. It was hot, there were screaming kids everywhere, and the scents of popcorn and cotton candy mixed with the general odor of animal and dung. It was a perfume that specifically said "zoo" and instantly brought him back to his many trips here in his youth.

Michelle grinned and elbowed his side. At some point they'd started holding hands, like a real couple. He didn't know how it had happened. Maybe she'd taken his hand to pull him toward an exhibit, or he'd reached for her so as not to lose her in the crowd. But then . . . they hadn't let go.

"I'm just saying, you want to pay attention to how *all* the messaging reflects the brand's core values. Remember, the Bronx Zoo is run by the Wildlife Conservation Society, so you see the values of conservation and education all over the place."

She was right. Everywhere he looked, there were signs with information about each creature, maps with where in the world they could be found, endangered species list details, graphics of what the animals ate, and more.

"The 'story' of the zoo is present everywhere," Michelle went on as they passed a kiosk selling stuffed giraffes. "But of course, they also sell toys and food. That's the commercial aspect. First they sell you on the values, then they get you to buy the products."

"That makes sense," he said. "We're more likely to buy from a brand whose values align with our own."

"Exactly!" Her eyes shone with praise, and he was a little annoyed at himself for how much he liked it.

"So, what are the values of Agility Gym?" she asked, but answered before he could speak. "It's in the title. Movement, flexibility. How does that come through in the messaging?"

Gabe grunted. "It doesn't."

"Who cares if you show someone at peak physical condition being flexible? That wouldn't make me want to go to a gym. I want to see a regular person working out, to know that it's a place where I can fit in and feel comfortable."

"You *are* in peak physical condition."

She gave him a look up and down. "One of us is, and it's not me. I'm not saying I don't look damn good, but I'm not eighteen anymore. My body has definitely changed, and I'm okay with that. Cellulite and stretch marks are natural."

He stopped and cupped her face in his hands. "I have always thought you were beautiful. Now even more so. You take my breath away, Mich."

Her chin trembled and there was wistfulness in her eyes before she looked away. "Gabriel, this is a family establishment. Stop seducing me at the zoo."

His lips quirked, but he dropped his hands. "That's fine. I'll wait until we get home."

Home. Fuck. What was he saying? He didn't mean that. New York *wasn't his home.*

Michelle cleared her throat. "So, yeah . . . movement, flexibility—"

"It still sounds like you're talking about sex," he muttered, and she elbowed him again.

"—body parts working in harmony—"

"Still sex."

"—feeling at home in your own body *and not fighting it.*" She sent him a glare, but the corners of her mouth tugged upward. "What are you trying to do?"

"What are *you* trying to do?"

Her grin was sassy and he loved it. "You hired me, and I'm actually trying to do my job."

She was right, and he should be glad one of them was staying on task.

Gabe looked down at his hand—the one that wasn't currently folded around Michelle's. He remembered being smaller and slipping his fingers through the fence to feed pellets to the goats in the Children's Zoo, the way their sticky tongues had licked him.

Maybe he'd come back here again and bring Nikki's kids.

Shit, he should really tell his sister he was here. She was going to be so pissed if she found out he'd been in the Bronx and hadn't told her.

But that was a problem for another day.

They passed another kiosk, this one selling popcorn, and Michelle gestured to it. "The product you're selling is memberships, right? You want people to sign up for your gym and pay a monthly or yearly fee. But the service is the gym itself and the amenities."

Unbidden, another memory popped up. In it, Gabe was five, maybe six, and visiting the zoo with his sister and their parents. He'd begged his father to let him get ice cream on a cone, instead of in a cup, promising over and over that he wouldn't drop it. But of course, being a small child, he'd managed to lick the rapidly melting ice cream right off the cone. It had tumbled down his overalls before splattering on the hot pavement—and his sneakers. His parents had been furious. Gabe vaguely remembered that they were going somewhere after the zoo, and his mother had bemoaned bringing a dirty kid with her, while his father had yelled at him for wasting money and food.

Gabe never got ice cream at the zoo again, even after he was old enough to walk or ride his bike over here after school with Michelle.

"Right." Gabe focused on the conversation, instead of unwanted childhood memories. "The memberships are the main product, although we have some other branded items for sale on-site and online."

As they walked, she asked him about the other products and the gym's various partnerships. He answered the best he could, feeling frustrated by some of the questions—or by his own answers. When she asked, "Why did you start the gym?" he'd answered, "To help people feel better in their bodies and achieve a full range of motion." But when she'd inquired about the clientele, rattling off the names of celebrities didn't quite match the original vision.

He just didn't know what to do about it.

Or about Michelle. It was so fucking nice walking around with her like they were two normal people on a date, instead of former childhood friends with years of baggage and hurt who'd found themselves in some kind of sexual truce.

Finally, while touring the Madagascar exhibit, which was new to him, he found a shadowy corner blessedly devoid of children. He pulled Michelle in close and leaned down to kiss her softly.

"No more work, okay?" he murmured. "Let's just . . . enjoy this."

"Okay." She sounded surprised, and Gabe couldn't blame her. He was surprised at himself. His life was all work all the time, and taking a break in the middle of the day was completely unlike him. He'd told himself it was fine because they were still talking about the gym, but now . . . he just needed a break from it all.

Soon, he'd return to Los Angeles, and god willing, he wouldn't have to come back often. So why not make the most of the little time they had together?

Unable to help himself, he kissed her again, more deeply this time. When her tongue slid against his, he groaned and tightened his arms around her. Luckily, a group of children burst into the space a second later, their high-pitched "indoor voices" reminding Gabe where they were. He eased away from Michelle, running his tongue over the lower lip she'd just nipped. He didn't miss the sultry smile she sent him. Maybe the things they'd done that morning hadn't been a onetime thing after all.

Thinking about what they might do when they got back to

the house that night, he slipped an arm around her waist and led her through the rest of the exhibit.

"THAT WAS DELICIOUS." Gabe stretched his legs as much as he was able to in the front seat of Michelle's Fiat.

"I don't think I've ever had a bad meal there," Michelle agreed as she drove up Morris Park Avenue.

After leaving the zoo, they'd stopped at one of the Bronx's famous Italian restaurants, where Gabe had worked as a valet his senior year of high school. They'd gorged on pasta and seafood, and after a waiter recognized him, a glass each of white wine. Gabe couldn't remember the last time he'd consumed so much butter in one sitting, but he had no regrets.

Lulled by carbs, wine, and the familiarity of the road, Gabe noted each house as Michelle drove to their old street—he wouldn't think of it as "home" again. As Michelle started to turn the car into her parents' driveway, Gabe's gaze continued on to his own house, an old habit, just in time to see the front door open and his father step out.

"Shit!" Gabe ducked down in his seat, nearly wrenching his shoulder when the seat belt pulled taut. "Keep driving!"

"What the fuck?" Michelle jerked the wheel and sped up, stopping briefly at the stop sign on the corner before turning. "You nearly gave me a heart attack."

Gabe felt like he was nearly having one himself. His pulse skyrocketed, and his skin felt clammy.

"That was my dad," he mumbled.

He hadn't seen his father in nine years, hadn't even really

gotten a good glimpse of him before ducking out of sight, but he'd know Esteban Aguilar anywhere.

If they had pulled into the driveway just three seconds earlier, he would have come face-to-face with him while getting out of the car.

"Gabe, stop being such a baby," Michelle snapped as she circled the block. "He's your father, not a serial killer."

He gaped at her. "Are you serious? He almost caught us!"

Me. He almost caught me.

"And I almost hit your mom's car because you scared me. How would I explain that? *Lo siento, Norma. Your son, who you don't know is here, startled the shit out of me while I was parking and I took out your taillight. My bad!*" She pulled over to the curb and pointed. "Look, there he goes. We're in the clear."

Gabriel did not appreciate her sarcasm. "One of the conditions of me staying with you is that my parents do *not* find out I'm here."

"That wasn't one of the original conditions," she said in a snotty voice he remembered all too well.

"Only because you lied to me about where we'd be staying." He knew he was getting loud, but his heart was still pounding with the shock of seeing his father.

"Are we back on that again? I didn't *lie*, exact—"

"Get out of the car."

She shot him an incredulous look. "Excuse me?"

"Michelle, ¡salte del carro!"

"Mira, comemierda, este es *mi* carro."

Gabe took his hat off and shoved his hands through his hair, groaning in frustration. "Okay, pero let me drive it around the corner so I can get out closer to the gate and sneak around the house like a fucking burglar again. And this time open the goddamn basement doors so my mother doesn't almost see me too."

"Whatever you want, Gabe!" The way Michelle said it did not match the accommodating words, but she left the engine running and opened her door. They both climbed out and stomped around the car—Gabe around the trunk, Michelle around the hood—before getting back in. Gabe drove around the corner in silence, still shaken by the close call. Michelle sat with her arms folded across her chest and a dark scowl on her face. He parked in the driveway and Michelle grabbed the key fob the second the emergency brake was engaged, sweeping from the car in high dudgeon.

Once upon a time, Gabe would have tried to placate her. She had a temper, and he'd always tried to soothe her when she was in a mood. But now? Fuck it. He was pissed. This was exactly why he hadn't wanted to stay here.

He ducked out of the car and around the side of the house, easier this time since he was coming from the driver's side and wasn't carrying a suitcase. From the steps, Michelle activated the locks on the car doors. Gabe had been so careful on the way out, making Michelle keep tabs on where his parents were in their own house before sneaking out to her car and diving into the back seat. They should have been more careful coming back, but the trip to the zoo and the restaurant had lulled him into a false sense of security.

In the backyard, he waited by the sliding glass doors longer than it should have taken Michelle to get there, and he figured she was punishing him for yelling at her. He wasn't proud of it, but he couldn't take this shit anymore. She had no respect for his feelings where his parents were concerned.

At least the motion sensor light didn't out him this time. He'd remembered to disable it before they'd left.

When Michelle finally appeared on the other side of the glass, she glared at him for a long moment. Then she unlocked the door and slid it open, turning and heading back up the basement stairs before he could even step through.

"Oh, it's like that, huh?" he yelled after her. The basement door slammed shut in response.

Yeah, it was like that.

Fifteen years ago

Celestial Destiny: Episode 3 Planning Session

Michelle:

   All right, time to plan episode 3. Riva is pissed at Zack.

Gabe:

   This should be in her POV, which means you should write it.

Michelle:

   But I have Into the Woods rehearsals every night!

Gabe:

   And I have baseball practice every morning. I still wrote all of
   chapter 2, which was three times as long as chapter 1.

Michelle:

   Maybe I can come by the store this weekend while you're working.
   I'll bring my laptop and we can work on it when there aren't any
   customers.

Gabe:

   Which is, like, all the time now.

Michelle:

   If anyone does come in, we'll say we're doing homework.

Gabe:

We SHOULD be doing homework instead of writing fanfiction.

Michelle:

But this is so much more fun! I also got a great idea for this chapter while I was in the shower.

Gabe:

. . . the shower?

Michelle:

Yeah, it's where I get all my best ideas. Don't be a perv.

Gabe:

You're the one who brought it up! You could have left that part out.

Michelle:

ANYWAY . . . I think Zack should get amnesia.

Gabe:

You know that's not real, right?

Michelle:

Amnesia?

Gabe:

Yeah. In real life, people forget memories but they don't actually forget who they are.

Michelle:

Well, these people are running around in spaceships and there was a Groundhog Day time loop episode about getting sucked into a black hole, so I'm not really concerned with accuracy here.

Gabe:

Okay, true.

Michelle:

And since Zack never told Riva his powers, he forgets what they are!

Gabe:

How does he get amnesia?

Michelle:

> Remember how Zack warned Riva to double-check her equipment
> after the mechanics worked on her ship in chapter 1?

Gabe:

> Yeah . . .

Michelle:

> Well, what if she didn't?

Gabe:

> They can get attacked by space pirates as they're leaving the
> planet where his mom is hiding, and because she didn't check the
> diagnostics or whatever, they crash-land on a different planet.

Michelle:

> And Zack hits his head and loses his memory!

Gabe:

> Doesn't Riva have healing powers? She'd be able to heal his amnesia.

Michelle:

> Maybe, but what if she just . . . doesn't?

Gabe:

> Harsh.

Michelle:

> Zack isn't planning to go along with the mission, and Riva wants to
> save the galaxy. So she lies to him about who they are.

Gabe:

> She can say they're smugglers or something. And it would make Zack
> believe that they have to be careful about not getting caught.

Michelle:

> Right. Maybe she makes up a threat, someone who's trying to capture
> them.

Gabe:

> Someone IS trying to capture them. His father, the king.

Michelle:

> This'll be fun. Riva can tell him real memories from their childhood, and made-up memories of their smuggling career.

Gabe:

> You're definitely writing this chapter. Backstory is not my strong suit.

Michelle:

> Don't worry, Gabe. I'll remember our backstory for us. ☺

Chapter 11

Michelle had already been rage-cleaning for hours by the time Gabe came downstairs the next morning. She'd scrubbed the kitchen and downstairs bathroom until they sparkled, and she was in the middle of cooking a giant—but healthy—breakfast when Gabe entered the kitchen with a bewildered look on his handsome face. Maluma crooned softly from the mini-speaker connected to her phone.

Before Gabe could say anything, she blurted out, "I'm sorry I called you a baby."

His dimples flickered like he was suppressing a smile. "Is *that* why you think I'm upset?"

"*And*," she continued, not willing to let his smart remarks derail her, "I'm sorry for not taking your concerns about your parents more seriously."

One of his dimples deepened. "Thank you. I didn't mean to startle you, but seeing my dad . . . it took me by surprise. I haven't talked to my parents in nine years."

"*Nine?*" The spatula skidded in the pan, causing her to flip the egg white and spinach omelet with more vigor than was strictly necessary.

He shot her an incredulous look. "You really didn't know that?"

"I thought my mom was exaggerating when she said you didn't talk to them. Like maybe she meant you hadn't visited in a while. You know how Puerto Rican mothers are."

He shook his head. "No contact since my sister's wedding."

"I'm sorry. I didn't know that. And yesterday wasn't my finest moment," she admitted. "But I don't want to spend the precious little time we have together fighting. Besides, we have a busy day ahead, and it'll be a hell of a lot easier if we're on speaking terms."

"Mich." Gabe leaned against the kitchen counter. When she turned to look at him, he said, "I'm sorry I yelled at you."

She shrugged. "I can handle yelling. You've met my family."

"Doesn't matter. I try not to raise my voice or speak in anger, but I did that to you yesterday. And I'm sorry for it."

Damn, how could anyone resist a man who delivered such a heartfelt apology?

"Apology accepted," she said primly. "Do you want bacon?"

"Of course I want bacon. What kind of a question is that?"

"How should I know?" She gestured at him with the spatula. "You clearly have a *my body is a temple* thing going on, and I would imagine that life doesn't include a lot of greasy breakfast meat."

He sputtered out a laugh. "You're right, but I make exceptions when I'm not at home. Otherwise I try to eat healthy most of the time."

"So do I, but that doesn't explain why you look like you lift weights every day."

"Not *every* day. I take rest days, as one should."

"Gabe. Don't try to tell me you're not in a gym every single day."

"I *work* in a gym."

"You know what I mean."

"Working out clears my head, helps me focus. It gives me a sense of . . ."

"Control?" she suggested.

His brow creased, like he was thinking about it, but then he nodded. "It improves my mood, helps me feel stronger—all the typical benefits of exercise. But yeah, I can probably be a little . . . militant about my diet and lifestyle."

Knowing the details of his upbringing, Michelle could understand why he'd been drawn to activities that allowed him full control over himself. For so long, he'd been subject to his parents' demands, forced to do things their way. But she didn't bring that up.

Instead, she asked, "I guess this means your pot-smoking days are over?"

"Oh god. I haven't done that in years. You?"

"I don't need to anymore." She showed him the prescription container stationed next to the electric kettle.

"What are these?"

"Anxiety meds. I started them after I quit my job. They calm me down, help me feel . . . steadier."

He nodded. "Steady. Yeah. That's how working out makes me feel."

"Get plates," she told him. "Food's done."

They kept the conversation light while they ate, discussing the itinerary for the day. First, they were meeting with the real estate agent to look at a few locations. Then there was a meeting with the investor and a possible celebrity spokesperson.

"Who's the celeb?" Michelle asked, spearing a piece of avocado with her fork.

"You'll see when we get there," Gabe said. "Don't freak out."

"Pfft. I can be cool. You know my cousin Jasmine is a movie star now, right?"

His lips curved in a slight smile. "I might have watched *Carmen in Charge*."

"What did you think?" She pointed her fork at him menacingly. "If you hated it, don't tell me."

Gabe's grin was full blown. "I loved it. Jas was great. You must be proud of her."

Michelle set down her fork. "I am."

Some part of Michelle appreciated that, even though Gabe hadn't reached out in all these years, he'd watched Jasmine's show.

"I'll play chauffeur today," Michelle said, getting back to the topic at hand. "No offense, but I don't trust you to drive my car around Manhattan. I'll bring my laptop and do some work in cafés, or in the car if we can't find parking."

Gabe frowned. "Why would you do that?"

"Because you'll be in meetings."

"So? I want you there." He said it like there could be no other option.

It made logical sense, so she nodded. Seeing the potential spaces and meeting the celebrity they were thinking of working with would help her formulate the best plan for the campaign.

But inside, warmth kindled at the thought that Gabe wanted her with him for his business meetings. Whether it was because he valued her input or couldn't bear to be apart from her, she didn't know. The possibility of either made her a little giddy.

Instead of her usual tank-top-and-jeans combo, Michelle put on a royal-blue dress from her Rosen and Anders days and a pair of red wedges. She swapped out her Captain America–themed mini-backpack for a red Kate Spade shoulder bag, and left her hair down instead of sweeping it into a messy bun. When she met Gabe in the living room, he did a double take.

"Never mind," he said. "I think we should just stay here. In bed."

It was hard to say no when he was looking so good in dark slacks and a button-down shirt, the sleeves rolled up to expose his exquisitely muscled forearms. But Michelle wanted to see Business Owner Gabe in action, so she grinned and shook her keys at him. "Let's go."

AFTER VISITING FIVE locations with Carter the real estate agent, Gabe welcomed Michelle's suggestion that they stop at a café before driving uptown for the next meeting. With his oat milk latte in hand, Gabe leaned back in the front seat and took a long, slow sip, trying to forget that he'd quit caffeine years ago.

He and Michelle had viewed potential spaces all over Manhattan from Harlem to Soho, and gotten stuck in traffic twice, where they were forced to make small talk with Carter, a sandy-haired guy who looked to be about thirteen. Carter was a self-proclaimed HGTV addict.

"I never want to hear about *House Hunters* ever again," Gabe muttered, lowering the to-go cup.

Michelle snickered. "It's a whole channel devoted to his profession. I'd be more concerned if he *didn't* watch HGTV. I hope he knows most of those shows are fake, though."

"Don't tell him that. You'll ruin his life."

She took another sip of iced tea, then set the cup in the holder between them. "Did you prefer any of the spaces we saw? You played it pretty cool, so I couldn't tell."

He'd worried she was going to ask that. "I don't know," Gabe finally said. "The Soho space was nice. I could see it matching the vibe of the Los Angeles location. High ceilings, lots of glass, et cetera."

"Do you want it to have the same vibe?" Michelle asked. "Or do you want it to be its own thing?"

"I don't know," he said again. "Fabian is supposed to do this part. I'll send him the pictures and let him decide."

"We should talk about your audience," she said, starting the car. "Have you analyzed your social media following to see where they're located? I'm guessing most will be in the Los Angeles area, but we're going to want to build out your New York City and tri-state area audience, because they're going to be your new customers."

"Um, Fabian would know."

She was quiet for a moment. "Should I email Fabian about some of these things?"

"Yeah, probably." Gabe hated that he couldn't answer her questions, but all of this was Fabian's area of expertise. Gabe trained the employees and worked on classes and curriculum.

He connected with vendors and equipment providers, and handled the hiring and firing. Fabian was the one who usually interacted with the investors, bank, and anything having to do with décor or social media.

"Okay, I'll email him, maybe set up a call," Michelle said, pulling out of their parking space. The woman had a sixth sense for finding parking spots in Manhattan. "What's next on the agenda?"

"We're heading to a restaurant near Columbus Circle to meet our investor, Richard Powell, and the celebrity spokesperson he has in mind."

Michelle shot him a quick look. "Shouldn't it be who *you* have in mind? Or Fabian?"

Gabe shrugged. "Powell has a lot of strong opinions. And this actor is a member at the gym."

"Ooh, it's an actor? Let me guess." She tapped her chin in thought. "Sylvester Stallone."

"What year do you think it is?"

"John Cena?"

"Only in my dreams."

They chatted about their celebrity crushes while she drove, with Michelle even going so far as to provide infomercial-like introductions to Agility Gym in their voices. By the time they made it to the restaurant, Gabe was laughing so hard, he was near tears.

Michelle couldn't find a space, so she dropped Gabe off and went to circle the block.

Alone on the sidewalk, Gabe slipped on a pair of sunglasses and took a deep breath. Something about Powell made him nervous, and he never liked meeting him without Fabian present. It wasn't that Powell was mean or evil or anything like that. He'd even helped Gabe set up a legal aid fund for people in ICE custody. But the guy was just a little too . . . forceful. Or maybe *pushy* was a better term. When Powell had a vision, it was hard to deter him from it.

Even when it didn't match your own.

Gabe straightened his shoulders and strolled into the restaurant. The interior smelled heavenly, like garlic and basil, and was less pretentious than Gabe had expected, considering Powell had picked the place. The hostess brought him to their table.

"Hey, Gabe!" Richard Powell shot to his feet and rounded the table to take Gabe's hand and give him a one-armed hug. "Good to see you, man."

Sometimes Powell made Gabe feel like he was still that kid from the Bronx who didn't know anything about the world. But he knew, at the very least, that Powell admired his physical prowess, so Gabe always tried to appear confident in their meetings.

Powell was a few inches shorter than Gabe and probably twenty-five years older, with bright blue eyes, a ruddy complexion, and an excess of energy. He was in great shape for a man his age, and Gabe had a nagging suspicion that hanging out with fit younger guys—who were, often, POC—made Powell feel cool.

The other man at the table was about as tall as Gabe but leaner, with a fighter's build and dark, serious eyes. Rocky Lim, the handsome Chinese British star of a series of martial arts movies involving race cars, reached out a hand to Gabe, who shook it.

"Hey, mate," Rocky said, his voice still carrying a British accent despite his years in Los Angeles. Gabe had known Rocky since the actor had started coming to Agility to train for a role a couple years earlier. "How's it going?"

The table was square. Powell and Rocky sat perpendicular to each other, and Gabe sat on the other side of Powell, leaving a chair between him and Rocky. He'd alerted them in advance that he would be bringing a colleague, so Powell had made the reservation for four. Some part of Gabe didn't want Michelle sitting next to Powell. Rocky, on the other hand, had always been unfailingly polite to the women who worked at Agility, and Gabe trusted him to be the same with Michelle.

"Surprised to see you here in New York," Powell began, and Gabe resisted the urge to grit his teeth.

"Well, you know about everything happening with Fabian," Gabe said lightly. "Plans change."

"That they do." Powell gestured at the table, which was covered with no fewer than five platters and a basket of bread. "Are you hungry? I got here early and ordered some appetizers to start. I wasn't sure what you or your assistant might want."

Gabe opened his mouth to reply, but before he could get a word out, Michelle's voice came from over his shoulder.

"I'm not his assistant," she said, with the perfect amount of breezy confidence and flirtation only she could manage. She slid into the empty seat before any of them could get up. "Good afternoon, gentlepeople. I'm Michelle Amato, marketing consultant for the New York expansion."

Powell's eyes lit up when he saw her, and he stood to reach across the table to shake her hand. "You're the genius behind the Victory ads?"

She inclined her head, easily accepting the compliment. "That I am."

"Richard Powell, of Powell Enterprises. Great to meet you. I was thrilled to hear you were taking this on."

"Thrilled to be here," she said easily, then turned to Rocky. "Well, you don't look familiar at all."

Rocky flashed her a genuine smile. "Rocky Lim. Pleasure to meet you."

"Charmed." She shook his hand, then reached for a plate of calamari. "How did you know my weakness, Mr. Powell?"

"Call me Richard, please." And from there he proceeded to focus approximately 91 percent of his attention on Michelle, offering to order food or wine, asking what it was like to grow up in New York—as if Gabe hadn't grown up literally next door to her—and picking her brain on what Broadway musicals he should see while he was in town. He wasn't hitting on her, per se, but he was too ingratiating for Gabe's liking.

Michelle, for her part, handled it beautifully. She slipped in an impressive amount of questions about the gym, Rocky's involvement, and her own insights about the locations they'd seen that day. At no point did she seem uncomfortable, and she managed the flow of conversation with grace.

For the 9 percent of the time Powell talked to Gabe, Gabe was distracted by the conversation going on to his right. It seemed like Rocky and Michelle were bonding over black-and-white photography.

"Who are some of your favorites?" Rocky asked, leaning toward Michelle with an elbow on the table.

"I mean, it's hard to top Cartier-Bresson," she answered easily. "The decisive moment, and all that."

Powell was still talking, though, and Gabe reluctantly turned his attention back to his investor. He flashed a smile, since he'd long ago learned that was the best way to make it seem like you were listening. And like Michelle said, it was his moneymaker.

This kind of shit—meetings, schmoozing, cutting deals—wasn't for him. Fabian was good at this stuff, whereas Gabe preferred to be on the ground, working with regular people. Not movie stars and venture capitalists. But as the business had grown, he'd spent more time behind his desk and less time on the part of it he loved—training clients, teaching classes, or doing bodywork on PT patients.

For so long, Gabe had told himself the business tasks were the trade-off for success. And for the most part, Fabian had carried this particular part of the load.

It's not forever, Gabe told himself. Soon Fabian's schedule would free up, and he'd be able to handle the rest of the New York launch.

You think his schedule is going to free up after the twins are born? a little voice in the back of Gabe's mind nagged at him.

He pushed it aside. It had to. Because aside from Michelle's hand patting his thigh comfortingly under the table, he was fucking miserable.

And deep down, he knew he couldn't do this forever.

Chapter 12

Powell was quite impressed with you."

"Yeah?" Michelle gave Gabe a quick glance as she drove them through Hell's Kitchen to her apartment. The contractor had texted that morning to let her know the new toilet had been installed. The bathroom was still covered in plastic and there wasn't a sink, but since the toilet was hooked up, she could be in the apartment if she needed to be. She'd told Gabe she wanted to check it out while they were in the city, but really, she wanted to show him her apartment and see his reaction.

It was a hot August evening, and tons of people were out choosing between the little restaurants and bars that dotted the first stories of many of the buildings in her neighborhood. Michelle was on a quieter side street that was mostly residential, aside from a laundromat and a parking garage.

"Well, I am pretty impressive," she quipped, in the hopes of making Gabe laugh. It worked, and he let out a low chuckle.

He'd been moody since she arrived at the restaurant. She didn't know what had happened while she was parking the car, because he'd been laughing and joking with her right beforehand. Not that he'd said or done anything unprofessional. He'd been serious, which made sense, considering he was talking with his investor. But it was the sort of serious she remembered from their youth, when she'd seen him around his father. At her house, he'd been silly and fun, but in his own home, he'd been more subdued. Serious Gabe was almost . . . quietly macho. He stuck to short answers, with fewer flashes of dimples and a slight deepening to his voice.

Not that Michelle had minded that last part. The deep rumble had done things to her while she'd chatted with Rocky, who was unexpectedly down-to-earth. As they'd talked, she'd been hyperaware of Gabe to her left. The low notes of his voice. More enunciation, less of an accent, less slang. He held himself still, his posture unwavering throughout the meal, fully embodying his size and stature.

She'd found it sexy as hell, but she didn't know why he felt like he had to do all that posturing with Powell. The guy had seemed to like Gabe a lot. He'd been easygoing, informal, and excited about Agility's growth. In fact, she'd gotten more concrete answers about the gym and the brand from him than she'd gotten from Gabe. Even Rocky had only good things to say about the gym. He seemed to enjoy training there, and said Gabe was a great PT. She could already see how Rocky would be an excellent celebrity spokesperson.

Except none of it jibed with what Gabe had told her about his original vision for the gym.

To help people feel better in their bodies and achieve a full range of motion.

She couldn't imagine Rocky didn't already feel good in his body. And she'd seen his movies. There was not a damn thing lacking in his range of motion. The man did all his own stunts, for fuck's sake.

But at one point he'd turned sideways to show Michelle the line of his neck where it led to his back.

"See how straight that is?" he'd asked, in those lovely clipped vowels. "That's all Gabe. Whenever I start to hunch, he works on me, gets my muscles and joints moving in harmony again. It's like magic. Painful, beautiful magic."

As far as testimonials went, it was perfection, and Michelle had jotted it down on her phone verbatim the second she'd had the chance.

Meeting Rocky had made her wonder something, and now seemed as good a time as any to bring it up.

"So, Rocky . . ." she began, and Gabe turned a wary look on her.

"Are you going to fangirl over him now?"

"I'm way too cool for that. But I am curious. Did you and he ever . . . ?"

Gabe huffed out a laugh. "No. Not that I didn't think about it. I mean, you've met him."

"Gorgeous, charming, and not a jerk. Hard to find someone with all three qualities these days."

"Especially in LA. But he's a client, and I have rules about that."

"Don't shit where you eat?"

"Exactly."

"That makes sense." A car pulled out of a spot right in front of her building as they approached, and Michelle slid her car right in. "We're here."

Gabe peered outside and mumbled something about her being a parking psychic. She grinned and swung out of the car.

Michelle lived on the second floor of a redbrick five-story walkup. It wasn't fancy, but the management company weren't total dicks and the building's super kept everything clean as a whistle. He was also Puerto Rican, and he said Michelle reminded him of his daughter, so nothing in her apartment ever stayed broken for long.

She used her keys to let them into the lobby, paused to check her mail since she hadn't done it in a week, then led the way up the narrow staircase to the second floor.

"God, that ass," Gabe muttered behind her, and she let out a surprised laugh.

At the landing, she unlocked the door to her apartment and was about to say "Welcome to my humble abode," but what came out was "Mi casa es su casa."

Oh god, she had not just said that.

She turned her face away as her cheeks heated. For one thing, it was the most cliché thing she could have said, even more cliché than what she'd originally intended to say. But it also didn't sound like a joke, especially when he was currently staying with her at her parents' house. Bringing him into her own space felt even more intimate than that.

She quickly stepped inside and turned on the light, illuminating her combination living/working/kitchen space.

"Shoes off," she murmured, bending down to undo the straps on her sandals. Gabe unlaced his stylish leather sneakers and set them on the mat beside the door, next to a small basket of Jezebel's toys. Then he straightened and took in the apartment.

Michelle was proud of her home. It was small, but it was *hers*. She'd busted her ass to buy it, working long hours at the office while commuting from the Bronx and saving every penny she could. Sure, her living room also served as her office, the kitchen led right into the living area, and the bedroom was teeny tiny. But the apartment had high ceilings and got a fabulous amount of reflected sunlight through the living room windows. The street was quiet, and her upstairs neighbor was hardly ever home. Plus, it allowed cats. What more could she want?

She wondered how Gabe saw it. He probably thought it was too small, like her family did. That hadn't stopped them from helping her with the down payment, though. Technically her dad owned a third of the apartment, but he said she'd saved him money by getting scholarships and choosing a state university, so he was happy to help. And owning real estate in New York City was always smart.

After moving in—and making a shit-ton of repairs and upgrades—Michelle had decorated slowly and thoughtfully. She didn't want a home full of hand-me-downs from her parents or tías. That didn't stop them from trying to push off everything from sofas to flatware on her, but she turned them all down, or donated the things they refused to take back.

She wanted her home to be hers. Every bit of it. From the black and white furniture with red accents to the explosion of houseplants hanging above her desk, which was positioned near the windows.

Gabe wandered a few steps in while Michelle fidgeted with her purse strap.

Nerves kicked in and she couldn't stay quiet anymore, waiting to see what he thought. "It's small but—"

"Really nice," he said, sending her a quick smile. "It's perfectly you."

Fuck, her cheeks were getting warm again. "Thanks."

She gave him the nickel tour, starting with the living room and her office setup.

At her desk, he crouched next to the ergonomic chair, eyeing the dual monitor setup critically. "This is an okay work-from-home setup, but you probably want to raise your main screen an inch or two and get a different mouse pad."

"Sure thing, Dr. Gabe," she teased.

He sent her an amused smirk that made his dimple flash, then peered around a little more. "To be honest, I thought there'd be more nerd shit everywhere."

"It's here and there, if you look closely." She went over to the kitchen and took down the oven mitts to show him the tiny Mickey Mouse heads printed on them, black on red. "For example, all my kitchen textiles are Disney."

"Classy."

She put the mitts back on their hook and when she turned, Gabe was behind her.

Tension thickened the air around them, making her heartbeat quicken and her skin hypersensitive. All of her awareness narrowed in on her own body . . . and his.

"I need you, Mich." His voice was raw with longing, and all she could do was close the distance between them.

He slipped his arms around her waist and pulled her close. His mouth came down on hers and she shivered at the first taste of him. Her fingers were shaking when she reached up to tunnel them through his hair, and she clung to him to steady herself.

When he dragged his mouth away to press burning kisses down her neck, she struggled for air.

"What's wrong?" he whispered, and she realized his fingers were pressed to the pulse in her neck.

"Nothing," she said, her voice broken and breathy, but that wasn't true. "Why does it feel like this?"

He cupped her cheeks and peered into her eyes. "Like what?"

"Like I'm going to fall apart if you don't touch me?"

She hadn't meant to say it, but nothing felt real right now. Why not say what she was thinking?

His lips parted but he didn't answer. She didn't feel like her usual flippant self. She felt as raw and needy as he'd sounded.

She cleared her throat. "Do you want to see the bedroom?"

His gaze heated as it swept up and down her body. "Yeah, I do."

She took his hand and led him down the narrow hallway. The bedroom door was closed to keep out the dust from the bathroom renovation. She opened it and stepped inside.

As always, entering her room brought her a feeling of peace. It was small, with dark hardwood floors, and it didn't receive a lot of natural sunlight. To brighten it up, she'd decorated with light colors and earth tones. The bedding was white with tan accents, and she'd covered the wall behind the bed with removable wallpaper that resembled a misty gray forest with skinny trees.

Gabe followed and closed the door behind him. He didn't touch her, but the look on his face stole her breath.

"Gabriel," she whispered.

"I've got you." The words were almost lost, so quiet they were, and then, oh god, those wonderfully soft lips were moving over hers. He murmured her name between kisses, trailing his mouth down her throat as his fingers drew the fabric of her dress up over her thighs. She gasped at the feel of his hands on her bare legs. They were so hot, and with his PT expertise, he probably gave *amazing* massages.

Michelle was floating on a cloud of pleasure and anticipation when Gabe hooked his thumbs into the sides of her panties and slid them down.

Bad enough that her parents' home was full of memories of him. Now, every time she entered her bedroom, she would remember him here.

And she would cherish it.

Gabe wrapped one arm around her waist, supporting her. Then his big hand slipped between her legs and he stroked her folds gently, tenderly, with one finger.

Her back arched and she gasped at the touch, at the flash of sensation that shot through her body.

He held her like that, pressing hot, openmouthed kisses to her neck while he touched her. He didn't penetrate, barely even touched her clit, but by the time he picked her up and laid her on the bed, she was panting his name, tugging at his shoulders, and begging him to touch her *for real*.

He stretched out on the bed next to her and proceeded to seduce her into a state of utter bliss with slow, drugging kisses and a thorough exploration of her pussy with his fingers. He trailed his fingertips up and down her vulva, tickling the trimmed hair, before slipping between to trace the full length of her slit. Whenever he found a particularly sensitive spot that made her hips jerk, he slowed down and explored it further. Only then did he dip a finger inside her, and only partway, until she was pleading for release.

Her toes curled and flexed as he patiently rubbed his wet fingers over her clit. Michelle often didn't bother trying to come during sex—it took too long and it was easier if she did it herself using the collection of toys stashed in her closet. But Gabe didn't seem to be in any hurry. And what he was doing felt so amazing, she wasn't inclined to make him stop.

By the time he slid a second finger into her, she was wild with need. He had a huge dick, and while she hadn't let him prepare her the first time—her own fault—she was ready now. She was so fucking ready for him to fill her with his cock and—

Gabe pressed her clit with his thumb and gave it a little nudge.

The orgasm blindsided her.

Michelle's heels dug into the mattress and she cried out in ecstasy. Her back bowed and her hips bucked as ripples of sensation coursed through her body, going on and on as he pumped into her with his fingers and stroked her clitoris, giving her the best orgasm of her entire life.

When he'd finally wrung her dry, she fell back on the pillow, breathing hard.

She was never going to be the same after that. It was the kind of orgasm that changed someone forever.

Yesterday, when they'd fucked, she had fought against this level of intimacy with him. But it had been a futile effort. Everything about him demanded her attention, from his dazzling smile to the way he touched her. Softly, languidly, but with single-minded focus. Even his kisses were unhurried, as if he had all day to make her come.

The man was making it very difficult for her to keep her feelings in check.

Gabe shifted away and slid her skirt back down over her thighs.

"What are you doing?" Her voice was thick and drowsy, her thoughts slow.

"We don't have any condoms," he replied, dropping a kiss on her forehead. "But I wanted to touch you, and I couldn't resist watching you come."

"Is that what you think?" She reached behind her and stuck a hand in her purse. After rummaging around for a moment, she withdrew the box of condoms.

Gabe's jaw dropped and his eyes lit up like it was fucking Christmas. With a relieved chuckle, he wrapped his arms around her and pressed his face to her chest.

"I didn't take your dress off because I knew if I saw your gorgeous breasts, it would have been over for me."

"Well, since that's all that was holding you back . . ." Michelle sat up and swept the dress up and over her head. Gabe let out a groan at the sight of her lacy black bra, reaching out to cup her breasts reverently in his large hands.

"Mich, you still have the most beautiful boobs I've ever seen." The look on his face was one of pure wonder.

Michelle smoothed his hair back when he buried his face in her cleavage. "Thanks. I think they're pretty great too."

"This is a very nice bra," he said, kissing the tips of both of her breasts through the lace, "but right now it's in my way."

He reached behind her to unhook it, then tossed it aside.

"Much better," he murmured, gazing down at her naked form. Then he bent his head to take one of her nipples in his mouth.

Arousal coursed through her as he closed those soft, sexy lips around her pebbled peak. Despite the glorious orgasm he'd just given her, her body was already gearing up for the next one.

"Gabe?" His name came out breathless, more whine than word.

"Hmm?"

"Will you strip for me?"

He froze with her nipple in his mouth, then released it with a surprised laugh. When he raised his head, humor gleamed in his dark eyes. "Will I what?"

"Strip."

His dimples flickered in his cheeks. "I'm assuming you don't just mean take off my clothes."

"Well yeah, but in a sexy way."

He stared at her, then ducked his head and chuckled.

She peered closely at him. "Are you *blushing*?"

"Maybe." He released her and sat up. "I've never done this for anyone."

"Really? No lo creo." She was having a very hard time believing no other person had asked him to do a sexy striptease.

"Es la verdad," he confirmed.

"I mean, I would do it first, but . . ." She gestured at her body. "I'm already naked. You'll have to wait until next time."

His gaze took a leisurely path down her curves. "I'm going to hold you to that."

"So you'll do it?" She clasped her hands in front of her breasts and gave him a hopeful smile.

After a moment, he gave a single nod, then got to his feet and stood at the end of the bed. He raised his hands, hesitated, then put them on his hips.

"I have no idea where to start," he admitted.

"Do you need some music?" Michelle got her phone, trying not to laugh as she chose the song. A second later, "Boombastic" by Shaggy played from the speaker.

Gabe glared at her. "You're not helping."

She bit back a grin. "What's wrong with this song?"

"It's old. What about that song from *Magic Mike*?"

"You know that song is just as old, right?"

"It's slower, at least."

"Man, the nineties had some great sex jams." She pulled up "Pony" by Ginuwine on her phone. "Here you go."

The familiar melody began, but Gabe just stood there.

"I don't know what to do," he said, sounding helpless.

Michelle set the phone on her dresser and stood.

"Vas a perrear. Just pretend you're grinding on me at a high school dance. Or that you're in a Bad Bunny video."

He narrowed his eyes at her, but she turned her back to him and started swaying her hips. A moment later, Gabe's hands landed on her waist and his chest pressed against her naked back. His fingers tightened on her bare skin and he gently pulled her butt into alignment with his pelvis. And then he began to move his hips in time with the slow, heavy beat.

Oh *fuck*. Michelle's pulse skyrocketed as she leaned back against him, rocking and swaying. There was something so delightfully *nasty* about grinding together while she was naked and he was fully dressed.

When the lyrics kicked in, she slipped away and perched on the edge of the bed to watch.

Gabe kept his hips moving and his eyes on her as he reached up and began unbuttoning his shirt.

"Slowly," she said in a stage whisper.

His hands slowed, fingers slipping one button loose at a time, gradually revealing his defined abs.

"Ooh yeah, baby, take it off," Michelle cooed in a sultry voice once he'd reached the last button and pulled the shirt from the waistband of his pants. "I would give you all my dollar bills, if I had any."

She held back a laugh at the exasperated look he sent her, but he did a little shimmy when he shrugged out of the shirt.

When he got to his belt and unbuckled it, she let him undo the button at his waistband, before she interrupted him.

"Go slower," she prompted.

"I'm trying, baby."

"You're doing great." She slid to the edge of the bed and beckoned him closer. "Come here."

When he was within reach, she captured his waist in her hands and leaned her face toward his crotch. She caught the zipper pull of his fly in her teeth. Above her, he sucked in a breath, then muttered a litany of curses as she carefully tugged the zipper down over his bulge.

"Fuck, Mich. God, that's so fucking hot. You're amazing. I—"

He broke off with a groan when she completed the task and leaned back.

"Pants off," she said silkily, and helped him pull them down over his gyrating hips. When he was clad in nothing but a sexy pair of tight black briefs, she couldn't hold back. She palmed his ass and pulled him forward, opening her lips around the outline of his dick.

They both moaned as she mouthed him through the fabric. He was so fucking big and she was so turned on, not just from the orgasm he'd given her, but from his willingness to pleasure her first, and to do something he found mildly embarrassing simply because she liked it.

Gabe bent and kissed her fiercely, pushing her back on the bed and climbing on with her. Together they shoved his underwear down, and from there, they were a wild tangle of limbs as they tried to kiss and touch each other everywhere. His mouth found her breasts and he stroked her pussy, sliding two fingers into her when he found her still wet.

"You liked my striptease?" he asked, sending her a wicked grin before sucking her nipple into his mouth again.

"I loved it," she said, panting, as she reached down to cup his balls.

He surged up to kiss her again, swiping his tongue against hers in rough caresses. Then he broke away and reached for the condom on the bed.

"I need you. I need to be inside you, I—"

"Yes, now, Gabe." She opened her legs for him and in seconds he'd rolled the latex on and knelt in front of her. He pulled her knees up around his hips and bent over her, bracing himself on his elbows so he could kiss her. Then he entered her in one long, strong slide.

She moaned into his mouth, her thighs tightening around his waist. He was so big, he took her breath away, but this time she was more than prepared, and he sank right in.

He started to move before she could catch her breath, and she gasped and clutched at the sheets as he pounded into her. Sweat broke out on her skin and all she could do was hang on for dear life.

Gabe, meanwhile, nodded his head at the forest wallpaper and said conversationally, "I like the trees. It's just like doing it outside."

Michelle gasped out a giggle. "Shut up."

His hips continued to move in a steady rhythm to the music. "I hope we don't get interrupted by a bear."

"Gaaaaabe."

"You think the deer are watching us?"

She covered her face to hold in laughter. "You're supposed to be fucking my brains out, not cracking jokes."

He put his mouth next to her ear and gave it a nip with his teeth. "Oh, is that what I'm supposed to be doing?"

"Yeah." It came out like a whimper. Truth was, he was already fucking her brains out, and she didn't think she'd have any left if he kept this up.

"Challenge accepted." Rearing back, Gabe pulled out of her, flipped her onto her stomach, and slid back in.

Michelle sucked in a breath. At this angle, he felt even bigger and she fucking loved it.

"That okay?" he asked.

"God yes."

She gripped the blankets as he pumped into her, but then he stopped.

"I need to touch you." His breath was hot on the back of her neck as he wrapped an arm around her waist and lifted her. "Come on, baby. Up."

Her limbs felt limp, as if pleasure had sapped all her strength, but with his help she got on her knees and pressed her hands to the forest wallpaper. When he angled her hips and entered her from behind, her head fell back. Her throat worked like she wanted to say something, but he'd rendered her speechless. It was so good, almost too good.

"Okay?" he whispered in her ear.

She nodded, unable to speak as his hand slid down to where they were joined. He touched her clit lightly, then paused.

"I need you to tell me, babe. If something isn't working for you, you gotta tell me."

"It's working," she ground out, pushing her butt against him to urge him on. "It's really fucking working."

"Awesome." He expelled the word in a rush, then began to move.

Michelle braced herself against the wall, taking everything he gave. She tried to buck her hips but it was all she could do to stay upright as he moved inside her. He was glued to her back, his arms wound around her. She was losing all sense of herself. There was only her body, his, and theirs together.

It scared her to be this close, this unguarded, with another person. But it was also so perfect, so beautiful, even her fear was silenced. For perhaps the first time in her life, Michelle just let herself *feel*.

Gabe's hand palmed her breast, rolling her nipple between his fingers and mimicking what his other hand was doing between her legs, circling over her clit as he pounded into her from behind. Intense waves of pleasure consumed her. And all at once, the orgasm was within reach. She stretched for it as he shuttled in and out of her. The pressure built, tensing her muscles.

"I'm going to come," she said, breathless.

He growled something into her neck and caught her earlobe between his teeth. The sound of his harsh breath was the last straw. He was as undone as she was.

"I'm going to—" she said again, and then it was there, crashing over her and wringing a cry from her lips as she broke apart.

As aftershocks soared through her, her fingers traced one of the skinny trees silhouetted on her wallpaper. She'd never look at this forest the same way again. Gabe was imprinting himself on every part of her life.

And, unfortunately, on her heart.

He was still fucking her, and her pussy was wetter and more sensitive now, the waves of bliss carrying her along and scattering her thoughts. She let out high-pitched little moans with each of his thrusts, her body moving perfectly with his.

"Fuck," he growled into her hair, one arm braced against the wall and the other holding her tight around her middle. "Michelle. God. I need—"

He stiffened. Her eyes rolled back at the feel of that hard body flexing behind her, around her, inside her. Surrounding her. His hips jerked and he let out a low groan as he came.

Michelle shut her eyes and pressed her face to the wall. She couldn't move. Couldn't think. Could only breathe—and feel.

She'd felt everything. Taken everything he'd had to give and held back nothing. And it had brought her to greater heights than she'd ever imagined.

Two more days. How was she ever supposed to let him go?

They stayed like that, their bodies linked, their breath like bellows, until Michelle's thighs trembled. Gabe slipped out of her and helped her onto the mattress when she would have just melted into a messy puddle. Once she was horizontal, he crashed down next to her and they lay with their heads on the same pillow, gazing at each other.

"Why is everything ten times better with you?" he said softly, lifting a hand to brush her hair back from her temple. There was a note of wonder in his voice, in the light in his eyes. "Not just sex. Everything."

"I'm just that awesome, I guess." But it didn't come out flippant. It came out . . . sad.

He stroked her chin with his thumb. "You don't sound like you believe it."

She rolled onto her back and stared at the ceiling. He knew her too well. Still. And after what they'd just done, she was having a hard time keeping her usual walls up.

This was why she didn't get close. If anyone looked too deeply, they'd see she was nowhere near as confident as she claimed to be.

"What made you want to work freelance?"

She shot him a startled look. "What?"

He shook his head, his eyes blinking drowsily. "I was just thinking about your office setup. You did the whole Victory campaign with that firm, but now you're working from home."

She sat up, heart pounding for a different reason. "But you asked me after sex. Why?"

Lounging on the bed next to her, he looked like a god at rest. "I just can't figure out why you quit. You're clearly great at your job. And just now, you sounded like . . . I don't know, like you don't think you're amazing. So I wondered if these things were connected and—never mind. I'm sorry for asking."

"I guess I shouldn't be surprised you connected the dots."

"You don't have to tell me."

"No, it's okay. I should." She let out a long sigh and lay back down, folding her hands over her stomach. "I had a fling with one of my coworkers. We worked on the Victory campaign together. It was my project, all of the original concepts were mine, but he helped execute it. And then, when there was a promotion at the California office, he got in there first. Talked up his work on the campaign, played down my desire to go further in the company. He used this apartment and my family against me."

"How did he do that?"

"He claimed I never wanted to move away. Told the higher-ups that all my family was here in New York, that I'd bought an apartment. They never even fucking talked to me about it, those shitheads. Never even gave me the option. He got promoted, and I got a severe case of burnout. So I quit."

And then, since she was clearly in a sharing mood, she turned to him and added, "That's partly why I took this job, you know. I was worried that if I turned you down, you'd hire *him*."

Gabe's jaw tightened, but his fingers were gentle when he trailed them over her hip. "I'm really fucking glad Fabian was able to track you down."

Something in her chest twisted, and she turned her attention back to the ceiling. "Me too."

Fifteen years ago

Celestial Destiny: Episode 4 Planning Session

Michelle:

Our readers LOVE the amnesia story line.

Gabe:

They love that Riva hinted to Zack that they might be a couple.

Michelle:

Lots of people like a romance!

Gabe:

I was worried they'd abandon us because so much time passed between when we posted the chapters, but I think this is the most comments we've gotten so far.

Michelle:

The school year's almost over so let's try to get the next chapter up sooner.

Gabe:

I already have some ideas for the next one.

Michelle:

Ooh. Does Zack still have amnesia?

Gabe:

> Everyone really liked it, so let's keep that going. I think some tragedy should befall them on their way back to the crash site. Maybe something involving the wildlife on this planet.

Michelle:

> That will give it some variety.

Gabe:

> And as they're escaping, they lose some of their camping equipment.

Michelle:

> Oh yeah. Good source of conflict.

Gabe:

> I was thinking . . . what if they're left with only one sleeping bag?

Michelle:

> ¡Qué escándalo!

Gabe:

> Our readers will eat it up.

Michelle:

> They totally will. Let's do it!

Chapter 13

With the interior of the car lit by the streetlamps over the West Side Highway, Gabe eyed Michelle in the driver's seat and asked the thing most pressing on his mind.

"You wanna tell me why you own a car when you live in Manhattan?"

Michelle sputtered out a laugh. "How long have you been wondering that?"

"Since you picked me up at LaGuardia."

Her lips curved in an easy smile as she watched the road. "I needed it when I was living in the Bronx, and it seemed easier to keep it, since I drive up to visit my family a lot. Sometimes I leave it there and take the train, but as you've seen, I have amazing luck at finding parking spots."

"It must be brujería. There's no other explanation."

She laughed again, and the sound reached inside him and alleviated a weight he hadn't even realized he'd been carrying.

The day had been a whirlwind of emotions, but Michelle had been a steadying force for him through it all. It had also been that way when they were kids. After getting into it with his dad, he could always rely on Michelle to cheer him up.

"There's something I've been wondering too," she said.

"Oh?"

She cut him an apprehensive look, and he had a feeling he knew where this was going. "You said this morning that you hadn't talked to your parents in nine years."

"That's right."

"Did something . . . specific happen?"

He raised his eyebrows. "No one told you?"

"What do you mean?"

"My sister's wedding. Your parents were there. Monica and Junior too."

Her face scrunched up in thought. "Where was I?"

"In Paris with Jasmine."

"Oh right. Something happened at the wedding?"

Gabe leaned back in his seat, stunned. "I can't believe they didn't tell you."

Her face shuttered. "They knew how your leaving affected me, so I can only guess they made a secret pact to never mention you again."

He reached over and put a hand on her thigh, sliding it up and down in a gentle, soothing motion. "I hate that I hurt you."

"Likewise," she said quietly. "I should have been a better friend."

"You know, I used to fall asleep narrating emails to you in my head," he confessed.

"You did?" She said it like she didn't believe it.

"I missed you so much, Mich." For some reason, in the darkened car, with the white noise of traffic all around them and the smoothly flowing Hudson River stretching alongside on the left, it was easier to confess the depths of his feelings for her. "Especially when it was quiet."

She snorted, but her expression softened. "It's never quiet when I'm around."

"Exactly." A smile curved his lips, unbidden. "You used to fill the silence, with stories, questions, memories, whatever. I always knew what you were thinking and feeling. And then, suddenly, I didn't."

"I emailed you," she murmured. "More than once."

"I know. There was so much I wanted to say, and I didn't know how."

"Like what?" she whispered.

Like "I love you." But he still didn't know how to say that, so he didn't.

"Like what happened at my sister's wedding. You would've gotten a kick out of it."

"Really?"

He was relieved she accepted the return to a somewhat lighter subject. "The drama of it all. My brother-in-law, Patrick, owed Nikki twenty bucks."

"For what?"

"Nikki bet her husband that my dad and I would cause a scene. Patrick—bless him—was sure we wouldn't. Or maybe it was just wishful thinking."

"And Nikki was right." Michelle sighed. "What happened?"

"Tío Marco—you remember him?"

"Of course. Your godfather."

"Right. He made some crack about me playing for the Yankees. He was kidding, but that set my dad off."

"Why did you stop playing baseball, anyway?"

"Hurt my knee, got more interested in sports medicine and rehab."

"And that led to physical therapy. Gotcha."

His chest warmed, glad that she was able to make those kinds of connections about him. "My dad said some shit about me thinking I was too good for the Yankees—"

"Um, excuse me, Esteban," she cut in, addressing Past Dad as if he were in the car with them. "Who thinks they're too good for the Yankees?"

"Not me. I reminded him that I'd gotten injured, which led him to bring up my student loans. You know how my dad feels about debt."

"Oh, I remember. I was present for some of those conversations."

Conversations was putting it mildly. Even *lectures* didn't come close. They were more like tirades. Gabe shook off the memories.

"He started in on my job at the time. I was working as a personal trainer, building up my client base, while looking into physical therapy programs. And he acted like I was just hanging out, lifting weights for fun."

Try as he might to squash it down, the memory of old hurts rose up. Gabe had been so fucking done that day. Done being belittled and talked down to because he'd dared have dreams of his own. Because he'd had the gall to follow those dreams, even though it meant leaving his family—a cardinal sin, in his father's eyes.

His parents had acted like it was fucking *easy* to leave everything he'd known to move across the country. Like he hadn't worked his ass off. And when he'd finally found the thing that fulfilled him, they'd treated it like it was nothing, because it didn't fit their dream for him.

Gabe remembered the next part clearly. His mother had tried to shush him, but he'd stood up to his father, once and for all.

Even if I carry it with me to my grave, every cent of debt is worth it. It got me away from the store. It got me out of the house. And it got me away from you.

Gabe had gotten up to leave then, feeling like shit for ruining his sister's wedding, his father's shouts echoing behind him in Spanish. And then, in English . . .

"Don't come back," Gabe repeated out loud, the words overlapping with his father's voice in his mind. "That's the last thing he said to me."

Michelle sucked in a breath. "That's what *I* said to you," she whispered, shooting him a pained look.

Whatever, Gabe. Run away to California. Run away, and don't ever come back.

"I remember," he murmured.

"God, no wonder you left all of us behind." Her voice held anguish. "None of us got it. Got *you*."

"I had this feeling that if I stayed in New York for college, my life was never going to be my own." It was more than he'd planned to say, but it was the truth. He'd needed space to grow up outside the family unit, away from the crushing weight of his father's expectations.

He just wished it hadn't meant leaving Michelle too. At the time, it seemed necessary. And it was yet another thing he blamed his parents for.

He shifted in the seat. "I'm just surprised your sister never told you about the wedding."

"Monica? Why?"

"She came out to talk to me when I was waiting for a taxi. Told me you were okay, had a good job."

Michelle narrowed her eyes, as if looking back into the past. "I was already at Rosen and Anders by then."

"Monica said it paid well."

"It did. Until I decided the cost to my health was too damn high."

She'd mentioned burnout before. But they'd poked enough old wounds for one night, so he tried to lighten the mood.

"Seen any good movies lately?" he asked.

"You're changing the subject."

"Damn right I am."

And maybe she was also feeling emotionally wrung out, because she asked if he'd seen the *Beyond the Stars* fifteenth-anniversary panel at Comic-Con, and when he said he hadn't, she launched into a play-by-play of the banter and behind-the-scenes gossip.

And for a moment, it felt just like old times.

But better.

MICHELLE HAD FORGOTTEN the condoms in her apartment, but that didn't stop them from getting creative in Gabe's bed after they returned. To her own surprise, Michelle actually let him go down on her. It wasn't something she did often—it felt more vulnerable, like losing control, something she'd previously avoided at all costs. But with Gabe, it had felt okay to release the reins and see what kind of pleasure he could bring her.

And boy, had he delivered.

After that, Michelle made good on the striptease she owed him, and proceeded to blow his mind in every sense of the word.

Once they were done and had cleaned up, Michelle made him flip over onto his stomach so she could thoroughly examine the tattoo on his back. It was fairly large, taking up about a fifth of the real estate, and blended the flags of Mexico and Puerto Rico with flora and fauna, forming a cohesive whole.

"Is this your only one?" she asked, trailing her fingers over the ink.

"You've seen every inch of me, so if there were more, I don't know where I'd be hiding them."

She grinned and gave him a poke. "I knew someone in college who had a tattoo on the inside of their lower lip."

Gabe narrowed his eyes at her from where his cheek was pillowed on his arms. "Michelle, I do not have a tattoo inside my mouth."

"Just checking." She returned her attention to his broad back. "When did you get this?"

He hesitated before answering. "After I stopped talking to my family."

She'd suspected as much. It broke her heart to imagine Gabe as a young man, alone and cut off from his family, his heritage.

She kept her voice light. "Can I guess what it means?"

He closed his eyes. "Go for it."

"I recognize this one. It's the Taíno symbol for the coquí. And is this one . . . an eagle?"

He nodded. "An Aztec eagle."

Michelle studied the tattoo, the meanings whirling in her

head. The coquí were a species of frog native to Puerto Rico. The little frogs were small but resilient, and they made their voices heard. They came out at night, whereas the strong and majestic eagle symbolized the sun, and the place where the Aztec people had founded what was now Mexico City.

"The styles represent the original inhabitants of the places where you're from, before colonialism attempted to wipe them out," Michelle guessed. "Am I right?"

"One hundred percent." Then he pulled her close and kissed her until she was breathless.

She fell asleep in his arms, but halfway through the night she got up and slipped through the adjoining bathroom to her own bed in the craft room.

As she tried to fall back to sleep with Jezebel snuggled into her side, she was forced to admit she was already breaking too many of her own rules with Gabe. Orgasms during sex, letting him go down on her—she swallowed hard at the memory of his tongue between her legs—talking about her *feelings*. Sleeping beside him, being completely vulnerable in repose, was the last barrier remaining.

And she needed it. If she let herself get used to sleeping with him, even for one night, it would make the pain of his inevitable departure unbearable.

She rolled onto her side and petted Jezebel, who let out a grunt at being disturbed. As the cat settled down again, Michelle reflected on their conversation in the car.

She understood now why Gabe had been so anxious to leave the Bronx, and so angry at her for dragging him back here. She'd always liked his parents, and she could see now that while they'd been kind to her, Gabe had suffered under the weight of their expectations more than she'd ever realized. He had good reason to be estranged from them.

His life was in Los Angeles now. She got that. But maybe opening another gym in New York would give him a reason to visit more often. And maybe that would allow them to continue exploring this new evolution of their old friendship.

Michelle didn't need to spend every second of every day with somebody. The whole reason she'd worked so hard to buy her apartment was so she could have a place that was hers and hers alone. Unlike the rest of her marriage-obsessed family, Michelle was fine on her own.

But she wasn't opposed to occasional companionship. If Gabe were to visit New York on a regular basis . . . well, that could be enough.

Lying in her bed with him had been too easy, had felt too right. Seeing him walking around her apartment in his underwear, perfectly at home, had, for the first time in a long time, made her wish for more. Someone she could talk to and share experiences with, someone who would *see* her.

The way Gabe had when they were younger.

Plus, Jezebel liked him. On the way to the real estate office, Gabe said he'd woken up that morning with Jezebel curled up against his neck—although he'd made it sound like he'd wished it had been Michelle in bed with him instead.

It was hard not to take that as a sign.

Maybe, after all this time, they were being given another chance.

HALF ASLEEP, GABE stretched his arm across the mattress, reaching for Michelle. The other side of the bed was empty and cold, until he reached a pile of warm, purring fur.

He cracked his eyes open to find Jezebel watching him with an enigmatic gaze.

"Where'd she go?" he grumbled at the cat. Jezebel took it as some sort of invitation and padded over to drape her body across his neck, nearly suffocating him. "Fine, I'll pet you."

Ten minutes later, Gabe found Michelle in the kitchen loading the dishwasher. "I was looking for you."

"I'm right here." She bent over to jam utensils into the holder. "Coffee's on the counter."

Gabe glanced at the little mug of café con leche and, after only a moment's hesitation, grabbed it and took a sip. His eyelids fluttered shut as the first heavenly taste hit his tongue, a reminder of his old coffee habit. Michelle must have made it especially for him, since she was primarily a tea drinker. But he wouldn't allow it to distract him from the conversation at hand.

"I meant I was looking for you in my bed."

She shrugged and fit drinking glasses into the top rack. "I don't sleep with people."

Gabe let out a snort and set down his mug to pass her the dishes from last night's dinner. "Could've fooled me."

"No, I mean I don't share beds overnight with sexual partners."

Gabe frowned as he gave the frying pan another rinse before handing it to her. "Is this some *Pretty Woman* shit? Like how Julia Roberts wouldn't kiss Richard Gere?"

She straightened, a look of surprise making her amber eyes go wide. "You remember that?"

"Come on, Mich. You made me watch that movie at least a dozen times."

"And how many times did you make me watch *Scarface*?"

"Touché."

She closed the dishwasher and turned it on, then moved to the sink to rinse her hands.

"And yes," he heard her mutter, barely audible over the sound of running water. "It is some *Pretty Woman* shit."

Chuckling, he came up behind her and slipped his fingers under the hem of her shirt, skimming them up her ribs to tease the undersides of her breasts.

"Don't start something you can't finish," she warned. "We don't have any condoms, remember?"

"Hmm. Right."

It was Thursday. He was leaving later the next day. They hadn't made a ton of progress on the campaign—or at least, he hadn't. Hell, he couldn't even decide which of the five locations he liked best. Michelle's laptop was already open on the dining table, surrounded by a slew of fancy pens and pencils he wasn't allowed to use and a sketch pad he wasn't allowed to look at. Meanwhile, the worksheet she'd given him Tuesday was still only halfway done.

He heard the slam of a car door and sneaked into the living room to peer out the window. Through the lace curtains, he could just make out the form of his father sitting in the SUV parked in his parents' driveway. The car started, then backed out and took off down the street.

Gabe went to the kitchen doorway. "My dad just left. I can run to the pharmacy for condoms if you give me your car keys."

"What?" She looked up from the laptop screen and blinked at him. "Oh. The key fob. It's in my bag."

She pointed at the red purse sitting on the kitchen counter and he sifted through at least half a dozen lipstick tubes before he found what he was looking for.

"Can you pick up one of those presentation boards for me?" she asked. "I want to put together a mood board."

"A—" He didn't even know where to begin with all of that. "Never mind. Sure, I'll get it. Is the big pharmacy still on Williamsbridge Road? The one where you used to get pictures printed?"

"Yeah." Her smile was a little wistful, although he didn't know why. "It's still there."

After peeking out the kitchen window to make sure his mom was still sweeping the backyard next door, Gabe hurried out the front door, down the stairs, and into Michelle's car. He was wearing his Yankees cap and dark sunglasses, but he knew what this neighborhood was like. If anyone saw a strange man running in and out of the Amato house, there was a good chance they'd report it to Michelle's parents.

He started the car and navigated to the drugstore like he hadn't been gone for nearly a decade. People had a certain image of New York City, like it was all glass and steel skyscrapers, populated by businesspeople and models. In reality, the outer boroughs were all a collection of neighborhoods, a mix of houses and buildings, corporate brand stores and mom-and-pops, and home to families who'd called the city home for generations.

Morris Park had changed in the years he'd been gone, but in so many ways, it was still the same.

The drugstore had a sizable parking lot attached. Gabe found a spot near the entrance and pulled in. As he was getting out of the car, his phone buzzed. He checked it, thinking maybe Michelle had forgotten to ask something. But it was Fabian.

Fabian: EMERGENCY

Gabe: What's wrong?

Fabian: Everything. AC is out. Ventilation system down. Lights flickering.

Fuck. Gabe took a deep breath and ran through each problem in his head, lining it up with a solution.

Gabe: Hold on. Sending numbers for repair services.

Gabe scrolled through his phone's contacts as he walked, glancing up every so often to make sure he was heading the right way. After he'd sent Fabian the info for the electrician and the HVAC, he found the condoms in an aisle near the pharmacy counter, a full shelving unit of brightly colored boxes with names that didn't actually describe anything useful.

It had been years since he'd had to buy condoms for himself. For one thing, he was too busy to need them often. The gym also kept free Agility-branded condoms in the locker rooms for members to take. He had a whole stash at his apartment, yet hadn't thought to bring a single one with him to New York.

Before he could even begin to make a decision, his phone buzzed again with more incoming texts from Fabian. Gabe peered at the screen to look at the pictures Fabian had sent, but couldn't see them well. He tore off the shades to take a better look. Water . . . some kind of leak. Fuck, he was going to have to call and help troubleshoot from here. He shot off a quick text.

> **Gabe:** Don't touch it. Will call in a minute.

He slipped the phone into his pocket and examined the dazzling array of condom boxes. There were too many fucking choices, and he had to get out of here. He picked up a couple to read the labels. What the hell was the difference between Ecstasy and Double Ecstasy? Was there a Triple Ecstasy option, and if not, why not? Where did the ecstasy end? Did it go all the way to infinity?

He was sure Michelle would have something pithy and insightful to say about the branding. *Notice the way the logo's helmet resembles a dickhead, thus revealing the brand's core values!*

Gabe stifled a laugh at the thought, then found the MAG-NUM condoms. There, decision made. But wait, there were "thin" and "ribbed" options. He bit back a groan. Did condom companies *want* to cause decision fatigue?

Fuck it. He had to call Fabian. Grabbing both boxes, Gabe turned toward the pharmacy desk to pay.

And came face-to-face with his father.

Chapter 14

This was his own fault, really. Gabe should've known better. Yesterday, he'd joked about brujería then talked about his father, all but summoning him. And now here the man was, as if conjured by the Universe to appear at the *worst possible moment*.

A myriad of emotional responses battled within Gabe. There was the adolescent embarrassment of getting caught by his *dad* while buying *condoms*, amplified by the fact that they hadn't seen each other in *nine years*. Add to that approximately thirty years' worth of pent-up anger and resentment, along with a sprinkling of something like regret as he noted the signs of aging on his father's face. There were lines around Esteban Aguilar's eyes, and his hair was almost entirely gray, which surprised Gabe almost more than anything else.

Gabe did the math quickly in his head. His father would be sixty now. How the fuck had that happened?

But regret was a feeling Gabe didn't have time for.

Underlying the other emotions was the familiar urge to run. How could he possibly explain what he was doing here? The absolute last thing Gabe wanted to do was tell his father about the gym and everything else. He didn't need a single second more of this man doubting him, interrogating him about his life choices, or making him feel small and stupid and worthless. Those days were *over*.

All this passed through Gabe's mind in an instant. Maybe his father hadn't recognized him. Maybe Esteban would pretend not to know him, or deliver some cutting remark like *I told you not to come back*. Maybe Gabe could just slip his sunglasses back on and—

"Gabriel?"

The shock of recognition reverberated through Gabe at the sound of the voice he knew better than his own, but hadn't heard in years.

"Papi," he said, even though he hadn't called his father Papi since he was small.

The last time they'd seen each other, they'd said horrible things, and Gabe braced himself for an argument, for accusations and recriminations. All the things he'd been running from.

Adrenaline and training meant he noticed when his father lurched toward him. Gabe flinched—

But Esteban only caught him in a tight hug.

The air whooshed out of Gabe in a rush. Not from the force of the embrace, but from shock. Of all the reunions Gabe had imagined over the years . . . he'd never pictured this.

"Ay, mijo," Esteban murmured. He clapped Gabe hard on the back, and Gabe was struck by another sense memory. His dad smelled the same—like aftershave and the slight whiff of cigar smoke. Back then, Esteban had enjoyed one a week, sitting out in the backyard. Gabe and his sister weren't allowed outside while Esteban smoked, and while Gabe was sure part of the reason was their tender lungs, he suspected as he got older that it was also his father's only downtime during the whole week.

Belatedly, Gabe raised his arms and hugged his dad back, just before Esteban finally released him.

"¿Qué estás haciendo aquí?" Esteban asked, then looked at Gabe's hands.

That was when Gabe remembered he was still holding a box of condoms in each hand.

"Um . . ."

"This part is obvious," Esteban said, his mouth twitching like he was trying not to laugh. "I mean, ¿qué haces en el Bronx?"

As much as Gabe wanted to throw the success of Agility Gym in his father's face, he didn't want to do it now, like this. He wanted to do it at the right moment, when the New York location was an indisputable fact. So Gabe did something he wasn't totally proud of.

"Michelle," he blurted out. He couldn't tell his father about the gym, and Michelle was the only other reason Gabe's poor misfiring brain could think of in the moment. "Michelle and I are . . ."

Gabe trailed off, and his father filled in the blanks on his own.

"¡Por fin!" Esteban threw up his arms like this was something to celebrate. "Estabas tan enamorado de ella."

That brought Gabe up short. He hadn't realized his father had known Gabe was *so in love with her* back then.

"Yeah, we . . . um. Yeah." Gabe shrugged.

"¿Por qué no nos dijiste?" Esteban crossed his arms.

"Ah, porque . . ." Gabe cast around for an answer to why

they hadn't told anyone and settled on one that sounded legit. "We knew you'd all make a big deal about it."

"Verdad. Tu madre . . ." Esteban shook his head. "She's going to lose her mind. You're back, and you're with Michelle. It's all she ever wanted."

Fuck. Gabe had forgotten to consider his mother's response in all this. How could he have forgotten about his mom?

"¿Dónde te estás quedando?"

"I'm staying, um, me estoy quedando . . . con Michelle." Gabe's voice cracked and he cursed himself for not thinking of a lie. Hotel. He should've said he was staying in a hotel! And then he could have raced back to the house, grabbed his suitcase, and escaped forever.

Michelle would probably kill him for leaving her again, but death would be an improvement over whatever hell he was currently trapped in.

"¿En la casa de Dominic y Valentina?" Esteban raised his eyebrows and gave Gabe a look like, *Dude, that's bold.*

It was. Shit. What had he been thinking, having sex with Michelle *in her parents' house*? All of this was a giant mistake!

"Vendrás a cenar esta noche," Esteban said in a tone that brooked no argument. "Michelle también."

"Uh, okay. Sí." Fuck, why had he just agreed to have dinner with his parents that night?

He was regressing. Two minutes in his father's presence and Gabe couldn't think of a lie to save his life, couldn't say no, and couldn't set clear boundaries like a fucking adult. *This* was why he'd needed to leave.

"I better go," Gabe muttered, and made a move to stash the boxes back on the shelf.

His dad put a hand on his arm to stop him. "¿Qué haces, muchacho? You're not married to her yet. Necesitan practicar safe sex."

Gabe's heart stopped. This was it, this was the moment he died. In the condom aisle of a CVS, at the age of thirty-one, because his father had told him to *practice safe sex.*

Because his father was watching, Gabe held on to the boxes and got on line to buy them.

Esteban waited with him, since he was there to pick up his blood pressure prescription. He peppered Gabe with questions in a mix of Spanish and English, and by the time Gabe was able to get away—after promising that yes, he and Michelle would be over for dinner at 6 P.M.—Gabe no longer had any idea what he'd replied. It was like some kind of out-of-body experience.

Gabe hurried out of the store and lost a few moments looking for his black Audi hybrid before he remembered that he was in New York and had driven Michelle's teal Fiat.

Once in the car, he pulled out his phone to call Michelle, but his hands were shaking so badly he almost dropped it. Never mind. He'd be back at her house in a few minutes. Taking a deep breath, he started the car and drove back as quickly as residential speed limits allowed.

MICHELLE WAS IN the basement printing pictures for her presentation when she heard pounding footsteps and Gabe shouting her name. She abandoned the printer and ran upstairs.

"I'm here!" she called, heart racing. Had something happened with her car? Was he hurt? Did he—

Gabe met her in the kitchen, eyes wild. He shook a white paper pharmacy bag at her. "We're caught."

Michelle looked him over, checking for blood. "What?"

Gabe sucked in a breath and let it out in a rush. "My *dad* . . ."

Michelle's stomach sank.

"Saw me . . ."

She clapped her hands over her mouth. It was obvious where this story was going.

Gabe squeezed his eyes shut as if in pain, then yelled, "BUYING CONDOMS!"

Michelle bit down hard on her lower lip. If she laughed now, he would never forgive her. Maybe in ten years they'd be able to joke about this, but right now he was looking apoplectic, so she took his arm and pulled him over to the sofa.

"Let's sit down." Channeling Ava, Michelle adopted a soothing tone. "Why don't you tell me what happened?"

Gabe sank into the cushions and covered his face with his hands. "It was awful, Mich. I couldn't decide between the condom brands' core values, and then suddenly my dad was *right there*."

She opened her mouth to ask what he meant by that, then thought better of it. "What did he do?"

"He *hugged* me." Gabe sat up and rested his arms on his knees. "Like . . . what the fuck?"

Poor guy. After what he'd told her about his sister's wedding, she could only imagine how confusing that must have been. Michelle placed a hand on his thigh, wishing she could find the right words to help him. "And then?"

"I told him we were together."

She balked. "You—what? *We* as in *you and me?*"

"I'm sorry." Gabe buried his face in his hands. "He was asking me all these questions, and I was still holding the condoms, and I didn't want to tell him about the gym—you were honestly the first reason I could think of for why I'm here."

It shouldn't make her happy but . . . damn it, it did. "You told him we're together in what sense?"

He raised his head and his expression was bleak. "We have to go over there for dinner tonight and pretend we've been secretly dating."

Secretly dating, huh? That was certainly simpler than trying to explain their current situation, although it implied a greater level of commitment. Michelle tried to look on the bright side for his sake.

"That shouldn't be too hard. We're already secretly screwing, right?" Clearly it was the wrong thing to say, because Gabe groaned and covered his face again. "What's wrong?"

"He also guilted me for sleeping with you in your parents' house, and when I tried to put the condoms back, he lectured me about safe sex. So then I *had* to buy them."

"Well, that's good, right? At least we have condoms?" Again, finding the silver lining. Ava would be so proud.

"I don't think I can ever have sex again after that conversation," Gabe mumbled. Then he gave Michelle's boobs a sidelong look. "Never mind. I take that back. Somehow I'll find the fortitude."

"I'm sure you will." Michelle patted his back. While part of her felt bad for his obvious distress, another part of her perked up in hope. If Gabe reconciled with his parents, maybe he'd visit more.

Or maybe he'd stay.

Above all, Michelle wanted Gabe to be happy, and she suspected that until he dealt with his feelings about his parents, he was always going to be running away from them in some sense. Maybe if he faced them, he could finally stop running.

"Okay, well, what's done is done," she said. "We still have work to do."

"Work? How am I supposed to work when my life is imploding?"

"I want to show you my preliminary ideas. Did you buy the board?"

"Sorry, I forgot. When I saw my dad, I think my brain short-circuited. And then I had to stand on line with him to buy the condoms."

"Oh my god. That's terrible. I'm sorry, babe."

"You have no idea."

And then he wrapped his arms around her, pressing his face into her neck. "Mich, what do I do?"

She rubbed slow, comforting circles on his back. "We'll go to dinner, and I'll be right there with you. You're not the boy you were when you left. What can they do to you now?"

He mumbled something, but all she heard was "doubt myself." She squeezed him tight and let him hold on for as long as he needed.

IN THE KITCHEN, Michelle's phone rang. At the sound of the ringer, she stilled.

"What's wrong?" Gabe asked, lifting his head.

"That's my mom."

"Oh fuck."

Fuck indeed. Gabe released her and she hurried to pick up the phone before it went to voicemail.

"Hi, Mom!" she said, aiming for a combination of cheerful and *nothing to see here.*

"Is Gabriel Aguilar in my house?"

Wow, trust Mom to cut to the chase. No matter. Michelle could play this cool.

"Yes, he is. Did you want to talk to him?"

Gabe appeared in the kitchen doorway, eyes wide with horror. He mouthed *NO!* at her.

On the phone, Valentina stifled a begrudging laugh. "Ha. Don't get smart with me. Why is Gabriel there?"

Time to spin this thing. "You know how we were really close when we were younger? Well, we recently reconnected online, and you know, one thing led to another. We wanted to test it out, but we knew if we told *anyone* in our families, you'd all make it a big deal."

She paused, to imply that her mom calling her right this moment was proof of their concerns.

"So we decided to keep it a secret for a little while. You know how it goes, Mom."

It was a well-known family story that her mom had started dating her father while she was still in high school, and there had been a fair amount of sneaking around. Michelle's mom couldn't begrudge her having a secret relationship in her early thirties.

"Fine, but why is he in *my* house?"

"Your house is bigger," Michelle replied, and Gabe slapped a hand over his face in exasperation. "And because mine *just* got a toilet yesterday."

"Oh, they installed the new toilet? How is it?"

"Amazing. You wouldn't believe how quiet the flush is."

"I keep telling your father we need to upgrade the toilets in the house to ones that use less water."

"We'll make him test mine, and then he'll see how great it is."

"I can't believe you're talking about toilets right now," Gabe hissed at her.

"Is that Gabriel?" Valentina asked. "Tell him I said hi."

"Mom says hi," Michelle repeated dutifully.

Gabe shut his eyes like he wanted to disappear. "Hi, Valentina," he called.

"He says hi," Michelle reported back.

Gabe's phone rang and he took it out of his pocket. "Coño. It's my sister."

Michelle's phone buzzed and she pulled it away from her ear to look at the screen while her mom reported all the gossip from her friends and extended family in Florida.

> **Jasmine:** What

> **Jasmine:** The

> **Jasmine:** Fuck

Oh hell. Jasmine knew. Michelle was *never* going to live this down after all the shit she'd given Jas about dating Ashton.

In her defense, she and Gabe weren't working togeth—

Wait. Yes, they were. He'd hired her to consult for his business. *Damn it.*

Another text popped up.

> **Ava:** My mom just called to ask if you have a man living with you at your parents' house.

Since Valentina was still bochinchando about Florida chisme, Michelle typed back a reply.

> **Michelle:** Cat's out of the bag. I'm on the phone with my mom now.

> **Ava:** Are you okay? Do you want me to come over?

From the living room, Michelle heard Gabe saying, "Nikki, listen to me. I was going to tell you but—"

"—to the quinceañera," Valentina was saying, so Michelle brought the phone back to her ear.

"What's that? Sorry, Jezebel did something."

When in doubt, blame the cat.

"I was asking if you're bringing Gabriel to Ronnie's stepdaughter's quinceañera this weekend."

"No, I didn't RSVP with a plus-one and you know how Ronnie—"

Valentina sucked her teeth. "No es nada. There's always room for one more person."

Michelle had a feeling her mom also wanted to show off to the entire family that Michelle was finally dating someone.

Fuck. Maybe the fake dating pretense wasn't such a great idea after all. Her family had a tendency to blow anything relationship-adjacent out of proportion.

Michelle eyed Gabe, who was pacing the living room. There were worse things than having Latino Superman on her arm at a quinceañera. Plus, it would get on Ronnie's nerves, which was a good enough reason to bring him.

Michelle and Ronnie had been frenemies since they were ten, when, while practicing triple axels in Abuela's living room, Ronnie had broken a window and blamed it on Michelle. It wasn't the indoor figure skating that caused the accident, but the baseball Ronnie had thrown at her older brother Sammy after he gave her a low score on her short routine.

"You *have* to bring him, Michie," her mom was saying. "Everyone will want to see him."

Especially since everyone already seemed to know Gabe was here. If Michelle didn't bring him, the Rodriguez family would spend the entire quinceañera lamenting his absence.

Another text popped up.

> **Abuela Esperanza:** ¿Tienes un novio?

Oh no. Even her *grandmother* knew about Gabe. Instead of answering whether or not she had a boyfriend, Michelle sent a winking emoji in reply and brought the phone back to her ear.

"I'll ask him," she hedged. "We'll see."

God, Gabe was going to hate this. She had to get off the phone before her mother pressured her into something else. Like a proposal.

"I gotta go, Mom. Jezebel is puking."

Jezebel was currently curled up on one of the dining chair cushions taking a nap, oblivious to all the turmoil surrounding her.

"Not on my rugs!" Valentina cried.

"No, Jez, not there!" Michelle said, so convincingly that the cat raised her head and sent her an affronted look. "Bye, Mom."

Michelle ended the call as Gabe wandered back to the kitchen doorway with a dazed expression on his face.

"My sister wants me to visit her," he mumbled.

"And my mom has insisted I bring you to a quinceañera this weekend."

Gabe frowned. "I thought your family didn't do quinces. You didn't have one."

"It was a widely held belief among my mom and her siblings that quinceañeras and Sweet Sixteens were a waste of money, especially since all the girl cousins were such brats at that age. Except Ava, of course. Ava was perfect."

"Nikki had one. Our entire family was there, even people I'd never met before. Whose birthday is it?"

"My cousin Ronnie's stepdaughter."

He squinted, like he was trying to remember. "Have I met Ronnie?"

"A long time ago," Michelle replied. "Ronnie's half Jamaican, but her husband is Mexican, and this is his daughter's fifteenth birthday. Ronnie loves being the center of attention, and she's starting an event planning business, so this is her chance to shine. It'll drive her nuts if I show up with you, because everyone will be talking about us."

"Fuck." Gabe rubbed his hands over his face. "I'm supposed to be leaving tomorrow."

"What did you think would happen if you told your dad we were together?" Michelle asked gently. She didn't question why he hadn't told his father about the gym. They could dig into that later.

"I don't know what the hell I was thinking. Let's get through dinner with my parents tonight. Then I'll think about the quince and my return ticket."

"Fair enough. We'll consider it a dress rehearsal, and then decide if we want to go through with opening night."

"Deal."

Fifteen years ago

Celestial Destiny: Episode 5 Planning Session

Michelle:

    AHHHHHH

Gabe:

    Are we famous?

Michelle:

    Maybe Internet famous.

Gabe:

    At least fandom famous.

Michelle:

    I don't think that counts.

Gabe:

    Probably not, but for two teenagers in the Bronx, this is pretty big.

Michelle:

    I can't believe Celestial Destiny has so many views.

Gabe:

    I thought we'd be lucky if a dozen people read it.

Michelle:

    You didn't even want to post it online in the first place!

Gabe:

I stand corrected.

Michelle:

We have to step it up in the next chapter.

Gabe:

I'm leaving for Puerto Rico in a few days. I'm not sure what my abuela's wifi situation is like.

Michelle:

And I'll be at Disney World when you get back. ☹

Gabe:

How could you be sad about Disney World?

Michelle:

I'm not sad about Disney World, I'm sad about not seeing my bestie for such a long time.

Gabe:

We can try to start the chapter before I leave, and maybe I'll have time to work on it while I'm in PR.

Michelle:

Yeah right. Your mom is going to drag you around to see every single distant relative who still lives there. That's what mine does when we visit the island.

Gabe:

Probably, but I'll still try.

Michelle:

We should plan it out now. I'm leaving for a sleepover at Ava's soon.

Gabe:

We need to escalate the conflict. It's been a while since Zack's family was involved, so I think the king's guards should find them.

Michelle:

And Zack still has amnesia.

Gabe:

Really? He doesn't wonder why the royal guards are after them?

Michelle:

Riva warned him that someone was chasing them. This will prove her right. Besides, we have to milk this story line for all it's worth. For the fans.

Gabe:

All right. For the fans.

Chapter 15

He knows we're having sex," Gabe muttered darkly as Michelle locked the front door of her parents' house. Focusing on his embarrassment over the Condom Aisle Confrontation kept all the other uncomfortable feelings at bay, but it required constant effort.

"Gabe, you're thirty-one, not sixteen. Chill." Michelle took his arm and steered him toward the steps. The only benefit to getting caught by his dad was that he no longer had to sneak in and out through the back of the Amatos' house.

Gabe was wearing the same slacks he'd worn the day before and the nicest of the T-shirts he'd packed, but he kept touching his neck like he should be wearing a tie or something. Michelle had put on black jeans that made her ass look fantastic, and a sleeveless red wrap top that emphasized her hourglass figure.

"Should I go back and shave?" Gabe touched his cheek, felt the beard growth there. "I should shave."

"You don't need to shave. I like your face as it is." She sent him a saucy grin and kept hold of his arm, probably so he couldn't make a run for it.

They'd come up with a story to explain why Gabe was there,

seeded with snippets of truth. According to the fabrication they'd concocted, Gabe had seen one of Jasmine's Instagram pictures, which had led him to finding Michelle's account. He'd DMed her—Michelle had insisted on this part, as penance for all the years he *hadn't* replied to her messages—and they'd started talking. As they rekindled their old friendship, one thing led to another. Gabe had come to New York to stay with Michelle for a few days, to see if the spark they felt online existed in person, and he'd just gotten there the night before.

Why all the secrecy? Because they knew everyone would make a huge deal about it, and since this was so new, they wanted time to explore it alone before bringing their big nosy families into it, especially with Gabe's complicated history with his own parents.

Michelle had crafted most of the story, and Gabe had been too absorbed in ironing his T-shirt to give much input. But something about it reminded him of all the times they'd brainstormed plot points for their fanfic together. Back and forth, coming up with bigger and more outrageous galactic adventures for Zack and Riva. He'd missed that.

Even armed with what Michelle had claimed was a convincing lie, Gabe's stomach was still tied in knots as they made their way over to his parents' house and up the steps to the front door.

Part of him wanted to run all the way back to California and pretend none of this had ever happened.

Another part of him just wanted to get this over with.

And yet another part wanted to see his mom again. She'd reached out to him after the blowup with his dad at Nikki's wedding, but as he had with Michelle, Gabe had ignored her entreaties.

At the door, Michelle slid her hand down his arm to lace her fingers with his. She gave his hand a light squeeze.

"You should ring," she said softly, smiling up at him. "It'll be okay. I'm right here."

Gabe took strength from her reassuring smile. As much as he wished he'd never started this ruse, and as much as he wanted to blame her for dragging him back to the Bronx in the first place, he was glad to have her by his side so he didn't have to do this alone.

Clinging to her with one hand, he raised his other one and rang the doorbell.

The familiar *bing-bong* he remembered from his childhood rang out, and he held his breath. A moment later, the door swung open, and his mother's face appeared on the other side of the screen.

"¡Mi Gabriel!" she cried, then pushed open the screen door to let them in. "Ay dios mío. Get inside, get inside."

"Hi, Mami." Gabe stepped into the house and was hit with the familiar aromas of lemon polish and his mom's cooking. It slammed him back to his past just as his mother threw her arms around his neck and hugged him so tight he thought he would choke.

"Ay mi nene," she crooned. "Mi bebe."

Gabe hugged her back, astonished by how small she felt. She'd always been short, but now she seemed tiny. Was he really that much bigger? Or was she shrinking with age?

That thought upset him, so he pushed it away, holding his mother while she rocked him.

Finally, she released him, and lifted a hand to wipe her eyes. Fuck, he'd made his mom *cry*.

"Mami, no llores," he pleaded, feeling like the worst son in the world.

"Estoy bien," she said, brushing him off. Then she clapped her hands on his shoulders and squeezed his biceps, shooting Michelle a knowing look. "Mira, qué grande y fuerte."

Michelle smiled easily and leaned in to kiss the older woman on the cheek. "Hola, Norma. Nice to see you."

Norma looped her arm through Gabe's and walked him toward the kitchen. Despite the years, his mother's brown skin remained smooth and her spiraling curls were still dark, with only a little gray at her temples. "Oye, muchacho. I wanted to go over there right away, pero your father told me lo que estabas comprando, y él lo dijo qué I shouldn't interrupt you."

Gabe's face burned and he wanted to die. His father had told his mother about the condoms. Because of course he had. Why should anyone have privacy or secrets in a Latinx family?

"Anyway, I'm so happy you two are finally together." Norma grabbed Michelle's hand with her free one and beamed at her. "I always knew it would happen. Gracias, Michelle, por devolverme a mi hijo."

"I wanted him back too," Michelle admitted, then sent Gabe a quick glance that had his heart flipping over in his chest.

In the kitchen, Gabe was in for another shock. His father was at the stove—*cooking.*

Not just cooking. He was pan-searing a slab of fish like a pro.

"Ay, bueno. You're here." Esteban gestured toward the table with a tilt of his head. "Siéntate ahora. This will be ready en un momentito."

Gabe turned to his mom in wonder. "Papi's cooking?"

"He cooks all the time." She released him and gestured to the dining table, which was new, and not covered in a plastic tablecloth. "Sit, both of you. Michelle, you want wine?"

"I'd love some." Michelle sent her a winning smile.

Norma bustled over to the counter and leaned down to open—whoa, was that a wine cooler?

"¿Qué tipo de vino?" Norma called out, peering at the bottles stacked in the mini-fridge. "Tenemos rojo, y blanco, y verde . . ."

"Red is fine," Michelle replied, raising her voice to be heard over the exhaust fan blasting over the stove.

"Perfecto. I have a Pinot Noir chilling in here to go with the salmon." Norma straightened and came up with a dark bottle. Then she expertly uncorked it and poured the wine into the four glasses waiting on the counter above. She carried two over to the table.

Gabe could barely mutter a *gracias* because he was so dumbfounded by the situation.

And it only got stranger from there.

His mother carried over a large bowl of arugula salad, something Gabe would have bet money his parents didn't even know existed. And his father—wearing a navy-blue linen apron tied around his waist—plated the fish, adding slices of lemon and sprigs of dill for garnish. Gabe thought he spotted rice on the side, but to his utter amazement, it was *quinoa*.

Gabe looked around. Was this the right house?

Michelle, of course, got along with his parents beautifully. She'd seen them many times over the years, and they'd always thought the world of her. While part of Gabe resented them for it when he was younger, he couldn't blame them. She was amazing.

He just wished they could have spared some of that praise for him once in a while.

Michelle and his mother carried most of the conversation, keeping it light. They talked about Jasmine's latest film project, about Nikki's kids, about Michelle's parents. And every time his dad got close to asking something about why Gabe hadn't been in touch, his mother jumped in with a question or comment, then shot Esteban a dark glare when she thought no one else was looking.

Who *were* his parents? They knew about wine pairings and had a wine refrigerator installed under the counter. His father was searing salmon rather competently. His mother was interfering before his father could pick a fight—also competently. Where the hell had this side of her been during his youth?

Because as much anger as Gabe carried toward his father, he reserved some for his mom too. She'd stood by and let his father berate him and control him for years. She'd taken his father's side when it came to Gabe working in the stationery store, leaving Gabe to advocate for himself when he had baseball practice or school events his father had deemed a waste of time.

Gabe ate his food—which was fucking delicious—and tried to reconcile what he was seeing now with his memories from before.

When Gabe started high school, he'd gotten more health conscious. He'd begged his father to change his eating habits, but Esteban loved his meat and rice, and he'd refused to listen, regardless of what Gabe or his doctors said.

It looked like someone had finally gotten through to him.

Gabe found himself getting quieter as the meal went on, as memories pressed him from all sides. The plates were different, but the framed mosaic of La Virgen de Guadalupe was the same. One side of the fridge was still covered with magnets from Puerto Rico and Mexico, but it was a new fridge. Gabe was consumed with the urge to wander the house looking for things he remembered and noting the changes, but this wasn't his house anymore. And it was still ingrained in him not to leave the table during dinner. He couldn't just get up and go snooping around.

The sensation of being a stranger in his own home was overwhelming, even more so than when he'd been at Michelle's.

It hurt to admit it, but he'd missed this house. Missed this neighborhood. Missed his *parents*.

The nostalgia was killing him.

Suddenly, all he wanted to do was blurt out the news about the gym expansion. To fill them in on all the things he'd done and accomplished since the last time they'd seen him. To show them he was a *success*, damn it.

But one of his earliest regular PT clients had been a therapist, and Gabe had done a lot of talking while he'd worked on the guy. He understood enough about himself now to know this urge came from a need for validation from his father, and Gabe refused to indulge that need anymore.

As lukewarm as he'd once felt about bringing Agility to New York, now, more than ever, Gabe wanted it to be a hit. No matter what it took, he was going to make it happen.

When the meal was over, his mother brought out home-made flan for dessert.

"He always loved my flan," Norma gushed to Michelle as they dug in. "¿Te gusta, Gabriel?"

"Sí, me gusta. Tan delicioso." Despite the words of praise, Gabe's voice came out strained. He shot a look at Michelle, who was watching him carefully. How could he tell them the sweet, slippery dessert tasted like home?

When they were done, his father got up and began collecting the dishes.

Michelle jumped to her feet. "I'll help you, Esteban."

"Ay, nena." Esteban made a shooing motion with his free hand. "Siéntate. No es necesario."

"My mother would kill me if I didn't help clean up after enjoying such a wonderful meal." Michelle took Gabe's plate and gave him a meaningful look, then she was gone, leaving Gabe and his mother alone.

Norma reached across the table and took Gabe's hand in both of hers.

"It's good to see you," she said, patting his hand.

"You too," Gabe said in a low voice. Even with all the years and bullshit between them, it was true. He'd missed her.

Then she shot a look over her shoulder, to where Michelle and Esteban chatted easily over the running water in the sink.

"It's been a long time," his mother whispered, turning back to Gabe. "I know you were angry. But please don't disappear again. He couldn't take it if you did."

Defensive anger rose up in Gabe. *He?* That was rich. She expected him to believe Esteban was upset at his disappearance? His father was the one who'd told him to go and never come back. All the calls and texts after that had come from his mother's cell phone, until, in a moment of resentment and despair, Gabe had finally blocked the number.

In response, Gabe just gave a noncommittal nod. He wouldn't make any promises on that front.

Michelle came back, wiping her hands on a paper towel. "Ready?"

Gabe got up and the four of them walked to the front door.

"Visit again, okay?" his dad said, slapping him on the back. "Before you go back to California."

Gabe hesitated. He was supposed to leave the next day. But between the quinceañera this weekend, his sister's demand that he visit her, and whatever was happening here with his parents—not to mention Michelle—he clearly needed to extend his stay.

"Okay," he said. And then he was surprised when his dad smiled.

"Bueno. Hasta luego, mijo."

Yes, Gabe would see them later. And he had a feeling they wouldn't hold back next time.

They all hugged and kissed goodbye, and Gabe put his arm around Michelle as they walked the short distance back to her family home.

"You all right?" she asked in a quiet voice.

"I don't know," he replied honestly. "But . . . I'm glad you were with me."

She slipped her arm around his waist and gave him a squeeze. Then released him to climb the steps and unlock the door.

Once they were back inside, Gabe's shoulders sagged. "God, I'm exhausted."

"That's a shame." Michelle toed off her sandals. "You went through a lot for those condoms. But if you need to rest, that's fi—" She ended with a squeal as Gabe spun her into his arms for a kiss. When they came up for air, she looked dazed.

"You seem to have caught your second wind," she murmured.

"I always have energy for you," he said, because what he really wanted to say was *I'm under a lot of emotional stress and I need you*. When he kissed her again, she wrapped her arms around his neck, rising up on tiptoe. Gabe grabbed her butt and lifted her further. When she locked her legs around his waist, he carried her to the stairs and up to his room. And then, for just a little while, he let himself get lost in her. Completely.

Chapter 16

Gabe: Hey, I tried calling you.

Fabian: Sorry. Shit's crazy right now. I'm at the hospital.

Gabe: What happened? Is it Iris?

Fabian: My mom broke her leg.

Gabe: Oh shit. I'm sorry to hear that.

Fabian: Yeah. It's not a bad break, but with the twins on the way and Dad's surgery, it's not ideal. Anyway, what's up? How's it going over there?

Gabe: I have to extend my time in New York.

Fabian: Because of the gym? Or because of her?

Gabe: What?

Gabe: No.

Gabe: I mean, kind of. I saw my dad.

Fabian: Oh damn. How?

Gabe: I'll explain later. But I have to stay a few extra days. I'm going to miss the Monday meeting.

Fabian: Honestly dude, there's so much going on right now, I can't even think about next week. Just do what you went there to do. See you when you get back.

Gabe: Take care of your fam.

Fabian: I'm trying!

Chapter 17

Michelle pulled into the parking lot and searched for an empty spot. The quinceañera was being held at an event space in the Hudson Valley, which was lush and green in late summer. It was hot, but less humid than it had been in the city. Above them, the skies stretched out bright blue, with only a few wisps of clouds. The drive up had been pretty, but once the glow of morning sex had faded, Gabe had started freaking out again.

"We're late," he said for at least the tenth time.

Michelle shrugged and navigated to the overflow lot behind the venue. "Well, someone bought two whole boxes of condoms . . ."

"Please, Mich, for the love of all that's holy, don't talk about the condoms while we're around your family."

"You're kidding yourself if you think *your* mom hasn't already told *my* mom about it."

He groaned and leaned back in the seat.

Michelle gave him an appreciative once-over, then found an empty spot right near the side entrance.

The two of them looked like they'd just pulled off a heist and needed to ditch their disguises. Michelle was clad in black full-body shapewear and gold sandals. Gabe was wearing boxers and a black sleeveless undershirt, plus his socks and chanclas.

In reality, they'd left late enough that they wouldn't be able to check in at their hotel first. Rather than make the whole drive sitting in their fancy attire—after running around yesterday to find a pair of pants and a shirt that would fit Gabe's muscles—they left their freshly steamed clothes hanging from hooks in the back seat and made the drive in their underthings.

"Is anyone around?" Michelle asked, looking out the windows.

"We're late. Everyone is probably inside already."

She rolled her eyes at him. "This is my family we're talking about. I'd be surprised if half of them are here. And you know Ronnie is not going to start this thing on time."

They pushed their seats back and twisted around to retrieve their clothes, then set about shimmying into them inside the car.

Michelle's dress was tangerine orange, with a deep vee and a flared skirt. She was able to slip it on, but when she turned to Gabe to ask him to zip her up, she stifled a laugh. He'd put his shirt on and buttoned it, but he was having trouble getting his long legs into the pants while sitting in the Fiat.

"Gabe, just get out," she said. "No one is here."

He sent her an aggrieved look, but he opened the car door and climbed out, holding the pants over one arm.

Michelle got out, too, rounding the car so he could do the zipper on her dress.

The venue's back door opened and Ava walked out. She stopped short, eyes going wide when she saw them.

Gabe let out a strangled squawk and dove back into the car. Michelle waved.

"Hi, Ava. Can you zip my dress for me? Since Gabe is struggling to put his pants on."

"Michelle!" Gabe yelled from inside the car, sounding absolutely scandalized.

Ava shook her head, but walked over to them. "Why is Gabriel always half naked when I show up?"

Michelle turned so Ava could pull up the zipper. "Just your good luck, I guess."

"Ha," Ava muttered. "No, really. Why doesn't he have pants on?"

Gabe stuck his head out of the car. "We were running late and Michelle suggested we drive up in our underwear so we didn't wrinkle our clothes."

"Brilliant idea, right?" Michelle grinned. "Hurry up, Gabe."

Gabe stalked over to them, grumbling and tucking his shirt into the pants, which were now on his legs.

Which was a shame, since the man had stunning thighs.

"Do you need help with your tie?" Michelle asked. They'd co-opted one of her father's ties for the occasion.

"Sure." Gabe positioned the tie under his shirt collar and faced her, but Michelle stepped back.

"Ava, would you?" Michelle gestured at Gabe's neck. When he gave her a look, she said, "What? You think I know how to tie a tie?"

Ava sighed, but she stepped forward and made quick and efficient work of Gabe's tie.

He watched her hands, then looked up with a confused expression. "Was that a Windsor knot?"

"Yes." Ava turned back to Michelle. "Go inside. I'll be there in a minute. Titi Lisa asked me to get something from her car."

Michelle caught her arm. "Is everyone talking about us already?"

"Do you even have to ask?"

Michelle's shoulders slumped as Ava left them. "That means yes."

Gabe came up beside her and they watched Ava go. "It's not too late, you know."

"For what?"

"To run away."

"That's your MO. Not mine." Besides, she'd never live it down. "Remember our story?"

"*Celestial Destiny*? Of course."

She shot him an amused smirk. "No. Our fake dating story."

"Oh. Yeah."

She took his arm and they entered the venue together.

THE BALLROOM WAS a madhouse. The Puerto Rican Rodriguez cousins were mixed in with Ronnie's Jamaican relatives and her husband's equally large Mexican extended family, and likely his ex-wife's family too. Michelle couldn't be totally sure who was related to whom. A cacophony of Spanish and English and Spanglish and Jamaican patois threatened to overpower the music supplied by the DJ, who was one of Michelle's distant cousins.

Eyebrows raised when they entered the room, and Michelle

shoved her anxiety down into a little ball. This was the first time she'd ever brought someone to visit her family, and she was sure they were going to be completely extra about it.

Michelle and Gabe greeted everyone with a kiss on the cheek, answering each obligatory "¿Cómo estás?" with English— Michelle—and Spanish—Gabe. They made their way through a crowd of tíos, tías, and cousins, many of whom remembered Gabe from Michelle's childhood birthday parties, before finally reaching Michelle's parents, Dominic and Valentina. They had returned from Florida that morning and retrieved their car from Dominic's brother who lived in Queens.

"There you are!" Michelle's mom reached for her, giving her a hug and a kiss that would undoubtedly leave pink lipstick on her face. Sure enough, Valentina swiped a thumb over Michelle's cheek as she eased back. "You look great, honey. Love this orange color on you."

"Thanks, Mom." But Valentina, barely Michelle's height with wavy black hair and a deep tan from the Florida sun, was already turning to Gabe and giving him a look up and down. "Well! You sure grew up nicely, Gabriel."

Michelle pinched the bridge of her nose. "Oh my god, Mom. Don't flirt with him."

Her dad, a quiet Italian man with an olive-toned complexion and thinning brown hair, stepped forward to give Michelle a hug. "Hi, honey," he said. "Now what's going on here? I didn't understand your mother's explanation."

Michelle repeated the lie about reconnecting on Instagram. Her dad grumbled, "I still don't see why you had to bring him to *my* house," but otherwise, he was civil.

Until Michelle overheard him telling Gabe, "Remember what I said."

Abuelo came over to greet them. Michelle gave him a big kiss on his lined brown cheek and a tight hug. Then, while her parents were distracted, she pulled Gabe aside. "What did my dad mean?"

Gabe ducked his head and scratched the back of his neck. "Oh, when I was around . . . twelve, I guess, your dad made some light threats about what would happen if I ever touched you."

Michelle narrowed her eyes. "Like what?"

"Vague stuff, like . . ." Gabe made a menacing face and drew his finger across his throat.

"Jeez, Dad. Way to be a stereotype." She shook her head. "Is that why you never made a move until after we graduated high school?"

"What? No. I wasn't even thinking about any of that yet. And later . . . I didn't think you were open to being more."

She sighed. They'd both been so foolish then, Gabe too scared to make a move and Michelle too scared to hope.

Maybe the timing was better now. Maybe she didn't have to be afraid of wanting more.

Valentina butted in. "You have to say hi to Abuela. She's over there by the cake table."

Michelle gave Gabe's bicep a squeeze, as if to draw strength from him. "Gird your loins, buddy. Into the dragon's den we go."

They made their way to where Esperanza Rodriguez, clad in a yellow floral dress with lots of ruffles, held court next to a four-tiered pink-and-gold cake topped with a glittery number fifteen. Multiple family members stopped them as they went, and they had to pause to greet each one. By the time they reached her grandmother, Michelle was clinging to Gabe's arm for dear life.

"You all right there?" he asked out of the corner of his mouth.

"This is the worst part. Let's get it over with." Michelle loved her grandmother dearly, but the woman was a force to be reckoned with, and you never knew what was going to come out of her mouth.

Esperanza whooped with delight when they approached her, and Michelle released Gabe to give her grandma a hug.

"Hi, Abuela."

"Ah, Michie!" Esperanza enfolded Michelle in her vanilla-scented embrace before saying in a loud whisper, "¡Por fin tienes un novio!"

Michelle winced, but when she pulled away, she fixed an easy smile on her face. "Yup. Finally got myself a boyfriend."

Esperanza leaned in conspiratorially and gave Michelle's dress strap a tug. "I told you these tetas were too good to waste."

Michelle just smirked. "I never said they were going to waste."

Esperanza cackled in response, then moved on to Gabe. She hugged him and made a lot of comments about how well he'd grown up, how big and strong he was, and how much he'd loved her arroz con pollo when he was a little boy.

Michelle let out a breath. Somehow, this whole thing was easier than she'd expected. And it made her sad. Because this was just for show, to keep Gabe's gym plans secret from his dad. But it didn't feel like acting. Everything about it felt natural.

Don't get it twisted, girl, she scolded herself. *This isn't real.*

But . . . wasn't it?

For her, this was the realest relationship she'd ever had. She was opening up during sex, letting down her guard and accepting the vulnerability that went with it. She was talking about how she felt instead of relying on humor as a shield for her emotions.

And she knew this wasn't just a fuck-and-run for Gabe either.

I need you, Mich.

Fuck, they had no business involving their families when *they* didn't even have a handle on it.

"Has the birthday girl arrived yet?" Michelle asked her abuela.

Esperanza flicked her wrist, waving that away as if it were a ridiculous notion. "Ay no. Maybe in an hour. They're having a hair emergency."

The DJ switched to a Luis Fonsi song and Michelle perked up. "I love this song."

Gabe gave her his hand. "Bueno, vamos a bailar."

He led her to the dance floor, which was already full of people, many of whom Michelle was related to. But when Gabe put one strong, solid hand on her waist and pulled her close, everything else fell away. It was just the two of them and the music.

They eased into a sensual Dominican bachata with small sliding steps and swaying hips, adding double and triple steps to the footwork as the beat picked up. The height difference should've made it difficult, but Gabe was so light on his feet, so in control of his body, it was easy to surrender and let him lead her.

As the rhythm pulsed, Michelle flipped her hair and Gabe spun her out and back in. Holding her close against his hip, his thigh pressed between hers, their hips rocked together in time with the music, moving in perfect harmony. They threw in body rolls and hip rolls, having fun with it, but their eyes never left each other's.

In short, they danced like they were *not* surrounded by her immediate family.

When the song ended and shifted into something by Taylor Swift, Michelle and Gabe came to a stop. She closed her eyes and pressed her forehead to his chest.

"I'm afraid to look," she muttered, breathing hard and sweating a little.

Gabe rubbed her back comfortingly. "Why, because everyone is staring at us?"

"If they weren't talking about us already, they are now."

"Am I supposed to apologize?"

"You should." She gave him a saucy grin. "Because you've ruined me for all other dance partners."

A familiar voice called her name. "Michelle?"

Michelle squeezed her eyes shut. "Oh shit."

Caught in the act. Michelle stepped away from Gabe's side and squared her shoulders, preparing to face the music as her cousin Jasmine wiggled her way through the crowd, with Ava in hot pursuit.

Jasmine, a TV and movie actress, was stunningly beautiful, with thick dark hair and golden brown skin. At the moment, her famous face was fixed into a disapproving glower.

"You're welcome for letting you finish the dance," Jasmine told Michelle, barely sparing Gabe a look. "Hi, Gabe. Welcome back. Been a while."

Michelle sucked in a breath. "Look, Jas—"

"Don't worry." Jasmine put her hands up, her tone all innocence. "We're not gonna make a scene here, but we *are* going to discuss this later. Trust."

Ava blinked. "We?"

Jasmine narrowed her eyes at their taller cousin, and then her mouth dropped open. "What the hell, Ava? You knew about this?"

Ava's shoulders hunched with guilt and Jasmine rounded back on Michelle. "When I told you not to tell Ava about me and Ashton, you flat out refused."

Affronted, Ava put a hand on her hip and turned to Jasmine. "You told Michelle not to tell me about you and Ashton?"

"I was in denial about my feelings," Jasmine said with a shrug. Then she shook her head at Michelle. "I'm not mad, I'm just disappointed. But I'm also mad."

Ashton Suarez, Jasmine's boyfriend and an award-winning telenovela star, appeared over her shoulder. "Hola, primas," he said, then extended a hand to Gabe. "¿Cómo estás? I'm Ashton Suarez."

Gabe shook his hand. "Gabriel Aguilar."

"Jasmine said you own a gym?"

"I do. Agility Gym in Los Angeles."

Ashton nodded. "I've heard of it. If you ever open a location in New York, let me know. Vamos, Jasmine. I think your abuela is looking for us."

As Ashton led Jasmine away, Michelle nudged Gabe and gave him a meaningful look. "Potential testimonial?" she whispered.

He had a speculative look on his face. "Maybe . . ."

They danced more together, and took turns dancing with Michelle's niece and nephew, then found their seats once the festivities got underway. Michelle sat at a round table with Gabe and her parents, plus her older sister, Monica, Monica's husband, and their three kids. Her brother, Junior, was out of town, so his family wasn't there.

Monica was the only one who'd taken Gabe's presence in stride.

"I always figured this would happen someday," she'd said, but Michelle didn't get to ask her why.

Ronnie's stepdaughter looked beautiful in a hot-pink princess dress, but still so young, as she went through some choreographed dance routines with her friends. The kids were great, and you could hardly tell three of them had been crying not half an hour earlier—gossip courtesy of Michelle's chismosa mother.

Michelle looked at Gabe seated next to her, remembering when they were fifteen. Back then, she'd felt like she knew it all, like she was practically a grown-up. But that was also the year they'd started writing *Celestial Destiny*, two kids still playing out their favorite stories. They'd been so young. And now here they were, playing out another story.

The food was good, the music was great, and Michelle found herself having a genuinely good time. But she'd underestimated the number of people who claimed to be *so excited* that she *finally had a boyfriend*. It had never bothered her before that her family was obsessed with marriage and kids, or that they acted like she was weird because she'd never once brought a significant other to a family event. In fact, that was why she never told anyone, not even Ava or Jasmine, when she was fooling around with someone. If you wanted to keep a secret in this family, you kept it to yourself.

As she'd planned to do with Gabe. Except now every-damn-body in her family knew about him. Which meant that after he left, every-damn-body would ask about him for the rest of her life. It had been bad enough when they'd been younger and her relatives inferred he was actually her boyfriend. She'd known the truth. And after he left and people still asked about him, her mother had intervened, warning all the tías not to mention his name.

This was going to be a hundred times worse.

By the end of the night, Michelle's ability to maintain her good humor was being severely tested. After she said goodbye to everyone she was related to, and gave the birthday girl a hug, Gabe pulled her aside.

"Hey, are you okay?" His brows knit with concern. "You seem down."

She let out a long sigh. "I feel like we just fucked this up more by involving all of them. It feels too real, Gabe."

"It is real," he murmured, pulling her into his arms. "Just for this weekend. Let it be real."

How was she supposed to argue with that? Especially when he leaned down to kiss her deeply.

In the background, no less than three people whistled and someone else let out a grito. It was like the Latinx version of an audience reaction when the actors kissed on a sitcom.

Michelle broke away and grabbed Gabe's hand. "Let's get out of here. I'm tired of having an audience, and I have big plans for you tonight."

Chapter 18

Gabe paused in the doorway of the hotel room. "There's only one bed."

"I know." Michelle swept past him and sat in a high-backed armchair to swap her heels for indoor chanclas. "I wasn't expecting to share the room with anyone, and with so many of my relatives hanging around in the lobby, it would have looked suspicious if I'd asked to change it."

Gabe watched her carefully as she bustled around, noting her body language and nonverbal cues. She was doing her *la la la, I don't have a care in the world* act, which meant there was something she wasn't saying. "Are you okay with that?"

"It's fine." Michelle pulled her toiletry bag out of her suitcase.

"I can call downstairs and ask them to book me a separate room if you want privacy."

"No need." With a toss of her hair, she carried the toiletry bag to the bathroom at the other end of the room and shut herself inside. The lock clicked behind her.

Huh. That wasn't convincing.

Gabe closed the hotel room door behind him, then turned to study the bed. It was a king-size mattress with an enormous wooden headboard. Definitely big enough for both of them, and it faced a Victorian-style wood-mantled fireplace. It couldn't be more romantic if he'd planned it. But as much as he wanted to fall asleep cuddled against her and wake together all warm and cozy before starting the day, Michelle had been clear: she did not sleep in the same bed with sexual partners. He didn't want her to do something she didn't want simply because of circumstance, because of a lie he'd told his father. If that was her way of keeping distance between them, he had to respect it. After all, he was leaving in a few days, although he had yet to buy a new return ticket to Los Angeles.

He thought back to what he'd told her at the venue.

It is real. Just for this weekend.

If it was real, did that mean sharing a bed? It seemed strange that this was the line they hadn't crossed, but nothing was normal about their situation.

Shit, maybe she was letting him stay because she was worried about hurting his feelings or something like that. The thought made his stomach sink, and he crossed the room, raising his voice so she'd hear him through the bathroom door. "I'm just saying, you've already gone above and beyond helping me keep the gym a secret from my dad, so if you want me to—"

"I said it's fine, Gabe! Relax!"

She sounded annoyed, so he let it go and tried to take her advice.

Relax. Okay, he could do that.

He removed the ill-fitting dress shirt—the department store tailors had done the best they could in limited time, but he missed his own tailor in LA—and the pants that fit better than he'd expected. He hung them up and pulled on a pair of basketball shorts, just in case Michelle changed her mind and kicked him out.

Shopping for his quinceañera attire with Michelle had reminded him of the old days. Sure, he'd tried to coax her into a dressing room with him more than once, which wasn't something he'd done when they'd been teens wandering around Fordham Road in the Bronx or St. Mark's Place in Manhattan looking for clothes. But they'd joked around and had a good time.

"Remember the makeover episode of *Celestial Destiny*?" she'd asked while he was trying on shirts at Macy's.

"That chapter was *your* idea," he'd reminded her from inside the fitting room stall. "During the interminable amnesia story line."

"Hey, our readers loved the amnesia story line."

"It lasted for *seven episodes*. And then you made me end it with a makeover."

"I'd just gone back-to-school shopping with Jasmine and I thought it would be fun for Zack and Riva."

"Fun in theory, but you forced me to watch hours of makeover shows on TV before I wrote it."

"If I recall correctly, you had very strong opinions about pleated pants by the end of it," she'd teased, and then snuck him a kiss when he'd stepped out to model yet another boxy button-down shirt.

Smiling at the memory, Gabe moved their suitcases closer to the wall, where they wouldn't risk tripping over them if they got up during the night. There was something nice about having such an extensive shared history with someone he was . . . not dating, exactly, but . . .

Involved with. There. That sounded better than *someone he was fucking*, and even though they were definitely fucking, he'd be an idiot to think that was all that was going on here.

Michelle had been his first love, and while he'd later tried to dismiss those feelings as "just a crush," they felt strikingly similar to—while also a pale shadow of—what he was experiencing now.

All he could do was stay in the moment with her for however long that moment lasted. And when it ended . . . well, he'd do what he'd always done. Throw himself back into his work.

While he waited for Michelle to come out, he examined the fireplace and found a remote control to turn it on. The night was cooler here in upstate New York than down in the city. Not cold enough for a fire, but he could leave it on low for atmosphere. The bathroom door opened and Gabe turned to ask Michelle if she wanted to order anything from room service, but the thought flew right out of his head when he saw her.

He didn't know what to call what she was wearing. Lingerie, probably, but that seemed like too tame a word, evoking images of silk and lace.

Michelle was instead clad in some sort of . . . contraption. There was lace, yes, little black scraps of it, but the rest was made up of crisscrossing straps and ties that accentuated her curves and somehow cupped and lifted her breasts in a way that was truly magnificent.

"Cat got your tongue?" The words were teasing, but her smile was wicked, like she knew exactly what this outfit was doing to him.

"Did you buy this yesterday?" he asked, because *let me worship you* seemed like too much. During their shopping expedition, she'd ducked away while he was trying on pants, claiming she needed to go to the bathroom. She'd been gone a long time and it would've been rude to comment on it, so he hadn't.

"I did." Michelle strolled into the room slowly, wearing black high heels that she absolutely hadn't been wearing at the party. "Do you believe me now when I say I don't want you to get your own room?"

"I'm having trouble believing any of this." Gabe closed the distance between them and reached for her hips, but at the last second he paused, not touching her. Instead, he hovered over her lush curves, his fingers nearly trembling with anticipation.

"You can touch me," she whispered. "I want you to."

Slowly, with reverence for the gift he was being given, Gabe rested his hands on her waist and looked his fill. The lacy bits were sheer, and he could see the outline of her dusky nipples and the shadow of neatly trimmed hair at the apex of her thighs. He skimmed his hands over her hips, letting his thumbs tug lightly on the satiny elastic straps, before he spun her around to get a view of her from behind.

Holy fuck.

The lacy panties were a thong, with a tiny triangle of black lace right at the top and straps outlining her fantastic ass.

With a strangled laugh, he slid his hands around her waist and dropped his head onto her shoulder, speaking into her neck.

"What's all this for, Mich? I love it, but don't think you need to do all this for me."

He almost added, *I love you in anything or nothing at all*, but held his tongue.

She lifted a hand and stroked his cheek. "Like I said earlier, I have big plans for you tonight . . . if you're up for it, that is."

"Oh, I am *up* for anything." He shifted his hips, letting her feel his erection against her ass.

She gave a little laugh, but he detected nerves. "I was hoping we could play out a fantasy of mine."

"Tell me your fantasy, Mich," he murmured, pressing kisses to her neck. Whatever it was, he'd do it. He'd do anything for her.

"Well, I don't usually orgasm with other people."

Confused, Gabe lifted his head and turned her to face him. "What do you mean? I've seen you do it."

"Yeah, well . . . it's different with you." She worried the corner of her lip, and her gaze bounced around the room, not meeting his. "Usually I don't bother to try. It takes too long—"

"No, it doesn't." He cupped her face and waited until she looked at him, instead of at the watercolor landscape over his shoulder, before he went on.

"However long it takes, your pleasure is worth it. Anyone who's made you feel like it wasn't . . ." He worked to get the anger out of his voice, because he wasn't angry at *her*. "I'm just sorry anyone ever made you feel that way."

Her lashes fluttered, like she couldn't hold his gaze any longer. "I'm not sure why, but I prefer to do it alone. Probably to avoid emotional intimacy or whatever."

"Why now?" he asked, when he really wanted to say, *Why me?*

She shrugged. "I didn't feel comfortable doing all this in my parents' house, and we should make the most of this room. Plus, you're, like, really good at it, and I . . . trust you."

Her trust overwhelmed him. It was more than he deserved. He placed his hands on her shoulders and kissed her forehead. "Thank you."

She shifted restlessly. "Anyway, my fantasy is to come. A lot. By someone else's hand. Or . . . parts."

"Challenge accepted. And, Mich?"

"Yeah?"

Her tone was apprehensive, like she expected him to turn her down, so he slipped his arms around her and tried to let all the desire and love he felt for her show in his eyes, in his voice. "If I come—and I might, because seeing you in ecstasy brings me pleasure too—it doesn't mean the night is over. We'll go for as long as you want. Okay?"

She gave him a small smile that wasn't anything like her usual smirks or flirtatious grins. This one was real and a little nervous. "Thanks."

WHEN MICHELLE HAD conceived of this plan in the Macy's menswear department, she hadn't doubted Gabe would be on board. Sex was the easy part with him—it was everything else that was complicated.

What she'd doubted was her own courage to go through with her request.

She'd bought the sexy bralette combo and packed the heels and some other goodies, but it wasn't until they were leaving the party that she found her resolve.

After he'd said, *Let it be real.*

Admitting she hadn't orgasmed with anyone else during sex was as real as it got. She hadn't planned to say that, but Gabe was so easy to open up to, it had slipped out.

And now he was looking at her like he was a wolf about to devour her.

"Are there any boundaries?" he asked.

She shook her head. "Not with you."

Some emotion she couldn't name passed across his face, but he only tightened his arms around her and pulled her closer. He was still in his undershirt and a pair of shorts, and she was dressed like some kind of sex superhero.

"There are some presents for you in the bathroom," she said, nodding her head toward the door. "Take a look."

He released her with great reluctance, and while he was retrieving the bag she'd left him—packed with condoms, lube, and a travel-size wand vibrator—she pulled the blankets back and climbed onto the middle of the bed. He returned wearing only a wolfish grin and black boxer briefs. She expected him to join her, but instead, he hooked his arms under her thighs and dragged her to the edge of the mattress. He spread her legs wide, then he dropped to his knees between them. And even though his intent was clearly telegraphed by the ravenous way he stared at her, she still jumped when his tongue swiped over the sheer lace covering her pussy.

He paused and gazed up at her from between her legs. "Problem?"

Yes, she did have a problem. The sexiest man in the world

was about to eat her into next Tuesday, and she was on the verge of a massive anxiety-induced laughing fit. "Nope."

His eyes narrowed. "You're nervous."

She bit her lip. "Um, maybe."

Sliding his arms under her legs, he rested his head on her inner thigh and folded his hands over her belly, as if he were settling in for a fascinating conversation. "Why?"

"I don't know." She let out a slightly hysterical giggle and slapped her hands over her rapidly heating face to cover the blush. "Not like we haven't done this before."

"Is it because you gave up control? Asked for what you wanted?" His voice was low and silken, compelling her to lower her hands and look at him. She did, and his dark gaze captured hers. "*Let me in.*"

Michelle couldn't tell if the last was a question or a demand. It didn't matter. Yes, she was nervous about letting him in— into her life, into her heart, into moments that would become memories.

But yes, she would do it anyway.

In answer, she spread her legs wider for him.

Something intense flashed in his eyes before he shut them and pressed a soft kiss to her inner thigh.

"Don't worry, Mich," he murmured. "I'll make your fantasy come true."

And yes, *oh hell fucking yes* he did. Gabe did her in every position he could think of, going above and beyond even her wildest fantasies. Sitting on the side of the bed with her straddling his lap, lifting her up and down while he worked his hips like a piston beneath her. Bending her over the side of the mattress and plowing her from behind. In between fucking, he went down on her, licking her until she came. When he was inside her, he used the vibrator or his hand.

And then there was the dirty talk. Gabe was good with his tongue in more ways than one, and Michelle was living for it.

They were on the bed, spooning with one of her legs thrown back over his hips so he could touch the vibrator to her clit. His other hand cupped her breast, rolling her nipple and giving it light pinches.

"I wish I could lick you while my dick was inside you," he murmured into her ear. "But I guess this'll have to do." He pressed the vibrator to her and she exploded.

He fucked her slowly through it. She swallowed, her lashes fluttering. Then she opened her eyes and met his gaze.

"Harder," she said.

He stilled, reading the desire in her face. "You like it a little rough, don't you?"

At her nod, he bent her in half and gave it to her how she wanted it, tossing the wand aside and using his hand.

"¿Así?" he asked her repeatedly. "Like this?"

Every time, she said *yes*.

As much as she tried to keep track, Michelle lost count of how many times she came.

"I'm close, babe." His breath was harsh and hot against her ear. "You got one more in you?"

"I don't know," she said brokenly. Her body was awash in sensation, no longer tethered to this plane. There was only Gabe and all the amazing things he made her feel.

"Whatever you want, I'll give it to you. But you gotta tell me what you want."

"I want . . . you." She finished in a whisper, the admission wrenched from her by the thrust of his body in hers and the hold he had on her heart.

His arms tightened around her and he groaned into her neck. "God, Mich. You annihilate me."

"Is that a good thing?" she whimpered as his fingers picked up the pace between her legs, just how she liked it.

"The fucking best."

His strokes deepened, becoming erratic. His loss of control, which he'd kept a tight rein on the entire night, was what undid her for the last time. The orgasm hit like a lightning bolt; sizzling lines of electric pleasure zinged through her nerves and wrung ragged sobs from her throat.

It carried through to Gabe, who thrust his hips hard against her ass and came with a long, agonized groan.

When it was done, they lay on the bed side by side, sweaty and wrecked, but holding hands.

"Do you remember the only-one-sleeping-bag scene of *Celestial Destiny*?" she asked hoarsely.

His breathing was heavy and fast. "That was my favorite scene in the whole fic."

"Whose idea was it?"

"Mine. Absolutely mine."

She was silent for a moment. "I should've known," she said. "How you felt about me. I'm sorry I didn't see it then."

He shifted closer and nuzzled his face into her shoulder. "It was better that you didn't. I was pretty stupid back then.

I would have ruined it somehow. And then we wouldn't be here now."

"But we could've had . . ." She trailed off and squeezed his hand tight. "This. We could've had this."

"I always wondered," he admitted. "But I had to leave, Mich. I had to get away from him so I could become my own person."

His father.

"I understand. I'm sorry I didn't see that back then either."

"We were young," he said easily. "And it means a lot that you see it now. But, Mich, I missed you. Every day."

She turned to him, let him enfold her in his strong embrace. With her eyes closed and her face pressed to his chest, she whispered the thing that scared her. "Why does this feel so right?"

He rubbed her back with those big, hot hands of his. When he held her like this, she felt safer than she ever had. Like nothing could go wrong.

"We were always good together," he mused. "As friends. I guess this is an evolution of that."

Friendship 2.0, she thought, remembering her list. "I don't think we can cling to that 'just friends' nonsense anymore."

He let out a surprised chuckle. "No. I think we're well past that."

Well past that and on their way to where?

She was afraid she knew the answer, at least for herself.

Let it be real.

Fourteen years ago

Celestial Destiny: Episode 9 Planning Session

Gabe:

I think we've run this amnesia story line as long as we can.

Michelle:

Yeah, we've stretched it out for more episodes than even I expected.

It's time to give Zack his memories back.

Gabe:

We need something big to prompt Riva to heal him, though.

Michelle:

Like what?

Gabe:

They're exhausted from a series of constant attacks and narrow

escapes. And we've been managing the will they/won't they thing for

multiple episodes. I think it's time to give the readers what they want.

Michelle:

Are you saying what I think you're saying?

Gabe:

That Zack and Riva should kiss?

Michelle:

Yeah.

Gabe:

Uh, I guess that is what I'm saying.

Michelle:

Okay, but he has to be the one to do it. It'll make Riva feel guilty about lying to him and then she'll finally heal his amnesia.

Gabe:

That works.

Michelle:

Zack is gonna be PISSED.

Gabe:

Oh yeah. He is.

Chapter 19

The next morning, Michelle gave Gabe the keys to her Fiat so he could visit his sister in Yonkers, then she met up with her parents in the lobby to ride back to the Bronx in their van. It was less than ideal, since her mother spent most of the drive talking about how *thrilled* she was Michelle and Gabe had finally gotten together.

"I always knew," Valentina kept saying in a smug voice.

"Well, I didn't," Michelle finally grumbled from the middle-row bucket seat, and her father took that opportunity to turn the music up.

Michelle tried to numb out to Bon Jovi's greatest hits, but she couldn't stop replaying the things she and Gabe had said to each other the night before.

I missed you. Every day.

Why does this feel so right?

Let it be real.

When they drove up to the house, Michelle spotted a blue Prius parked out front, and Ava's white Toyota across the street. She groaned.

"Why did we ever give Ava a set of keys?"

"For emergencies," her mother replied. After all this time, Valentina thought nothing of coming home and finding the Primas of Power in her house.

Michelle's father had a different reaction. "I'll be in the basement. You can all go yell at each other upstairs."

After an extended period of time with the Rodriguezes, Dominic Amato usually needed some alone time. And he often complained Michelle and her cousins were "too loud" when they got together. But then, he said the same thing about his wife and her siblings.

"As if your Italian family is any quieter," Michelle retorted. Her dad sighed and pulled into the driveway.

Inside the house, Michelle found her cousins sipping coffee at the dining table. "Upstairs," she said. As they trooped past her parents, Ava and Jasmine leaned in to give their tía and tío kisses on the cheek, then followed Michelle upstairs.

"Oh hey, coffee," Dominic said from behind them.

"That's for you, Tío," Ava called.

"Grazie, Ava!"

Michelle ushered them into the craft room, which she'd cleaned up before driving upstate the day before. It had occurred to her at the last minute that her parents would expect her to be sleeping in the same room as Gabe. She wasn't thrilled about it—sleeping in separate beds had been the last remaining wall she'd kept up against him—but she hadn't seen a way around it.

The hotel room had been different. She wouldn't be returning there, and it had been like a getaway, time out of time. Sharing her brother's old room with Gabe was going to be weird.

As soon as the primas were all seated in the craft room with the door closed—Michelle and Jasmine on the bed, Ava in Valentina's ergonomic crafting chair—Jasmine started in.

"I can't believe you kept this from me, especially when Ava already knew."

"Ava wasn't supposed to know either," Michelle grumbled. "Nobody was."

"That's not the point. *I'm* not allowed to have any secrets about my relationships."

"No, you're just terrible at keeping secrets, so it's easier to pull them out of you all at once instead of waiting for you to spill them drop by drop." Michelle didn't comment on Jasmine's breakup the previous year, which had been splashed all over the celebrity gossip rags. That would've been a low blow, and it wasn't Jasmine's fault.

Ava, ever the peacemaker, intervened. "Michelle, we're just worried."

"And we want to know what's going on." Jasmine leaned forward, cupping her mug with both hands. "You've *never* brought someone to meet the family. You don't even talk about dating. And then you show up with *Gabe*, of all people?"

"You told me the other day he was here to work on a project," Ava prompted.

"If he's here to work on a project, why parade him around the party like that?" Jasmine asked, bewildered. Michelle couldn't blame her for being confused.

"Just please tell us what's going on." Ava's eyes were patient, but concerned.

Michelle looked from one cousin to the other. It was true,

she was usually tight-lipped about anything to do with sex or relationships. Old habits died hard, but even she could admit she was in over her head. Maybe she did need advice from her primas. She grabbed Jasmine's mug and took a fortifying sip of the bitter black brew.

"All right," Michelle said. "You want to know what's going on? We gotta go back a little bit. Remember how Gabe left after high school?"

Jasmine's expression darkened. "How could we forget?"

"And you remember what I told you we did before he left." Ava nodded.

"All right, now we need to jump ahead. Because I never told you two about Nathaniel."

Jasmine took her coffee back. "Who the fuck is Nathaniel?"

And so Michelle explained about Nathaniel, her coworker, and how late nights working on challenging projects had brought them closer together. Nathaniel had always been conscientious, but the more time they spent together, the flirtier he got. One thing led to another, and soon they were blowing off steam after long workdays.

It wasn't serious, Michelle insisted. But she'd liked spending time with him, and she could talk to him about work. They talked about other things, too, like their families. And when the next promotion came up, Nathaniel used that against her, ingratiating himself with their bosses and cutting her out. And then he was gone, off to the Los Angeles office with the job that should've been hers.

Michelle had stayed at Rosen and Anders for a short time after that, but the feeling of betrayal, combined with the long work hours, finally broke her, and she'd ended up in the emergency room with a diagnosis of "stress and exhaustion."

"That's why you quit," Jasmine murmured. "I always wondered if there was more to it."

"Yeah. I mean, I was burned out too. But that shit with Nathaniel sure didn't help."

Ava's eyes shone. "Why didn't you tell us?"

Michelle shrugged. "Why didn't you make me a cup of coffee?"

At Ava's narrow-eyed *Don't try to change the subject* look, Michelle sighed. "You both have your own problems. I don't like to burden anyone else with my feelings."

"A burden shared is a burden halved," Ava quoted, and Michelle rolled her eyes.

"I'm not one of your students, A."

"Aren't you?" Ava's eyes twinkled with mischief as she raised her mug and drank.

Jasmine rubbed Michelle's back. "Mich, you're always there for us. You have to let us support you too."

"I know it goes both ways," Michelle said, more touched by her cousin's words than she wanted to admit. "It's just hard."

"Well, start now, and tell us what's really going on with Gabe. Because I'm not buying that *We reconnected on Instagram* basura for a minute."

Michelle should've known Jasmine wouldn't be fooled. She told them about Fabian's email, about the Pros and Cons list, and about fearing that Nathaniel would get the job if she turned it down.

"No better way to ruin Gabe's life than to drag him to a

family gathering," Jasmine commented when Michelle was done, raising her mug in a toast.

"I was kidding about ruining his life. Besides, he was supposed to leave on Friday, before my parents got back."

"Why didn't he?" Ava asked.

"We got caught." Michelle explained how Gabe's father had discovered him buying condoms, and how Gabe didn't want to tell his dad about opening a gym in New York.

Jasmine's smooth brow creased in confusion. "Why didn't Gabe want to tell his dad about the gym?"

"He's been estranged from his parents for years. Their relationship is . . . complicated."

"I can understand that," Jasmine murmured.

"And of course, Gabe's dad told his mom, who told *my* mom, who then told our entire family. And here we are." Michelle raised her hands, then let them drop into her lap.

Jasmine was quiet for a moment, then she sent Michelle a side-eyed glance. "But you *are* having sex with him, right?"

"Oh yeah. All the time. It's amazing."

Jasmine raised an eyebrow. "Well, that's something, at least."

But Ava sighed. "I'm glad you're having great sex, Mich. Truly, I am. But . . . you two have such a messy history."

"And you're technically working for him," Jasmine added, grimacing a bit. "I know it's freelance, and you're revisiting old territory with the touch-and-tickle, but trust me, it's not a great idea."

"Worked out well enough for you."

Jasmine smiled. "Only because I had two primas to talk some sense into me."

"I know. You're right. It wasn't my intention when I brought him here."

"So what *was* your intention?" Ava asked.

Michelle sighed and leaned back, bracing her arms on the mattress. "I just wanted to see him again," she said in a small voice. "And I wanted to know why."

"Why what?" Ava asked in a gentle tone.

"Why he completely abandoned me." Michelle shrugged and looked away. "Since then, I've never wanted to get close to anyone romantically. It's like if I don't let myself get fully invested, it won't hurt when they inevitably leave."

Jasmine let out a slow breath. "What are you going to do when Gabe goes back to California? I'm assuming that's his plan."

Michelle stared up at the ceiling. "We haven't discussed anything that far ahead, but . . . I guess we'll tell everyone we tried and it didn't work. Gabe's life is in Los Angeles. Mine is here."

Ava leaned forward, resting her elbows on her knees. The look in her eyes was intense. "Michelle. How do you feel about Gabe? Really. No bullshit."

"No bullshit?" Michelle sucked in a shaky breath and hated the way her throat grew tight. "You want the truth?"

When her primas nodded, Michelle pressed her fingers to her eyes to alleviate the building pressure. "I'm so happy when I'm with him. I want to figure out a way to keep it going, but I don't know how. And on top of all that, I'm enjoying the work."

She dropped her hands and looked at her cousins. The words spilled out of her in a rush, like the dam she'd placed around her feelings for all these years had finally cracked.

"The truth is . . . I've felt so stuck lately. I've been taking easy design jobs because I was burned out, but they're so fucking boring. Consulting on this campaign has made me feel alive again. And being with Gabe is . . . it's just the best. I don't know how else to explain it. It's like he's been holding a piece of me all this time and I just got it back."

Her voice broke at the end and both of her cousins grabbed her in a hug.

Michelle laughed through the sob in her throat. "When was the last time we did a group hug?"

"I don't know, but it's been too long," Ava murmured against the top of Michelle's head.

After one last squeeze, they released her, and Jasmine sent her a sympathetic look. "You know you're never going to hear the end of this from the family."

"I know. I didn't think it would be such a big deal, but with the way everyone reacted yesterday . . ."

"You're not the only one who'll have to deal with their family," Ava added. "Gabe has a lot of work to do when it comes to his parents."

Michelle sighed. "I hope he doesn't shut them out again. They were so happy to see him. I don't think he even realizes it."

"Probably not," Ava agreed. "But you can't heal that rift for him."

"Yeah, I know." But she would if she could. "He's at his sister's today, but he'll be back tonight."

"When is he leaving?" Jasmine asked.

"He doesn't have a return ticket yet, but probably in a few days." That was the plan, but Michelle was hoping against hope that he'd stay in New York until the new location was complete.

More time. That was all she wanted with him. A little more time.

But what happened when she got more time? She'd want more, and more, and more. It would never be enough.

She wanted all of him.

"Just be careful, okay?" Jasmine said.

"I will." She was trying, but she had so few defenses left.

"And talk to us," Ava added. "We're here for you. No matter what."

Michelle nodded. "I know. Thank you. Both of you."

She would need them, she realized. After Gabe left, she'd need them to run interference with the family.

But more than that, she'd need their help to once again put all her pieces back together. Because the thing she hadn't told them was that she was fairly certain she was head over heels in love with Gabe.

GABE HAD FORGOTTEN how exhausting Tío Duties could be. Since it was his first time visiting Nikki's kids at their home, they'd taken it upon themselves to be good hosts. Seven-year-old Oliver had endeavored to show Gabe every single Lego set he owned, along with a detailed commentary on the "special features" of each one, and nine-year-old Lucy had insisted they play all the outdoor games she could think of, from tag to water guns to pony rides. That would've been okay, except Gabe was the pony, and the kids had taken turns leaping onto his back and screaming in his ear to *run faster*. After hours of this, Oliver and Lucy were wiped out, and Gabe figured he'd done more than his share of cardio for the day.

Once the kids retreated indoors for air-conditioning and video games, Gabe sat with his sister on the deck, drinking beer.

Nikki and Gabe had the same dimples and coloring, but her curly hair and petite stature came from their mom, while Gabe favored their dad. She sent Gabe a glare through eyes nearly identical to his own. "I'm still annoyed that you came to New York and didn't even tell me. What if we'd been out of town?"

Gabe sighed and took a long pull from the bottle. He should pace himself. This was the only one he was having before he drove back to the Bronx.

"I'm sorry, Nik. Nothing about this trip has gone as expected." Total understatement.

"Man plans, God laughs," Nikki muttered, and Gabe raised his beer in salute.

"Are you going back to California?" she asked.

"Yeah, in a few days."

"Permanently?"

"Of course. That's where I live."

Nikki twisted in her deck chair and pinned him with that older-sister look, the one that reminded him all too much of their mother.

"So what the hell are you doing here?" she demanded.

Gabe frowned. He'd told her about launching an Agility location in Manhattan. "I'm here to open a—"

"No, I don't mean what are you doing with the gym, I mean what are you doing in the *Bronx* with *Michelle*?"

"Oh." Gabe looked down at his beer as if it held the answers, which he knew full well it did not. It was why he rarely drank. Alcohol never made him feel clearer on his problems and, if anything, led him down the path of second-guessing his life choices. "We, um, we reconnected—"

"Don't give me that bullshit story you told Mom. I don't believe it for a second."

Gabe let out a heavy sigh. It was almost a relief to be called out, because he needed to talk to *someone* about Michelle. Fabian was busy, and Gabe wasn't in the mood for *I told you so* anyway. He'd explain to his friend later. For now, his sister was the next-best option.

"Michelle is actually helping us with the new gym," he admitted, and then he told Nikki the whole story.

She listened, asking questions for clarification but offering no opinions. Until the end.

"All right, look," she began, and Gabe knew he was in for it. "I've known Michelle just as long as you have. Longer, even, if you consider that I've seen her plenty of times since you two started college, and you haven't. I know both of our families very well. So believe me when I tell you, you better figure out what the hell you want before you drag her into this any further."

Gabe scowled at his sister's accusatory tone. "What are you talking about?"

"You have her working on this New York project—which, let's be real, is clearly some sort of bid to get Dad's attention—and now you're prancing around with her like you're the greatest love story of our generation. Wake up, Gabe. This isn't going to turn out how you want."

"I don't even know what I want," he shot back, and she raised her eyebrows.

"Therein lies your problem."

Fuck, she'd talked him into a corner, just like she'd done countless times when they were kids. "Opening an Agility location here is part of the investment agreement. Fabian was supposed to handle it."

"Yet here you are."

Here he was. Mixed up with Michelle, and Powell, and their families—

Shit, Nikki was right. He had no idea what he wanted, from any of them.

Gabe set his beer on the patio table and dropped his head into his hands.

"What am I doing?" he moaned.

Nikki patted his shoulder. "You gotta be clear on what you want, Baby Gaby."

"For god's sake, Nik. Don't call me that."

She grinned wickedly at his response to the old nickname. "Then stop acting like a little kid. What do you *want*?"

Gabe sat up and said with as much conviction as he could muster, "I want Agility to be a success."

Nikki stared at him impassively for a long moment, then sipped her beer. Finally, she asked, "And what does that mean?"

"It means . . ." Shit, what *did* that mean? Talking points swirled in his head, from the gym's tagline to publicity buzz to what he'd told Michelle.

Agility can be yours!

#5 on Hollywood's Hottest Celebrity Gyms List

To help people feel better in their bodies and achieve a full range of motion.

Was Agility's success about fame? Money? Helping people?

Or was it all about proving to his father that he hadn't needed him after all?

The thought made Gabe's head hurt.

Nikki cut into his conflicting thoughts. "Let me put it this way. Michelle is working for you on the New York campaign, which you don't want to be doing, because you want to stay in Los Angeles. But while you're here, she's also pretending to be your—what, girlfriend? To save you from telling Dad about the gym. What happens when you go back to California?"

"It's temporary. She knows I'm leaving soon."

"Except *she will still be working for you*." Nikki enunciated each word as if to make sure he didn't miss a single one.

Gabe began to sweat, and it wasn't because of the August humidity. "Fabian's going to take it over."

Nikki raised her eyebrows. "Oh really? While he has two infants at home?"

Fuck. Everything was so tangled up now that he'd let all these people back into his life. Gabe had been ignoring reality for the past few days, telling himself it would be easy to pack up and leave again like he'd planned. But even when he returned to LA, things would be different. He and Michelle had told a giant lie, all so he could protect himself from facing his father's judgment, and she was going to be left holding the bag, while still technically working for his business. For *him*.

Gabe let out a long sigh. "I should've never come back to New York."

"But you did. And now you have to clean up the mess you've made."

"I don't even know where to begin."

"You begin with what you want, regarding Michelle, the gym, and Mom and Dad. I didn't tell you this before, because I knew you weren't ready to hear it, but they were devastated when you left. We all were. Well, except for me, because you'd at least reply to my texts. Mom, Dad—hell, even our aunts and uncles were pissed at you for disappearing after my wedding. Only Tío Marco got it, and I think he tried to talk to Dad, to explain. I did too. But they were so hurt, Gabe. You have no idea."

He forced himself to take a small sip of beer. "I was hurt too."

"I know you were. And I understand why you felt like you had to leave. But if you think you can just waltz back to Los Angeles like nothing's changed . . . maybe you'd better think again."

He had thought that, but now he could see he'd been fooling himself.

What do you want?

His sister's question echoed in his mind. Gabe shut his eyes and tried to think.

He wanted . . .

Michelle.

No shit. He'd always wanted her.

But what did it mean, to want her? Beyond sex, beyond a shared past.

He didn't know. Once, he'd wanted a future with her, but his plans had changed and he'd realized it was impossible. She was firmly entrenched in his old life, and he couldn't stay here, not even for her. And he'd never ask her to leave her family for him.

The reality was, he didn't have a future in New York, and

he didn't have a future with Michelle. It didn't matter what he wanted.

It was painful to think about leaving her, so he turned his thoughts to Agility.

This, at least, was becoming clearer. He missed the real work of helping people recover from injuries and improve their mobility, to live better lives in the bodies they had now, instead of whatever kind of body they wished they might have.

But he was currently the owner of "Hollywood's 5th Hottest Celebrity Gym," and he had an obligation to expand that brand into a new market.

As for his parents, he didn't want anything from them, except to prove his father wrong and show them that he could be a success all on his own. For that, he needed the gym expansion to go well, and that meant he needed Michelle to stay on board.

He had to stop doing anything that would jeopardize Agility. Including messing around with Michelle.

"Have you decided what you're going to do?" Nikki asked.

Gabe pushed the beer bottle farther away from him. Now was not the time to introduce more self-doubt. "I'm going to buy my return ticket to LA."

Nikki sighed and shook her head. It clearly wasn't the answer she wanted to hear, but it was all he had.

Somehow, he had to untangle himself from Michelle. From his parents. And, if he could manage it, from the responsibility of managing the New York location.

Fourteen years ago

Windows Messenger Chat Transcript

Celestial Destiny: Episode 10 Planning Session

Michelle:

Our poor fans.

Gabe:

We're going to rip their hearts out.

Michelle:

They really think this story is almost over.

Gabe:

We're just getting started.

Michelle:

It's been fun to watch them speculate about who's on the ship that just landed.

Gabe:

Little do they know things are about to get very bad for our intrepid heroes.

Michelle:

Daddy's home!

Gabe:

What?

Michelle:

Zack's dad. King Salazar should finally appear in this scene.

Gabe:

Oh I thought you were saying YOUR dad is home.

Michelle:

LOL he is, but no, that's not what I meant.

Gabe:

Mine is at his store, thank god.

Michelle:

Good, you can work on this chapter in peace.

Gabe:

Me?

Michelle:

I wrote a lot of the last chapter, and since Zack has his memories back and is seeing his dad again for the first time in years, you should write this one. He's your character.

Gabe:

No, they're OUR characters.

Michelle:

That's right. ☺

Chapter 20

Gabe stood next to Michelle in her brother's old room, staring at the bed like the floral coverlet concealed bear traps.

"I didn't see this coming," he said in a low voice. "I figured they'd make me sleep on the sofa. Or in the backyard."

While Gabe had loved sharing a bed with Michelle at the hotel, after his talk with Nikki, he was finally seeing the wisdom behind Michelle's no-bed-sharing rule. They needed *more* space between them, not less.

"I kind of did expect it," Michelle admitted. "That's why I washed the sheets from the other room and made up the bed like I hadn't been sleeping in there."

"Ah. I was wondering why you'd decided to do laundry at the crack of dawn before we drove upstate."

"Clearly my mother has decided it's better to risk un escándalo than get in the way of our secret romance. We should make sure the condoms haven't been tampered with."

Gabe shuddered. "I hope you're kidding."

"I am. Mostly."

"That's not comforting."

"Look," she said. "The bedrooms are connected. We'll wait

until my parents go to sleep, and I'll sneak into the other room through the bathroom. Then I'll get up early and remake the bed so my mom doesn't know I slept in there."

He shook his head. "Your mom will definitely know. These walls are thin, and as you might have noticed, we're not great at sneaking around."

Michelle pressed the heels of her hands to her eyes and groaned. "God. You're right. We suck at this."

"I could go sleep next door in my parents' house."

"How the hell would you explain that? You'd have to tell your dad the truth about why you're in New York. Are you ready to do that?"

No. He wasn't. "Should we tell them we had a fight?"

"They'd ask a million questions, and our moms are *super* excited about this dinner tomorrow. It would crush them."

It echoed what Nikki had said earlier, and Gabe felt a pang of regret. He should've just told his father the truth—that he was in New York for work and Michelle was helping him.

But he still would've had to explain the condoms. And why he'd been sneaking around next door. And why he hadn't called them in nine—

Never mind.

"We technically shared a bed last night," he pointed out. As awkward as the whole thing was, part of him really looked forward to cuddling with her all night again.

"That was a hotel," Michelle replied softly, and Gabe understood the distinction. It had been a place where they could play pretend and indulge in all their fantasies together. But now, back in her parents' house, they were confronted with reality.

And a lack of privacy.

"Besides, your parents are right down the hall," he added.

"Having loud sex where my parents can hear it would really sell this fake dating story."

Gabe rubbed a hand over his face. "Your father would kill me."

"Plus it's only a queen-size bed." She looked at it skeptically.

"We'll manage," he said, then remembered what Nikki had told him that afternoon.

You better figure out what the hell you want before you drag her into this any further.

Was he leading Michelle on? Giving her false hope?

"I'm going to buy my plane ticket tomorrow," he blurted out. Might as well get it out there before this went any further.

"Oh?" Michelle leaned over to move the pillows around, and he was momentarily distracted by the way her shorts rode up. "For what day?"

"Soon. I'll talk to Fabian tomorrow."

"Okay." Her tone was deceptively breezy as she peeled the blanket and sheet back, and Gabe realized he was talking to the old Michelle. The Michelle he remembered from their teen years, who appeared unconcerned by the actions of others, who took everything in stride or turned it into a joke. Now that he'd seen another side of her, he recognized this for what it was: a defense tactic. She was hiding her feelings from him.

And maybe from herself.

Over the past week, they'd managed to build something new on the ashes of their old friendship. It was fragile and un-defined, but it was real.

Whatever it was, it would be demolished when he left. It would hurt both of them, and he had no idea how to avoid it. He *had* to go back.

"Let's go to sleep," Michelle said, sounding tired.

Side by side, they brushed their teeth at the mirror in the adjoining bathroom. Michelle wore the same pajama set from their first morning together, and Gabe couldn't help watching her tits jiggle in the mirror as she brushed her teeth.

She spat and rinsed, then gave him a smirk. "Were you looking at my boobs?"

"Always," he admitted, and she laughed. The tension in him eased, and as they returned to the bedroom, things didn't seem so bleak.

Michelle adjusted the ceiling fan setting and pushed back the blankets.

"Do you have a side of the bed you sleep on?" she asked.

"Well, since I sleep alone, I sleep in the center."

"That's fair," she said, grinning. "I'll probably have to get up to pee in the middle of the night, so I'll sleep on the side closer to the door."

"That works."

Gabe climbed in first, moving over to make room for her. Michelle sat on the edge of the bed and turned off the lamp, then stretched out under the covers next to him.

Gabe lay quietly for a moment, barely breathing. Every one of his cells was hyperaware of Michelle beside him. The night before, they'd fallen asleep sprawled together on the big hotel bed, exhausted by their sexcapades. There hadn't been time in the morning for awkwardness, because they'd had to hurry and hit the road. He should take Nikki's advice and put space between them. Let Michelle sleep on her side of the bed and above all, don't touch her.

But he didn't want to.

Rolling onto his side, Gabe found her in the dark and kissed her shoulder. "I want to cuddle with you."

"Okay." Michelle's voice was soft in the darkness, but she turned her butt toward him so he could be the big spoon. Gabe pulled her closer, pressing his thighs against hers and tucking his knees into the backs of her legs. Her hair was in his face, but he didn't mind. The sweet herbal scent of her shampoo soothed him. There wasn't an inch of space between them.

And it felt so, so right.

He tried to sleep. He really did. But it was hard. *He* was hard. How could he not be with her gorgeous ass pressed into his crotch?

Her parents were down the hall, so sex was out of the question, but maybe . . .

Gabe raised his head to whisper in her ear. "I want to make you come."

Michelle's breath caught, and he felt her tense. "Now?"

"Right now."

She parted her thighs to give him access. Her immediate acceptance of his offer showed how much had changed between them in a few short days.

He dragged his hand down her body, traveling over her hip to the waistband of her sleep shorts, where he slid his fingers underneath and into her panties.

When she made a little noise, his hand stilled. "Shh. You have to stay quiet, babe."

She huffed. "I'll try."

He touched her again, stroking gently between her lower lips until she opened for him, soft and wet.

"God, I want to fuck you so bad, baby." He breathed the words into her ear as he caressed her, shifting his hand to slip his fingers inside her. "Just like this. I'd slide into you from behind, and—"

He broke off and pressed his face into the nape of her neck when she bit back a moan. As much as he was doing this to tease her and bring her greater pleasure, he was teasing himself too.

"What else?" she asked, her voice raspy with desire. "What else would you do to me?"

He let out a shuddering breath. This was torture of the most exquisite sort.

"I'd slide into you and you'd take every inch," he went on, moving his wet fingers to her clit and circling it as he spoke. "I'd start off slow, but then we'd go faster. You like it hard, don't you, babe?"

"*Yes.*" Her reply was barely audible amid her harsh gasps as he matched the speed of his touch to the images he was spinning. She was close, so he shifted his fingers down again, pressing two into her pussy. He thrust them back and forth, mimicking what he wanted to do with his cock. Her hips bucked, and when she let out a series of soft whimpers, he captured her mouth with his in a kiss before bringing his fingers back to her clit.

She shook beneath his touch, moaning quietly into his mouth.

And Gabe knew he'd held back when Michelle asked what else he would do with her. He wanted to do more than just fuck her. He wanted to hold her like this while she came around his cock, swallowing her gasps of ecstasy.

He wanted to cuddle with her through the night and wake up with her every morning.

A few days and nights weren't enough. One weekend of pretending wasn't enough. He wanted more with her. More time, more . . . everything.

And it scared the shit out of him.

He didn't belong here. He'd thrived in Los Angeles. He'd grown into a person he liked and respected. He couldn't throw all that away and come back to who he used to be.

Not even for Michelle.

She sagged against him, panting. "I think I'm ready to sleep now," she mumbled, and Gabe stifled a chuckle.

"Glad to be of assistance."

"What about you?" She cupped his cock through his shorts, but he gently moved her hand away. All the scary thoughts were bringing him down, and he truly didn't want to get caught having sex by her parents.

"I'm good, babe. Just let me hold you, okay? That's all I want."

But instead of spooning her this time, he wrapped himself up in her, tangling their limbs. For this one night, at least, he didn't have to let her go.

DESPITE BEING A heavy sleeper, Gabe woke periodically throughout the night to check if Michelle was still there.

She was.

By morning, he was attuned to her, and he stirred when he felt her getting out of bed. He pulled her in for a hug, breathing in her woodsy, cinnamon scent. She gave him a kiss on his forehead, then slipped away. He drifted off again and slept deeply.

When Gabe woke up for real, he was groggy, and Jezebel was curled up where Michelle had been. The cat raised her head, peering at him with big yellow eyes, before slinking over and headbutting his cheek.

Who was he to ignore an invitation like that?

After petting Jezebel for a few minutes, Gabe threw on some sweatpants and stumbled downstairs to brew coffee, only to be drawn up short at the sight of Michelle's dad using the espresso machine.

Dominic gave Gabe a sidelong look. "Looking for coffee?"

"Uh, yes, please. Thanks."

Dominic poured a shot into a little cup and passed it to him. Gabe blew on it quickly and took a sip. He preferred to add a lot of milk, but he needed to wake up. Fast.

"Never thought I'd see you around here again," Dominic said conversationally as he fixed his own cup.

"I never thought I'd be back," Gabe answered honestly, then drank some more. His brain clearly wasn't functioning at full power yet.

"What's this I hear about a gym?" Dominic asked.

"Well, I own one." What did the guy want to know? "I'm also a licensed physical therapist."

"No shit?" Dominic raised his eyebrows like he was impressed. "What is it, one of those bodybuilder gyms? Boxing?"

"Not quite. We do bodywork and movement training, also fight training for actors."

Dominic gestured at him. "With the way you look now, I figured you were into competing and stuff."

"I've thought about it," Gabe replied. "Did a few competitions when I was younger. But I just like the routine."

"Probably been hard to keep up with here." Dominic gave a nod toward the basement door. "Our home gym is pretty pathetic. Val uses it more than I do. I still swing by the firehouse when I want a real workout."

"You're retired now?"

"Yeah, a few years ago." He shrugged. "I don't know what the hell to do with myself anymore. I started working security part-time just to have something to do. Val has her arts and crafts stuff upstairs. You probably saw it."

"I did, although I can't say I knew what any of it was."

Dominic barked out a laugh. "I don't ask anymore. And now she wants to open something called an Etsy store for her jewelry. I built her the photo corner with lights so she can take good pictures. It makes her happy, and her jewelry is really good."

It was probably the most Dominic had ever said to Gabe directly, except for the couple of times he'd threatened him. To be honest, Gabe had expected more threats, but no, they were able to talk one-on-one. Like adults.

Dominic clapped Gabe on the shoulder as he passed by on his way to the basement door. "Michie's downstairs, using the printer. You should probably use the desk in the craft room if you want to get any work done. Val will be back soon and she's going to be cooking and cleaning for tonight. She already gave me a warning that she'll be assigning me some projects, so I'm going to relax while I can." He held up his cup in salute. "See you later, kid."

Gabe mumbled a goodbye, then glanced at the clock. Fuck, he had little more than ten minutes before the manager meeting started.

In his pocket, his phone chimed with a calendar alert.

Make that exactly ten minutes. Despite telling Fabian he wouldn't be able to make it, Gabe would feel too guilty if he skipped it.

He grabbed smoothie ingredients from the fridge and freezer, mixed them up, and rinsed out the blender in record time. Then he bounded upstairs, threw on a T-shirt, and opened his laptop with seconds to spare. At the last second, he slapped a Yankees cap on his head, since he hadn't combed his hair yet.

One meeting led to another, which led to a never-ending stream of emails. He was behind on his inbox after not checking it much over the last three days, and when he opened it that morning, he wanted to cry.

Fabian had missed the meeting and hadn't replied to any of Gabe's texts, which was unlike him. Gabe shot him an email, then followed up with Powell, the real estate agent, and even Rocky Lim. He also finished Michelle's worksheet and typed up all the answers in an email. He sent it to her, although he had a funny feeling that a bunch of his answers were somehow . . . wrong.

She replied a few minutes later with a text.

Michelle: Come downstairs.

Gabe checked his watch. He'd been working for four hours straight, and he was famished. It was a good time to take a break. He closed the laptop, finally combed his hair and gelled it back, and went downstairs.

Michelle was in the living room, and to his surprise, she had a whole presentation set up on the coffee table. He had a flash of memory of Michelle's school projects. She'd always loved a presentation board.

"What's all this?" he asked.

"The storyboard for your campaign."

"But I just sent you my answers five minutes ago."

She waved that off. "I never really expected you to fill that out. I've been listening to you talk about yourself and the business for days. I also did an analysis of your website and social media, and between my own market research for Victory and what Fabian sent me for Agility, I had enough to put together a preliminary pitch. Are you ready to hear it?"

Gabe studied the board, which was divided into three color-coded sections: Consumer Insights, The Idea, and Activation Plan. Each area contained data and printed pictures.

"When did you do all this?"

"Here and there." Michelle patted the seat cushion next to her. "I'm good at my job."

"But you don't do this exact work anymore, right?"

She looked at the floor. "No. I don't."

Salsa music played in the kitchen and Valentina sang along off-key. From the backyard, Gabe heard the sounds of hammering. One of the projects Dominic had alluded to?

Gabe was hungry, but Michelle was giving him an expectant look. She seemed so pleased with herself, he sat on the sofa without any further questions.

Michelle started with an analysis of the research, throwing around terms like *social listening, unmet needs,* and *gaps in the marketplace.*

"New York City is a crowded market for gyms," she explained. "You want to show your consumers that you have a differentiated approach that will meet their needs better than your competitors will."

Gabe nodded. He vaguely remembered this stuff from when they'd launched Agility in LA, but, of course, Fabian had been in charge of this part, and Powell had weighed in heavily with his ideas.

Michelle continued by highlighting the opportunity to refresh the brand with a new logo, a revamped website, and a clearer mission statement, to reach the people Gabe really wanted to help. The storyboard included mock-ups of potential designs.

"We'd have to market-test them with consumers," Michelle explained. "But it's a start."

Then she focused on the second section of her pitch, The Idea.

"The focus of your gym is on helping people achieve a full range of movement, right? Let's lean into that for the ad campaign, getting aerialists and contortionists and the like and photographing them in regular fitness wear and working out on gym equipment. And we'll get people in a range of ages and body types, races and ethnicities, genders and abilities, to show that your gym is inclusive and everyone is welcome there."

The board included a brainstorm of taglines, like "Bodies in motion stay in motion," "A movement solution for every body," and "Harmony of movement." He liked all of them better than "Agility can be yours!" He was pretty sure Powell's team had come up with that.

Michelle launched into the Activation Plan, spinning out a story using the visuals on the board.

"People pay for experiences," she said. "For the launch, let's invite them into the gym for a live experience. You know those immersive theater shows where audiences are included within the performance itself? We could work with a theater company to conceive the story and characters, and get an athletic brand to sponsor the costumes, which will just be gym clothes with their logo on it. The performers will be like the ones in your ads, but people will see them come alive here, interacting with the gym and the equipment. It can be a story of movement, of achieving full range of motion. Consumers will associate this story with the Agility brand. And maybe you hold the event every so often as a surprise, like a secret pop-up performance. New Yorkers love a live show, but they especially love one that'll give them bragging rights."

Michelle finished with a rundown of final suggestions, then waved her hands with a flourish. "And there you have it. Agility Gym takes New York."

Gabe's mind whirled with the images and ideas she'd presented. He could see it so clearly, and it excited him more than anything marketing-related ever had before. Trung, who managed Agility's client schedule, would be ideal to take part in the campaign, and Gabe was sure they'd love the chance to get back to their acrobatic roots. Michelle was a genius.

"Wow. I just . . . wow, Mich. This is way more than I expected, especially after only a few days."

Her smile was a little sad. "I like doing this."

"And you're amazing at it." This felt important to tell her. Gabe knew she'd been burned in the past, but she had a gift for this kind of work.

"But you haven't said yet if you think it's the right direction," she pointed out.

He hadn't. Because as much as Gabe loved the idea, he could already imagine Powell's reaction. The investor likely wouldn't think it was "cool" enough. He'd insist on more celebrities, more idealized bodies, more flash. Michelle's idea got to the core of what Gabe had set out to do. Unfortunately, it didn't match what the gym actually was.

Although it did match what he'd always wanted it to be.

That was when it hit him. He was still getting steamrolled, still letting someone else influence his decision-making. When he'd been younger, his dad had made all the choices for their family. Gabe had been forced to go along with them, regardless of what he wanted. School, friends, baseball, college—his dad had placed all of those second to family obligation, which, during Gabe's teen years, consisted of working at the stationery store.

Ever since Gabe had met Powell, the investor had done the same thing, pushing Gabe and Fabian to include stuff like fight choreography training, to make choices that would appeal to celebrity clients, to open a New York City location even though Gabe had been adamantly against it.

Gabe had gotten away from his father, only to replace him with Powell.

The thought gave him a sick feeling in his gut, so he shoved it away.

"I like it," he told Michelle, because he did. "I think it's brilliant and fun, and will speak to people. But we'll have to run it past Fabian and Powell too."

"Understood. And remember, this is just the preliminary concept. There's still a lot more fine-tuning involved, or we can go back to the drawing board."

"Right. Thank you for . . . all of this."

And because the words weren't enough, he cupped the back of her head and pulled her in for a kiss.

He didn't care that her mom was in the kitchen or that her dad might walk in at any moment. The presentation had brought up so many conflicting feelings inside him, feelings that had nowhere to go. He needed this connection with Michelle to ground him, to give some of his emotions a home. Love. Appreciation. Hope. He didn't even know what else. All he knew was that she made him stronger.

Michelle didn't question him or make a joke. She just leaned in, meeting his mouth with hers and opening for his tongue. Gabe kissed her slowly and thoroughly, trying to show her without words how much she meant to him.

Her hand fisted in his T-shirt and she tugged him closer. Gabe slid his fingers into her hair, angling her head so he could tangle his tongue more fully with hers. The kiss deepened and heated. Their mouths fused together until they were both gasping for air whenever their lips parted.

Gabe was on the verge of dragging Michelle onto his lap and grinding against her through their clothes, but her mom was in the next room, just an open doorway away. Instead, he eased back with a reluctant groan.

Michelle's honey-colored eyes were dazed and dreamy. She blinked slowly and licked her lower lip. "What was that for?"

What could he say to that?

For being incredible.

For seeing me and my vision clearly.

For caring about my gym.

For caring about me.

Before he could settle on a reply, Valentina called to them from the kitchen. "Oye, nenes. ¿Quieres comer?"

Gabe jolted at the sound of Valentina's voice, and the moment was lost. Michelle shifted away from him and Gabe didn't say any of the things that were on the tip of his tongue.

"Do you ever think they'll stop calling us children?" Michelle muttered, folding up the presentation board.

"Never."

Gabe was glad for the interruption, which had kept him from revealing too much. And in a weird way, he liked the reminder that there were people older and wiser looking out for him. It was something he hadn't experienced in nearly ten years.

As he followed the scent of tostones to the kitchen, he realized that it wasn't just his feelings for Michelle that were delaying his purchase of a return flight. The sense of home, of family, of being cared for, was nearly intoxicating. He couldn't let himself get used to it, but he could enjoy it while it lasted.

And a small part of him was even looking forward to seeing his own parents again that night. He wasn't sure why or how it had happened, but for once, he decided not to fight it.

Chapter 21

The doorbell rang for the umpteenth time and Michelle went to open it with Gabe on her heels.

"This is not a small family dinner," Gabe hissed.

Michelle snorted. "According to my mother, it is."

"There are already more than thirty people here!"

"Exactly. A small family dinner." Michelle laughed at the look of distress on his face and pulled him down for a kiss. "Relax. They're just here to eat."

The doorbell rang again, more insistently this time.

"Somebody get the damn door!" Valentina yelled from the kitchen.

"I got it," Michelle yelled back.

"I forgot how loud our families can be," Gabe muttered.

"This is nothing." Michelle opened the door and rolled her eyes when she saw her cousin Sammy standing on the other side with his wife and kids. Sammy was Ronnie's brother and the oldest of the Rodriguez cousins. He was also a giant pain in the ass.

Michelle stepped aside to let them in and kissed each of them hello. "Sammy, what are you doing here? Looking for free food?"

"I heard it was an engagement party, so I brought a present," Sammy joked, and at Michelle's withering glare, he laughed. "Relax, *Mitch*. Your mom asked me to pick up a box of cannoli from Arthur Avenue." He handed over a large white box tied with red-and-white string. Michelle could smell the sweet aroma of Italian bakery wafting from the edges.

"All right, you're forgiven for the engagement party crack, but only because you brought cannoli. And don't repeat the joke because that's how rumors start and it's the absolute last thing I need right now."

Sammy laughed, bumped fists with Gabe, and moved on into the house.

Despite her reassurances to Gabe, Michelle had to admit that this seemed like more than just a family barbecue. Her dad and Gabe's had removed part of the fence separating their backyards so various Rodriguez and Aguilar relatives could move between both houses with ease. Her sister and brother were both there with their spouses and kids. Gabe's sister was there with her family, and it seemed like all of his aunts and uncles had shown up, along with some cousins. Ava and her mother were there, and Jasmine had brought Ashton and his son, Yadiel. Michelle's Puerto Rican grandparents were there, along with her mom's sister and her dad's brother.

Large house parties weren't uncommon in her family, but Sammy's joke made Michelle wonder what exactly her mother had told everyone the occasion was. She wouldn't put it past Valentina to claim this was a "pre-engagement" party, despite the number of times Michelle had told her she didn't plan to ever get married.

Her suspicions grew as the night wore on and she and Gabe fielded increasingly invasive questions. The most common was "When's the wedding?" but everyone also wanted to know if Gabe was moving back to New York. Titi Nita, Sammy and Ronnie's mom, announced that she'd had a dream where Michelle moved to Los Angeles to take over Jasmine's empty apartment. Jasmine made a mad dash out of the room when that one came up. And at least two people asked Michelle when she was going to get a "real job" again. She didn't have the energy to fight back with more than "I already have a real job."

When Michelle had quit corporate and made the decision to go freelance, no one had understood why she'd give up a secure position—with benefits!—to work from home. One of her great-aunts had even implied that Michelle—and her entire generation—were lazy, and Ava had dragged Michelle away before she told a viejita what she could do with her opinions about millennials.

After Sammy toasted Gabe with his beer and gave an elaborate speech welcoming him to the family, Ava pulled Michelle aside.

"This is getting out of hand," Ava warned in a low voice. "I wouldn't be surprised if Abuela's already booked a priest."

"I'm not getting married and even if I were, it certainly wouldn't be in a church," Michelle retorted. "Why do they all have to be so extra about everything?"

"Not everything," Ava mused. "Just relationships."

Michelle patted her cousin's hand. A few of their relatives had acted like it was *such a shame* that Ava had gotten divorced, like she was defective in some way. The number of times they'd heard "Ay, qué pena" that year had irritated Michelle to no end, but Ava had forbidden her from telling them off.

It was a recurring theme. Michelle wanted to curse someone out, and Ava talked her down.

Now, Ava was looking at her with unmasked concern. "How much longer are you two going to let this go on?"

It was a good question, but one Michelle didn't have a clear answer to. Originally it had seemed like they were just going to enjoy this time together while he was here, but now, everyone else was involved too. Would they expect that she and Gabe would still be together every time he traveled here for something related to the gym? What did Gabe expect? What did he want?

Michelle knew what she wanted. She wanted more of him, however she could get him.

But it didn't seem like he wanted that.

"He said he was going to buy his return ticket today." Michelle worried her lower lip with her teeth. "Other than that . . . I don't know."

Since she hadn't seen Gabe in a while, Michelle decided to go looking for him. This house party was exactly the kind of situation he'd been trying to avoid, and he'd already tried to make a run for it once. She wouldn't put it past him to do it again.

AFTER NOT SEEING any close relatives other than his sister for nearly a decade, Gabe was completely and totally overwhelmed.

His parents' house was a little smaller than Michelle's, and his mother had a fondness for oversized furniture and ceramic knickknacks. As a result, the Aguilar home was always a little tighter and more cramped than strictly necessary—probably why Gabe valued open space and a lack of clutter in his own habitat. Now, filled with all the aunts, uncles, and cousins who still lived in the tri-state area, the Aguilar house felt stuffed to the gills. No one had wanted to miss the return of the prodigal son, a phrase Gabe heard no less than four times over the course of the night.

Nikki drove down with Patrick and the kids, and Lucy and Oliver grabbed Gabe's hands and dragged him up to his old bedroom as soon as they arrived. Upstairs, they peppered him with a million questions and asked if they could have his old toys, which, to Gabe's surprise, were boxed up and still in his closet.

At the bedroom door, Nikki sent Gabe a disapproving grimace. "I can see our talk really sank in," she murmured.

"I'm working on it," he ground out in response, and then lost his breath when Oliver leaped onto his back and demanded a piggyback ride.

Later, after eating his fill of carne asada, Gabe was in the living room catching up with a couple of his cousins when Tío Marco barreled into the house like a freight train.

"Where is he?" Marco yelled, and when he spotted Gabe, he made a beeline for him and caught him up in a bone-crushing hug.

"Hey, Nino," Gabe said, returning the hug.

"You finally came back, huh, Squirt?" His uncle clapped him hard on the back.

The old nickname drew a laugh from Gabe. Their bond, at least, was like no time had passed at all, but he was struck by how alike they looked. Marco could have been his older brother.

Gabe's parents had been born in Mexico and Puerto Rico, and while most of their immediate families had also ended up in the New York–New Jersey area, Tío Marco had been Gabe's closest adult support. He'd only been twenty-one when Gabe was born, and he'd taken his role as godfather seriously.

Marco eased back, but he kept an arm slung around Gabe's shoulders. "Remember," he said, leaning in so the relatives swarming the living room wouldn't overhear, "if you need help dealing with him, just ask."

Gabe swallowed hard. "I know. Thanks."

After Nikki's wedding, Tío Marco had texted Gabe to say he understood where Gabe was coming from and he'd respect his choices, but if he ever wanted help bridging the gap with Esteban, he'd be there. More than anyone, Marco understood what it was like to be raised by Esteban, who was ten years older than him and had become a surrogate father figure after their own father passed away.

"And what's this I hear about una mujer?" Tío Marco raised his eyebrows.

Gabe didn't have the heart to tell his godfather the truth about him and Michelle, so he just nodded, and a moment later his parents came over to greet Marco.

Somehow Gabe ended up back over in Michelle's backyard, and after her abuela confessed to shoulder pain, he'd escorted the older woman inside for a quick treatment in the Amatos' living room, the only quiet spot in either house. That was where Michelle found him.

"What are you doing to my grandmother?" Michelle asked, walking over to them.

Esperanza looked up with a grimace. "Tu novio está arreglando mi hombro."

"Fixing your shoulder?" Michelle frowned. "What's wrong with your shoulder, 'buela?"

"Estoy vieja," Esperanza said with a laugh, then winced. "Ay, mira, Gabriel. Cuidadito con mi cuerpo."

Gabe smiled widely to set her at ease. "No te preocupes, señora. I'm very careful."

Michelle sat and watched while he pressed his fingers into the space around Esperanza's scapula, instructing her to move her arm back and forth. If this hadn't been second nature for him, Michelle's curious gaze might have distracted him. When he was done, he stood back.

"How does it feel?" he asked.

Esperanza moved her arm experimentally, and then her eyebrows shot up in surprise. "Es mejor."

"See?" Gabe helped her to her feet. "Sometimes there's a little discomfort but it's better in the end. Please remember to ice it."

"Es un milagro." Esperanza took Gabe's face in both hands and patted his cheeks. "Gracias, muchacho."

"De nada, Doña Esperanza."

Esperanza turned and gave her granddaughter a wink, then left them alone in the living room.

Gabe sank onto the sofa and sagged forward, resting his arms on his knees. Michelle rubbed his back, her hand warm and comforting through the fabric of his T-shirt. While he was tempted to curl up with her right here in the quiet living room, he was too worn out.

"What the fuck are we doing?" he whispered, his voice bleak.

She let out a soft sigh. "Ava thinks we should give up the ruse."

"So does Nikki." He rubbed his face with one hand, but the other reached for Michelle's, and he twined their fingers together. "She cornered me in my old bedroom next door. Did you know my stuff is still over there?"

Michelle shook her head. "I haven't been in your house much since you left."

Of course she hadn't. Why would she?

"I mean, it's all in boxes in the closet. But there's the same furniture, and my mom didn't throw any of my things away. She said she was keeping it for when I came back." He pressed his fingers to his eyes, trying not to think about how awful he'd felt when his mom had dropped that tidbit. "I don't know how we get out of this, Mich. They're all expecting . . . something."

"They're imagining wedding bells," she mused. "Alas, they're in for a disappointment."

Gabe met her gaze, a pit opening in his stomach, despite all the Mexican, Puerto Rican, and Italian food he'd consumed that night. "You're the one who's going to bear the brunt of it when I leave."

Because he was watching her carefully, he noted the moment her eyes shuttered and her chin firmed. But she didn't reply. Instead, she got to her feet and gave him a tug. "Come on. If we disappear for too long they're going to expect me to come back with a ring."

Gabe groaned, but let her pull him to his feet and back out to the party.

That night, they collapsed into bed next to each other, exhausted.

"I forgot what these family gatherings are like," he muttered.

"It's so much worse being the center of attention," she agreed, sounding tired. "Did you buy your plane ticket?"

"Fuck. I forgot." He exhaled heavily. "I'll do it tomorrow. My parents asked me to come over to talk before I leave."

It amazed him that he'd managed to put off this conversation as long as he had. His parents had been civil all evening, playing the charming hosts, but Gabe knew their patience was running out. They were going to want answers.

He still had no idea what to tell them.

Michelle stayed quiet, rubbing his bare chest in soothing circles. Gabe caught her hand and pulled her closer. And despite his bone-deep weariness, he didn't drift off until she'd fallen asleep in his arms.

MICHELLE WAS ALREADY gone when Gabe woke the next morning. Before he could even stand from the bed, his phone buzzed with an incoming call. It was Fabian. Gabe subtracted three hours from the time and—fuck, it was super early in California. After nearly a week in New York, Gabe was just starting to acclimate to the time difference. Why the hell was Fabian even awake?

He quickly accepted the call and held the phone to his ear.

"Fabian? What's up? Everything okay?"

On the other end, Fabian let out a long, slow sigh. "Man, you don't even know . . ."

"Tell me. Is everything okay?"

"It's Iris. She went into labor earlier than we expected. We went to the hospital, they did an emergency C-section, and the twins, they're . . ."

"They're what?" Gabe's hand clenched around the phone as he waited to hear.

"They're fine. More than fine, actually. They're beautiful, they're perfect, but they're *here*. Now."

"Whoa. Congratulations, man."

"Thanks. But now my wife is recovering from labor, my mom's leg is in a cast, and my dad is still having heart surgery in a week. Plus I have two premature babies to take care of. The fucking nursery isn't even done yet."

"Shit. Is there anything I can do? Do you need help?"

"Thanks, man. My sister is flying in from Florida tonight. She's going to stay for three months. We'll make it. But Gabe— something's gotta give."

Gabe's skin chilled at Fabian's fatalistic tone. "What do you mean?"

"I mean, I need more flexibility right now. More time. And not just right now, but for the foreseeable future. What I'm saying is—" Fabian took a deep breath, let it out. "I'm saying we should sell the gym. Powell is ready to buy us out. We're already in over our heads with one location. How are we supposed to handle New York too? And I know you don't want to be going out there all the time for every little thing. This is the best deal we're going to get, and I think we should take it."

"Wait." Gabe pressed a hand to his forehead. "Powell already approached you about selling?"

"Dude, Powell's *been* on me about selling. For, like, two years. He wants to turn it into a franchise. I told him we weren't interested. But after meeting you and your girl last week, he called me and sweetened the deal. Sorry to spring all this on you at once. I should've told you about Powell's offer as soon as it happened. With everything going on, I haven't had a chance to think about it myself, let alone tell you the details."

"What's the offer?" Gabe asked numbly.

Fabian recited a number that made Gabe's stomach drop.

"Holy shit," he whispered.

"I know. He thinks the New York location is going to be a hit. He's offered to buy me out and partner with you, or he'll buy both of us out and take it from there. If you did that, you'd be free. No more New York trips. No more calendar alerts. No more emails."

Gabe blinked, lost in his own thoughts. A week ago, that's all he would have wanted, a reason not to manage the New York branch, a way out of coming back home.

But deep down, he'd also wanted for it to be a knockout success, so he could finally prove to his father that he didn't need him.

And maybe, finally, receive the validation he'd always craved.

It was all slipping out of reach now, his dreams turning to sand and falling through his fingers. Part of Gabe wished he could tell Fabian to figure it out, that they were in this together, that they couldn't give up.

Another part of him wished he were strong enough to do this on his own, without Fabian, without Powell. If he didn't need them so much, he wouldn't be proving that his father had been right all along.

He couldn't do it alone.

And he had to admit part of him wanted the excuse to visit New York more frequently. And while it was mostly to explore whatever he had going with Michelle, it was also so he could see his family. His parents, his sister and her kids, even his aunts and uncles. He'd missed them all. The party last night had shown him he had a lot of lost time to make up for.

But selling the gym hadn't been on his radar. It was *his*, the closest thing he had to a baby. To sell it all off in one fell swoop seemed wrong. It felt like giving up.

Fabian had his family, a home, and now, his children. His life was full without Agility.

But it wasn't Fabian's name on the gym, it was Gabe's—the proof that he'd made something big of himself, that he'd done what his father couldn't.

That leaving New York—leaving *Michelle*—had been worth it.

"I gotta think," Gabe finally said. "Go be with your family. We'll talk later."

"Let me know. And Gabe—I'm sorry, man. I know this isn't an easy choice."

It is for you, Gabe thought. But he just wished his friend well and hung up.

It was easy for Fabian because he had something more important in his life than the gym. But for Gabe, the gym was part of his identity. Without it?

He'd have nothing. He'd *be* nothing.

But shit, it was a lot of fucking money on the table.

What else could he do? He couldn't buy out Fabian's share of the company himself. And the thought of running the business with Powell made him cringe.

Already, he could feel it slipping away from him. Fabian would sell. It was the right choice for him, and Gabe couldn't fault him for that. With Fabian's education and experience, he'd be able to book a consulting gig or pick up a teaching contract no problem, something with fewer hours and less responsibility.

Gabe, on the other hand . . .

He thought about Michelle's presentation, and the truth he hadn't wanted to see. Her observations had highlighted the glaring disconnect between what he'd envisioned for the business and what it had become.

A calendar alert beeped on his phone. He was supposed to visit his parents this morning, to "talk." He'd come all this way to prove to his father that he was a success. And in the end, he was going to have to go over there and admit he was a failure. Because what else could he do but sell?

Sell, and be left with nothing to call his own. Or keep the gym and partner with Powell, who would steamroll him at every turn, or use him as the face of the company and nothing more. A poster boy. A diversity prop.

Fabian deserved an answer soon, so he could focus on his family. It wasn't fair for Gabe to drag this out, to leave it hanging over Fabian's head while he labored over the decision, pushing it off until he tied things up here with his parents and Michelle.

If only he could go to his parents for advice. His father had been in this position before, had made the hard decision to close his business. But what if he'd regretted it? He'd hated the retail manager job he'd been forced to take after closing the store. Maybe he'd advise Gabe to tough it out, to hold on no matter what. Or maybe he'd tell him to take the money and move on.

It didn't matter, because asking for advice was out of the question. Too much time had passed, and Gabe had worked too hard to get his father's voice out of his head. He had to sort this out on his own. He'd gotten into this mess, and he was the only one who could clean it up.

He didn't have time to dig into the past with them like he suspected they wanted, but the least he could do was say good-bye in person.

And Michelle. What was he supposed to say? *Sorry for dragging you into this, but I'm either selling the gym or partnering with the investor, and even though I think your idea is perfect, he isn't going to go for it.* Fuck, what a mess. And it told him all he needed to know about how much his own business had already gotten away from him.

The whole thing was fucking embarrassing. After all they'd gone through on this trip for the sake of the gym, he had to admit that it was a failure. He'd make sure Michelle got paid for the work she'd done, and after that . . . he didn't know what they were going to do. He had nothing to offer but old memories and a big dick. She was smart and funny and beautiful, and she deserved more.

For now, he had to get out of here. This wasn't his life anymore. His life was back in Los Angeles, and he'd already been gone too long.

Before he could change his mind, Gabe pulled up the airline app. There was a flight in a few hours. He bought a ticket and started packing.

Fourteen years ago

Celestial Destiny: Episode 11 Planning Session

Gabe:

I think I wrote us into a corner.

Michelle:

Don't worry, we'll figure out how to free them from the dungeon.

Gabe:

In a way that isn't totally contrived?

Michelle:

Zack has his memory back, so he knows what his powers are.

Gabe:

But he hasn't used them in years.

Michelle:

Maybe he tries to use them to get out but fails.

Gabe:

That's gonna kill him.

Michelle:

Not literally!

Gabe:

No, but he's going to hate failing.

Michelle:

So what? They're not at the end yet. He can't have too much growth by this point. Let him mope for a while.

Gabe:

Fine, but you're writing the moping scenes.

Michelle:

But you're so good at moping! 😜

Gabe:

Chapter 22

Michelle was in the basement at her father's desk, working on a new vector design for the Agility logo, when Gabe came downstairs.

She turned to him with a smile, which faltered when she saw the downcast look on his face.

"What's wrong?" she asked, getting to her feet and going to him. "Did your parents—"

"I'm leaving."

"Oh." This was her chance to drop hints about continuing to explore what was growing between them. "Will you be coming back at some point to—"

"No. We're probably selling the gym."

The words hit her like a punch. They were the absolute last thing she thought he'd say.

"What? I thought you were opening another location."

Gabe's voice was clipped and formal. "The situation has changed and the best option now is to sell. I appreciate all the work you've put into this, but—"

"Gabe, what *happened*? Yesterday I gave you the presentation and today you're saying it's all over." Michelle didn't like this bleak, guarded version of Gabe, or the feeling that the gym was the only thing keeping him in her life. Because without it . . . where did that leave them? "Why is this the best option?"

His tone was full of bitterness. "Fabian's out and Powell's ready to buy immediately. The smart choice is to throw away everything I've worked for."

"But you're selling it," she said, trying to understand. "You're not throwing it away."

His lips compressed and he shook his head. "Feels the same."

"Why don't you sit down? We'll brainstorm. You don't have to make this decision alone."

"I do," he said stubbornly. "It's all on me."

"Gabe—"

"Anyway, I came down to tell you I'm leaving." He wouldn't meet her gaze.

Her breath caught. "When?"

"Now."

A chasm opened inside her, threatening to suck her in. This was happening sooner, and faster, than she'd expected. But she gathered her mettle and spoke the question in her heart. "Can't you stay a little longer?"

"Michelle, my business is falling apart."

"Maybe if we talked about it—"

"What is there to talk about?" Gabe ran his hands through his hair. "You knew I was going to leave. And now it's happening. I would've been gone already if I hadn't run into my dad."

Michelle had no idea how they'd gotten from planning the expansion to a corporate takeover, but that wasn't the point here. Gabe was clearly conflicted about the decision, and if she could only get him to calm down and discuss it with her, she was sure they could work it out.

And maybe, they'd be able to work something out between the two of them too.

Thirteen years earlier, Gabe had told her he was leaving.

Damn it, she wouldn't make the same mistake she had last time.

"Gabe. Please stay."

There. She'd said it. In no uncertain terms. She was putting her heart on the line, making herself vulnerable. It was scary as hell, but worth it.

He was worth it.

"Mich, I *can't*." Anguish roughened his voice, and his eyes pleaded with her to understand. "I have to go back and deal with this."

Michelle waited, but he left it at that. Nothing about how he'd come back after it was taken care of, or how he'd call her once he was in a better frame of mind. No mention of the future at all.

Because she, clearly, *wasn't* worth it.

It was on the tip of her tongue to say the other piece, the thing that had been brewing inside her for a few days.

I'm falling in love with you.

But she wouldn't use that on him. Not like this. So she locked it away inside what was left of her heart.

"All right." Her voice was brittle, and she felt like she was about to break into a thousand pieces.

He gave her a pained look. "I have to do this, Michelle."

"What about us, Gabe?"

"I don't know what to tell you. My life is in LA. You knew that."

"So you're just going to pretend like nothing happened?"

"Michelle, whatever we've been doing here, playing house, isn't real life. My real life is falling apart and I have to go fix it."

It didn't matter that she'd opened up to him more than she ever had with anyone else. It didn't matter that they were good together. It didn't matter that she loved him.

She'd loved him before—granted, not like this, but she had—and he'd still left. And according to him, he'd wanted her back then and left anyway. Cut her out *because* of his feelings for her.

Was it any surprise he was doing the same thing now?

As much as Michelle wanted to wish otherwise, she knew that once Gabe left, she wouldn't hear from him again. This was it. She could either argue with him or scream at him like she had before, or she could say goodbye and accept the truth.

Let it be real.

But it wasn't real. He'd just said so.

He was leaving, and they were over.

"Good luck," she said. Because what else was there to say? She'd known this was coming. From the beginning, he'd been clear that he was going back. It was her own stupid heart that had hoped he might change his mind. Or that even if he left, he'd do it sweetly, with assurances that he'd return.

Except it wasn't meant to be. He was leaving her. Again.

It was as Michelle had always suspected. Love was for other people. And she was meant to be alone.

If even Gabe didn't think she was worth sticking around for, who would?

He turned and headed for the stairs. Halfway there, he stopped. His hands clenched and unclenched. Then he spun around and stomped back to her. The look on his face was fierce and hungry, and she was already moving toward him when he caught her around the waist and pulled her in for a kiss.

Michelle slung an arm around his shoulders and went up on tiptoe, pressing their bodies together, soaking in the feel of him. Gabe held her close, and she poured everything she felt for him into the kiss. It was pure heat, the intensity drawing whimpers and moans from their throats as their tongues tangled and their teeth nipped. It was a wild, unspoken war of all the things they had and hadn't said.

It was goodbye.

As she had in this very basement all those years ago, Michelle reached for the waistband of his pants, yanking at the elastic in desperate movements. Before she could free his cock, he gripped the back of her thighs and lifted her, carrying her to the desk. He deposited her on the surface and shoved her laptop and notebooks aside. She didn't even care that the pencil case fell to the floor, her collection of colored pens spilling out across the beige carpet. Urgency was the only factor here.

Their mouths parted long enough for Michelle to lean back on her arms, lifting her hips so Gabe could yank her shorts and panties down her legs. He shoved his own pants and briefs to mid-thigh as she hurried to find a condom in her zip-around Wonder Woman wallet. She ripped open the wrapper and gripped the base of his dick, holding him still as she rolled the condom down his hard length. He hissed in pleasure, his eyes rolling back as she sheathed him, but he didn't say a word and neither did she.

There was nothing left to say. There was only this.

Gabe hooked his arms under her knees, angling her hips so they aligned with his cock. His mouth found hers again in a searing kiss, and she reached down to guide him into her. She was wet, but not enough, and it was her turn to hiss as he stretched her. She scooted forward as much as she was able, urging him on, and he pumped his hips to work his way in.

From there, he set the pace for a hard, fast fuck.

Face-to-face, with barely a breath between them, Michelle could barely hold a thought in her head. Everything about him overwhelmed her senses, from his size, to his heat, to the sound of his harsh breaths and his clean, soapy scent. She took everything he gave and committed it all to memory. She kissed him so hard her lips felt bruised, but she didn't care. She needed as much of him as she could get before he was gone.

His eyes were closed, like hers had been the first time they'd had sex, and she couldn't blame him. It gave her the opportunity to study his face as he fucked her, to memorize the crease between his dark brows, the way his jaw tightened and his lips parted to reveal a flash of clenched white teeth.

But eventually the sensations became too much for her, and her own eyes drifted shut. Michelle stopped thinking and just let herself feel. From this angle, his cock was rubbing both her clit and her interior walls in the most delicious way. She moaned as he moved inside her, and the feelings intensified. She tightened her thighs around him as her body wound with tension.

Holy fuck, she'd never felt this close to a vaginal orgasm before. Her toes curled against his ass and she threw her head back, giving herself over to him. He took her cue and ran kisses up and down her neck, swirling his tongue against the sensitive skin as he picked up the pace, grinding deeper and harder.

The climax hit her fast, sudden and devastating. She cried out, digging her nails into his shoulders as she shook and shattered. A second later, he groaned and pressed his forehead to hers, his body heaving as he came.

And then it was over.

Tingles still spiraled through her, but he'd stopped moving. Her heart pounded like it was going to jump right out of her chest and follow him to California.

Gabe finally opened his eyes and met her gaze. His expression was bleak, but he raised a hand and brushed aside the hair that had fallen into her face during his vigorous attentions. Then he reached for the box of tissues—and froze. Michelle glanced over to see what he was staring at. When Gabe had pushed everything aside, a yellow legal pad had shifted out from beneath the pile of notebooks.

And on it, her Pros and Cons list.

With a shuddering sigh, Gabe slipped out of her and backed away, grabbing a handful of tissues from the box on the desk. He wrapped them around himself, then raised his pants before walking into the bathroom and shutting the door behind him. A moment later, she heard water running in the sink.

Michelle let out a long shaky exhale and slid down, trying not to think about the fact that she'd just had her bare ass on her dad's desk. Thank god her parents had left early that morning to go to the beach.

She retrieved her panties and shorts and put them on. She could leave the basement while he was in the bathroom. Just go and lock herself in one of the upstairs bathrooms, waiting until he'd left. But she wouldn't make this easier for him.

Besides, she wanted one last look at him.

Michelle relived the last few minutes in her mind as she waited and tried not to cry. She'd never felt this way with anyone else before, and she knew no one in the future would ever come close. Gabe was special. He was hers.

But it wasn't meant to be, and she had to get used to that fact.

She was still leaning against the desk with her arms crossed when Gabe exited the bathroom a few minutes later. He paused when he saw her, like maybe he'd expected her to be gone, but he crossed the carpet and, with the gentlest movements, took her face in his hands and pressed a soft kiss to her forehead.

Michelle's heart twisted into a knot as she watched him walk away. A heavy sense of finality settled over her.

This was truly the end.

Without a word, and without looking back, Gabe went up the stairs and disappeared from sight.

Michelle waited until she heard the door at the top of the stairs close. Then, with trembling fingers, she pulled out her phone and sent a message to the Primas of Power group text.

Michelle: He's leaving.

Ava's reply came a second later.

Ava: I'll be right there.

Upstairs, Gabe took a quick shower and packed the last of his belongings.

He hadn't planned to have sex with Michelle, but damn it, he hadn't been able to walk away from her without at least one last kiss. And when she'd reached for him, he'd given in to the impulse to be with her.

One last time.

No matter how much he'd prepared for this moment, it was still tearing him apart to leave her again. He'd thought doing it a second time would hurt less than the first, but if anything, it was worse. As close as they'd been as kids, it was nothing compared to how deeply they'd connected over the past week. Walking away from her downstairs had felt a bit like dying.

It was tempting to leave now and head straight for the airport, thus avoiding yet another uncomfortable goodbye. But he recalled Michelle's words from a few days before, from outside the quinceañera venue.

It's not too late, you know.

For what?

To run away.

That's your MO. Not mine.

She was right. His natural inclination was to run away from emotionally uncomfortable situations, to protect himself by avoiding whatever was making him feel too much.

Just like her MO was to make a joke, using humor to dispel the tension and change the subject. They both had their patterns.

But Gabe had told his parents he would be there, and he couldn't bring himself to bail on them.

Hefting his suitcase and laptop bag, he went downstairs and out the Amatos' back door. He didn't see Michelle on his way out, and ignored the sense of unease that came from already missing her. Outside, he crossed the backyards—now connected through a gap in the lattice fence—and strode up to his mother's kitchen door. As Gabe let himself in, a knot formed in his stomach at how much it felt like the old days when he was a kid running back and forth between the two houses.

This wasn't even his house anymore. He probably should have knocked. But his mother looked up from the sink and greeted him with a big smile, so he knew it was okay.

The kitchen was warm, and Gabe was immediately hit with a sweet, familiar smell. He sniffed the air as childhood memories assaulted him, and his mouth watered. "Mami, are you making pan dulce?"

"Sí. I made mini conchas. You used to love them." After Gabe dutifully kissed her cheek, she flipped back the towel covering a basket full of the round pastries.

Damn, Gabe hadn't had a concha in years. The Mexican sweet bread had been a staple of his childhood, but despite living in Los Angeles all this time, he hadn't found himself frequenting any Mexican bakeries. Not when he so closely monitored his sugar intake. Gabe inhaled deeply, the smell of pan dulce easing some of his stress. It was hard to feel like the world was ending when you were surrounded by fresh-baked goods.

"Toma uno," his mom prompted, so Gabe picked one out of the basket and took a bite.

"Ay dios mío," he mumbled as sweetness exploded on his tongue. It was just as delicious as he remembered, although sweeter than he was used to now.

"¿Te gusta?" his mother asked.

"Sí, Mami. Está perfecto."

She gestured toward a tray with three bowl-size mugs of café con leche. Gabe lifted one and washed the bite of concha down with the sweet, milky coffee.

Gabe heard footsteps on the stairs and a moment later his father entered the kitchen. To Gabe's surprise, his father hugged him before reaching over and snagging a concha from the basket.

"Should we sit in the living room?" Norma asked, but Gabe shook his head.

"I can't stay," he admitted, and he didn't miss the way his father's mouth tightened. "There's an emergency at the gym and I have to fix it."

His mother knotted her hands together. "When will you come back?"

"I—I don't know how long it will take." He'd been about to say *I don't know*, but he couldn't do that to them again.

For all these years, he'd thought this door was closed. But it was open again. Or maybe it always had been, and he'd just refused to walk through.

His mother nodded, like that would have to be good enough.

"We still have things to talk about," his father said mildly.

"I know. We will."

It was the best he could give them right now.

"Pues, hasta luego." Esteban clapped him on the shoulder. "See you next time."

There *would* be a next time. Gabe didn't know when, but the answer wasn't "never" like it had been just a week earlier. For now, he had to close another chapter of his life before he could even think about starting a new one.

"You should give some of the conchas to Michelle's family," Gabe suggested as his mother packed one for him in a plastic container.

"Aren't you going back over there?" she asked.

"No, I—" *Can't.* "I'm not."

Esteban eyed him warily but said nothing. Norma glanced at the suitcase by the kitchen door. "Oh. Sí, I'll bring them over. Don't miss your flight."

"Do you want me to drive you?" Esteban asked, but Gabe shook his head quickly. After what had just happened with Michelle, he couldn't take another drawn-out and emotionally wrenching goodbye with someone he had years' worth of baggage with.

"Está bien. I'll take a cab."

Gabe kissed his mother goodbye, gave his dad a quick hug, and went out to the sidewalk to secure a rideshare to take him to the airport.

When the SUV showed up at the curb, Gabe turned for one last glimpse of the houses where he'd spent the majority of his time from ages six to eighteen.

When he'd come back a week earlier, the sense of coming home had scared him.

He wasn't afraid of that feeling anymore. Not when his future had become so much scarier than his past.

Pulling out his phone, he snapped a quick picture of the houses. Then he got in the car and began the trip back to his real life.

Chapter 23

Through the living room window, Michelle saw Gabe get in a car and leave. He didn't come back over to say goodbye.

Some things never change, she thought bitterly.

After cleaning up in the bathroom, Michelle returned to the desk to wipe it down and right all the things she and Gabe had displaced during their frantic lovemaking. She collected all the pens from the floor, closed and stacked her notebooks, and repositioned her laptop back in the center of the desk.

The Pros and Cons list was ripped up and flushed down the toilet, never to be spoken of again.

Tapping the touch pad to wake up the laptop, she sat down and moved all the files related to the Agility campaign into their shared folder, then moved them off her laptop onto a USB stick, which she tossed in her dad's drawer.

Before she could talk herself out of it, she invoiced Agility. And added a 20 percent cancellation fee.

She'd just sent the email when she heard Ava's voice calling for her.

"Down here," Michelle yelled. She shut the laptop and went upstairs.

Ava was in the kitchen unloading cans of chickpeas from a canvas tote. Four bottles of wine already sat on the counter.

"Jasmine's on her way," Ava reported, putting the food processor together. "There's traffic, so it might take her a little while to get here from Brooklyn."

Michelle climbed onto one of the high chairs stationed at the counter. She didn't sit in them often, because her legs were just barely long enough to rest her feet on the rungs, but she wanted the comfort and familiarity of watching Ava in the kitchen.

Ava plugged the processor in, then grabbed the corkscrew and opened a bottle of red. She retrieved three glasses from the cabinet, poured wine into two, and pushed one across the counter to Michelle.

"Here. We can wait to talk until Jasmine gets here, if you want."

"Thanks. I don't want to go through it twice." Michelle raised the glass and took a sip.

"Oh, there was a package for you by the door." Ava handed Michelle a cardboard tube.

Michelle took it and glanced at the label. "Wow, this got here fast."

"What is it?"

Michelle didn't want to tell her. But she was trying to change, trying to let her cousins in.

Even if it meant they saw her for the sentimental sap she was.

"Right after we graduated, I made Gabe a photo collage of the two of us. A memento since I'd be away at school." She turned the tube over in her hands but didn't open it. "This weekend I got the idea to make a new one, using the photos we've taken here, to replace that one."

What a stupid, ridiculous idea. She'd made the collage on her phone during the drive back from the quinceañera, and ordered it on the spot. She hadn't expected it to get here so soon, yet here it was.

And Gabe was already gone.

Michelle passed the tube to Ava. "Throw it out."

"I want to see it."

Michelle shook her head. "I don't. Just toss it."

Ava sighed, but she put it in the recycling bin under the sink. Then she turned on some music and opened the cans of chickpeas to make hummus from scratch.

By the time Jasmine arrived, Ava had arranged a whole spread while Michelle sat at the counter drinking wine and singing along with K-pop songs. The coffee table was laden with hummus, pita chips, vegetable slices, and cubed cheese. And, of course, wine.

Michelle met Jasmine at the door with a full wineglass. Jasmine slipped out of her sandals, took the wine, then enfolded Michelle into a tight, one-armed hug.

"Stop," Michelle muttered. "I'm not ready to cry yet."

"Then we'd better get started." Jasmine sipped from her glass and headed into the living room.

The three of them sat on the floor around the coffee table and dug in.

"So, he's gone?" Jasmine asked, her tone hesitant, like she was worried about bringing up the subject of Gabe.

But he was why they were here, wasn't he? Once again, he'd left her, and her Primas of Power were putting the pieces back together.

"He left for the airport right before Ava got here." Michelle toyed with the stem of her wineglass, the pressure of all she was holding back building in her chest.

"And?" Ava prompted. "Did he say anything?"

"He said he might be selling the business."

Ava and Jasmine exchanged a glance.

"The gym?" Jasmine asked. "He's selling the gym? Why?"

Michelle shrugged. "He wouldn't talk to me about it. He just said he had to deal with this on his own, and he was leaving."

Ava's voice was gentle. "Did he say when he was coming back?"

"No. He's not coming back." And that had hurt more than his departure.

Ava gripped Michelle's arm. "Michelle," she said quietly. "Stop fighting it. Just talk to us."

Heartache threatened to overwhelm her. Michelle's immediate urge was to wrestle it down and lock it away so she could carry on like normal.

But where had that ever gotten her?

"I don't even know how," Michelle admitted in a dull voice. What was the harm in letting it out? Why was it so hard to let her cousins see her?

"Are you worried we're going to judge you?" Jasmine asked.

"Logically, I know that you won't." Michelle sighed. "And I know you've both gone through worse. In comparison, this is nothing."

Ava was divorced, and Jasmine's last breakup had become national news. It felt silly for Michelle to cry to them about Gabe leaving.

"It's not nothing to you," Ava murmured, and that quiet acknowledgment broke the dam on Michelle's need to hold back.

"It hurts," she whispered, staring into her wine. "A lot. I told myself I've been in this situation with him before, that I could handle it when he left, especially since I knew it was coming."

"It's different this time," Jasmine said, reaching out and rubbing Michelle's back. Of course Jasmine would understand.

"I didn't count on getting so close to him. On—" Michelle faltered, then spit it out. "On falling in love with him."

Because she had fallen for him. Not as the boy she'd known, but as the man he'd become. She *loved* him.

It was so much worse this time around.

"I asked him to stay," Michelle admitted hoarsely, and the pressure in her chest and throat finally moved up and spilled out of her eyes as tears. "I didn't last time. But this time, I did."

"And what did he say?" Ava prompted.

Michelle's answer came with a sob. "He said we aren't real."

Her cousins passed her tissues and hugged her as she cried, and while Michelle wanted more than anything to declare that she was fine and that they should stop fussing, she let them coddle her.

Because she wasn't fine. Her heart was breaking, and it felt like she would never recover.

But Jasmine and Ava had. And they were here with her now, supporting her. If nothing else, Michelle had her primas. And they would help her through this.

AFTER A LAYOVER in Denver and flight delays on both legs, Gabe crashed hard when he got back to his apartment in Venice. He was so tired, he couldn't even enjoy the feeling of being back in his own bed.

On the plus side, he was so tired he didn't have the energy to think about Michelle's absence at his side. If he had, he wouldn't have been able to sleep at all. After just three nights, he'd already gotten used to falling asleep with her soft curves pressed against him.

The next morning, he dragged himself up, showered and dressed, and hit a Starbucks drive-through on the way to Fabian's new house in Brentwood.

By some miracle, there was very little traffic, and Gabe arrived at Fabian's quickly. He showed up at the front door with a to-go carton of hot coffee and a box of pastries.

Fabian's sister Shirelle let Gabe in, greeting him warmly and taking the box of baked goods off his hands. Gabe followed her into the kitchen, where the whole Charles family seemed to be gathered around the long rectangular dining table.

"Coffee!" Fabian's wife, Iris, exclaimed when she saw Gabe.

Iris, a petite Black woman with medium-brown skin and a short dark bob, got up from the table and walked stiffly over to the counter. Gabe remembered she'd had a C-section just a few days before.

"Should you be . . . walking?" He felt weird asking that of his friend's wife, but he was a health professional. She was clearly moving like someone in pain, and her normally bright eyes seemed dull.

"I'm okay, but you're sweet to be concerned. Put it down here, Gabe. Fabian, get milk and sugar."

Gabe set down the carton and passed her one of the paper cups. She took it and sent him a grateful smile. "Bless you, Gabe. None of us got around to brewing a pot yet. As I'm sure you can imagine, things have been a little hectic around here."

"I bet. Where are the babies?"

Iris pointed to the tablet propped on the counter, which showed split-screen video footage of two little lumps in bassinets. "Sleeping," she said. "Both at the same time. Thank god."

Gabe filled cups while Fabian set out skim milk, oat milk, half-and-half, and a variety of sweeteners. While Fabian fixed cups for his wife and sister, Gabe took direction from Fabian's parents about how they liked their coffee and passed them their drinks, while also promising Mrs. Charles that he'd happily help her with rehab services after her leg healed. Then he and Fabian poured and doctored coffee for themselves.

"You're a lifesaver," Fabian said as he took the first sip from his own cup. "Thanks for thinking of this."

"I figured caffeine would be welcome." Gabe drank deep from his own cup, heavy on the oat milk, with a hint of granulated brown sugar. It tasted like perfection.

Fabian's tired eyes sharpened. "Since when do you drink coffee?"

"Since staying with people who treat café con leche like a lifestyle," Gabe muttered.

A squeal came from the tablet's speakers. On-screen, one of the lumps started moving.

Fabian and Iris both moved to go, but Shirelle waved them off. "I'll get her," she said. "You two chill."

Wincing, Iris sank back into her chair at the table. She sent Gabe and Fabian a meaningful look.

"Go," she said. "We'll be fine. You two have things to discuss."

Fabian snagged a croissant from the box on the table and gestured at Gabe with it. "Come on. Let's go talk in my office."

Fabian's home office was in the back of the house on the first floor. A few streaks of test paint had been dabbed on the walls, but the last Gabe had heard, Fabian had yet to decide what particular shade of eggshell he wanted. The ceiling fan was still in its box, and Fabian's new filing cabinets sat empty with the drawers open, while cardboard filing boxes rested on top of them. A rolled-up rug was propped in the corner, and framed baseball memorabilia leaned against the wall under the window. The desk was brand-new but otherwise looked like Fabian's desk at the gym—covered in piles of paper and sticky notes—with a framed photo from Fabian's wedding sitting on the only clear space.

Gabe's desk at home sat in the corner of the living room and had almost nothing on it. Being in Fabian's house like this, surrounded by his family, it was hard not to compare it to his own cold, spare apartment.

Especially after being back in his childhood home, and in Michelle's apartment. She lived alone, too, but her apartment was vibrant and full of life.

Maybe he would get a plant.

Fabian sat behind the desk and Gabe took a seat in one of the leather armchairs facing him.

They were quiet for a moment, before Fabian said, "So we're really doing this."

Gabe shrugged. "What choice do we have?"

"There's always a choice, Gabe." Fabian steepled his fingers under his chin. "If you wanted to keep the business, I could help you figure it out. It doesn't all have to go to Powell."

"You have enough on your plate," Gabe protested. "This is the easiest and cleanest course of action."

And besides, why not now? If Gabe had to take out loans or find other investors so he could buy Fabian out, who was to say he wouldn't find himself in this position again further down the line? And without as sweet a deal as Powell was offering.

"I don't want you to do this only because of me," Fabian argued. "I want you to want this too."

Gabe spread his hands. "What do you want me to say? That I want to sell? I don't. But this is too good an opportunity to pass up, and I'm not going to drag it out when you need to move on."

And the thought of running this business without Fabian was terrifying. They'd been a team from the beginning. He'd never have that bond with Powell.

Fabian grimaced. "This was your dream. I don't want to be the one who makes you give it up."

"You're not." Gabe thought about Michelle's presentation. "And anyway, I'm starting to realize that what the gym is now . . . is not what I envisioned."

Fabian nodded and looked uncomfortable. "I thought about that sometimes. But everything seemed to be going well, so I figured it was okay. And dude . . . I don't want you to think

I'm bringing this up to influence you or anything, but you've seemed kind of . . ."

"Kind of what? Just tell me."

Fabian shrugged. "Like utterly fucking miserable. For at least a year now. Definitely since you took on more admin duties."

Gabe folded his hands over his middle and leaned back in the chair.

"I fucking hate calendar alerts," he admitted. "And emails. And meetings."

Fabian huffed out a laugh. "I know you do. You've made it pretty fucking obvious."

But Gabe also hated the idea of giving up, of throwing away everything he'd worked for and being left with nothing.

Well, money. He'd have the money.

But it had never been about the money. It had been about building something with his name on it. It had been about creating a space where he could help people with his own two hands.

Not that the money was nothing. He remembered the way his parents had struggled and saved back when the four of them lived in a small two-bedroom apartment. His father had been so proud of being able to buy the house they lived in now.

At the time, Gabe had been six, and he'd put his foot down. He hadn't wanted to move, so he'd insisted he would stay behind in their old apartment. His father had imparted the lesson he would then go on to repeat multiple times over the years.

You need family. No one makes it alone.

Gabe had set out at eighteen to prove him wrong. To prove he could do it himself, without his family. Here in Fabian's house, surrounded by his parents, his sister, his wife, and his two babies, it was hard not to see the truth of those words. Gabe was still sure he didn't want to be a father, and he wasn't sold on the institution of marriage. But companionship? A partner to stand by your side? The support of your community, whether it was biological or found family? He was starting to see the value of those things.

He was about to make the hardest, biggest decision of his adult life, and he didn't have anyone to discuss it with. There was Fabian, but Fabian was part of the decision. Gabe imagined Fabian had discussed it at length with Iris, who, in addition to being his wife, was a big-time Hollywood lawyer. He'd probably talked about it with his parents, too, and maybe even his younger sister.

Hell, Michelle had all but begged Gabe to talk about it with her, and he'd shut her out. He hadn't wanted to admit his failures, his doubts. Hadn't wanted to speak them out loud, to show her that side of him.

Michelle, who had seen him and his business more clearly than he had himself. She'd cut right to the heart of Agility. And he still hadn't let her in, insisting he had to make this choice alone.

But he was fooling himself. He'd traded his father for Powell, letting someone else roll over him and sway his decisions. So long as Powell was involved, Agility would never truly be his.

When Gabe had been younger and his father's store was failing, Esteban had refused to see the writing on the wall, sure that if they all just worked harder, it would pan out. His drive had stifled Gabe's own dreams, until the only recourse had been to leave. Gabe had tried talking to his parents about his future, and they'd shut him down. They needed him at the store, they said. Family worked together. No one could do it alone.

He'd been determined to prove them wrong. And now look where he was.

"How was it in New York?" Fabian asked, breaking into his thoughts. "With your dad and your girl."

Gabe shook his head. "She's not my girl."

The words felt wrong to him. Some part of Michelle belonged to him, just as part of him would always belong to her. Not in some weird possessive way, but in a way formed by entwined life experiences. Twelve years' worth of childhood memories weren't nothing. And now, he had a week's worth that had shown him how his life could have been if things had been different. If he hadn't made the choices he had.

But things weren't different. They had their own lives, far apart from each other, and his was in such disarray, he couldn't conceive of dragging Michelle any further into this mess.

"Not your girl, huh?" Fabian raised an eyebrow. "That's not how it looked in that video."

Gabe's gaze snapped to him. "What video?"

"I fell down an Instagram rabbit hole one night at the hospital. Trying to keep my mind off worrying, you know? Anyway, I saw a video of the two of you dancing. Here, I saved it and meant to send it to you with some shit-talking, but I forgot."

"Dancing?"

Fabian pulled out his phone and Gabe got up to look over his shoulder as his friend scrolled through countless pictures of swaddled bundles.

"Are those the twins?" Gabe asked.

"Yeah, aren't they perfect?"

Fabian tapped on a picture of the twins immediately after birth, which Gabe could have done without, but he just said, "They're beautiful. Can't wait to see them when they're awake."

"Heads up, Iris is going to ask you to be the godfather."

"No shit?" Gabe rocked back on his heels, stunned by the honor they were bestowing on him. "I—yeah. Of course. Wait, what do you mean by that, exactly? My own godfather would have been my legal guardian if something happened to my parents."

Fabian frowned at the phone as he continued scrolling. "Not like that—our families would fight you for custody, and I know you don't want kids. Just like a special uncle-type person."

This conversation had taken a completely unexpected turn and Gabe didn't know how to keep up. "Good. I mean, yeah, I'd be happy to be a tío to them."

"Make sure you act surprised when Iris brings it up. Ah, here it is." With a note of triumph, Fabian held up the phone and hit play. A shaky video showed Gabe dancing bachata with Michelle, their bodies glued together and their hips swaying and thrusting in a way that was inappropriate for even a Latinx family birthday party.

Gabe grabbed the phone and replayed the video again. And again. And again.

Shit, no wonder their families had been so obnoxious at the barbecue. He might as well have gotten down on one knee and proposed in the middle of the damned dance floor. That dance was a *declaration*.

He played it again. They looked so fucking good together. They *were* so fucking good together. She saw him in a way no one else ever had or probably would.

His heart hurt at being away from her. But he had a business to sell, and next steps to figure out.

What the hell was he going to do with the rest of his life?

"You sure she's not your girl?" Fabian asked mildly.

Gabe texted the video to himself. "I'm sure."

"Whatever you say, dude." Fabian took his phone back. "Now, about the gym . . ."

With a heavy exhale, Gabe threw up his hands. "Fuck it. Let's sell."

His friend gave him a long look, then nodded. "All right, I believe you."

"Believe me? About what?"

"That you want to sell. You didn't think I'd let you do it unless you really wanted to, did you?"

"I . . . I don't know." Gabe narrowed his eyes. "How come you believe me now?"

"Because I think you're finally starting to realize that the gym isn't the only thing of value in your life. Hold on, they're here somewhere." Fabian sifted through some papers, found the folder he was looking for, and held it up. "Here we go."

"What's that?"

"The papers detailing the sale."

Gabe swallowed. "This is moving faster than I expected."

"Did you see my kitchen? There are seven people in my house and I'm the only one who can work right now. I had our lawyer on this as soon as Powell emailed me, just in case. Was just waiting on you to decide if you were in or out."

Fabian stood and handed Gabe the folder.

"Take this. Read the whole thing. Call me or our lawyer with any questions, or anything you want to add or take out. We're only doing this if you're okay with it, and if you're not, we'll go back to the drawing board. Okay?"

"Okay."

"Good. Now let me introduce you to my kids."

And just like that, the ball was rolling.

Thirteen years ago

Celestial Destiny: Episode 12 Planning Session

Michelle:

> Okay, they've escaped, but before they go they have to retrieve the MacGuffin for Queen Seravida and destroy it.

Gabe:

> I've been thinking about this . . .

Michelle:

> Oh yeah?

Gabe:

> What if this thing the queen wanted them to destroy is something else? What if she had a secret agenda all this time, and she was using Zack?

Michelle:

> Omg what a twist. She lied to her own son?

Gabe:

> She already lied to him when she faked her own death and left him to fend for himself.

Michelle:

> Poor Zack. This is going to break him. His dad is using him for power, and his mom is using him for . . . what exactly?

Gabe:

> Zack and Riva showed up at the end of Beyond the Stars with this device that would remove everyone's powers, to level the playing field and bring stability to the galaxy. What if that's the MacGuffin the queen sent them to destroy?

Michelle:

> But in this episode they figure out it's not what they thought it was.

Gabe:

> So they go to confront Zack's mother.

Michelle:

> After hiding the device, because they might need it later.

Gabe:

> Right. And Zack gives up the mission.

Michelle:

> But there's still more work to be done.

Gabe:

> Doesn't matter. He's been betrayed and used. He thought there was a greater reason for why his life and his parents sucked, but there isn't. Some people are just horrible.

Michelle:

> That's a bleak outlook.

Gabe:

> Power corrupts. And Zack doesn't want any part of his family's power plays anymore. He's out.

Chapter 24

Late the next day, Michelle woke slightly hungover in her mom's craft room. Ava and Jasmine had spent the night, and they'd shared the bed in what Michelle now thought of as "Gabe's room."

That was stupid, though. It was the guest room. He'd been a guest and he'd stayed in the guest room and now he was gone. It was still just the guest room.

Jezebel was draped over Michelle's shoulder like a living feather boa, emitting soft kitty snores. Because Michelle wanted to cry, she pressed her face into Jezebel's fur. The cat purred, then stretched and rolled over. She climbed onto Michelle's belly and started making biscuits.

Michelle's chest rumbled with a laugh as she shifted away. "Jez, that tickles."

The cat curled up in the warm sheets and closed her eyes, still purring.

Michelle gave her ears a scratch. "At least I still have you, mamita."

Even though she felt a little unsteady, she climbed out of bed. After a visit to the bathroom, she forced herself to go downstairs.

Ava and Jasmine were already in the kitchen. The second

Michelle entered the room, Ava popped up from where she and Jasmine sat at the table drinking coffee.

"I'll make you tea," Ava said. "Have a seat."

Michelle sank into the chair next to Jasmine and groaned. "I feel like I've been hit by a bus."

Jasmine passed her the mug. "Have some. It'll help."

"Thanks." Michelle took a sip and closed her eyes, savoring the taste of rich, dark coffee. It was strong, the way Jasmine liked it. She passed the mug back. "You let me sleep late."

"We figured you needed it," Jasmine said. "Your dad is downstairs playing video games and your mom is out shopping with my mom."

"Any word from Gabe?" Ava asked.

Michelle shook her head. She didn't expect to hear from him. He'd gone back to his life in California, and she suspected he was going to do whatever it took to pretend there weren't people in New York who loved him.

She had, however, heard from the contractor, who'd texted to say her bathroom was all finished.

Michelle drummed her fingers on the table. "I'm going back to my apartment today."

Ava looked up from the counter, alarm written on her features. "You are?"

"Relax, Ava. I'll be fine."

She didn't feel fine, but she would be. She always was.

Michelle thanked her cousins and sent them on their way. She packed up everything she'd brought with her, coaxed Jezebel into her carrier, and waited until her mom got home before saying goodbye to her parents. She'd told them the night before that Gabe had a work emergency and had gone back to California, then did her best to brush aside her mother's follow-up questions. Her dad, bless him, must have noticed there was something wrong, because he changed the subject.

And then there was nothing to do but leave. Her dad helped her carry everything out to her car and got Jezebel settled in. The cat was meowing, so Dominic passed her a treat through the wire door. Michelle finished arranging bags of groceries in the trunk and slammed it shut.

"Everything okay, Michie?" her dad asked.

She sighed. Her dad was far more perceptive than he let on. "No, Daddy. But it will be."

He gave her a big hug and kissed the top of her head. "Let me know if you want me to . . ."

"Dad, don't be a stereotype," she warned.

"What? I was gonna say, let me know if you want me to leave bad Yelp reviews for his gym."

It made her laugh, which she guessed had been his intention. "I'll see you for dinner next week."

He patted her shoulder, then went back into the house.

Michelle opened the driver's door and slid behind the wheel. Before she started the car, she stared for a long moment at Gabe's parents' house. Part of her felt like she should go say goodbye to Norma and Esteban. But if she went inside, she'd start crying, and Norma would probably start crying, too, and then it would just be a whole big mess. Michelle didn't know how Gabe had left things with his parents, didn't know what he'd told them about her, and honestly, she didn't want to know.

She just wanted to go home.

After firing up her K-pop girl groups playlist, she hit the road. She'd beaten rush hour, so she reached Hell's Kitchen in less than forty-five minutes. It took a few trips around the block before she found a spot near her building, then she started the process of bringing everything inside.

She hauled Jezebel up the stairs first and left her in the carrier with the apartment door propped open while she went back to the car. Jezebel was meowing her head off by the time Michelle had retrieved the last of the groceries. Jezebel was normally a quiet kitty, but she didn't like being left alone in her carrier for long stretches of time.

"Chill out, Jez," Michelle muttered as she locked the apartment door behind her. "I put the air-conditioning on for you, didn't I?"

Jezebel yeowled in response.

Michelle bent to the carrier and released the beast. Jezebel leaped out and began a curious circuit of the apartment, smelling everything.

Michelle stood for a minute watching her.

"It's just you and me again, Jez." Then she hung her keys on the hook and toed off her sneakers.

She'd gotten her life back, just as it was before. No more staying at her parents' house. No more marketing projects.

No more Gabe.

She felt shaky, like her insides were trembling, and it had nothing to do with the wine she'd consumed the night before. Because she wanted to break down and cry in her bed, she forced herself to get to work. There were groceries to put away, plants to water, a cat to feed.

And if she went into her bedroom, she'd be inundated by memories of him. Of his adorable striptease. Of him fucking her against the forest wallpaper.

Why is everything ten times better with you?

Screw it. She was sleeping on the sofa tonight.

GABE SAT ON his couch, reading through the papers that would take his company away from him. These were the preliminary steps, he could see. There was room for his own negotiations and requests. And Fabian had already included a lot of the things Gabe would have asked for—for example, being able to use some form of the word *agility* in the future, since they'd chosen it because of the similarity to Aguilar.

As the original owners, they'd have lifetime access to the Santa Monica gym and any New York City locations that were opened, but since Powell planned to franchise the name, they wouldn't be granted memberships at locations owned by other people.

And so on, and so on. An incredible number of tiny details, all of which Gabe was expected to weigh in on.

Coupled with that was the guilt of ignoring the daily operations at the gym. Fabian had left it in Charisse's capable hands, but Gabe felt bad about having been gone for more days than he'd planned, and now that he was back, he was sitting at home planning to sell it.

Gabe made a few notes about what sort of packages would be given to employees who chose to leave. He wanted all of them taken care of, the ones who left and those who chose to stay. Treating his employees well was something he'd been adamant about as owner, and he didn't want that to end.

When he felt like his eyes would cross if he looked at one more clause, he set the papers aside and stretched out on the sofa. Maybe it was jet lag, maybe it was the lower-quality workouts he'd managed while in the Bronx, but his body felt heavy and sluggish. Likewise, his brain felt dull and distracted, his thoughts pinballing around with no sense of direction.

He'd kept his phone on silent, and when he checked the time, he saw he had a missed call from his parents and a few texts from his sister. He stared at the notifications for a moment, then set the phone down without opening the messages. While he could no longer get away with avoiding his family forever, he couldn't face them right now. They'd ask about what was happening with the business, or worse, with Michelle. He didn't want to tell them about selling the gym, and he didn't know what to tell them about Mich.

If Fabian hadn't emailed her, they never would have found each other again. Gabe would have continued on with his life, never knowing how good things could be with Michelle.

Never knowing how easily he could fall in love with her again.

All the things he'd once dreamed about, and told himself were simply the musings of a youthful crush, he now had specific memories for. The way she sighed his name. The way her breathing changed when she fell asleep. The way she stress-cleaned and how she preferred her tea. Along with countless other little details he hadn't known, despite half a lifetime of friendship.

He couldn't believe he'd gotten her involved in the expansion, only to drop it after she'd put so much work into it. He felt bad about that too. It was embarrassing, and added yet another layer to his feelings of failure.

So many hours, days, *years* of his life had been funneled into the gym. Who was he without it?

He didn't know the answer yet, and until he figured it out, he wasn't fit to even think about next steps with Michelle either.

Selling the gym felt like a loss, like a death. Like someone close to him had passed, or like a piece of him was dying. It was going to take time to get used to his life without Agility in it.

Yes, he still had his degree in physical therapy. He had the experience of running his own business. Those couldn't be taken away from him. Yet the thought of going to work for someone else felt like a step down from where he'd been. He could do it, but it wouldn't feel as fulfilling.

He picked up one of the many sheets of paper in front of him, then put it back down. He already knew he was going to sell. And while he still had a few more questions and negotiations to work out, right now, he needed a break from it.

Dragging his laptop across the sofa to him, Gabe opened it and hovered the mouse over his email icon, out of habit.

No, he didn't want to do that either.

Looking around his apartment, there wasn't a single thing he *did* want to do.

He didn't want to call his parents or sister back just yet. He didn't want to talk to Fabian. He didn't want to get caught up in the endless loop of social media. He didn't want to watch TV or exercise. What did other people do with free time? He wasn't used to having it.

Gabe squinted at the titles of the small pile of books stacked on the shelf above his desk. He didn't keep many physical copies of books on hand—part of his mission to cut back on clutter—and there wasn't anything he particularly wanted to read. Besides, he suspected if he sat around reading or watching ScreenFlix, he'd feel guilty about wasting time.

But really, when had he last had time to waste? Before going to the Bronx, his only downtime was his workouts, which he did at a friend's gym because he needed a break from being in his own.

Gabe thought of the hours he and Michelle had spent wandering the Bronx Zoo, of petting Jezebel in the mornings—and petting Michelle at night. The time he'd spent with Michelle, he'd been fully present and in the moment, for once not thinking at all about work.

Aside from when they'd collaborated on the campaign for Agility. And at those points, his brain had gotten squirrelly because what she was showing him about his intention for the gym didn't match what he had.

He thought about the night they'd spent in the Hudson Valley. It had been one of the most stunning and revelatory of his life. For one night, he'd gotten a taste of everything he could have with Michelle.

And he wanted it. He just didn't know how to go after it. He hadn't known how to fit her into his life as it had been, and now that life was falling apart. He had nothing to offer. His sense of self-worth had come from the gym, and without it . . . he was worthless.

Memories of the king-size bed they'd shared reminded him of the "only one sleeping bag" chapter of *Celestial Destiny*, the one Michelle had mentioned when they'd been lying beside each other. Since his laptop was open, Gabe began a search for the thirteen-year-old files. They had to be somewhere—he wouldn't have deleted them—but he hadn't looked for them in years and damned if he could remember what he would have named them.

After a few minutes of frustrated searching, he found them in a folder labeled "G and M Story." Past Gabe sure hadn't wanted to make it easy for Future Gabe to find. He copied the folder to his desktop and renamed it "Celestial Destiny," which was what he should have called it in the first place. Inside, there were saved copies of each chapter, along with copy-pasted messenger chats detailing their brainstorming process for each "episode," as they'd called them. He'd even saved screenshots of reader comments.

Gabe opened the first chapter and read the heading and disclaimer, which hit him with a wave of nostalgia.

Celestial Destiny: A Beyond the Stars Season 2 Fanfic
Episode 1
By BxGamer15 and ChelleBlockTango

Disclaimer: We don't own the rights to Beyond the Stars, we're just two fans who are mad that we finally got Latinos in spaaaaace but they were canceled after one season.

He'd written it based on other fanfic disclaimers he'd read at the time. In the back of his mind, he'd worried that the studio who'd made *Beyond the Stars* would sue them.

He remembered the day he and Michelle had decided to write this. How full of hope and possibility he'd been. How much closer it had brought them, an activity full of inside jokes only shared between the two of them.

Except they'd never written the end. Just one more bit of unfinished business between them.

Gabe's eyes traveled down the screen and over the first few lines.

Zack was working his shift at the Gardaron Port cantina when someone he didn't recognize walked in.

Gabe smiled for the first time since Fabian's phone call the day before, and settled in to read.

Celestial Destiny

A Beyond the Stars Season 2 Fanfic

Episode 1

By BxGamer15 and ChelleBlockTango

Disclaimer: We don't own the rights to Beyond the Stars, we're just two fans who are mad that we finally got Latinos in spaaaaace but they were canceled after one season.

Zack was working his shift at the Gardaron Port cantina when someone he didn't recognize walked in.

This wasn't unusual. Planet Gardaron was a tiny outpost on the Outer Rim, but everyone who landed here went through the port. Zack was used to strangers at the cantina. In fact, it was one of the reasons he'd come here. Gardaron Port was an easy place to disappear.

So it wasn't strange that Zack didn't recognize this person. What was strange was that he felt like he should.

He kept wiping the bar as he watched them approach from the corner of his eye. There was something about their height, the way they walked, that pinged his memory, but he couldn't place them. So he waited for them to reach the bar before he lifted his head.

"What'll you have?" he asked.

The person wore a dark visor over their eyes and a cloth mask over their nose and mouth. Their head was wrapped in a scarf. He thought they might be human, but couldn't be sure. All Zack knew was that his instincts were on high alert.

"A Vika cooler," the person replied, their voice slightly muffled.

Were his ears playing tricks on him, or was the voice familiar? Zack just nodded and moved down the bar to retrieve a chilled glass. As he got it, he slipped his go bag onto a crate that needed to be put in the storeroom. Then he poured citrus fizz and a splash of Vika liquor into the glass and passed it to the familiar stranger.

"Any idea how long the Gardarian mechanics take?" the stranger asked. "The ones closest to the port."

"Not long," Zack replied. "But you'll want to check all your diagnostics before you take off. They're notorious for unfinished business."

"I know all about unfinished business," the person muttered, and slapped some credits on the bar. They were Salazarin coins. Those plus the scar on the back of her—he knew it was her now—hand told Zack all he needed to know. He scooped up the credits, tossed them into the register. Ignoring the group of Remyrian traders at the end of the bar trying to get his attention, Zack hefted the crate—and his go bag—and headed for the back room.

As soon as he was out of sight of the bar, he ditched the crate, strapped on his backpack, and slipped on his own mask. The air quality on this planet wasn't great, plus the mask helped disguise his identity. Pulling his hood over his head to cover his hair, which he'd let grow long while in hiding, he ducked out the back door and took off at a run.

Halfway down the alley behind the cantina, a stun shot hit the wall beside his head and he veered off to the side. A quick glance over his shoulder told him what he already suspected: she was following him.

"Stop running away!" she shouted after him.

"Not a chance in Volcanor," he muttered behind his mask, and ran harder. If he could just make it to the port's main hub, he could catch a ride on the next ship—any ship—off planet. And then he'd find somewhere else to hide.

A shame, really. He was finally getting used to Gardaron.

He was almost there when someone turned a corner and crashed into him like a rampaging trihorn, taking him to the ground. They fell in a writhing tangle of limbs and Zack, though bigger and expertly trained by the finest soldiers in the Salazarin army, soon found himself facedown on the dusty ground with a stunner pressed to his throat.

His attacker spoke. "I could stun you, but then I'd have to drag your heavy ass back to my ship, and I'd rather not do that."

Zack sucked in a breath, the mask sticking to his face. "I knew it would be you."

She hesitated before asking softly, "How?"

Part of me has always been waiting for you, he thought. But he didn't say that.

Instead, he hardened his voice. "Tell my father I'm never going back."

"I would, but it was your mother who hired me."

"My mother?" Shock mixed with fear, betrayal, and something close to happiness. Heedless of the stunner, Zack rolled over to look his old friend in the face. "She's alive?"

She pushed the visor up on her forehead, revealing the amber-colored eyes that would've given away her identity immediately. Dark wisps of hair were visible at her temples, and despite the mask, his brain filled in the remaining details of the face he'd known so well. A mouth that was made for smirking and smiling, a nose she turned up at him when he was being an ass, despite his higher status.

"Riva . . ." he whispered, reaching for her.

A jolt of electricity tore through him, scrambling his thoughts and stealing his consciousness.

She'd stunned him.

Chapter 25

Michelle did what she always did after emotional upheaval. She flirted with burnout.

There was regular client work, and a few other inquiries had come in while she was with Gabe. She accepted everything and overloaded her schedule, which gave her the perfect excuse to turn her cousins down when they tried to get her to leave her apartment.

Except, this time, work wasn't cutting it. Simple layout designs and social media graphics weren't providing the kind of challenge she needed to make her stop thinking about Gabe. They filled the hours, but not her thoughts.

Not only that, Michelle was sad to let the Agility project go. She'd enjoyed working on it, flexing those muscles that she hadn't used since quitting her job. While she'd drummed up enough freelance work to pay her bills and keep herself busy, she'd stuck to simpler projects that didn't require a ton of input or creativity from her, mostly just moving text and pictures around on the screen. It had been a while since she'd led a project, doing all the research and ideation, formulating a plan, and she'd missed it. She'd been looking forward to the rebrand, too, and had put together a whole package for Gabe to take back to his team.

She'd started drafting at least twenty emails to him, and twice as many text messages, but she'd deleted them all before sending. The bedroom was still off-limits, so she'd been sleeping on the sofa since returning home. It was mostly fine, but her pillow had fallen on the floor the previous night and she hadn't noticed, so she'd woken that morning with a vicious crick in her neck. Yoga had helped a little, but not enough, especially since she'd been spending so much time sitting at her desk. She'd been thinking about installing a standing desk—or rather, having her dad install it—but she had twelve browser tabs open for different desk options and hadn't gotten around to ordering one yet.

In short, she was a mess.

Michelle was sending final image files to Jamilette, a regular client who owned a Dominican hair salon uptown, when a new email landed in her inbox, from one Rocky Lim.

Her heart beat double time when she saw the name, and for a second she was sure Rocky was reaching out to her on Gabe's behalf. But the subject line read "Marketing project," so that seemed unlikely.

Still, her throat was tight when she clicked on the email to open it.

After skimming the details, she relaxed. Rocky had been impressed with her after their meeting, and he was wondering if she'd take him on as a client to help him launch a men's cologne.

Michelle jotted down ideas in her notebook as she read through the email again, her mind already whirling. Opening a new browser tab, she took a quick look at other fragrance campaigns to see which stood out to her, and which were blah. She looked at Rocky's website, reading over his bio and film credits, then checked out his Instagram. He had a huge following on there, and a ton of modeling shots for other brands and publications. It made sense for him to come out with his own product.

Two hours later, her eyes were glazing over, and she realized she hadn't gotten up to eat, drink water, or go to the bathroom at all during that time. Glancing down at her notebook, she flipped through the notes and sketches she'd jotted down, and was amazed to see she'd filled six pages.

Wow. She hadn't even felt the time passing. Her mind had been fully engaged by researching and brainstorming a project she wasn't even officially attached to yet.

She dashed off a reply to Rocky, letting him know her availability so they could set up a call. Then she closed her laptop and got up to stretch, feeling better than she had in days.

As she took care of basic needs—using her brand-new bathroom, drinking a large glass of water, and eating what was left of her chicken shawarma pita from the night before—she thought about how differently she'd responded to Rocky's email compared to her current workload. Rocky was asking for the same kind of work she'd done for Gabe, and she could no longer ignore how much she'd enjoyed working on Gabe's project, and how much more fulfilled she felt when she was engaging those creative parts of her brain.

The truth was, she wasn't content to do basic layout design for the rest of her life. She wanted to get all up in a project, from the beginning stages to the final steps. She wanted her fingerprints all over it and the freedom to make decisions, instead of the graphic design equivalent of busywork.

When she returned to her desk, she opened up the back end of her own website. On a whim, she changed the copy on the "Services" page, expanding it to include branding and marketing packages, and raising the prices. Then she registered a new domain name and an LLC, rewrote her bio, redesigned the website layout, and sketched out a new logo.

By the end of the day, Jezebel Creative Solutions was live.

Michelle glanced at the time. Shit, she had to get moving. But there was one more thing to do.

She drafted a quick email to all of her clients, notifying them that she was getting back into the marketing and branding game, and linking the new "Services" page. And she offered a 15 percent discount for those who contracted with her in the first month.

After she sent the email, she sat back in her chair and just stared at the screen.

She'd done it. After almost two years in limbo as a freelancer, she'd taken the step to officially start her own business and get back to the work she loved doing.

And it was all thanks to Gabe.

Beyond spending time with him, she'd enjoyed the work. It had made her feel more like herself than she had in a long time, and not just because Gabe was there, reminding her of who she used to be. It was something clients like Jamilette had begged her to do, but she'd resisted, packing that part of herself away because it had reminded her of Nathaniel's betrayal and brought up the fear of burning out again.

But who was she really punishing here? Not Nathaniel, who probably never spared her a second thought.

Not her old bosses, who didn't give a shit if she had good work-life balance or not.

Only herself.

And wasn't it time she stopped doing that?

Jezebel Creative Solutions was the first step. The next step was right behind a door at the end of her hall.

It was also time she stopped sleeping on the sofa.

Yes, the bedroom reminded her of Gabe. Yes, it hurt that he'd left. Yes, she'd asked him to stay, and he hadn't.

But at least this time, she'd asked for what she wanted. She hadn't let anger get the better of her, making her say things she later regretted. As much as it pained her to think of him, she didn't regret opening up. Those days with him had been the most emotionally satisfying of her life. She'd allowed herself to be vulnerable. To be seen. To ask for what she wanted. How many people never felt that in their whole lives?

She'd once been one of those people. And now that she'd felt it, she'd always know.

She deserved better. And she would survive, no matter what.

After a quick shower, Michelle did a light cleaning pass over the apartment before Ava arrived, so it didn't look like the home of someone in the throes of heartbreak.

When Michelle had canceled on family dinner with her parents, her mom had texted Ava, pinging her Primas of Power radar. Like the Capricorn she was, Ava had sent a firm *I'm coming over and making you dinner* text. Jasmine was in Los Angeles doing a press junket, or else she'd be showing up at Michelle's door tonight too.

When Ava arrived, Michelle had spread out light appetizers and wine on the coffee table, and put all her bedding from the sofa back in the closet. No one needed to know about that part.

They sat on the sofa with Jezebel between them, and Michelle showed her cousin the new website.

"This is amazing, Mich," Ava exclaimed. "You did all this today?"

Michelle nodded. "Getting that email from Rocky lit a fire under me. This is really what I've wanted to do all this time."

She'd just been scared to take the leap. For all this time, she'd been doing something she was *good* at, instead of what she was *great* at.

Ava clicked the "About" page and even though Michelle had written it, she read her new bio over Ava's shoulder.

Located in the backyard of New York City's Theater District, Jezebel Creative Solutions brings drama, excitement, and flare to our clients' strategies and visuals. Founded by Michelle Amato, an award-winning marketing and branding consultant, we offer out-of-the-box campaign solutions to corporate clients and small businesses alike, to help you turn ideas into reality and dreams into success.

After Ava finished reading, she passed the laptop back to Michelle and reached for her shoulder bag.

"I think it's the right time to give you this," Ava said, pulling out a cardboard tube.

Michelle took the tube and examined the label. "This is the collage. I told you to throw it out."

Ava's smile was smug. "And I didn't. Because I knew at some point, you'd be ready to see it. I think you're ready now."

Grumbling, Michelle used the cheese knife to slice the packing tape at the end of the tube. Opening it, she reached in and gently pulled out the rolled sheet of photo paper. Her heart twisted when she looked at it, but a smile tugged at her lips.

She'd compiled photos of herself and Gabe from their visit to the Bronx Zoo, their day in Manhattan, the shopping trip, and the quinceañera, combining them with a few old photos from their childhood and high school years. There was a Halloween picture from the year Gabe had dressed as a Jedi and Michelle had been a vampire. Another from Michelle's thirteenth birthday party, when they'd gone to Jones Beach. Gabe in his baseball uniform and Michelle in a school play, the two of them sitting on the steps of her house and playing on the swings in his backyard, the first day of middle school and their high school graduation.

Across the bottom, in bold script, it read:

Part of me will always be waiting for you.

"What do you want to do with it?" Ava asked.

Michelle didn't answer. Instead, she grabbed her phone and sent a text message.

> **Michelle:** I need his mailing address.

Chapter 26

Gabe read over the page he'd just written. Was it picking up the story threads well enough? Fuck, he couldn't tell. His eyes were bleary and he couldn't remember the last time he'd eaten something. Or showered.

He'd been working on the fanfic all week, ever since he'd signed the papers turning the gym over to Powell. It was all up to the lawyers and the financial folks now, but Gabe suddenly found himself in possession of a lot of money and a lot of free time.

Having never been in this position before, he hadn't known what to do with himself. So he'd turned to the only thing that had brought him joy during this darkest of times.

Celestial Destiny.

It was a little ridiculous how happy rereading the fanfic had made him. It had lifted his spirits, bringing him back to a time and place where the possibilities had felt endless, where he'd indulged in his creative whims and controlled the fates of characters he'd grown to adore. And most of all, it reminded him of Michelle. Of the story decisions they'd made together. Of the drawings she'd made of their characters—some of which still lived on his hard drive. Of the hours they'd spent talking about

Beyond the Stars, theorizing about what could have been going on behind the scenes in the space kingdom so they could bring it to life in the pages of their shared story.

It had been a simpler time, and the memories brought him a sense of contentment and optimism he never could have predicted.

He really loved this silly story.

Reading over it now was a trip. For one thing, he had some writing tics that made him smile and shake his head every time he saw them, like a tendency to overuse the words *suddenly* and *shrugged*. Some things he didn't even remember writing, and he mumbled, "Who wrote this?" more times than he could count.

But the biggest surprise was . . . himself. He'd written himself into the character of Zack in a way that was glaringly obvious, and as a result, reading the story was like opening a time capsule and finding Teenage Gabe.

Zack Salazar, a Latinx space prince with telekinetic powers and major family baggage, was slow to trust and second-guessed himself and others constantly. He went through periods of extreme caution before throwing it all to the wind in an impulsive act fueled by emotions. And he had been head over heels in love with Michelle's character, Riva.

Riva, as Gabe had written her, was daring and smart, brave and beautiful, and far too cool for Zack. She was, in essence, how Gabe had always seen Michelle.

It was while reading episode 9, the one where Zack and Riva kissed, that Gabe had realized the truth. Michelle was the love of his life, and she always would be.

Which meant he had once again tossed aside something most people only dreamed of.

After finishing his *Celestial Destiny* read-through, he'd gotten his shit together to sell the business. One step in front of the other, Gabe had worked with Fabian, Powell, and a team of lawyers. It had gone smoothly. They'd broken the news to the employees and gym members. Shortly after, Rocky Lim had texted, saying he was sorry to see Gabe leave Agility, but he hoped to hire him for one-on-one sessions if Gabe was willing to take on private clients. Gabe said he was open to the idea but needed to think about it, only to get a number of similar messages over the next few days from other clients, both famous and not.

If he wanted it, the next phase of his business was there. But right now, he still needed to come to terms with closing out this chapter of his life. Needed to let himself mourn the loss, even though he could now see it was the best decision all around. The thing he'd loved the most had been choking him. And while he'd never thought of ending it this way, he was free now. He just needed to figure out what to do with that freedom.

The first thing he'd done was paste *Celestial Destiny* into a new document. Then he'd started revising it from the beginning, fixing typos and clunky sentences, filling in details and beefing up story lines that had gotten dropped. It was hard work, employing skills he hadn't used in what felt like a million years. He went for long runs on the beach when he needed to think out a plot problem, something he hadn't had time to do in ages. The repetitive, methodical act of running gave his brain the space to

problem-solve, and in the process, it crunched the experiences
of the past few weeks.

New York.

Michelle.

His parents.

Powell.

Inside, Gabe felt like he was healing a wound he hadn't even
known he bore.

And then he'd set out to write the final chapters of *Celestial
Destiny.*

Back in the day, he and Michelle had discussed how it would
end, and he still had some notes from their chats. But after
reading over everything, he had a few new ideas that eighteen-
year-old Gabe never could have dreamed of.

Teenage Gabe had felt like the whole world, or at least his
parents, was against him. That he'd had to fight alone to get
what he wanted. That he had to cut out the naysayers before
they drowned him in doubt.

He hadn't seen that he'd internalized that doubt and made
it his own, carrying it with him wherever he went, allowing it
to run his life.

And wasn't that a kick in the ass.

Wasn't it time he started *really* believing in himself?

The sound of someone knocking on his door pulled Gabe
from his reverie. He looked around like he was coming out of
a trance. There were mugs on his desk, dishes on the coffee table, and a pile of running sneakers in a heap by the front door.
His usually spotless apartment was, by his standards, a mess. And

since he'd been home, he'd postponed the cleaning service that stopped by once a week.

The knocking continued. Who the hell could it be? It was—he glanced at his laptop screen—three in the afternoon on a Wednesday. And his apartment had a buzzer.

"Who is it?" Gabe yelled.

"You need to sign for a package," a muffled voice said from the hallway.

Oh for—fine. Gabe couldn't even imagine what he'd ordered, but the last few days had been a blur.

"Be right there," he called.

Grumbling, Gabe gulped down the last of the cold coffee in his most recent mug—the caffeine habit was back in full swing—and swiped a hand through his hair. He hadn't styled it, so his loose curl pattern was unrestrained, and he hadn't trimmed his beard since—shit, since he'd returned from the Bronx.

He was wearing only a pair of basketball shorts, so he grabbed a tank top from the arm of the couch and threw it on, shuffling to the door in his socks and chanclas.

He swung the door open and froze.

His parents beamed at him from the hallway.

"Surprise!" his mother yelled, throwing up her arms.

"Yeah." Gabe blinked at them. He was sure the hell surprised. "Uh, come on in."

His mom took his face in her hands and kissed his cheek, then wrinkled her nose. "Gabriel, ¿qué pasó?"

His father gave him a one-armed hug on the way in. "¿Estabas durmiendo?" he asked.

"No, I wasn't sleeping, I was"—*Writing fanfiction*—"working. On my computer."

He closed the door behind them and watched in a speechless stupor as his mother parked her suitcase by the entrance to the kitchen, then walked around picking up dirty dishes. She tsked and muttered, "Qué sucio," when she saw all the cups on his desk.

Gabe hunched his shoulders. It was the kind of thing that would've gotten him grounded as a kid.

"What . . . what are you two doing here?" he asked, since neither of them had explained why they were in California—in his *apartment*—yet.

"We came to visit you," his father said, as if it were a perfectly obvious and natural thing for them to do. "We have things to talk about, and you were taking too long."

"How—"

"Nikki gave us your address, and your friend Fabian picked us up at the airport. He gave us keys to the building, but we didn't want to just barge in." His mother gave the pile of plates in her hand a meaningful look, while completely ignoring the fact that they *had* barged in, while also pretending to be a delivery person.

"¿Dónde está el baño?" his father asked, and Gabe pointed down the hall, then winced when he remembered the three days' worth of running clothes on the floor by the shower.

"My apartment is usually very clean," Gabe told his mother, following her around and picking up the other odds and ends that had gotten out of place. "I've just been . . . busy."

"With the gym emergency?" she asked, loading the dishwasher.

"Yeah. It was—yeah."

While his mom cleaned his kitchen, Gabe went into his bedroom and pulled fresh bedding down from the closet. He didn't know what else to do. His parents were in his apartment for the first time ever, and of course it was the only time his place was a mess. But since he wasn't going to tell them to leave or stay in a hotel, the only thing to do was make his bed for them. His dad came in a moment later and, without a word, helped him change the sheets and pillowcases.

While flipping the comforter back over the bed, Esteban winced and rubbed his left shoulder like it pained him.

Gabe's eyes narrowed. "What's wrong?"

His dad waved it off. "Es nada. I'm just getting old." His words held a trace of humor, but the corners of his mouth were pinched.

Gabe knew what someone in pain looked like, but he let it slide. For now.

Instead, he went back out to the living room to retrieve his parents' suitcases. Then he ducked into the bathroom and picked up all his dirty clothes before his mom could see them. While he was at it, he also replaced the hand towels and wiped down the sink too.

In the kitchen, he found his mother cooking chicken in a pan. "What are you doing?"

"Making dinner," she replied, like it was obvious. "It's evening for us."

Sure enough, his father was already setting the table—something that had been Gabe's job when he was young.

The scene was so . . . normal. Somehow, it felt natural for his parents to be in his space, even though they'd never been here before, and he'd hardly spoken to them in a decade. They'd shown up on his doorstep in Los Angeles and picked up right where they'd left off.

No, not where they'd left off. This was worlds better than it used to be.

All this time, Gabe had been feeling like he had nothing without the gym, because the life he'd built was falling apart. But maybe that wasn't true.

Many years ago, he'd cut his parents out of his life to save himself. And while he was a firm believer in upholding healthy boundaries against toxic people, even if those people were related by blood, he could acknowledge that he'd also done it to hurt them. But in doing so, he'd hurt himself too. He'd distanced himself from his family, but he'd never put down the anger, the pain, the validation-seeking. All this time, he'd been carrying those around with him. Wasn't it time he put that shit down?

Maybe this was the wound that was healing.

Not everyone got these kinds of second chances. Some families started out dysfunctional and stayed dysfunctional. But ever since running into his dad in the condom aisle, Gabe had wondered if his parents had changed enough for him to give them another chance.

If *he'd* changed enough to give them a second chance.

Esteban went into the bedroom and came back holding a bottle of Sauvignon Blanc.

Gabe stared. "Did you bring that from New York?"

His father gave him a bland look. "No, your friend gave it to us when he picked us up."

Fabian really was the best friend a guy could ask for. He would've known Gabe didn't keep alcohol on hand, so he'd gifted them a bottle. Gabe could imagine his parents arriving at the airport, having come all this way and not knowing what kind of reception they'd receive, and how much it would have meant to them that Fabian not only picked them up, but brought them a present.

"Gabriel, ¿dónde están los vasos de vino?" his mother called from the kitchen.

Gabe didn't have wine, but he did own a few wineglasses, leftovers from his relationship with weekend-getaway-obsessed Olivia. He pointed to the correct cabinet, and his mother waved his father over to reach the glasses, which were on a high shelf.

Esteban reached for the glasses, then hissed in pain and jerked his arm back down.

"Coño," he muttered, rubbing his left shoulder.

"You have to remember to reach with your right hand," Norma reminded him.

"I can't help it. I'm left-handed."

"Papi, why don't you let me work on your shoulder?" Gabe offered, moving into the kitchen and taking down the wineglasses himself. "There's no reason to live in pain if you don't have to."

"I don't want to trouble you," Esteban insisted.

Since when? The man had troubled Gabe for the first eighteen years of his life and had now shown up uninvited on his doorstep. But they were getting along well, so Gabe didn't say that. "Come on, Pop. This is literally what I do every day. Let me help you."

That wasn't precisely true. Once upon a time, physical therapy was the thing Gabe had done every day. Before his schedule had been consumed by phone calls and emails and meetings, which was exactly why he'd sold. Still, he knew what to do.

"You should let him help you," Norma said, uncorking the wine. "Never turn down free medical care."

Esteban sighed, but finally he said, "Okay, you can try."

"Come on," Gabe said. "I'll get a hot compress on you while I set up my table."

Gabe directed his father to sit on the sofa, then went into the kitchen to pop a hot/cold pack in the microwave for twenty seconds.

"Do a good job, okay, mijo?" his mom said under the cover of the microwave hum.

As the words filtered in, Gabe was able to read between the lines. She wasn't saying it because she didn't believe in him, but because she knew he was worried about his father's response. She wasn't telling him to do a good therapy session, but to have a good interaction with his father.

Had his mother always been this way? Saying one thing and meaning something else? Why was he only able to see it so clearly now?

Because you're an adult now, his brain supplied.

Before he'd left at eighteen, Gabe had still viewed his parents through the lens of a child, interpreting their actions only in relation to himself. He hadn't yet learned to see them as real people. Now, he'd been gone so long, it was like seeing dual images of them: the parents he remembered, and the people— older people—that they were now. He was forced to confront the truth that they were fully formed humans beyond their roles as Mami and Papi.

Not only that, they'd all changed during the time apart. His parents seemed much more mellow than he remembered, and Gabe noticed he was better at managing his own emotional responses to them. He didn't get as riled up as he once had.

"I will, Mami," he said. The microwave beeped and he removed the hot pack.

And mentally prepared to be alone with his father for the first time in years.

AFTER MOLDING THE pack around his father's shoulder, Gabe pulled his portable treatment table out of the hall closet and carried it to the bedroom. There was just enough space by the windows to set it up.

It had been ages since he'd used this thing, since he'd worked on someone in his home. As he opened up the table and got it ready, he realized that he'd missed the literal hands-on aspect of physical therapy. He'd been working on the business side for years now, managing other PTs and trainers. And of course, the tables at Agility were maintained by assistants. Gabe couldn't even remember the last time he'd had to spray and wipe down a treatment table himself. He grabbed a pillow from the bed and called his dad into the room.

"Lie on your back here," Gabe said, setting the pillow at one end of the padded table.

"Should I take off my shirt?"

"Only if you want to."

Esteban hesitated, then unbuttoned his plaid shirt and draped it over the closet doorknob. He sat on the table and seemed to test it for sturdiness before stretching out on his back.

Gabe had always known he took after his dad, but it was weird to get a glimpse of what he'd look like in thirty years. Esteban was still pretty fit, but his chest hair had gone gray and his skin had changed. His shoulders sloped more than they had before. Gabe noted the small changes with the eye of a physical therapist: the curve of the spine, the angle of the neck, the tilt of the pelvis, the swelling in his dad's hands. Gabe would have bet his entire business—if he still had it—that his father had more pain than just in his shoulder, but of course Esteban would never admit it.

Well, Gabe would start where he could, with the pain his father couldn't hide or ignore. Beyond that . . . well, they'd see. He lotioned up his hands and got to work.

"The shoulder consists of three bones," Gabe explained as he explored the area with his hands. "Together, they make a ball-and-socket joint."

Years of training took over as he palpated the joint, gently moving his father's arm to observe the range of motion. He asked questions in a low voice as he worked. "Does this hurt? Can you move it this way?" And mentally noted his father's answers.

Once he'd assessed the issue, Gabe moved into a combo of manual therapy and soft tissue mobilization, coaxing the muscles and tendons to release tension.

As always, Gabe went into the zone as he worked, the back of his mind wandering as his fingers and hands found the physiological connections in a patient's shoulder and encouraged them to relax.

But this wasn't just any patient. This was his father. In his mind, their complicated history merged with the present moment, his awareness of his father's body, his ability to visualize what was going on beneath the skin through touch and years of education. Gabe found the pain points and channeled his own energy into releasing them, which made it sound magical, but it was really just about his movements helping someone else move better. It was the thing that had drawn him to PT all those years ago while recovering from his knee injury. Gabe had been fascinated by the way the sports doctor had explained the connections in the body and how to release pain and tension, as well as how much better he felt and was able to move after what he'd initially called "torture sessions." How could jabbing your fingers into a joint release swelling? He'd been determined to find out, and it had changed the course of his life.

The intersection of pain and movement, the absolute beauty of the human body's inner workings, the ability to help people through touch, had set Gabe on this path.

"Ow," his dad grumbled.

Gabe suppressed a smile. "Hurts?"

"You know it does."

Now Gabe grinned. "Sorry. It'll help in the long run, I promise."

He explained what he was doing as he worked, suspecting that the steady stream of one-sided conversation would put his dad's mind at ease. Some clients preferred quiet while they were worked on, others chatted up a storm to take their mind off the pain, or because they were worried, or lonely.

So Gabe talked, leaving gaps in the flow of words in case his father wanted to respond. And eventually, he did.

"How many hours have you put into this?" Esteban asked.

Gabe blew out a breath as he tried to think of an answer. "Oh, I don't know. Thousands, probably."

"¿Verdad?"

Was it his imagination, or did his dad sound impressed?

"At the beginning I was trying to learn everything as fast as I could, to get through my training in record time. I did as many sessions as I could fit into a day, on anyone who would let me."

"That's because you know how to work hard," Esteban said, then added, "Ow. Carajo."

"Sorry."

Gabe replayed his father's words in his head. *You know how to work hard.* They sounded like praise. Once, Gabe would have taken them as a dig, like he owed his work ethic to his father. But . . . maybe he did.

All those hours Gabe had put in at the store, stocking shelves, creating displays, prepping the bank deposits, and taking inventory. The endless tasks, on top of homework and baseball practice, had taught Gabe to focus his attention and manage his time, and had prepared him to run his own business when it came to it.

Or maybe Esteban was also just acknowledging that Gabe was a hard worker. He'd worked hard then, and now. Maybe his father did see that, had always seen that.

Back then, Esteban wouldn't have said it out loud, so perhaps this was progress.

As Gabe worked on the tension his father held in his body, he thought about the responsibility Esteban had carried. And the worry. Now that Gabe worried about his niece and nephew, about his parents and their health, he could recognize how much worry must have been his father's constant companion in those years.

There was a lot he could blame the man for, but he had to admit, his father had prepared him for adulthood well. He'd forced Gabe to sit beside him and learn how to manage the finances for the store, which had made Gabe feel more than comfortable when he was paying bills and doing payroll for his own business.

Gabe's mind wandered to those early years of doing PT work, and he had a flash of remembered feeling—the sense of satisfaction he'd gotten after working on a patient, when they told him how much better they felt, as he noted their progress on his chart. He looked down at the light brown skin of his father's shoulder, just a shade darker than his own hands, and remembered.

This was why he'd started. This was what it had always been about for him.

Doing the hands-on work, helping people one at a time. He opened the gym so he could help more people on his own terms, assisting them in living lives free from pain to be more present and happier in their own bodies.

But somewhere along the way he'd started spending more

time in the office than at the treatment table. The needs of a growing business had distanced him from the physical work. No wonder he'd been so miserable and burned out.

Agility had gotten on the radar of celebrities, leading to more success, but they weren't who the gym was for. Agility Gym hadn't been designed with celebrities in mind, but for real people with real bodies and real pain, to help them increase their mobility, decrease pain, and improve the quality of their lives.

Even the location of the gym had been Powell's idea. Establishing it in Santa Monica meant they'd have a certain kind of clientele. And while Gabe was grateful to celebs like Rocky Lim who'd put Agility on the map, they had access to all kinds of additional body help that regular people didn't. And once celebs started frequenting a place, it changed.

Fuck. *He'd* changed.

Gabe wasn't some celebrity trainer. He was a physical therapist. A health-care provider. Not a PT to the stars.

Without Agility and what it had become hanging around his neck, Gabe had an opportunity to shift course. He just had to be brave enough to go for it.

As he rotated his father's arm, noting the range of motion, Esteban turned to Gabe and pinned him with a look.

"Tengo una pregunta," Esteban said, and Gabe knew which question was coming. "¿Por qué?"

There could only be one thing that *Why?* referred to, but Gabe asked anyway. "Why what?"

"Why didn't you come back? Until now."

"I thought it was the only way," Gabe said in a low voice.

It wasn't what he'd meant to say. It wasn't his typical defensive thought. Maybe he'd gotten those out of his system.

"The only way to what?" his father asked.

"To grow."

A long moment passed before Esteban spoke again, switching into Spanish. "I was hard on you," he admitted. "I thought I knew better, and I didn't—I didn't know how else to prepare you for life. It was how your grandfather raised me."

Esteban rarely spoke about his own father. He'd died well before Gabe had been born, when Esteban had been a teenager in Mexico.

Gabe looked at his father's body, at the minor scars, the signs of age. Life had been hard on this man. As a father, as the head of the household, as a small business owner, as an immigrant. Gabe had only one of those responsibilities, and he felt like he was drowning most of the time. Was that how his dad had felt? He must have, with two little kids at home, a wife, a store, employees, and customers. It would have been impossible to meet their needs and expectations 100 percent.

"I've talked to your mother," Esteban went on. "We should've considered what you wanted, should've let you make more of your own choices, follow your own dreams. We realize now, there were other ways. But back then? We didn't know. Lo siento, mijo."

This was it. The thing Gabe had wanted for as long as he could remember. Acknowledgment and apology from his father.

But it didn't heal him as much as he'd thought it would. There was no sense of instant satisfaction, no validation balm applied to his soul. He'd wanted to show his father he was wrong. Well, mission accomplished.

And so what?

Gabe had still lost nearly a decade with his father due to their anger and inability, or unwillingness, to see eye to eye. Granted, maybe Gabe had needed the distance in order to take ownership of his choices and grow up. The time apart meant he couldn't blame his doubts or his failures on anyone but himself.

Yes, there'd been tension during his childhood. Raised voices and too much responsibility. But Gabe had been in his early twenties, technically an adult, when he'd decided estrangement was the only option.

And maybe he'd been wrong.

"Why were you angry all the time when I visited?" he asked in a low voice.

Esteban sighed. "I was sad and worried, and I didn't know how to show it. Nikki says it's something called *toxic masculinity*."

Gabe decided not to comment on that part. "You were worried about me?"

"Of course. You were three thousand miles away, all alone, and you barely knew how to do your own laundry."

Okay, that much was true. But Gabe had known how to work hard. Thanks to his dad.

All this time, he'd thought his father didn't care, that his family probably hadn't even thought about him while he was gone. But that was stupid. He'd still thought about them all the time, even when he wasn't in communication. Their presence in his life, in his memories, had never gone away. Of course it must have been the same for them.

Gabe tried to imagine having a kid. Sure, he'd want his child to work hard and know the value of his own skills, but he'd also want them to have it easier than he did. It would be a hard balance to strike, he could see that now. To pass on your core values—in the case of his father, those values were hard work and the importance of family—while still preparing them for life in the real world.

His parents had challenged what Gabe said he wanted to do, and he'd taken it to mean they didn't think he was capable. But why would they have trusted him with as much as they had if they hadn't believed in him? They'd *wanted* him to stay. For the store, yes, but if the store was a symbol of familial connection, it wasn't just to keep him on hand for cheap labor. And if he'd really had as much confidence in his choices as he claimed to have, it wouldn't have mattered whether they'd doubted him or not.

What if he was the one who doubted himself all along?

He thought of the final *Celestial Destiny* chat transcript he'd saved. Even though Michelle hadn't known what Gabe was planning back then, she'd all but told him his way of thinking was flawed. At the time, Gabe hadn't been able to see it.

"I understand it more now," Gabe said slowly. "I'm . . . I'm sorry I stayed away so long. I won't do that again."

"Good," Esteban said, as if it were that easy.

Maybe it was.

Gabe picked up the towel and wiped the lotion off his dad's shoulder. "All done," he said. "You can sit up when you're ready. And we'll put ice on you after dinner."

Esteban swung his legs over the side of the table and sat up. He moved his arm experimentally. His eyebrows shot up in surprise.

"Better?" Gabe asked.

"Sí. Se siente mejor." There was surprise in his father's tone too.

"I'll show you some exercises to keep improving it," Gabe said. "And I'll get you some massage balls, a mat, and a foam roller."

His dad side-eyed him. "¿Massage qué?"

Gabe stifled a laugh. "They're like tennis balls," he said. "You roll your muscles on them."

"Hmm." Esteban still looked skeptical, but he got to his feet. Then, to Gabe's utter shock, he gave him a hug and said, "Gracias, mijo."

Unlike the apology, the thanks was like a blast of warmth through Gabe's chest. Was this what he'd been waiting for all this time? To feel like his dad valued him? Appreciated him for who he was?

Maybe Esteban hadn't known how to show it. And maybe Gabe had been too wrapped up in his own fears of inadequacy and powerlessness to see the signs clearly.

"No problem, Pop."

Esteban put his shirt back on, a little more easily than he'd taken it off.

Gabe packed up the table and put it away. When he went back to the kitchen, his father was pouring wine into glasses while his mother plated the food. Gabe helped her carry everything to the table. She'd cooked up a mouthwatering chicken and vegetables dish from whatever had been in the fridge. But there was something familiar about the smell . . .

Gabe glanced back at the counter and spotted an easily recognizable container.

"Mami, did you bring that adobo three thousand miles to California?"

"I knew you wouldn't have it," Norma said defensively. "Now, vamos a comer."

They all sat down and dug in.

Gabe was only halfway through his first glass of wine when his father set down his fork and steepled his fingers. "We have more to catch up on," he said. "Where do you want to start?"

Once, Gabe would have reacted defensively to the question, viewing it as a command. Now, he just set down his own fork and washed down the chicken with some wine. "Let's start with the gym."

He started at the beginning, telling the story mostly in Spanish, so his father could catch all the nuance, but switching to English when he didn't know how to translate a word or phrase.

His mother wanted to know more about Agility, so Gabe pulled out his phone and showed her the website and Instagram account. She scrolled through the feed, exclaiming over the décor and the photos of Gabe, but Gabe felt his father's watchful gaze on him.

"¿Y qué es el problema?" Esteban cut in. His arms were crossed over his chest in a pose Gabe knew well. He was in for an inquisition, although it didn't scare him like it once would have.

"Why do you think there's a problem?" Norma asked in alarm, looking up from the phone.

Esteban gestured toward Gabe with his chin. "Míralo."

Norma looked at Gabe. Her mouth pinched in sympathy. "Sí, yo lo veo."

Gabe fought the urge to touch his face or look in a mirror. What? What did they see?

Then he remembered the state of his hair and overgrown beard, and what his apartment had looked like when they'd arrived. It was pretty clear what they saw.

"Dime qué está pasando," his father said, getting right to the point. "¿Qué fue la emergencia?"

No more beating around the bush. "I sold it," Gabe blurted out. And he braced himself, for their disappointment, for the feeling of failure and disgrace.

Except it didn't come.

"Okay." Esteban nodded. "¿Por qué?"

His tone was reasonable. He was just asking why. But with the wisdom of age, Gabe knew that this simple question would have thrown him into a tailspin when he was younger. He would have gotten defensive, feeling like his dad was accusing him of something. Now, though, he could see that Esteban was just asking for more details.

So he gave them.

"It has to do with the real reason why I was in New York," he began.

"Not for Michelle?" his mother asked, and this, Gabe knew, was going to hurt them more than the news about the gym, which they had no attachment to.

"Well, kind of. But not like that."

He told them about the investment agreement and the expansion, about Fabian emailing Michelle, and Michelle insisting that Gabe come stay with her to work on the project. That meant he also had to admit that he'd never intended to come to the Bronx and that he'd been staying next door, sneaking around for days, before getting caught.

His mother looked scandalized, but Gabe was pretty sure his dad's sudden coughing fit hid laughter.

"You came to New York to work with Michelle?" his mother clarified.

"Sí."

Norma threw up her hands in disbelief. "¡Pero los condoms!"

Gabe rubbed his eyes. "Mami, please don't talk about those anymore."

"Pero no entiendo. Why did you need those if you were just working?"

Esteban cleared his throat and muttered, "No creo que solo estuvieran trabajando."

He was right, they hadn't only been working, but Gabe was still reluctant to admit that to his parents.

"But you *are* dating Michelle," his mother said, hope in her voice. "Right?"

"Ah . . ." How the hell did he answer that? "Not quite."

"Not quite?" Norma repeated, her voice edging toward shrill. "¿Qué es eso? Something for los jovenes like *hooking up* or *friends con benefits*?"

Gabe choked on his wine. "Mami!"

"You think I don't know about this stuff? I have ScreenFlix and chill."

"Oh my god," Gabe muttered, unable to believe how comfortable his parents were discussing this with him. When he'd been a teenager, the only times they'd mentioned sex had been to warn "Don't get her pregnant!" whenever he had a girlfriend.

And that, more than anything, showed Gabe how much his parents had changed. He didn't know how it happened or why. Maybe it was because he'd left, maybe it was because they were older. Or maybe, without the stress of their jobs and their children, having finally achieved the American Dream comfort level they'd worked so hard for, they'd been able to chill the fuck out.

Either way, *these* were people he could be a family with.

"I didn't go to New York to date Michelle," Gabe finally said. "I went to work with her on the launch campaign for the new location. We . . . I don't know what to call what we were doing. But when I saw you," he addressed his dad, "I didn't want to talk about the gym yet."

"So you put the blame on her," his father said, shaking his head. "You made her pretend that whole thing"—he waved a hand, encompassing the events that had transpired—"so you could avoid talking to us, to *me*, about why you were really there."

"I . . ." Gabe opened his mouth to dispute it, but his dad was right. He'd dragged Michelle into this ruse with him, rather than acting like a fucking adult and facing his dad with the truth.

"Yeah," he finished, because his dad had hit the nail on the head.

Except for one thing. They hadn't actually been pretending.

Esteban looked sad, but he nodded. "Yo entiendo."

"How do you feel about her?" Norma broke in. "Because I know you used to—"

"The same," Gabe muttered. "I feel the same about Michelle as I did—"

He stopped, because no, that wasn't right. However he'd felt about her in their teens was a pale shadow to what he felt now.

"No, actually. I feel . . . more. A lot more."

"You should tell her," his father said decisively. "Now go back to the part where you sold the gym."

Gabe explained how Powell's offer coincided with Fabian's life changes, leaving Gabe in the position of buying him out or working with a board of investors. So he'd decided to sell.

"It's hard to run a business alone," his father said knowingly. "You made the right choice."

"Sí, mijo." His mother nodded. "And it means you built something really valuable if this Power guy wants it."

"Powell," Gabe corrected, then huffed out a laugh. "Although *Power* is pretty accurate, since he held all of it."

"What about the work Michelle was doing?" Esteban asked.

"I still have it," Gabe admitted. "And we paid her. But I left suddenly, and I didn't explain everything to her."

"You should do that," Norma said in a mild tone.

"I'm working on it," Gabe said. "That's what I was doing when you got here."

His father rapped his knuckles on the table like a gavel. "Okay, mijo. You fixed things with the gym. You fixed things with us. Now you fix things with Michelle."

A smile tugged at Gabe's lips. "I will, Pop. Don't worry."

"We've missed you so much, mijo," his mother said, blinking back tears.

Gabe swallowed hard, and told them the truth. "I've missed you too."

Something eased in his parents' faces, like those words were enough. And hell, maybe they were, to start. But they had to be backed by actions.

And despite the confidence in his voice, Gabe *was* worried. He'd already left Michelle twice. Would she give him a third chance?

He could only hope his words to her would be enough, and that he'd have the courage to follow through on his plans. Because once again, he was going to need her help.

And not just hers. His family's too. His days of trying to do everything alone were over.

Thirteen years ago

Celestial Destiny: Episode 13 Planning Session

Michelle:

   I don't think Zack should leave.

Gabe:

   Why not?

Michelle:

   He should stick it out with Riva, even though it's difficult. Together, they can make things better.

Gabe:

   No, Riva should leave with him. They can give up everything related to their old lives and go off to have more adventures across the galaxy for season 3.

Michelle:

   Riva won't leave, though. That would be out of character. Badass bounty hunter, remember? She never gives up.

Gabe:

   Even if it's a lost cause?

Michelle:

    Never.

Gabe:

    Well, maybe she should.

Michelle:

    She wouldn't.

Gabe:

    I have to go. My dad is yelling at me about the store.

Michelle:

    Just think about it, okay?

Chapter 27

That's it," Gabe said in awe. "It's done."

His mother looked up from the kitchen counter, where she was packing a box of homemade conchas—a thank-you gift for Fabian's family, to go with the mountain of diapers, toys, and clothing she'd bought for the twins. Gabe had explained in no uncertain terms that he was never having babies, so she should enjoy shopping for his godchildren while she had the chance.

She had taken him at his word, and come back with a slew of shopping bags.

"What's done?" she asked.

"*Celestial Destiny*. It's finally complete."

His mother just sighed. Gabe's parents didn't understand how finishing "el fanfeek" was going to win Michelle back, but they encouraged him to do whatever he thought would work.

"Flowers are always a good idea," his father grumbled as he rolled the suitcases over to the apartment door. He'd consented to more treatments for his shoulder and his knee, which he hadn't even told Norma was hurting him. Norma had been delighted to find out that Gabe could also do back and neck massages, and demanded he work on her too. The regular PT treatments had put a spring in their steps, but maybe it was also the California sunshine and reconciling with their son. Gabe had missed the worst of the wildfire smoke from up north while he was in New York, and the skies were clear again— aside from the usual smog—by the time he'd returned.

"If this doesn't work, flowers won't do anything. This is Michelle we're talking about." Gabe saved the file and opened a new email.

To: Michelle Amato
From: Gabriel Aguilar
Subject: Celestial Destiny

The end.

Love,
Gabe

Before he could talk himself out of it, he attached the document and hit *send*. A second later, the "Message Sent" notification popped up. It was truly done now.

Gabe leaned back in his desk chair, awash in satisfaction and exhaustion. Between finishing the story and spending time with his parents, he'd barely slept the last two nights. But now, something sixteen years in the making was complete.

Celestial Destiny had always been his way of showing Michelle what she meant to him. Maybe he'd been too subtle then, but not anymore.

He just hoped he wasn't too late.

"I'm taking the suitcases down to the car," his father called from the door, and Gabe jolted.

"Wait, let me help you." Gabe got up and felt a series of pops in his joints. He'd done way too much sitting over the last week. But he couldn't have his dad hurting his shoulder again right before he left.

At the open door, Esteban knelt and picked something up. "Tienes un package," he said to Gabe, handing over a cardboard tube.

"Did you order a poster?" his mother asked, coming over with the box of conchas.

"I don't think so," Gabe muttered. And then he saw the label, and his heart leaped. "It's from Michelle."

His mother bounced on her toes. "¡Ábrelo, zángano!"

Gabe shot her a wounded look. "Mami, don't call me zángano."

His father came over with a kitchen knife. "Here, open it."

Gabe took the knife and cut the packing tape, then popped out the plastic lid at the end of the tube. He passed the knife and lid to his dad, then stuck his fingers in to pull out a rolled-up piece of paper.

Tucking the tube under his arm, Gabe unrolled the paper. A huge smile broke out on his face when he realized what it was.

Michelle had made him another collage, a physical reminder of their friendship—just like the one she'd given him after high school graduation. Just as the story he'd sent her would—hopefully—show her what she meant to him, this showed him clearly what he meant to her. There were recent photos and older memories, all blended together to show him what he'd already known.

He loved her. Always had and always would.

And then there were the words scrawled across the bottom, a quote from the final episode of *Beyond the Stars*.

Part of me will always be waiting for you.

Hope lifted his heart. Maybe it wasn't too late.

"I need a shower," he said, leaping into motion. His mother helped him pack and his father helped tidy up the apartment and package the perishables from the fridge, which Norma had stuffed to the gills. Gabe bought a ticket for the same flight his parents were on, then called Fabian on speaker while he threw on some clothes.

"I need a huge favor," he said when Fabian picked up the phone.

"Anything, bro. Just name it."

When Fabian arrived, Gabe and his parents loaded up the car with their luggage and all the gifts for Fabian's family. They were also giving him all of Gabe's groceries, since Gabe didn't know when he was coming back. Fabian took a concha out of the box immediately and nibbled on it as he drove them to the airport.

"Señora Aguilar, these are the best conchas I've ever tasted," Fabian mumbled through a mouthful of pan dulce.

Gabe's mother preened. "Call me Norma. And don't forget to send me photos of tus bebés."

At the airport, they unpacked the luggage and Fabian said his goodbyes to Esteban and Norma. Then he turned to Gabe.

"You can do this," he said, clasping Gabe's hand. "Don't hold back."

"Not anymore," Gabe agreed, pulling Fabian in for a quick one-armed hug. And then he and his parents raced through the airport to make their flight.

Celestial Destiny

A Beyond the Stars Season 2 Fanfic

Episode 13

By BxGamer15

FOR CHELLEBLOCKTANGO

~~Zack returned to Gardaron Port.~~

Zack soared away from Planet Salazarin and prepared to engage hyperspeed. But as his fingers hovered over the ship's control panel, he paused.

What in the galaxy was he doing? Going back to his dead-end life working as a bartender in a port city? Leaving Riva, the one person who saw him not as a savior or heir to his father's throne but as a real flesh-and-blood person, after finally reconnecting with her after all these years? Turning his back on all the work that needed to be done?

You couldn't pick your family, but you could choose how you played the cards you were dealt.

So what if his father was a monster and his mother was a manipulative liar? Zack hadn't turned out like either of them, thanks to his aunts and uncles, and thanks to Riva's friendship, the grounding force in a life marked by chaos.

Yet here he was, choosing to fold and thus proving himself to be worse than the king and queen. He was a coward, running away from his responsibilities, leaving his mess for other people to clean up because he couldn't be bothered to face where he'd come from and what it might mean about him. He was too enamored with his own pain to set it aside and see what was really before him.

Riva.

His people who relied on him.

And the few who'd stayed behind to temper the king's worst impulses.

It was time to play his cards, for better or worse.

Zack engaged the navigation AI. "Set a course for the Salazar Compound."

"Are you sure?" the computer asked. "You just left there."

"I'm 100% sure."

"Well, if you're sure you're sure . . ."

With the ship on autopilot, Zack took the MacGuffin Device and went to the engine room. He stared at the cube for a long time. It looked so innocuous. Who would have thought it had the capacity to wield so much power?

He held the cube on the flat of his palm and squinted at it. Then, using his telekinesis, he flung it into the engine's reactor core.

Zack landed the ship right where he'd taken off from.

"Shut everything down," he told the AI. "I won't be going anywhere for a while."

"Very good, Your Highness."

Zack paused. The AI hadn't referred to him by his title in years, and if it had, he would've corrected it. But now? It fit in a way it never had before. Not like something unwanted, but also not like something he deserved.

No, it was more like something to grow into. To aspire to deserve. To prove himself worthy of.

Zack found Riva in the great hall, reviewing a holo-map with one of his uncles.

When he approached, Riva looked at him with a mix of apprehension and hope in her amber eyes. His uncle took one look at the two of them and scurried off, claiming he'd left the hoverdrive on.

"Where is it?" she asked.

"Gone," Zack said. "Destroyed. You were right. It's too dangerous to exist. No one should control something like that. Not even me."

"So you . . . came back to tell me that?"

He shook his head. "No. I came back to rule. On one condition."

The corner of her mouth quirked. "What's that?"

"I'd like you to rule with me." He took her hand. "My connection with you has always been the best part of me. If I'm going to do this, and do it well, I need you, Riva."

"You do. But you've been gone a long time," she said. "How do I know you won't leave again?"

"You don't," he answered honestly. "I can't guarantee I won't get the urge to run again, but I can promise I'll tell you when I'm feeling that way, and why. I hope you'll give me another chance, and love me through it when those feelings come up. I know it's a lot to ask."

"It is. Lucky for you, I'm an expert bounty hunter. If you try to leave again, I'll just track your ass down." Her voice softened, and the look in her eyes was pained. "But please don't make me."

"I won't." He slipped his arms around her waist and looked deep into her eyes. "I love you, and I'm sorry it took me so long to figure out where, and who, I need to be."

"I got used to it," she whispered. "Like I said, part of me has always been waiting for you."

"You don't have to wait any longer," he promised. And then he kissed her.

Chapter 28

Michelle was skewering vegetables in her parents' kitchen when someone knocked on the back door. Odd, since it was unlocked, and people had been coming in and out all day. They were having a family barbecue for her nephew Henry's seventh birthday. The combined Rodriguez-Amato family was so big, the tradition was to throw house parties for family birthdays, followed by a smaller "friend" party another day.

"It's open," Michelle called, and continued poking chunks of zucchini.

When the door remained shut, her mother spoke up from where she was stirring a huge pot of arroz con gandules on the stove. "Go open it. It might be Ava with her arms full."

Michelle went to open the door, but it wasn't Ava.

It was Gabe.

Michelle sucked in a breath, her heart pounding in her chest, but she couldn't stop the smile that spread over her face.

"It's you," she said, with something like wonder.

"I'm back," he said, and there was a note of finality in his voice, like this time, he was back for good.

Michelle would have told herself that was just wishful

thinking, if she hadn't received an email from him the day before signed *Love, Gabe.*

And if she hadn't read the story he'd attached to that email. But she *had* read it, and she'd been thinking about it all day.

Part of me will always be waiting for you.

She'd been waiting, knowing with certainty that this time, he would come back for her.

And here he was. Holding a familiar cardboard tube.

The basement door swung open and Ava entered the kitchen, her gaze bouncing like a pinball from Michelle, to Gabe, to Valentina, to the skewers.

"Go upstairs," Ava said quickly to Michelle. "I'll take care of the vegetables."

Michelle mouthed *thank you*, then grabbed Gabe's hand and towed him past her mother and cousin and up the stairs to the craft room, where it was blessedly quiet. For the most part, everyone else was in the backyard eating or playing video games in the basement.

"I read it," Michelle said, the second they were seated on the edge of the bed.

"All of it?"

"All of it." Her heart twisted and tears sprang to her eyes. "You were always trying to tell me. I'm sorry I didn't see it."

"You weren't the only one," he said, opening the tube. To her surprise, he pulled out not one but two rolled-up papers. One was the professionally printed collage she'd sent him, but the other was more delicate, the edges yellowed with time and old Elmer's glue. He unrolled it, and Michelle saw with a start that it was the first collage she'd made him, from actual photos she'd cut out and glued together onto card stock. Puffy foam stickers spelled out "BEST FRIENDS" across the bottom in rainbow letters.

Michelle took the first collage, spreading it out carefully on her lap. Gabe did the same with the new one, and they stared at them, side by side.

BEST FRIENDS

Part of me will always be waiting for you.

"It's Friendship 2.0," he murmured, referring to her list.

"Yeah," she said softly, warmth suffusing her chest at how clearly he saw her intent. "It is."

"This was made with love," Gabe said, touching the corner of the old collage, the one that showed them between the ages of six and eighteen. "I saw the 'best friends' part, but I didn't see everything else that went into it. I was too caught up in my own unrequited love story. And then when we finally . . . I thought it was too late, because I was already leaving."

His gaze shifted to hers, and she saw love there, but also fear. "Is it too late, Mich?"

She swallowed, glancing down at the new collage. *Part of me will always be waiting for you.* Did he even need to ask?

"Too late for what?" After the way he'd left, she wouldn't make this easy on him. Even though the story he'd sent had broken her heart and put it back together all over again.

He set the papers aside and took her hands in his. "For me to love you," he said softly. "I feel like I've been waiting forever to tell you that I—"

"I love you," she blurted out, then grinned at his look of surprise.

"I was trying to say it first," he protested.

"Sorry not sorry. You took too long. Now kiss me, you marble-faced nerd."

She leaned in, and the first touch of his tongue on hers opened the floodgates on her feelings. She'd been so scared she'd never feel this again. Never touch him or taste him again. So she poured all that fear, all her love, into the kiss. They were gasping and groping at each other by the time they finally came up for air.

"You left me again," she whispered against those soft, soft lips.

"I'm sorry. That was the last time. I promise." He pressed his forehead to hers, like he had when they'd argued by the front door that first morning. It felt like ages ago. So much had changed since then.

Except her feelings for him. She still wanted him. Still loved him. Still didn't want him to leave her.

His magic fingers slid around to cup her head, gently massaging the back of her neck and releasing the tension she carried there. "I was stupid. I thought I had to go through it alone."

"You don't, Gabe. You only have to be alone if you want to." Which was something she'd figured out for herself too.

"I know that now." He traced his thumb over the curve of her cheek. "I worried I was going to be too late. That I'd fucked up too much. And then I got your collage."

"When did you get it?"

"Yesterday. Right after I sent you the fanfic."

She smiled. "You put your heart in an email, and I put mine in a cardboard tube."

He nodded. "Thank you for waiting for me to figure my shit out. I'm sorry it took so long."

She shrugged. "I had my own shit to figure out too."

"There's also something else I need your help with."

"What's that?"

"You made me realize a lot of things about myself and my business. Your concept was perfect—for what I'd originally intended the gym to be. But it got away from me. I wasn't doing what I'd set out to do. Your presentation helped me decide to sell. No, wait, that's not quite right. I decided to sell because I finally realized my dad was right, and I couldn't do it alone. But you helped me realize that it was the right choice for me."

He pulled out his phone and showed her some property listings—in the Bronx.

She looked up at him in shock. "You're going to stay?"

"Yeah. At least, most of the time. I still need to go back to California a few days each month to work with the clients who want to stay with me."

Michelle threw her arms around his neck and hugged him tight.

He'd come back. He was staying. It was all she'd wanted.

"I started a business," she murmured.

Gabe eased her back. "You did what?"

"The Agility project made me realize I was playing small on

purpose, and only hurting myself. I'm going back to the work I love doing, but on my own terms." She pulled up the website on her phone to show him. "I'm already booked for the next three months."

"Damn, I was hoping I could hire you to help me get a PT clinic off the ground. Now I'm not even sure I can afford you."

"*Maybe* I'll give you a friends and family discount this time. If you're good. How do you feel about charcoal gray and light wood for a color scheme?"

He nuzzled her neck, and she found the courage to bring up something that had been on her mind.

"What if . . . you stay with me?"

He raised his head and narrowed his eyes at her. "Here in your parents' house?"

She laughed. "No, not this time. I was thinking this before, when I thought you were going to have the gym here. Maybe when you're in town, you stay in my apartment with me. And since I work from home, maybe I can sometimes go to California with you and stay at your apartment. We could try a sort of bicoastal part-time living situation thing. It's unconventional, but I think it could work for us. At the very least, we'll rack up a ton of frequent-flyer miles while we give it a try."

Gabe grinned at her, and she brushed her fingertip over one of his dimples. "I think an unconventional situation thing sounds perfect for us."

He leaned in to kiss her again, but she froze at the sound of a creak. Jumping to her feet, Michelle threw the door open.

And saw both of her parents, Monica, Ava, her oldest niece,

and Gabe's mother, all crowded in the hallway with guilty looks on their faces.

"I told you not to step on the creaky floorboard," Monica scolded Phoebe, her daughter.

"Did he fix it?" Norma asked in a stage whisper. "¿Con el fanfeek?"

Valentina looked scandalized. "¿Qué es un fanfeek?" She said it like it was some kind of filthy sex act.

"It's called fanfiction, Grandma," Phoebe corrected with an eye roll. She was eleven and absolutely lived for telling adults when they were wrong about things. Michelle adored the little brat.

"Yes, he fixed it," Michelle informed them. "Now go downstairs. All of you."

She waited until they headed down the stairs before she closed the door and turned back to Gabe.

He was still sitting on the edge of the bed, covering his face with his hands. His shoulders shook, and when she went over he dropped his hands and roared with laughter. She sat beside him and held him while he laughed. The sound—clear and loud, not holding anything back—reset something inside her.

He was really back this time. Gabe. Her Gabe. She hugged him tight.

As his chuckles abated, he shifted her onto his lap and held her, pressing his face into her neck.

"I've missed this," he whispered. "All of it."

She understood what he meant. He'd missed her, holding her, but he'd also missed being here, being part of a big, messy, meddling family. A family who cared. Maybe they showed it in ways that weren't always clear, or that could feel overbearing, but it was out of love.

"I love you," she whispered.

He lifted his head and kissed her softly. "I've always loved you."

She smiled. "I know."

Epilogue

One year later

Gabe stood in front of the Aguilar Clinic on Williamsbridge Road, just a block down from where his father's stationery store had once lived. This street held a plethora of memories, but they weren't bad ones, and now, he was here to make new ones.

Beside him, Michelle held his hand and stared up at the sign she'd designed. Gazing at it, Gabe felt more satisfaction than he would have previously thought possible. It was his name, his *full* name, not a bastardization to appeal to a so-called wider clientele.

Not only that, it was his father's name. The Aguilars were back, and they'd come a long way from where they'd been.

Gabe's mother greeted the friends, family, and neighbors who'd shown up for the launch party. Salsa music played all around them, courtesy of Michelle's cousin, the DJ. An all-girl mariachi band was on standby to perform in about half an hour, followed by a pop-up performance by a Bronx theater troupe. They'd adapted Michelle's "range of motion" idea that Gabe had loved so much, and there was a lot of anticipation for the event. Trung was taking part, and Charisse and some of the other former Agility employees had flown out to show their support.

Esteban, in his role as manager of the clinic, passed around pamphlets with information about the hours and services, also designed and written by Michelle.

In the center of it all was Ashton Suarez, the famous telenovela star—and Jasmine's fiancé—who'd signed on as celebrity spokesperson for the clinic. After Gabe had worked on Ashton's father's back during a family gathering, Ashton had offered to help promote the clinic. They'd settled on a nominal fee—Ashton wouldn't accept any higher, and Gabe wouldn't let him do it for free. Ashton had done some background research on physical therapy so he could talk to regular people about it in both Spanish and English.

Because that's who this clinic was for. Regular people— not celebrities—who were in pain and needed help improving their mobility. That had always been Gabe's goal. And while he'd veered away from it for a while, with the help of Michelle's brilliant mind, he'd gotten back on track. Besides, his detour had given him the funds and the experience to open this place. He got his license to practice in New York City, hired local therapists and PTs, and put his father in charge of it all. With Esteban overseeing the management of the clinic, Gabe felt comfortable keeping his clients in Los Angeles. He flew out for about a week every month to see them, and his hourly one-on-one fee more than paid for the costs.

The rest of the time, he lived with Michelle in her apartment. He'd worried it would feel cramped—the two of them in such a small space—or that they'd get annoyed with each other. But they didn't. Like everything else between them, creating a new life together had been easy too.

Gabe knew this was because Michelle had chosen to forgive him for "being an absolute bonehead," as she'd put it. In return, Gabe made a concerted effort to open up and talk to her about what he was thinking and feeling. And when small conflicts inevitably arose, they found ways to talk it out that usually ended in laughter and great sex.

As it turned out, neither of them needed to be alone.

Michelle's business was taking off too. Sometimes she went with Gabe to California to meet with her own clients, like Rocky Lim, who'd become a close friend of theirs. Sometimes she stayed in New York to work from home, or to spend time with her parents and nieces and nephews.

They both owned their own businesses, and were masters of their own fates. And now, those fates were intertwined.

"You did it," Michelle said, squeezing his hand.

"*We* did it." Gabe leaned down to kiss her. "Couldn't have done this without you, babe. Any of it."

The clinic, yes, but also coming back here. Reuniting with his family. Returning to his core values, as she called them.

Care. Connection. Community.

Gabe had always believed in the adage *You can never go home again.*

But now he knew that wasn't true. Home was whatever, wherever, and whomever he wanted it to be. Home was in Los Angeles, with Fabian and his beautiful family. Home was in the Bronx, with his parents, the Amatos, and now, the clinic.

Most of all, home was wherever Michelle was. And right now she was here, holding his hand.

Gabe raised their joined hands to his mouth and kissed her fingers.

He was home.

Acknowledgments

Thank you for reading *A Lot Like Adiós* and spending time with Gabe, Michelle, and their families. I was born and raised in the Bronx, and it has been my pleasure to bring a piece of that experience to you.

As I write this, there is still a lot going on in the world. I hope this message finds you happy and healthy, and that this story brought you a little bit of joy, made you smile or laugh, or at least gave you a few moments of respite from your troubles.

As always, I must thank my agent, Sarah E. Younger. There aren't enough words to describe how grateful I am to have her in my corner. (Which is why I send her fanart of *The Mummy* to show my appreciation.)

I also give tremendous thanks for my editor, Elle Keck, who is always able to see the potential and possibility in whatever kind of draft I turn in. My characters and I have a true champion in Elle.

Additional thanks go to Kristin Dwyer, publicist extraordinaire, who somehow manages to keep me organized and calm during a book release. (Not an easy feat!)

To the amazing team at Avon and HarperCollins—my

awesome publicist Rhina, cover designer Elsie, the production team (Jessica, Diahann, Marie, Pamela, Rachel), Kaitie in marketing, and everyone else who contributed—thank you all for helping this book realize its full potential.

Once again, my cover artist, Bo Feng Lin, has created pure magic. These covers are a dream come true, and I am eternally grateful you agreed to illustrate them.

Writing a book isn't easy. Writing a book during a pandemic was even *less* easy. But while I might have been isolated in my one-bedroom apartment with only my boyfriend for company, I never felt truly alone. I'm so grateful I was already doing regular video chats with writer friends, as what was once a weekly thing became a daily thing, allowing me to find writing company whenever I needed it.

With this in mind, I share my gratitude for my RW-chat mastermind group (Robin, C.L., Kim), my early morning writing crew (Adriana, Nisha, Tracey), all the Rebelles on Rebelle Island and in the Slogging Thread (shout-out to Susannah Erwin for Los Angeles info), the other three of the 4 Chicas (Priscilla, Mia, Sabrina), my fellow NYC romance writers, the Heart Breathings Writing Sprints hosts, and the Better Faster Academy Zoom office. I'm also thankful for the Writers Room group text, semi-regular Beer & Knitting Zooms, and the Latinx Rom Retreat, as well as my own Primas of Power group text (Kathryn, Lisa, CarlyAnn, Tara, Stephanie, Laura—love you all!).

I also send my thanks to a team of people who provided emotional support as I worked on this book—Kate Brauning, Tonya R. Gonzalez, Becca Syme, and especially Lou, who has seen me through my whole publishing journey thus far.

I am especially grateful for the beta readers who read an early copy of *Adiós*, including Ana Coqui, Robin Lovett, Evi Kline, and Adriana Herrera.

I thank my childhood friends, Annalissa, who helped with *Hola* and shared my nostalgia, and Siobhan, for checking in on me. I also thank my dear friend Shanise, who provided details about Michelle's career and videos of my beautiful goddaughter sending me kisses.

Mom, Dad, Claudia, Howard—I'm so lucky to have you all in my life.

And to Mike, who stays up late with me when I'm on deadline and says "You can do it!" at least a dozen times a day. Thank you for everything. ♥

Finally, I extend my gratitude to you, the reader. Thank you for picking up one of my books and giving it a chance. Being an author was my greatest dream (aside from "movie star"), and you have helped me make it a reality. I feel so lucky that I get to share these stories and characters with you. (Also, a special shout-out to my newsletter subscribers and the supportive readers and reviewers on Bookstagram! Thank you!)

About the Author

ALEXIS DARIA writes stories about successful Latinx characters and their (occasionally messy) familias. Her debut novel, *Take the Lead*, was a RITA Award winner for Best First Book, and *You Had Me at Hola*, the first book in her Primas of Power series, is a national bestseller, Target Diverse Book Club Pick, and *New York Times* Editors' Choice Pick. Alexis is a lifelong New Yorker who loves Broadway musicals and pizza.

And don't miss Jasmine and Ashton's love story,

YOU HAD ME AT HOLA,

available now!

Leading Ladies do not end up on tabloid covers.

After a messy public breakup, soap opera darling Jasmine Lin Rodriguez finds her face splashed across the tabloids. When she returns to her hometown of New York City to film the starring role in a bilingual romantic comedy for the number one streaming service in the country, Jasmine figures her new "Leading Lady Plan" should be easy enough to follow—until a casting shake-up pairs her with telenovela hunk Ashton Suarez.

Leading Ladies don't need a man to be happy.

After his last telenovela character was killed off, Ashton is worried his career is dead as well. Joining this new cast as a last-minute addition will give him the chance to show off his acting chops to American audiences and ping the radar of Hollywood casting agents. To make it work, he'll need to generate smoking-hot on-screen chemistry with Jasmine. Easier said than done, especially when a disastrous first impression smothers the embers of whatever sexual heat they might have had.

Leading Ladies do not rebound with their new costars.

With their careers on the line, Jasmine and Ashton agree to rehearse in private. But rehearsal leads to kissing, and kissing leads to a behind-the-scenes romance worthy of a soap opera. While their on-screen performance improves, the media spotlight on Jasmine soon threatens to destroy her new image and expose Ashton's most closely guarded secret.

And keep reading for an excerpt from
Alexis Daria's *Take the Lead*, the first
book in her Dance Off series.

Available now!

TAKE THE LEAD
A DANCE OFF NOVEL
ALEXIS DARIA

Chapter One

Gina Morales clutched the edge of her seat in a white-knuckled grip and gave her producer a side-eyed glare as he and the camera crew sorted through equipment.

A seaplane. They'd stuffed her into an honest-to-god seaplane. The aircraft was painted bright yellow and blue with a tiny propeller stuck to the nose, cute little wings, and pontoons positioned underneath. It looked like a model toy, not something rational human beings who valued their lives should travel in.

Yet here she was, flying in a tin can over a large body of water somewhere in Alaska, while the motor droned on like a monstrous mosquito and the faint scent of fuel tinged the air.

Now she understood why her mother used the rosary in

airplanes. It was to keep your hands busy so you didn't chew off all your fingernails in nervous terror. Noted. Next time Gina found herself on a seaplane, she'd bring a rosary.

For now, she prayed to the gods of reality TV.

Please, please, let him be a winter Olympian.

A skier would be good, or a snowboarder, or better yet, a figure skater. Olympians were the holy grail of celebrity dance partners. If one of those awaited her when she landed, this whole harrowing journey would be worth it. After all, what other kind of celeb would be hanging out in the uncharted Alaskan wilderness?

When she finally dared to peek outside, she could admit the view was picturesque. A rippling ribbon of water unfurled below. Tall evergreens speared a brilliant blue sky crowded with thick, puffy white clouds. A gust of wind teased the treetops, making the seaplane bounce in the air.

Gina clenched her jaw and looked away. Even the pretty scenery didn't distract from the bouncing. Where the hell were they going? And if they were meeting a skier or snowboarder, shouldn't there be more snow?

A tap on her arm drew her attention from the window. Jordy, her producer, pointed at the cameras. His voice came through the headset she wore.

"All right, Gina. Ready to start?"

Taking a deep breath, she nodded and rolled her shoulders to relax them. Nerves notwithstanding, she had a job to do. When Jordy gave the go-ahead, she waved at the camera.

"I'm Gina Morales, a pro dancer. I'm on my way to meet my celebrity partner for season fourteen of *The Dance Off.*" She gave the intro in a loud, clear voice. Or so she thought. She couldn't hear herself over the engine.

The crew exchanged glances. The sound guy looked up from a device in his hand and shook his head.

After adjusting the mic on her headset, Gina repeated the lines at a volume closer to a shout. When she received a thumbs-up, she continued.

"We're in a seaplane flying over a river in Alaska, and I'm a little worried my producers are trying to kill me."

Next to her, Jordy covered his mouth to stifle a laugh. He gestured for her to keep going.

"I've been on three planes so far, each one smaller than the last." She gave an exaggerated shrug and a grimace that wasn't faked. "What's next, a hot air balloon?"

Jordy smacked his forehead like he should have thought of that. She resisted the urge to flip him the bird.

The pilot cut in. "We're beginning our descent."

The plane dipped. Gina spun to face the window again, her pulse racing as the water zoomed closer. Were they going to make a water landing? They had to be. Despite climbing aboard at a marina, she hadn't allowed herself to imagine the landing. With every second, the glistening surface of the inlet raced closer, but Gina kept her eyes open. She could do this. She was strong.

And if she died, at least she'd see it coming.

The pontoons hit the water, skimming along and kicking up a wave under the wings. Her stomach bounced, but she'd braced herself for a rougher landing. As the plane pulled alongside a small floating dock made of barrels, Gina pried her fingernails out of the seat cushion. She focused on getting her breathing under control while they disembarked, climbed into a waiting skiff, and motored to shore. The air carried the scent of salt and wet soil, along with a crisp freshness she could taste on the back of her tongue.

Fresh air. What a novelty.

Once they were ashore, Gina and her crew gathered on a pebbly beach that led right into the water from a clearing. Ahead stood a line of trees the seaplane pilot had called Sitka spruce, the national tree of Alaska. Behind her, the water. Nothing else, aside from the seaplane, the skiff, and a second camera crew she didn't recognize. No stores. No houses. No cars. Just trees, water, and dirt. And sky. Lots and lots of sky.

Too much nature. Not enough civilization. Was it possible to feel claustrophobic in a big empty space?

Gina hunched into her big coat. "Where are we?"

Jordy didn't look away from the tablet he shared with the other crew's production assistant. "Alaska."

"I know that, but . . ." Searching the unfamiliar crew's clothing for logos revealed nothing. Gina pulled out her phone. No service. Of course not. Why would there be service in the middle-of-fucking-nowhere?

Better not to think about how far away they were from the rest of the world. Except now it was all she could think about. What if there was an emergency?

Eyeing the trees warily, she inched toward the boat. Growing up in New York City had given her a healthy distrust of forests. Forests had animals and serial killers hiding behind every tree. Didn't these people watch movies?

Before she could stop herself, her nerves slipped out of her mouth. "You know I'm from the Bronx, right? I don't do nature. I've never even been camping."

Damn it. Gina bit her tongue as one of the cameras swung her way. It was the perfect sound bite and would without a doubt be aired during the premiere. This was exactly what they'd hoped for—bring the city girl out to the wilderness, film her freaking out, then toss her at her partner before she could get her bearings. The producers would do everything they could to throw her off-balance in the name of good TV.

Gina took a deep breath, then another. The air chilled her lungs. It was colder here than it had been in Juneau, but so fresh, she couldn't stop swallowing it in deep, cold pulls. It helped focus her, but also made her giddy.

"You all right?" For the first time, Jordy looked concerned instead of gleeful.

"I'm fine." *Just having an existential crisis over the complete and utter remoteness of their location. No big deal.* She shoved her hands in her coat pockets and balled them into fists. "Let's go meet him."

The crew checked her mic, touched up her hair and makeup. After she fed a few more lines to the camera about how excited she was to meet her partner, they started the trek through the trees.

"Don't break an ankle," Jordy warned.

Gina pressed her lips together and didn't reply. If she'd known where they were going, she would have worn different boots. The soles of her shiny black boots were better suited to sidewalks than wet docks or dirt trails. They were currently caked in mud and sand, which crunched under her feet with every step.

Jordy was right, though. It would suck to get injured right before the new season started. With her eyes on the trail, curiosity about the man she was about to meet consumed her thoughts. What kind of a celebrity would he be? Would he be able to dance? And more importantly, was he popular enough to get lots of votes?

On Gina's first season, she'd been paired with a young singer who'd started his music career on YouTube. While he'd been a great dancer—if a little too energetic—with a vocal fan base, he didn't have the recognition factor needed to win over *The Dance Off*'s older audience. They'd only made it halfway through the season. Nostalgia could help, too, but Gina's partnership with an aging actor from a popular action movie franchise ended after three episodes due to his arthritis.

Despite entering her fifth season, Gina didn't have the fan following some of the other pro dancers did. Kevin Ray had been on the show since season one, and *The Dance Off* was now approaching season fourteen. Kevin had won four times. With his easy charm and incredible choreography skills, people voted for Kevin no matter who his celebrity partner was.

It made Gina want to pull her hair out. Kevin had reached the finals in season thirteen with a teenage makeup artist from Instagram, while Gina and her partner—a popular football player who'd shown marked improvement—had been cut in the semi-finals.

At least she wasn't the newbie anymore—that spot went to Joel Clarke, a Jamaican dancer who'd joined the cast a month ago.

Since it couldn't hurt, she sent up another prayer that her new partner would be up to the challenge. If he had even a modicum of dance skill and audience appeal, she'd do whatever it took to reach the finals and get a shot at *The Dance Off*'s gaudy golden trophy.

The trail ended in a large clearing with a two-story house made from planks of yellow lumber. A smaller house of dark, weathered wood sat to one side, and a hut made of . . . branches, maybe . . . sat on the other. A treehouse painted with a camouflage pattern perched in one of the tall trees.

Gina stared, taking it all in. *What . . . the . . . fu . . .*

This was . . . well, she didn't know *what* this was exactly, but there was no way the collection of makeshift homes was the training camp of a winter Olympian.

As her plans for an Olympics-themed first dance turned to dust, anger kindled in the ashes.

Damn her producers. They could have warned her. When Jordy said they were going to Alaska, she'd dressed for a meeting at a ski lodge or an ice rink, or at least somewhere *indoors*. And they'd told her to do full hair and makeup. She was going to look ridiculous wearing false eyelashes at a meeting on a rough Alaskan homestead.

Bye-bye, trophy.

"Reaction, Gina," Jordy said.

There was no way she could say how disappointed she was. Instead, Gina took a deep breath, and was assaulted by a medley of rich, earthy scents she couldn't even begin to classify. Somehow, the natural aroma soothed her, and she found her voice.

"Wow." It was the first word that popped into her mind. "This is like . . . stepping into another time. I mean, look at these structures. And is that a treehouse?"

There. They could splice her words with shots of the buildings, if they chose. It was the best she could do under the circumstances.

A loud, rhythmic thudding came from behind the biggest house. Gina didn't bother to ask what it was, as the other crew's producer was now guiding her toward the noise.

Years of stage training kicked in, washing away her irritation. It had no place here. She grinned at the camera, infusing her voice with excitement. "I hear something over there. I think it's him."

As she turned the corner around the back porch and got her first look at her new partner, her pulse pounded in her throat and stole her breath. She blinked and spoke without thinking. "Is he . . . is he mine?"

Mine. She hadn't meant to say that, didn't want to examine the mixed emotions the word sparked.

"Yes," Jordy said. "That's your partner."

Hot damn.

The bare-chested man chopping wood behind the main house was six-five if he was an inch, covered in rippling, bulging muscles and smooth, tanned skin. Obliques and delts flexed and released with each swing, highlighting his pure strength and perfect form. The rustic axe acted as an extension of his beautiful body and hit its mark every time.

He was the kind of man who'd look remarkable doing any activity, but he fit here, as if he'd sprung from the earth fully formed—and conjured by Gina's wildest fantasies—for the express purpose of chopping wood.

She wanted to lick him just to make sure he was real.

Jordy gestured her forward to confront the magnificent wood-splitting specimen. The camera crew surrounding him fanned out. Gina's heart rate had yet to return to normal, and she seemed to have swallowed her own tongue, but she obligingly took a step.

A twig snapped under her boot.

The small *crack* stopped the man at the top of his swing. His head whipped around in her direction. As he straightened, the hand holding the axe fell to his side, and he scooped back his long hair with the other. Their gazes met, the bright blue of his eyes visible across the clearing.

Chest heaving, he swung the axe into the wood stump, leaving it embedded and quivering.

If Gina wasn't careful, she'd start quivering, too.

A blondish-brown beard covered the lower half of his face, amplifying his intense masculinity to a thrilling degree and making him look wild, unpredictable, and . . . delicious. The defined muscles of his torso made her mouth water. She swallowed hard.

Work. Cameras. *Job.*

Ignoring her thudding heart and warm cheeks, Gina marched toward him. Around them, camera operators shifted to capture every nuance of their first meeting—every word, every reaction, every sign of nerves.

Despite her calm expression, this wasn't Gina's first day, and her mind whirled, connecting the dots as she approached her new partner.

Dot #1: The producers throwing her off her game with an unsettling seaplane ride.

Dot #2: Making sure she was perfectly groomed, with full hair and makeup.

Dot #3: Surprising her with half-naked wood-chopping and so many muscles, it bordered on rude.

Gina's steps faltered as the truth hit her. *Shit.* She should have seen it right away, and would have if the first sight of him hadn't short-circuited her thoughts.

This man would likely be the hottest guy in the cast, and Gina was young and single. It could only mean one thing.

They were being set up as this season's showmance.

ALSO BY ALEXIS DARIA

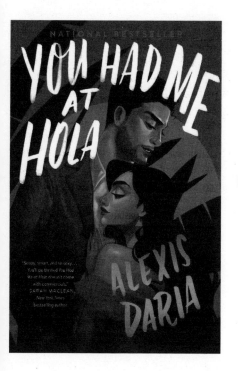

YOU HAD ME AT HOLA

"I could not get enough of Jasmine and Ashton! I adored Jasmine—her ambition, her confidence, her attacks of self-doubt, and especially her hilarious, snarky, and loving cousins. She and Ashton have such a steamy, swoony love story that I didn't want the book to end!"

—Jasmine Guillory, *New York Times* bestselling author

Alexis Daria brings readers an unforgettable, hilarious rom-com set in the drama-filled world of telenovelas—perfect for fans of *Jane the Virgin*.

After a messy public breakup, soap opera darling Jasmine Lin Rodriguez finds her face splashed across the tabloids. When she returns to her hometown of New York City, a casting shake-up pairs her with telenovela hunk Ashton Suarez. A disastrous first impression smothers the embers of whatever sexual heat they might have had, but with their careers on the line, Jasmine and Ashton agree to rehearse in private. But rehearsal leads to kissing, and kissing leads to a behind-the-scenes romance worthy of a soap opera. While their on-screen performance improves, the media spotlight on Jasmine soon threatens to destroy her new image and expose Ashton's most closely guarded secret.

DISCOVER GREAT AUTHORS, EXCLUSIVE OFFERS, AND MORE AT HC.COM